"Steven James knows how to tell a story that gets under your skin and challenges the way you think as only the most talented writers can. If you're looking for a mind-bending tale, strap in and take the ride with *Singularity*. I can't recommend it highly enough."

—Ted Dekker,
New York Times bestselling author

Praise for *Placebo*

"The writing, pacing, and plot lines are impeccable."

—*Publishers Weekly*

"The recipe for this one will be to take the darkness of Poe and the creativity of *The Matrix*, mix in science, and add a dash of faith/ religion."

—*Suspense Magazine*

"It's no surprise when the final act hits, the pages start flipping madly."

—Crosswalk.com

"*Placebo* is an edgy, multilayered thriller."

—*RT Book Reviews*,
4.5 stars

"*Placebo* is fast-paced, interesting, moving. All with James's signature style and flair."

—The Suspense Zone

SINGULARITY

Books by Steven James

THE JEVIN BANKS EXPERIENCE · BOOK 2

SINGULARITY

A JEVIN BANKS NOVEL

STEVEN JAMES

Revell

a division of Baker Publishing Group
Grand Rapids, Michigan

Published by Revell
a division of Baker Publishing Group
P.O. Box 6287, Grand Rapids, MI 49516-6287
www.revellbooks.com

Printed in the United States of America

Library of Congress Cataloging-in-Publication Data
James, Steven, 1969–
    Singularity : A Jevin Banks Novel / Steven James.
        pages cm. — (The Jevin Banks Experience ; Book 2)
    ISBN 978-0-8007-3426-8 (pbk.)
    ISBN 978-0-8007-1935-7 (cloth)
    1. Magicians—Fiction. 2. Friendship—Fiction. 3. Murder—Investigation—Fiction. I. Title.
    PS3610.A4545S56 2013
    813'.6—dc23   2013024128

Scripture quotations are from the King James Version of the Bible.

13 14 15 16 17 18 19   7 6 5 4 3 2 1

To Eddie Brittain and Rick Altizer
Friends for life

I had a stick of CareFree gum, but it didn't work. I felt pretty good while I was blowing that bubble, but as soon as the gum lost its flavor, I was back to pondering my mortality.

—Mitch Hedberg, comedian

It is not difficult to avoid death, gentlemen of the jury; it is much more difficult to avoid wickedness, for it runs faster than death.

—Socrates in *Apology*

PART I

Interface

15 miles northeast of Las Vegas, Nevada
Plyotech Cybernetics Research & Development Facility
Sublevel 4
9:32 p.m.

"Cream? Sugar?"

"No. Black. Thank you." Thad Becker had learned early on in this business not to allow anyone to add things to his drinks or season what he ate. It was a delicate balance—showing trust and exhibiting prudence. But in the end you can either be careful or you can pay the price.

He accepted the cup from the person he'd come here to see: a dark-haired, fit, Caucasian man in his late fifties who called himself Akinsanya—a Nigerian name that meant "the hero avenges."

Thad had done his research. It'd taken calling in quite a few favors, but he'd found out who the guy really was: a retired Army colonel named Derek Byrne. A former sniper instructor, Byrne was not a man to be trifled with.

He also knew about the kind of research Byrne was focused on here at Plyotech: a program that was not, according to any of the company's books, actually taking place. It was the kind of research the people who'd hired Thad had expressed keen interest in: robotics, mechatronics, informatics.

11

And, of course, cybernetics.

Which was what had brought him here.

They were in a high-tech conference room down the hall from where Byrne and his team did surgery on the primates, inserting the electrodes into their brains to see if the chimps could control mechanical apparatuses simply through the electrical activity generated in localized parts of their brains.

Here in the room where they were meeting, a robotic arm with an intricate and realistic-looking hand rose from a stand in the center of the table.

Byrne dumped a spoonful of light gray powder from an ornate ceramic bowl into his own cup. He swirled it into his drink until it disappeared, coloring the coffee a grayish-brown, then he took a sip.

It was not creamer. It was definitely not sugar.

Thad tried his coffee. As far as he could tell there was nothing unusual about the taste. "The people I represent," he said, "are very interested in seeing the results you spoke about on the phone."

"Yes." Byrne sat facing Thad and the two hulking former Special Forces soldiers turned mercenaries whom he'd brought along with him. They were here to do a little work on Byrne if necessary, if the results weren't satisfactory or if he proved too unwilling to share the findings. After all, Thad was a man of action and did not take kindly to people wasting his time.

An Indian gentleman in his mid-sixties and wearing a lab coat stood beside Byrne.

Thad took another sip, then set down his cup and gestured with an open hand toward the older man in the lab coat. "I was told we were going to be alone."

"This is Dr. Malhotra," Byrne replied. "He's part of my team."

Thad nodded politely to the doctor. "I'm pleased to meet you—and I mean no disrespect, but . . ." He eased his cup to the side, leaned forward, and eyed Byrne coolly. "I was told. We were going. To be meeting. Alone."

A moment passed. Byrne's eyes flicked to the two men Thad had brought along. In the end he said nothing about their presence, but simply addressed the man at his side: "Doctor, perhaps you could step into the hallway while I demonstrate our progress to our three guests here."

"Certainly," Dr. Malhotra said in a thick accent, but in a tone that was impossible to read. Thad gestured for one of his men to escort the doctor out of the room. While he did, Thad's other man unbuttoned his jacket, revealing his holstered 9mm Glock 17, and smiled intimidatingly.

Byrne did not appear intimidated.

Once it was just the three of them, Thad folded his hands, laid them on the table, and directed his full attention at Byrne. "Now. I believe you have something to show me, Colonel." He added that last word to make sure Byrne realized he knew his real identity, that this sophomoric game of using a code name was not going to get him anywhere.

Without a word, Byrne rolled up his left sleeve to reveal a bandage encircling the middle of his forearm. He unwrapped it carefully, exposing a healing incision just over three centimeters long.

"How many were implanted?" Thad asked.

"The array contains one hundred and twelve electrodes."

"I would've thought the incision would be larger."

"We've made great strides lately in reducing the size of the unit."

Thad shifted his gaze to the robotic arm in the middle of the table. "Show me."

Byrne depressed a button at the base of the stand that supported the arm. The mechanical hand closed once and then rested in a partially flexed position.

He laid his left arm palm-up on the table and then slowly curled his hand into a fist. As he did, the robotic hand replicated the gesture precisely, down to the minutest flexion of each finger. The colonel twisted his hand and then flattened it and formed a fist again, all gestures that were mirrored exactly by the robotic hand.

"The implant," he said, "is only four days old, and the body tissue around it is already pulling it into position in my arm, giving us every reason to believe that the permanent implants won't be rejected by the recipients."

"Yes, okay," Thad said somewhat impatiently, "you can remotely control the robotic hand when you move your hand, but that's not what we were promised; we've seen that before. I was told you were—"

"Neural impulses. The nervous system."

"Yes."

"Slide your coffee cup closer to the arm."

Thad did as the colonel requested, and then Byrne took two long, slow breaths, closed his eyes, and remained completely still.

A moment later, the robotic hand slowly opened and rotated counterclockwise. The mechanical arm angled toward the table while Byrne opened his eyes and concentrated, staring intently at the cup.

The arm bent at its artificial elbow and wrist, curled the pointer finger through the cup handle, and depressed the thumb and middle finger in opposition against the handle, just as a human might do when picking up a coffee cup.

The cup was close to the base of the arm, creating an awkward angle, and just like people would naturally do, the robotic arm slid it out slightly to create a less abrupt angle for the wrist and then raised it.

All the while, Byrne did not move his own arm or hand at all. His fingers didn't even twitch.

Finally, the robotic arm came to rest holding the cup in position as if it were about to lift it to someone's waiting lips.

Byrne let out a slow breath.

"All that just by your thoughts?" Thad asked quietly.

The colonel nodded. "The electrodes connect to my nerves, and the same impulses that would move my own muscles can be used to—"

"Yes, yes." Thad was already deep in thought and was not particularly interested in the physiological or neurological specifics—the people he worked for could work through all of that. "How long did it take you to learn to do that? To control it that well?"

"Nearly a month."

"You said this implant is four days old. How did . . . ?"

Byrne rolled up his other sleeve and exposed a series of six scars, some healed more than others, on his forearm.

"And you're saying this same technology can be used with soldiers to move exoskeletons?" The scene in *Aliens* of Sigourney Weaver using the giant exoskeleton to fight the mother alien came to mind. That, and the perhaps more applicable and contemporary example of Iron Man fighting other exoskeleton-equipped bad guys.

But even in the movies, the characters needed to move their muscles to manipulate the robotic exoskeletons. This bionic technology that Thad was looking at was in an entirely different league.

Byrne said, "With the lightweight exolimbs we're working on, direct brain-machine interfaces, targeted muscle reinnervation, and electrodes that are embedded in all four extremities, tomorrow's soldiers will be able to carry three-hundred-pound packs at sprinting speeds while exerting 90 percent less energy than they would if they were running with no pack at all."

"And"—Thad was musing aloud—"even if they get shot or lose the use of one or more limbs, they'll still be able to move the exolimbs through their thoughts."

"Eventually, that's what we're shooting for, yes. Paralysis will no longer be a detriment to battle readiness."

Thad evaluated that. Yes, the people he worked for were going to be very interested in this indeed.

He knew Plyotech did some contract work for the Department of Defense's research and development branch: DARPA, the Defense Advanced Research Projects Agency. And that might prove to be a problem here.

"And the Pentagon?"

"They're aware of our research but know nothing about our progress. You're the first group we've contacted."

As Thad was considering how to tell the colonel that he and his men would be needing to come with them now, tonight, he heard a heavy thud in the hallway. It was a sound he knew well—that of a body falling to the floor.

He gestured for the mercenary behind him to check it out, and the man whipped out his Glock and stalked toward the doorway.

Byrne watched silently from across the table.

Thad unholstered his own gun, but even as he did, he heard his man collapse behind him and felt himself becoming waveringly dizzy. He snapped around and saw the former Green Beret lying on the floor convulsing.

Thad spun and leveled his gun at Byrne, who was pulling on a pair of latex gloves.

"What did you do?" Despite his best efforts, Thad felt his arms growing heavy and slack.

Byrne spoke softly. "Put down your gun, Thad, before you hurt yourself."

He was about to squeeze the trigger, but before he could, both arms fell limply to his sides, causing his weapon to topple harmlessly to the floor.

"The coffee?"

No, that doesn't make sense because—

"No." Byrne shook his head.

"The grips," he muttered, "of the guns, you coated them . . ."

"With Dalpotol." Byrne stood and approached him. "Yes."

"But how did you . . . get to . . ." He was slumping in his chair now and finding it increasingly difficult to form his thoughts. His hands began shaking involuntarily.

"You and your men had an escort visit your room last night, my friend." He rose and kicked the gun aside. "You shouldn't have left

16

her alone, even for a minute. And you should have perhaps checked your weapons this morning. You can never be too careful about the people you trust."

A wave of convulsions began wracking Thad's body, and Byrne unpocketed a pill. "This is to stop the seizures." He placed it on Thad's tongue. "Do your best to swallow it."

Thad actually believed him, yet in an act of defiance he tried to spit it out, but the pill had mostly dissolved already and his muscles were relaxing, the convulsions dissipating—however, none of that offered him any strength to go after Byrne.

The colonel walked past Thad toward the downed man. A moment later a handgun's report echoed sharply through the room, and then Byrne returned and lowered Thad gently to the floor.

His head lolled to the side, and he saw that his man had been shot at point-blank range in the temple and was most definitely not twitching any longer.

Byrne straightened out Thad's arms and legs, and though he tried his hardest to stop him, he was unable to fight him off, to stand, to resist at all.

"Do you know what the problem is with most medical research?" Byrne asked him.

Thad's mind was reeling, his thoughts shifting across themselves, sliding into and out of focus. He tried his hardest to concentrate on what was happening, but he didn't feel like he was able to bring his attention back into alignment at all. "What is . . . ?"

"The problem. With most medical research today. Do you know what it is?"

Thad tried to sit up but found it impossible. "The . . ."

"Human trials. It simply takes too long for a drug or a treatment strategy to be approved for human trial. Monkeys, yes. Mice, no problem. But in this case, we need to know if it's possible for someone who has four paralyzed limbs to be able to use his thoughts to move the robotic ones, and we need to find out as promptly as we can if we're going to move forward with this project. To do that we have to test the implants in that situation, and since this research hasn't exactly been made public yet, we couldn't just pull in any quadriplegic off the street for the experiment. You can see why it's necessary to use a volunteer from the inside. You have the honor of being that volunteer."

The realization of what was happening finally struck Thad, and struck him hard.

Four paralyzed limbs.

Four paralyzed—

He heard another gunshot in the hallway and recognized it as coming from the 9mm SIG P226 his other man had been carrying. However, he did not hold out much hope that he'd killed the doctor, but rather guessed he'd met the same fate as the former soldier lying fatally shot just a few feet away.

"There are different ways we could do this," Byrne went on. "For most people it happens through an accident—horseback riding, a car wreck, sometimes a football player has a head-on collision and snaps his neck. I think you'll appreciate that I want to get this right the first time. Here"—he touched Thad's spine near where it connected with the base of his skull—"a scalpel is much more precise, more reliable, and you shouldn't leave something like this to chance. We tried drugs on two other people. Neither made it through without needing a ventilator, and that's just not the result we're looking for here. A scalpel is really the way to go."

The door to the hallway opened and Dr. Malhotra appeared, accompanied by two orderlies in scrubs, rolling a gurney.

"The people . . . I work for . . ." Thad struggled to get that much out, but then his voice faded away into silence.

Byrne nodded and continued Thad's sentence as if he were the one who'd started it: "Have spoken with me, and we all agreed you'd make a suitable subject. Good musculature, adequate intelligence, no close family. No one to miss you."

No, this wasn't happening, this could not be happening.

They're going to paralyze you.

They're going to—

"Technically, you'll be a C4 tetraplegic, or a quadriplegic, if you prefer that term. We're aiming for neck movement, so you should be able to turn your head, maybe even shrug slightly. You'll need assistance, of course, with dressing, bathing, self-care; you'll no longer be able to control your bowel or bladder functions, but we'll have people here to attend to you. With the implants, you should be able to learn to control your exolimbs. With time."

Thad struggled to move but couldn't even lift his arms.

The men lowered the gurney.

"On three," the colonel said.

No, please, no—

They positioned themselves around him.

"One. Two. Three."

The men eased Thad onto the gurney. As a precaution, they firmly secured his wrists and ankles with the wide leather straps riveted to the sides of the gurney, and then raised it again so they could wheel him out of the room.

He tugged desperately at the restraints, but it was clear he wasn't going anywhere. "I swear," he mumbled, "I'll . . ."

Byrne put a hand reassuringly on his arm. "Just relax, Thad. My people know what they're doing. I'll see you after your surgery."

Then he walked to the table and, using only his thoughts, made the robotic arm set down the cup, pick up the spoon, dip out some of the gray powder, mix it into the drink, and then hand it to him.

From where he lay, Thad saw it all.

The colonel was sipping the coffee when the orderlies wheeled Thad past the bodies of the two men he'd brought to protect him, and rolled him down the hallway toward the operating room.

Thad tried to scream out curses, threats, even a final cry for mercy, but it was too late for any of that. He could only make soft, unintelligible gurgling sounds that no one paid any attention to.

They stationed the gurney beneath a wide, bright light in the operating theater where they had done the implant procedures on the monkeys.

As the men prepared for surgery, Thad heard a woman's voice: "Lemme see him."

He couldn't be sure, but he thought he recognized that—

Leaning over him, she came into view.

Yes, he did know her: a stunning blonde in her mid-twenties, nubile, blue-eyed, and fair-skinned, a woman with a quiet, simple laugh and a svelte, well-toned body.

She was the escort he'd hired last night, the woman he and his men had shared. She called herself Calista, but he had no idea if that was her real name.

"Can you keep him awake while you do it?" she asked Dr. Malhotra.

"We should be able to get by with a local anesthetic. Sure."

She trailed her finger along Thad's cheek. "That'd be cool. He was totally rude to me last night. I wanna see the look in his eyes when it happens."

One more time Thad tried and failed to beg them to stop.

He felt a sting in the back of his neck as they injected the anesthetic. Then Dr. Malhotra began the surgery of severing his spinal column while Calista watched curiously and, admittedly, somewhat grossed out, holding Thad's hand in hers while it all went down.

PART II

Venom

The sun dips wearily into the evening mist hovering above the mountains as I watch my friend Emilio Benigno get buried alive.

One man cuffs his hands behind his back, two others lay him in the wooden coffin, and a fourth drops four Sri Lankan cobras in with him. They nail the lid securely shut, then lower him into the shallow grave and start shoveling dirt onto the coffin's lid.

We're in a cemetery, surrounded by ancient grave markers being slowly reclaimed by the jungle. Filipinos typically place their dead in cement tombs above the ground, but in remote areas like this, that isn't always feasible, so they're forced to plant their dead. Somehow this strip of cleared land beside the jungle seems glad to have the opportunity of swallowing this village's corpses.

Despite a recent downpour, the air is still thick and heavy with humidity. Puddles lie around us and dense clouds obscure the peaks of the nearby mountains. The rainforest that surrounds the village of thirty huts hums with unseen insects calling anxiously for night to come.

The evening is cool for this time of year, and a faint breeze fingers its way past the drenched rice fields and through the cemetery. The air is smudged with the sharp tinge of smoke from the wood fires of people cooking dinner in their bamboo huts. Everything smells damp and earthy and weary of the day.

One of the men who's standing beside the grave lights a kerosene lantern. Even though darkness hasn't devoured the jungle yet, the day is dim enough for the lantern to cast a blur of uneven light across the ground.

I picture Emilio lying motionless in the coffin, trying to calm his breathing. It would be pitch-black in there, the dirt sealing out any light that might be trying to sneak through the cracks between the lid and the sides of the coffin.

I imagine what it's like for him, hearing the sound of the soil landing on the wood just inches above his face, the noise getting more and more muffled with each shovelful of earth.

I've been in tightly enclosed spaces myself, struggled with claustrophobia for almost a year and a half now, and I know what it feels like when the walls seem to be closing in and there's nowhere to go and nothing you can do to stop them.

The whole event is being filmed, is being streamed live on the Internet. I have no idea how many people around the world might be watching, but based on the buzz leading up to today and the insatiable nature of human curiosity, the number might well be in the millions.

My friend is in the coffin, shrouded in the dark.

With his hands restrained behind him, Emilio is helpless to stop the four cobras from slithering across his body.

Though I'm no expert on snakes, my friend Xavier Wray knows his reptiles, and before we arrived here tonight, when all of this was still a possibility and not yet a reality, he told me about Sri Lankan cobras.

They're curious snakes and right now they would be exploring the confines of the coffin, passing over Emilio's legs, his chest, his neck

24

and face. He's almost certainly being careful not to move too much, not to let the sense of their thick, rope-like bodies startle him, or he might thrash around and agitate the snakes.

Sri Lankan cobras have one of the most toxic venoms of any subspecies of cobras. It's a neurotoxin that can cause respiratory failure.

But tonight their venom won't kill Emilio; this time if they bite him he will survive.

I tell myself this, try to comfort myself with this fact.

I'm guessing that now, as the men continue to toss the soil onto the coffin, Emilio is already out of the handcuffs, that he has slipped on the gloves he had hidden beneath his shirt to protect him if the snakes—which have had their venom glands removed but still have their fangs—were to bite him.

I glance at my watch.

He's been in the coffin for three minutes.

At any moment he'll be starting to dig.

His clothes are thicker than they appear, but with the amount of force the snakes are able to generate at the tip of their fangs, they would still be able to easily pierce the fabric. Any bites would still be painful. Venomous snakes can strike up to three times per second and if he responded impulsively or jerked from the bite of one of the snakes, it could make the rest of them aggressive—not at all what he would want, being sealed in a coffin with them.

We rehearsed for that, but you can never cover every contingency and you have to be able to respond when things don't go as planned.

Besides, his neck and face were still vulnerable.

Emilio even let himself get bitten by a cobra with its venom glands removed to see if he could remain calm and controlled. I know only a handful of escape artists who would be willing to go that far.

It took three months for me to train him for this escape. He's twenty-three, ten years younger than I am. He's been doing illusions and escapes since he was twelve, but he hasn't worked with snakes before.

I have—and I've been bitten: twice by rattlers and once by an Egyptian cobra. Those snakes hadn't had their venom glands removed, and I spent nearly a month recovering each time. I almost lost two fingers to the swelling in my left hand from the cobra bite.

Now, Charlene Antioch, my assistant in my stage show as well as the woman I'm seeing, squeezes my hand, just for a moment. A small gesture that speaks volumes.

Her walnut-colored hair makes me think of a rich, chocolaty waterfall. A year younger than me, she has an agelessness about her and could pass for twenty if she needed to.

We've worked together for going on seven years, and recently our relationship has blossomed into much more than just the platonic friendship we had before my wife committed suicide a year ago last September.

A born actress, Charlene has the uncanny ability to transform herself into whatever kind of woman the situation calls for, which is an amazing gift for her to have during the quick change segments in my show. With the bat of an eye she can move from cute to flat-out irresistible.

Charlene is experienced in emergency first aid, and even though the snakes have had their venom glands removed, I don't like to take any chances when the lives of other people hang in the balance, so she has several vials of antivenin with her in case something goes wrong.

Five minutes and forty seconds.

The men we've hired for this effect continue to shovel the earth onto the coffin that my friend Xavier designed.

Nearby, the snake wrangler, a Filipino man named Tomás Agcaoili, holds the canvas bag containing additional cobras. We told him we only needed four, but he insisted on bringing more to show the crowd and to "add more drama effect" for the video.

The crowd of nearly fifty people watches anxiously. Charlene, Xavier, and I are the only Caucasians here.

I glance toward Xavier, my effect designer. As a longtime veteran of working pyrotechnics for stage shows in Las Vegas, he met up with me just over three years ago when my show was doing a run on the Strip. He's fifty-two, lives by himself in an RV, still rocks out to the Grateful Dead, and has listened to every episode of *Coast to Coast AM* that's ever been aired. His job is to come up with effects that defy imagination and explanation. To, in essence, reverse engineer the impossible.

Bald, with a slightly graying goatee and mischievous yet steely eyes, Xav somehow looks both imposing and harmless at the same time. He's a wizard with anything electronic or incendiary and is a little antsy today because he hasn't blown anything up or burned anything down in over a week.

The coffin's side has a release mechanism that Xavier came up with, and to provide additional oxygen, a one-inch-wide plastic air tube runs down through the earth out of sight of the onlookers.

Emilio will press himself all the way against the left side of the coffin, swing the right side panel in, allowing dirt inside. Then, as he digs his way out, he'll continue to push the soil behind him and use his legs to kick it into the coffin so that, as he makes his way up through the earth, he fills the coffin behind him with the dirt he's digging through. We would retrieve the snakes later after the conclusion of the effect.

I've done similar escapes and the digging is terrifically exhausting work, made more difficult by the cramped quarters and, in this case, the presence of the cobras, which isn't going to allow him to make any quick movements that might make them aggressive.

I coached Emilio, taught him how to do this. He's good and has practiced each part of this escape dozens of times; I wouldn't be here encouraging him if I wasn't confident he had the skill to get out. But staying calm is just as vital as the technical aspects of an escape, and that's the hardest thing to teach—and to master—especially when the pressure is on.

Six minutes, fifty-eight seconds.

My attention is focused on the grave, but I notice Tomás pass to the back of the crowd.

Xavier gives me a look that to anyone else would mean nothing, but we've worked together enough for me to know that something is up.

A shadow of worry.

That's what I see cross his face.

He has a radio transmitter disguised as a nail in the side of the coffin, and in his earpiece he can hear everything that's going on inside.

Unobtrusively, he walks over and eyes the ground at the end of the tube we hid earlier, the one that leads to the coffin and could be accessed by pushing out a carefully concealed knot in the wood on the side panel.

As soon as Emilio's hands were free he would be able to pop the fake knot out, access the air tube, and get as much air as he needs.

Before we flew here to the Philippines I told him, "It's amazing how fast you use up air when you're digging—faster than you can imagine. You'll need the extra oxygen. So if you want me to help arrange this for you, we're going to use an air tube and we're removing the snakes' venom."

At last he agreed, Xavier and his team worked out the logistics, and here we are.

Soil quickly swallows the cries of people who are buried alive. Knowing Emilio, I don't think he will scream, but as the dirt piles higher, I hear a faint pounding sound, kicking. He's thrashing around inside the coffin.

"Hang on," I tell the men. "*Ihinto*. Stop."

I walk closer and listen carefully.

Xavier stands beside me. Things are quiet now beneath the earth. "Something's wrong," he says stiffly.

I turn to the men. "Dig him up."

"But—" one of the men objects.

"Do it."

They hesitate and I grab one of the shovels. "I said, dig. Now."

Xavier points to the person filming this. "Turn off the camera."

At last the men join me and the soil flies quickly. There aren't any shovels left for Xavier, so he gets on his knees and with his bare hands drags the soil aside.

"Turn off that camera!" he repeats roughly.

The crowd looks shaken. A few women hold their hands over their mouths.

After a few moments of furious digging, I drive my shovel into the earth and hear a dull thunk as the blade finds the top of the coffin. I call to Emilio but he doesn't answer. The soft, muted sound of the snakes hissing is faint, but even through the coffin I can hear it.

Yes, they're agitated alright.

"Emilio?"

No reply.

"Get this lid off!"

The men shoveling beside me look at each other uneasily, but I yell again for them to help me get the cover off.

Xavier and I brush dirt off the lid.

I can see that the right side of the coffin is tilted slightly inward, telling me that Emilio released it and started to dig, but with the angle I can't open the top yet. I'll need to get the cover off.

The release mechanism Xavier installed only works to open one side of it, not the top. Now he appears with a hammer to pry loose the nails holding down the lid. I take it from him and set to work.

"I'm coming, Emilio. I'm right here!" But he doesn't respond. And having rehearsed this so much together, I know he would if he could.

The nails were hammered all the way in, but the wood is slightly beveled, giving me enough space for the claw end of the hammer, and I go at the nails.

Did a cobra get mixed in there that still had its venom?

Charlene has already joined us and has the syringe of antivenin ready.

I don't see the snake wrangler close by. "Get Tomás over here," I shout, then scoot to the far end of the coffin and pry the final nail loose, edge over, plant my feet next to the coffin, and throw open the lid.

Inside the coffin I can see two, three—yes, all four of the cobras. One rears its head up at me as if to strike, but Xavier grabs a shovel from one of the men beside us and bats the snake violently away, then brings the blade down across its neck to stop it for good.

Emilio is still alive, his eyes are open and so is his mouth, but his lips are already turning bluish. His fingers twitch faintly.

Then I see it.

A baby cobra wriggles free from the end of the air tube, and as Charlene drops to one knee to open Emilio's airway and to get him the antivenin, another baby cobra eases out from between his lips. She jerks back involuntarily, but I move in, grab the snake, and fling it aside.

"Help me get him out," I shout to the men beside me.

We lift Emilio out of the coffin. Gasps rise from the crowd, and the men scramble backward toward safety.

"Where's Tomás?" I call urgently to the men. "Get him over here. Now."

The other snakes are already trying to find their way out of the coffin.

I can hear Xavier behind me taking care of the cobras before they get free—after all, if they still do have their venom we can't let them get loose with all these people around.

Charlene leans in beside me. "Jev, I've got it." She gives him the injection.

"You're going to be fine," I tell Emilio, but know it's probably a lie even as I say it.

The air tube. He put his lips up to it, sucked in to get air into his lungs, and a cobra ended up in his mouth instead.

I stand and study the terrified faces of those in the crowd, but one man does not look terrified and is easing back toward the path that leads into the rainforest. As he moves, Tomás is still holding his bag, heavy with the additional cobras.

He sees me looking at him and spins abruptly and sprints toward the trailhead to a jungle path that leads to a waterfall about a quarter mile away.

"Help Emilio," I call over my shoulder to Charlene, and then Xavier tosses his shovel aside and the two of us take off for the trail after Tomás.

Pursuit

Xavier is quick, but I'm a half-marathoner and I reach the trailhead first.

Despite the rain we've had, the path is surprisingly firm. Most of the water must have run off into the sloping ground and thick underbrush trailing down to both sides, and into the nearly impenetrable bamboo groves paralleling the trail. The right slope is steeper than the left, dropping off directly to the river.

I sprint through the darkening rainforest, but Tomás is still too far ahead on the winding path for me to see him.

For a little while I hear Xavier pounding behind me, but as I put more distance between us the sound soon fades. Apart from my own footfalls and breathing, and the unidentifiable jungle noises around me, I hear nothing.

The path is uneven. Narrow. I have to be careful to keep my footing.

I'd been hoping to see Tomás by now, but the trail zigzags in a series of tight turns on the way to the falls, and I still haven't caught sight of him.

It's possible he found a place to slip off into the jungle somewhere.

Yes, that's possible, but the tight clumps of bamboo trees leave very little room for someone to get off the trail, and I've been keeping a close eye on the jungle as I run and I haven't seen anything.

Though only halfway to the waterfall, I can hear it in the distance, thundering through the jungle.

Charlene and I hiked up here yesterday. The trail ends at a small scenic overlook. I'm not sure if there's anywhere beyond that to hide, but Tomás has been in the area a week already, and if there is another trail, he could have scouted it out earlier. Otherwise, I'm not sure why he would have fled on this path.

I round a curve in the trail and finally catch sight of him. I'm gaining ground, and there's only sixty or seventy feet between us.

As I sprint toward him, I can see that up ahead, the trail cuts sharply to the left to follow the escarpment of the cliff that plummets more than a hundred feet down into the valley.

Tomás disappears around the bend.

Easing up slightly so I can make the turn, I grab a tree with one hand to help me whip around the corner.

And as I fly forward, I almost step directly into the coiling mass of cobras Tomás left on the path in front of me.

I scramble to stop in time and barely manage to keep from trampling on the snakes.

Beyond them, Tomás disappears around the next turn.

Scanning the sides of the trail, I try to see if there's enough room to edge past the snakes, but the jungle is too thick.

Quickly, I snatch a sturdy stick from the underbrush. It's about four feet long, not ideal, but it'll have to do. There's no way to know if these snakes still have venom, but I don't have much choice. I move toward the cobras, prod the stick toward one of them, and manage to sweep it aside.

I tell myself that if I don't make any sudden movements, the snakes might just let me pass. However, as I move the stick toward the next one, it rears back and raises its hood, ready to strike.

I freeze, but before I can leap backward or knock the snake aside, it strikes at me with impossible quickness and latches onto my right forearm.

Dropping the stick, I grab the cobra's head with my free hand to pry it off, but it sinks its fangs in even deeper. I have to work at it, and finally I'm able to rip it loose, taking a meaty clump of flesh with it.

I sling the cobra into the jungle.

Maybe that snake had its venom glands removed and maybe it didn't. I feel a flash of pain, but at least it's not the same stinging, debilitating feeling that swept over me when I was bitten by the Egyptian cobra two years ago.

However, almost immediately my heart starts racing and I begin to feel like I did when I was struggling with claustrophobia and was sealed in a trunk and dropped into a shark tank.

Panic.

A rising, inexplicable, reeling sense of dread.

Calm. Breathe. Stay calm.

Xavier arrives at my side. The sound of the nearby falls makes it difficult to hear him, but by his gestures it's clear he's telling me to step back, to sit down.

He unbuckles his belt and snaps it out to wrap my arm in a rudimentary tourniquet, but I'm not about to have a seat; I'm going to catch the guy who left these snakes on the path, the guy who passed at least two cobras through the air tube Emilio was using.

My heart is jackhammering in my chest, and I can tell it's not just from the run and not just from adrenaline. It's something else. It's venom, it has to be the—

Get going, Jevin!

Stick in hand again, I shove one snake aside, giving me just enough room to get by. As soon as I'm past the cobras, I toss the stick back to Xavier and bolt forward again.

Blood flows freely from my arm. I ignore it and after maybe fifty yards I round the last turn and see Tomás.

He has reached the small clearing where a swath of forest was slashed away by the villagers to provide an overview of the waterfall, which drops ten stories into the gorge. He looks my direction, backs up two steps, and I have a feeling I know what he's about to do.

Trying to buy time until Xavier can get here, I hold up my hands to show Tomás that I'm not a threat. Slowly, I step forward.

Tomás glances toward me, then peers at the plummeting falls. I pause, then ease closer. He takes one more look at me and then spins and runs directly toward the edge of the cliff.

Time seems to slow as he strides across the ground, reaches the lip of the overlook at a full sprint, and launches himself off the edge.

A few seconds later I arrive and come to a halt near the place where he jumped.

You can catch him. You've fallen farther than this, you've—

Yes, but that was onto a stunt pad, not in a jungle river.

My heart is slamming hard against the inside of my chest, not just from the run but from the thought of what I'm about to do.

Shivers are still running through me; everything around me seems to shrink and grow larger at the same time. I've never hallucinated before, but this must be what it's like.

What is that? The venom? No, it can't be. It's—

Go!

After two decades of doing water escapes, I can hold my breath for close to three minutes.

But that's when you're sitting still, in calm water, not swimming through rapids!

In the fading light I can just barely make out Tomás's head emerge thirty feet beyond the base of the falls. He's moving toward shore. Still alive. Swimming. About to disappear into the jungle.

I take a deep breath.

No, you're not going to do this.

Actually, I am.

I'm backing up to get a running start when Xavier arrives, gesturing wildly for me to stop, but all I can think of is Emilio lying in that coffin, struggling to breathe, that baby cobra writhing from between his bluish lips.

Tomás did that to him.

And now he's getting away.

I dash forward and leap into the void.

Maelstrom

The cascading water envelops me as the world whips by.

My stomach seems to float up into my chest as the eternity of the fall wraps me in its drenching arms. Then I land, plunging into the water at the base of the waterfall, and everything is a swirl of black and I'm swimming hard, but it does no good. The rushing, tumbling river is tugging at me, dragging me down, holding me relentlessly under.

I should be able to hold my breath here without any problem, but whatever happened with that snakebite has affected my respiration and my pulse. The sense of apprehension is almost overwhelming. The water is shockingly cold and my lungs are already desperate for air.

Spinning.

Descending.

My left shin slams against a boulder, and a thick chug of pain pounds up my leg. The roiling water swivels me around but at least takes me to the surface briefly—just long enough for me to grab a breath before it sweeps me under again.

I try to swim up, but fail.

Calm.

Stay calm.

Just get to the surface.

I kick and stroke uselessly in the fearsome current, trying to make it to air, and at last the water spits me up, and I snatch another much-needed breath and swim hard toward the riverbank where Tomás headed a few moments ago.

But the river has hold of me and sweeps me swiftly downstream, past the clearing and toward the steep cliffs that tower high above me on both sides. Ahead of me, the water channels into another, smaller falls, but since the chute is so narrow, the current is even stronger here than it was at the base of the main falls.

Okay, this is where I need to get to shore.

Right.

Now.

I fight the current to get to a place on the right shoreline where a break in the cliffs just above the chute provides a spot that looks large enough to stand on. From there I'm not sure how I'll get up the cliff, especially if I have to climb it in the dark. But that side of the river is within reach. That's where I'm going.

It's the wrong bank to catch Tomás, but right now I'm more concerned with just getting out of this river and staying alive than anything else.

I swim fiercely toward the riverbank, and just when I'm starting to think I won't make it, the ground rises up beneath my feet, giving me enough footing to push off and propel myself toward the shallower water.

Chancing entrapping my foot between the rocks on the river bottom, I press off a boulder and scramble through the water that's still trying to sweep me under, and make it to the rocky edge of the break in the cliffs.

Exhausted, I crawl out of the river and use an outcropping on the rock face for balance as I hoist myself to my feet.

From here I have no way of getting across the river, but even though I can't get to Tomás, if I'm lucky I'll be able to scale this cliff and then scramble back up the bank and make my way to the trail again. Not easy by any means, but doable.

As long as I have enough light.

Xavier. He knows you're down here. He'll find you.

But darkness is already beginning to ensnare the jungle. Still, I can make out Tomás staring at me from the far shore. His face is hidden by shadows, but his form is visible.

He stands stoically for a moment, then slowly steps back and disappears into the trees. I watch to see if he'll reappear, but he does not. It's quickly getting so dark that it's tough to see across the river at all.

Leaning against the rock face, I close my eyes and try to catch my breath, but only find myself thinking of Emilio lying there struggling for breath himself—and of Charlene leaning over him, trying to save him.

I tell myself that my friend will be alright, that Charlene was able to get air past his swollen throat and into his lungs. I try my hardest to make myself believe it.

But right now I can't do anything to help him, all I can do is try to get back up the slope to the trail before the jungle becomes completely one with the night.

I inspect my wounded shin. It's bruised and already swollen, but passing my hand gently across it, I don't feel any fractures or obvious deformities. When I put pressure on it, the leg doesn't hurt like I imagine it would if there were any broken bones.

Taking off my shirt, I tie it tightly around my bleeding arm, study the darkening cliff for handholds, and begin to climb.

Dust to Dust

Emilio did not survive.

Xavier and three men from the village catch up with me as I'm picking my way through a narrow furrow in the trees, trying to locate the path. We don't find out about Emilio until we make it back to the village, but when I see him lying motionless with a sheet pulled over his head, it's clear what has happened.

Charlene approaches me silently as we emerge from the darkness and enter the uneven circle of light cast from the lanterns and torches that the villagers have left positioned throughout the cemetery and surrounding the body.

Her gaze lands on my arm, which is still wrapped with my shirt. Blood has stained the fabric dark red, and a question mark of deep concern crosses her face. I do my best to ease her worry, telling her I'm fine—and then I ask how she is and notice the trail of fresh tears on her cheeks.

She touches my shoulder lightly, then leans into my arms, and I feel her tremble as the shock of what has happened to our friend sweeps over her.

I don't know how long we stand there, but by the time she eases back, Xavier and the villagers have walked off and left the two of us alone.

I brush my finger across Charlene's cheek to press away the final tear that has slipped from her eye, but she shakes her head slightly and pulls away, as if suddenly my touch is disagreeable to her.

"What did you think you were doing?" Her tone is somewhat strained, but also delicate, like glass that's too brittle to stand on its own. "Going after him like that? You might have . . ." She catches herself and leaves the rest unsaid, but I can fill in the blanks.

It's hard to know what to say. "He got away," I tell her at last.

She gestures toward my soaked clothes. "The waterfall?"

"Yeah."

"Jevin, you didn't really jump off that overlook into the river." Her tone makes it clear that it's not really a question.

"I had to go after him, Charlene. He killed Emilio."

"But you didn't have to follow him off a hundred-foot cliff." There's sharp exasperation in her voice, making it clear that having this conversation right now is not going to lead anywhere productive, and all I do is end up agreeing with her.

"Right."

After a moment I realize we're both looking at Emilio's body.

"They've sent for some of the Philippine National Police," she tells me softly, "from Kabugao, but you know how far that is."

"They won't be here for, what, three, four hours?"

"At least. Do you have any idea why he did it? Why anyone would want to hurt Emilio?"

Charlene says "hurt" instead of "kill," and I figure it's just because actually putting into words the reality of what has happened would be too painful.

I shake my head. "No."

She looks at my wounded arm again. "What happened out there, Jev?"

"It's okay. I'm alright."

She reaches out tenderly to unwrap my impromptu blood-drenched dressing. "Did he have a knife? What is . . . ?"

I put my hand on hers to stop her. "It was a snake. One of the cobras. I had to pull it off—"

"What? You were bitten? We need to get you some antivenin right away and—"

"The snake didn't have any venom," I reassure her, but I'm not sure that's exactly true, not based on the reaction my body had after that cobra bit me. Regardless, whatever caused that uncontrollable rush of anxiety, the effect has been fading and I'm feeling more like myself again. "I'll be fine. Really."

"Well, I at least need to bandage that up properly." She takes my hand to lead me to the hut where we're staying. "Come on."

"Let me see him first."

"I don't want to go near him again, Jev. I can't."

People deal with death in different ways, and I sense that Charlene's urgency to treat my arm is, at least partially, her way of trying to wrap her mind around the situation—she can't do anything to help Emilio, but she can attend to my wound. It's not much, but at least it's something. And in times when things feel completely out of control, finding a way to manage at least one thing always seems to help, at least in a small way.

"I won't be long. Just give me a minute."

Her gaze shifts past me toward the dark fringe of the jungle. "Okay. I'll meet you by the hut."

"Right."

Then without another word she heads off, and it's just me in the graveyard with my friend's corpse.

Jagged shadows birthed from the flicking torchlight shift erratically across each other, giving the cemetery a ghostly, surreal feel.

As I walk toward him, the gravity of what has happened hits me full force.

My friend Emilio is dead. He will never smile again, never laugh again, never dream or hope or love again. It's over. Whatever he might have wanted to accomplish in this life will remain forever undone. His soul has escaped this vale of tears and slipped into eternity, and his body has been left behind for us to mourn and bury. Dust to dust. Life to death. Hope to grief.

I arrive at his corpse and stand for a moment looking down at the sheet covering his body. It strikes me that we cover the dead, we treat them with respect, not for their sake but for ours. We extend reverence to corpses in an attempt to affirm the value of our own lives and to mask the stark truth of our own mortality.

After all, if we just treated our dead like the skin-encased sacks of blood and bones and soon-to-be-rotten meat that they are, we would feel that—apart from the breath that separates us—we're as finite and susceptible to the grim reaper as they were. And that's just too terrifying a thought.

So we distract ourselves, divert our attention from all that, cover up the truth beneath the frantic, stifling busyness of our brief and worried days. If I were a devil trying to tempt people to squander their lives, I would simply keep them buried in urgency and obsessed with trivialities; otherwise they might just take the time to reflect on life and death and eternity and wake up to the things that matter most.

I kneel and gently pull back the sheet that's covering Emilio's face.

His eyes are closed, his lips blue, his face gray and clay-like. He's lying far more still than a living person ever could, and this thing that I'm looking at barely reminds me of my friend at all.

People speak of their loved ones passing away, but in this case that's not what happened at all. Emilio didn't pass away, he was viciously murdered.

No, when you die of asphyxiation because your throat has swollen shut, you're not just passing away, you're dying a strangled, horrible death. And the man who did this to him managed to get away.

There isn't always a silver lining or a pot of gold at the end of the rainbow. Eventually, bad things happen to all good people, and the dragon wins and death has her way. You can think all the positive, comforting thoughts in the world, extend so much love to others that it makes your heart ache and soar at the same time, but in the end everyone—everything—that has ever been born will pass from the world and end only in dust and rot and decay.

It's only wishful thinking to say that love conquers all. It doesn't. Death does. In the end, death even conquers love.

I feel the urge to touch Emilio's face, and I reach out slowly, but in the end stop short.

And as I lower my hand to the ground, it happens.

It doesn't surprise me, but still, it unsettles me and sends a terrible, oppressive chill winding down my spine.

I think of my family and what happened five hundred and two days ago when I stood on that shoreline and stared down at the three corpses, at the drowned bodies of my wife and our twin five-year-old boys, lying just as lifeless and still as Emilio does now.

Although I try to slide the memories aside, I know it won't help.

Whenever I remember what happened on that dark day, the images root themselves inside of me all over again, and it takes hours, sometimes days, before they leave. I can feel that happening right now—the grim memories gripping me, memories of Rachel and Anthony and Andrew lined up in a macabre row at my feet.

At the time, we were living in New Jersey during a run of my show in Atlantic City. On a quiet Saturday morning Rachel put the boys in the minivan and drove to Heron Bay. She passed through the parking lot and then accelerated off the pier with our twins strapped in their car seats in the back.

A little over two hours later I watched as the divers pulled up their bodies.

In the ensuing weeks when the police and the insurance company investigators inspected the minivan, they didn't find anything wrong with it. The truth, the heart-wrenching, terrible truth, became obvious and inescapable: Rachel did it on purpose.

There was no way she could have accidentally navigated through that parking lot, hit the pier at that angle, and guided the minivan all the way to the end where she drove off. No, it wasn't an accident.

But why?

Why did she do it?

That question has haunted me ever since.

In the months following their deaths, I searched endlessly through my memories and through Rachel's computer files, emails, text messages, and status updates looking for some clue as to why she took her life and took our boys with her. It was almost as if I thought that if I could find a reason, I might be able to accept it all more easily.

But I didn't find a reason, and with each passing day I only became more bewildered and felt more and more lost in a deep, confusing maze of unanswerable questions.

I wanted to hate Rachel for murdering my sons—and for murdering herself—but as hard as I tried, I couldn't do it. Love is a mysterious thing, and even after her unthinkable act, I never found a way to love her any less.

I should have seen something.

Should have been there to stop it.

That's what I told myself.

These days questions and pain still loom there, staring at me coldly, perched on the crest of my past, but at least I'm starting to move on. I'm with Charlene now. We're taking things slowly in our relationship, but at least it feels like a doorway has opened up and a new future is dawning with it.

But right now, in this cemetery with the corpse of my friend lying before me, all of the renewed hope is dimmed in the reality of his death.

Looking down at Emilio, I notice a curl of a delicate chain just below his neck, and when I pull the sheet back a little more I see that Charlene has laid her cross necklace on his chest. It's her most treasured piece of jewelry, and it just reiterates how much Emilio meant to her, to both of us.

I spend some time there with him and find that my thoughts have shifted into a kind of prayer.

He grew up in an orphanage here on this island. He was single, never married, had no children, and honestly, as far as I know, there are no next of kin to notify. So in the end, I don't pray for his surviving family members as much as I end up praying for myself and Emilio's other friends.

Before attempting escapes that can end up being fatal, all conscientious escape artists make plans for the possibility that they might not succeed, and I know that in the event that he didn't make it, Emilio desired to be buried here, near the jungle he learned to love as a child.

I'm no expert on how to talk to God, but I suppose sometimes the most eloquent prayers are those that aren't spoken at all but that rise to heaven directly from the fractures in our hearts, the places where words become superfluous, and now that's the kind of prayer I find myself praying.

Emilio was a man of faith, raised Catholic, but he'd recently joined a small conservative church—Baptist, I think. In any case, he was unquestionably more ready to face eternity than I've ever been, and that seems to bring me a small sense of peace—but it's nowhere near the peace I would be feeling if he were still alive.

At last I cover his head again and leave to find Charlene.

As I enter the hut, I see Xavier is waiting with her. They both look my way, and when he speaks his voice is soft yet intense. "I found something in Emilio's things."

"Tell me."

He shows me a scratched and well-used portable USB flash drive. It has the symbol for RixoTray Pharmaceuticals imprinted on the side.

I feel my hand forming into a fist. "Not those guys again."

"Yeah. Those guys again."

While She Sleeps

We first encountered RixoTray last fall while we were investigating a controversial mind-to-mind communication research program for a television show I had at the time. In each episode I would debunk the tricks of a different psychic or medium by using mentalism, illusions, and sleight of hand, then I'd demonstrate how the person faked his or her seemingly miraculous feats.

In the process of exploring how the RixoTray research might've been faked, Charlene and I stumbled onto a conspiracy involving the company's CEO and an assassin known as Akinsanya.

In the end, RixoTray's CEO was apprehended, but this guy Akinsanya was still out there somewhere. The FBI had interviewed us at the time and since then has continued to follow up with us every few weeks to see if he has contacted us.

Nothing so far.

Now, as Xavier hands me the USB drive, I ask him, "Do you have any idea what Emilio was doing with this?"

He shakes his head. "No. But I plugged it in my laptop. It's a 4 gig drive, but no files came up and only 2.7 gigs appear as available."

"So somehow there are 1.3 gigs of hidden data on the drive?"

"That's what it looks like. Yes."

I consider that. "It could be nothing."

"True." But the way he says that, it's clear he doesn't believe it. "But Emilio getting murdered with something like this from RixoTray in his things seems like an awfully big coincidence."

I evaluate what we know. It might be a stretch, but I throw it out there anyway. "You don't think Tomás could be Akinsanya?"

"Who knows. Maybe." Xavier rubs his chin thoughtfully. "In either case, Emilio is brutally killed as it's being filmed and watched by millions of people around the globe? Someone wanted to make a statement here."

There's no way to tell for certain, and speculating too much right now probably isn't going to move us any closer to finding out what happened here, but still, I find myself agreeing with him. I pass the drive back to him. "Did you find anything else in his things?"

"Nothing that struck me as unusual."

Charlene indicates toward the first aid supplies she has set out on the table, and I take a seat. She unwraps the shirt encircling my arm, shakes her head concernedly, and takes out some antiseptic.

"We need to find out what those files are," I say.

"Yes, we do," Xavier agrees.

"I think it's time to make a call."

"To who?"

"Fionna."

"Hmm." He nods. "I'll be right back."

He slips out the door and into the night.

The adrenaline must finally be draining from my system because the more Charlene works on my arm, the more it starts to really hurt, but I do my best to hold back from letting her see how much it's bothering me.

"How are you doing?" she asks.

"I'm good."

"It hurts like the dickens, doesn't it?"

"That's one way to put it."

She's being gentle, but as she spreads antibiotics on the sore, another sharp burst of pain shoots up my arm, and I tighten my jaw, try to distract myself.

For the time being, though, the discomfort in my arm is keeping me from thinking too much about my banged-up leg.

So at least there's that.

She's finishing bandaging my arm when Xavier returns with the satellite hookup that his team was using to transmit Emilio's escape live on the Internet. He runs the connect cord to his laptop and places a video call through to Fionna.

Fionna McClury is a single, stay-at-home mom who runs a cybersecurity consulting company out of her basement. Tech firms hire her to see if she can get past their firewalls, and she and her associates—who the companies don't realize are really her four homeschooled kids—rarely come up short. She makes reasonably good money, but two painful divorces cost her dearly, and these days she barely manages to sock enough away for the kids' college funds and keep the minivan filled up with gas and the fridge stocked—which is no easy task with two teenage boys.

I do my best to pay her what she's worth, and she's never let me down ever since she started doing projects for me a couple years ago.

Fionna answers the video chat request right away. Her frizzled red hair seems to have paused in the middle of an explosion.

Last week her five-year-old daughter Mandie informed me that her mommy's eyes were viridian. It was an impressive word for a kindergartner—I would have just said *green*—but as dedicated as Fionna is to homeschooling her kids, Mandie's vocabulary didn't exactly surprise me.

One of Fionna's eyes wanders, and I think sometimes she shifts which eye she's focusing on you just to mess with you.

As far as I know, she hasn't been in a serious relationship for over a year, which is something Xavier has mused aloud to me about more than once, wondering when I think she might be ready to date again. Just for curiosity's sake, of course.

I fill her in about what happened to Emilio and about the chase through the jungle after the snake wrangler, Tomás Agcaoili.

Fionna's eyes cloud as she listens, and at last she asks us to give her a minute. She turns away from the screen so we can't see her. I think we all know she's crying but just doesn't want us to see.

The three of us have all had at least a little chance to begin processing Emilio's death, and we give her some time to let the news sink in.

At last, when she gives her attention back to the screen, it's clear she's trying to be as detached and objective as she can, but still, her pain comes through in every word. "At first people on Twitter thought it was all part of the escape, but I could tell by your expression, Xavier, that something had gone terribly wrong." She takes a heavy breath. "There's still a lot of speculation online that it was all faked, that Emilio's really okay. I was hoping . . ." Her voice trails off. "I was hoping they were right."

It's a long time before anyone speaks, but finally Xavier does. He's never been good with calculating time zones, and when he asks softly if her kids saw what happened, Fionna reminds him that it's just now coming up on 5:00 a.m. there in Vegas. "They were all in bed. Thankfully."

Xav tells her about the USB drive, and when he holds it up she just shakes her head. "RixoTray? Really? How could they possibly be part of this?"

"That's something we're hoping you can help us figure out."

"And that, I'm glad to do. Stick the drive into your computer; let me see if I can pull anything up from here." He inserts it into the USB port and starts giving her his password to access his hard drive, but she cuts him off: "I already have it. I hashed it a couple weeks ago."

"You cracked my password?"

"You're a role model to my kids, Mr. Wray. I wanted to keep an eye on what sites you've been going to."

"I, um—"

"Nothing illegal, nothing immoral, no porn. I'm proud of you."

"Oh . . . Thanks."

"But you sure visit the *X-Files* archives a lot."

"I like the *X-Files*."

"Yes, you do."

"Best documentary filmmaking of the last twenty years."

"I really hope you're not being serious."

While she's talking, she's also studying her screen and typing. At last she shakes her head. "I might be able to do this from here, but I can tell you right now whoever did this is a pro. It'd be a lot easier if I had it in hand. When are you guys coming back?"

Fionna and her kids are house-sitting for me this week at my place in Vegas, but their home is in Chicago, and when she says "you guys" it sounds endearingly Midwestern.

"By Saturday afternoon," I tell her. I'm scheduled to perform again Saturday evening at the Arête, the newest resort and casino in Vegas. "Tomorrow morning we'll have to look into funeral arrangements, and I'm going to see if we can get anywhere with the police or maybe the consulate in Manila to find this guy Tomás Agcaoili. Then I imagine we'll fly back as soon as we can."

We have tickets for a very late flight Friday night but had planned from the beginning to get on an earlier flight if possible. Switching international flights isn't typically as hard when you're flying first class as it is when you're in coach.

"Alright. In the meantime I can do some checking—flight manifests, that sort of thing, see when Agcaoili arrived in the country, if he was traveling with anyone. Maybe I can find out more about where he's from or if he's booked any tickets to leave the country."

"Good. And the RixoTray connection, see if you can find out what Emilio might have to do with them or with Tomás."

"Done."

"One more thing. Can you remotely log into Emilio's computer?"

"Sure."

"I don't know why anyone would want to kill him, but he was wired into that machine like it was his lifeline to the world. If he was involved in something he shouldn't have been or found out something someone didn't want him to know—"

"It would be on his computer."

"Possibly, yes. Or at least footprints leading toward it would be."

"Hmm." She reflects for a moment. "I'll take a peek at his phone and iPad files too, do some searching, see if he used any kind of cloud-based backups. If he did, I should be able to access the data, download it onto a ghost drive."

Ah, yes. One of the disadvantages most people don't think of when they move to online backup services—you put your files on the web and anyone with a little motivation and know-how can get into them even if the devices are turned off. If people knew how easy it is for hackers to access data on the cloud, I doubt they'd be so quick to sign up for those services.

Emilio's house lies across town from mine, but it's within the city limits, and Fionna suggests that she contact the Vegas police.

"Why not?" I figure it's worth getting everyone we can involved in finding out what's going on. "Who knows, maybe they'll be willing to get to the bottom of this." I'm not holding out a lot of hope, though: Emilio was a Filipino citizen killed in his home country. "Okay, our plan for tomorrow—"

"Actually, for yesterday," Xavier clarifies, "for Fionna, that is."

"No, today," she corrects him. "At least as far as I'm concerned, but tomorrow for you, from your perspective. Remember, for me, this afternoon is tomorrow morning for you, so your yesterday evening will still be today for me."

"I have no idea what you just said."

"Xavier, Maddie is better at time zones than you are. And she's only nine."

A pause. "She's almost ten."

"Well . . . you have me there, Mr. Wray."

"So." I bring things to a close. "Fionna, you'll be diving into Emilio's data files; we'll see if we can get anywhere with the police and the American consulate in Manila and do our best to get back home by Friday night or Saturday morning."

We're all on board with the plan, and after ending the video chat, Xavier, Charlene, and I take off for bed to do our best to get some sleep before the police from Kabugao arrive.

2 hours 32 minutes later
Las Vegas, Nevada
7:31 a.m.

Colonel Derek Byrne, otherwise known as Akinsanya, stood beside the bed watching his partner Calista Hendrix sleep.

He liked to do this, to rise before she did and observe her when she had no idea that he was there.

Slowly, he pulled the covers away until only a single sheet was covering her.

The woman really was lovely.

She lay on her side, and he let his gaze move slowly down her body, tracing the curves of her impeccable figure outlined beneath the sheet.

He could touch her anywhere, run his hand across her arm, her back, her leg—light enough and she would never know, gentle enough and she would not even wake up.

She was his.

To do with as he pleased.

He bent closer and studied her face, then closed his eyes and drew in a long breath, smelling her clean, shampooed hair, still sweet and aromatic even after spending the last three hours nestled against her pillow.

Lavender.

Exquisite.

He stood.

From what he'd heard, things in the Philippines regarding Emilio Benigno had gone pretty much as planned, although Tomás Agcaoili had not been as clean about it all as he'd hoped.

Well, he would deal with that tomorrow afternoon when Tomás got back to Vegas and handed over the USB drive.

He walked to the living room and pulled out his cell phone.

It was still before office hours, but he put the call through to the person who was coordinating the project. All of their communication so far had been through encrypted files or electronically masked phone conversations, so Derek still didn't even know if it was a woman or a man, let alone the person's identity.

Derek was good at what he did, so he was impressed that so far he'd been unable to figure out the name of the person. Not even Mr. Takahashi, the CEO of Plyotech, had any idea who was pulling the strings and working in the background to mastermind the project.

But Derek wanted to find out.

After all, as they say, knowledge is power. While that might not always be true, knowledge was at least leverage. And when you have enough leverage, you can tilt even the most difficult situations to your advantage.

So, he was doing his own private research to find out who this person was, but for the time being he simply needed to find out if everything was still on track for Sunday night.

The person orchestrating the deal answered after one ring, and as always, Derek was the first to speak. "Emilio is dead."

"I saw the news. And the Filipino police?"

"Don't worry, they won't be looking any further into his death."

A pause. "Are we all set for Sunday?"

"I was just about to ask you the same thing. From my end, yes. I have a young woman here who's going to take care of everything."

"She can be trusted?"

"She can be trusted."

"And the engineer from Groom Lake?"

"Turnisen."

"Yes."

"We'll get what we need from him."

"You'll take care of that part yourself?"

"Absolutely."

And then a surprise. "I'd like you to meet with my associate in Phoenix tomorrow."

"I'll need to be back by five. I have a meeting scheduled with Tomás."

"That won't be a problem. I've already taken the initiative of booking you a ticket. You leave at 9:51 in the morning and will return on the 2:20 flight."

"And what will we be covering at the meeting?"

"The delivery of the merchandise. It's not something I wish to discuss over the phone."

That was certainly understandable. Considering what was at stake.

"Keep me informed if the schedule changes," Derek said.

"I will."

After the call, Derek took his morning regimen of forty vitamins and supplements, then brewed some coffee, mixed in the gray powder that he took every day, and worked out for an hour—core, mainly, since research showed that that was the most important muscle group for longevity.

He was taking all the steps he knew to treat his condition: reprogramming his body's biochemistry through supplements, diet, and gene therapy, exercising vigorously, eating only natural foods, pursuing the latest advancements in robotics, biogenetic engineering, and nanotechnology.

Because Derek, the avenging hero Colonel Derek Byrne, knew his time on this earth was limited.

He was dying.

Unless he had something to say about it.

Whether you believe we evolved from lower primates or were shaped uniquely by the hand of God himself, this much was undeniable: from the very beginning, ever since we first emerged on this planet, we, as a species, have been searching for the fountain of youth, for the secrets to living forever.

All across the globe, in every culture ever studied, *Homo sapiens* have sought eternal life.

In China alone there are at least a thousand different names for the elixir of life. Tales of the search for this "pool of nectar" or "dancing water" fill volumes of world history—from Gilgamesh's search for the answer to eternal life, to the legendary quest of Qin Shi Huangdi, the first emperor of China, to do the same, to the search for that elusive fountain of youth.

And where we fail to find physical immortality, religions spring up to offer us the next best thing—spiritual immortality, reincarnation, heaven, Nirvana, a paradise with seventy virgins at our beck and call. And on and on and on.

But now, in the twenty-first century, for the first time ever, our species was on the verge of conquering the grave.

Technology offered what biology never could: a chance to cheat death once and for all.

Derek returned to the bedroom, walked past Calista, who was still fast asleep, and entered the bathroom to take a shower.

He was an agnostic. He didn't believe in God, but he did believe in the possibility of God.

Yes, there were times when he even believed in the likelihood of God.

Because you had to give up an awful lot to be an atheist.

The idea of justice, for one thing, because some people really do spend their lives sexually abusing little girls in their basements and get away with it, and if there's no afterlife, they would just die like everyone else and be no better or worse off. In fact, looking at the world as it is, there's no legitimate reason to believe in justice. Why would you even delude yourself to think that it exists when there's no evidence of it at all in the natural world and, if there's no God, no one to institute it in the afterlife?

And you have to give up on the idea that your life has meaning—or at least any purpose beyond reproducing and hoping that eventually your genes will be good for the betterment of the race or the planet. And if they would not be, you'd have an obligation not to reproduce at all.

After all, there is no purpose inherent in naturalistic evolution. No goal. No intention. No design.

Without eternity, without God, hope is simply a sedative. It doesn't even rate as a helpful illusion because it isn't really helpful for anything other than numbing you, distracting you from the truth that, since the universe is winding down and dying, nothing you do ultimately matters, and your life, in the grand scheme of things, is nothing, contributes nothing, and will soon be forgotten and your name erased from the evanescent chronicles of time and space.

But, on the other hand, life would be so much easier, so much more carefree, if God wasn't there, if there was no higher moral authority to answer to. No ultimate accountability.

For Derek, that was perhaps the greatest attraction to being an atheist—the inevitable conclusion that morality is utilitarian, determined only by the biological imperatives of reproduction and survival.

What an enticing worldview.

Because, as philosophers have pointed out over the ages, if God doesn't exist then all is permissible.

Yes, very enticing.

Derek finished his shower, toweled off, and walked down the hall to his home office, where he kept the bionic arm to practice with when he wasn't at Plyotech.

Taking it with him, he returned to the bedroom and set it beside the bed.

He'd let Calista work last night and she hadn't gotten back to his condo until nearly four o'clock. But even then, she'd joined him for drinks. While preparing them, he'd slipped a couple pills into her margarita, and based on her body size and the amount of drugs and alcohol she'd consumed, Derek was confident she would be out until ten or eleven.

Which gave him plenty of time.

He had no idea how she would respond if she knew that he so often drugged her and then had his way with her like this in the mornings, but she did not know and he was not planning to ever reveal it to her.

"I love you, my little courtesan." His spoke the words softly and tenderly as he pulled the remaining sheet away.

She lay asleep before him. Drugged. Helpless. In only a nightshirt and panties.

He gently brushed a strand of hair away from her cheek, glided his hand along her thigh, and then pulled a chair up beside the bed. He hoped he wouldn't have to kill her when all of this was over. It just wouldn't be right using the thread and needle on her, marring such a flawless and magnificent body.

So beautiful.

So young.

So alive.

And all his.

He positioned her on her back, placed the robotic arm beside her, and sat in the chair to watch.

Then, using his thoughts, he uncurled the hand, leaned it out over her, and laid it gently on her shoulder.

And moved on from there.

Up in the Air

The four members of the Philippine National Police, or PNP, don't roll in until dawn. They do a cursory search of the trails surrounding the village, but there's no sign of Tomás, and they make it clear that they're not interested in tromping around the jungle any longer than necessary looking for him.

When I show them the thumb drive, they stare at me somewhat dumbfounded that I would think it has anything to do with Emilio's death.

They just shake their heads when they hear, through our translator, about the escape Emilio was trying to do, calling it a dangerous publicity stunt gone bad. Considering the circumstances, I'm amazed when they label his death accidental.

From past conversations with Emilio, I know that corruption is rampant in the PNP. Bribes aren't uncommon at all—in fact, they're expected—and I can't help but wonder if these officers might have been paid by Tomás or a cohort of his to turn their backs on Emilio's death.

My stage shows over the years have done quite well, and finances aren't a big concern for me. However, even after making it known that I have substantial resources at my disposal, I still get nowhere with the police, which tells me it isn't simply financial gain that's motivating them.

I can't think of too many things that are bigger motivators than greed, but I can think of one—fear.

What do they want?

What are they afraid of?

When all of that proves to be a dead end, I finally give up, realizing that our best bet will be talking with the US ambassador in Manila. Emilio might have been born here in the Philippines, but most of his life was spent in the States, and I'm hoping that Ambassador White-head will be able to pressure the government to have the authorities look into his death.

I'm not familiar with the specific religious beliefs of the people in this village, but I'm guessing that, like most of the indigenous people in the region, they practice a mixture of spiritist religions combined with strands of Roman Catholicism.

Whatever their religion is, it's clear that everyone here is deeply shaken by Emilio's death. They demand that we bury him quickly to avoid more calamities or curses. Based on what Emilio told me earlier about where he wanted to be buried if the escape proved fatal, we decide to hold a funeral right there at the graveyard, now, this morning.

Xavier and I say a few words, then Charlene, who isn't afraid of expressing her faith, gets up. She reads from 1 Thessalonians 4:13–14: "But I would not have you to be ignorant, brethren, concerning them which are asleep, that ye sorrow not, even as others which have no hope. For if we believe that Jesus died and rose again, even so them also which sleep in Jesus will God bring with him."

She speaks for a few moments about hope and how much it matters and how vital it is that we place ours in the right person—she says "person" rather than "place," which strikes me as a bit of an odd way to phrase things. The villagers and police officers listen quietly to her translator.

Finally, she recites the 23rd Psalm from memory, and a line about walking through the valley of the shadow of death strikes me. I guess I'd always thought the Bible said the "valley of death," but it's just the "*shadow* of death" instead. And if a shadow is covering the valley, it means there's a brighter light shining somewhere beyond the horizon.

That thought at least brings me a little comfort.

Then we lower Emilio into the grave again and, for the second time, cover his coffin with the damp jungle soil.

But unlike last night, this time I know there's no chance that I'll be seeing him rising from the ground alive.

To get to Manila we need to drive more than two hours through the jungle to Kabugao, then grab a charter plane. Xavier made prior arrangements, and it's waiting and ready for us when we get there.

The consulate is downtown in an older part of Manila. Battling traffic is a nightmare, and it's nearly six o'clock by the time we finally arrive. If we were in America, they might have already been closed for the weekend, but they're on Filipino time and Ambassador Whitehead is still in his office. However, he's packing up his things and obviously on his way out.

Xavier gets on the phone to work at trying to get us an earlier flight home while Charlene and I speak with the ambassador. I tell him about the USB drive, and although he seems doubtful that it'll lead to anything, he at last offers, "We could have someone dust it for prints."

Even though Xavier and I have already handled the drive, likely obscuring any other prints, I accept the offer. They take samples of our prints and lift Emilio's from his luggage, which we have with us because we weren't about to just leave it there in the village.

"We don't have the resources to run these here," the ambassador explains. "And it's a Friday night, so we're not going to be able to process them until Monday."

"Monday?" I shake my head. "That's—"

"We're not at the FBI Lab," he says curtly. "We're not set up for something like this. It's not what we do. We process visa applications, we're not a law enforcement agency."

He's being just as helpful as the PNP.

"You must have the ability to run this through some sort of fingerprint scanner."

"I'm sorry." But he doesn't sound especially sorry, and his attitude perplexes me.

I decide it'll be better to get the drive back to the states for Fionna to work on. Maybe the FBI or the Las Vegas PD will be able to run the prints.

With that settled, he makes me all sorts of promises, hands me a stack of papers to fill out, and then excuses himself for an important dinner appointment with some sort of cultural tourism group that's evidently trying to work more closely with Americans.

"Just fax those back to me or scan them in and email them to my office." He smiles in an artificial, political way that drives home once again how cavalierly he's taking this. "Honestly, I have to go, and there's nothing more you can do here. Go home. I'll do all I can to get to the bottom of your friend's death."

He checks the time, announces that he really must be leaving, and then reaches out to shake my hand, but I make no move either to leave or to take his hand.

"You're not going to do anything to find out who killed him, are you?"

"I just told you that I am."

"Yes, you did."

A stiff moment closes in around us.

At last he lowers his arm, and the look on his face is all the answer I need—even though he reassures me again, in well-practiced diplomatic tones, that he will do whatever it takes, I'm doubting that he'll do anything more than make a few obligatory phone calls.

Charlene is as exasperated as I am. "What if it were a friend of yours who was murdered?"

"I'm sorry for your loss. Truly, I am. I'll see what I can do working with the police, encouraging them to look into this, but since he's not an American citizen, I'm not sure what role I have in all this. I wouldn't want to make you any promises I can't keep."

"No." I don't take my gaze off his face. "You wouldn't."

His expression flattens. For a moment I have the sense that he's going to reply, but he holds back. He looks away, ushers his assistant into the room, excuses himself, and, without another word, leaves for his meeting.

Apparently, Emilio was too American to be investigated by the Filipinos and too Filipino to be investigated by the Americans.

Well, even if they are not going to do anything to get to the bottom of his death, I am.

On the way to the airport we connect with Fionna via another video chat and find out she hasn't located any record of Tomás leaving the country, but that's not entirely a surprise. He could have easily disappeared back into the population here or perhaps even left the country under an assumed name.

"I've been analyzing the files on Emilio's computer and his phone." She sighs, sounding both exhausted and exasperated. "Let me put this in an acorn for you . . ."

It takes me a moment before I catch on to what she's trying to say.

A nutshell. Yes.

She's going to put it in a nutshell.

Although Fionna is off-the-charts brilliant, when it comes to figures of speech she doesn't always hit the nail quite on the head—or nail things right through the brain, as she once put it.

She goes on, "All I'm finding are dead ends. I contacted the Vegas police, but they told me this is out of their jurisdiction—big surprise there. Anyway, I was searching for data strings that might be related to the name of the snake wrangler, RixoTray, and so on, but I'm not getting anywhere. I'm having to rewrite the search algorithms as I go along here. I need that USB drive. When will you get to town?"

Xavier answers for me. "With layovers and flight times it's going to be about twenty hours from now, so I guess we'll see you tomorrow night?"

"Not quite."

"Yesterday?"

"Actually, tonight."

"I'm never going to get ahold of this."

"I'll have Maddie walk it through for you."

"Ah. Thanks."

So, our itinerary: fly from Manila to Tokyo to Los Angeles to Las Vegas.

Tight connections all the way around. This is going to be a long night.

Or day, depending on how you looked at it.

After checking our bags, the three of us board the plane to start our journey home to see if we can untangle anything back in the States.

I'm not about to let the death of my friend get lost in a bureaucratic quagmire or get brushed under the carpet by police who've been paid off or intimidated.

No.

Not a chance.

PART III

Garbage Bags

The first time Calista Hendrix killed someone, it was a mistake.

It happened so quickly, so unexpectedly, that she hardly even realized what she was doing.

It was four years ago now, when she was twenty years old and still living in Florida.

One moment she was in her living room chilling to some Lady Gaga and flipping through *Cosmo*, and the next moment her friend Veronica was knocking at the door and then storming in and accusing her of sleeping with Jared Thacker, the guy she'd been going out with for three months.

Calista didn't want to hurt her feelings or anything, so she wasn't about to admit that she and Jared had been hooking up—what possible good could have come from that? So she denied it, even though sure, yeah, okay, she'd been sleeping with him pretty much the whole time Veronica had been seeing him. Instead, she told her no, no, no, of course not, no, she would never sleep with her best friend's boyfriend! *Not ever!*

But Veronica wouldn't let it drop.

Just wouldn't let it drop.

She kept saying that she had proof—*proof!*—and then she slapped Calista and screamed that Jared had told her everything.

Well, that wasn't very helpful of him.

Calista tried to explain that this was all just a big misunderstanding and if Veronica would just be quiet for a second, just *listen*, they could figure everything out. But Veronica got in her face, and Calista didn't like that at all and told her so, but it didn't do any good because then Veronica was crowding her against the couch that was pushed up against the wall beside her kitchen nook.

This girl was out of control, so Calista did what was natural, what anyone would have done—she tried to protect herself.

Veronica was so enraged that she was going to hurt her, maybe even *kill* her, so Calista reached across the counter, snatched a knife from the wooden block thing, and swiped it at her friend fiercely enough to scare her off.

But that's where the mistake part came in, because she didn't realize Veronica was quite that close.

Roni was wearing a halter top that left her midriff bare and the blade went right through the exposed skin and left a streak of seeping red across her stomach. Calista was still telling her to just be quiet and let her explain everything as Veronica shivered and stared disbelievingly at her stomach and pressed her hand against the warm blood and tried to push back inside of herself parts of her anatomy that were never meant to unfold into the day.

Then she staggered forward and fell into Calista's arms, completely ruining her blouse. Calista jerked back, shoving her friend to the floor and telling her *great, now look at what you did to my outfit!*

Veronica didn't die.

At least not right away.

Instead, her hands started twitching in this really weird way and thick blood oozed out all across the linoleum from the place the knife had gone into her. It was going to be a real bear to clean all that up.

Thankfully, the blood didn't spurt or squirt or anything, like it does in movies, because if it had, watching something like that would have probably made Calista throw up.

As her friend bled out on the floor, Calista tried to figure out what to do.

Mercy Memorial Hospital wasn't far. They might be able to get an ambulance over in time. She might still be able to save Veronica if she called 911 right away.

She unpocketed her phone.

But then had another thought. And paused.

Honestly, what good would that do, calling the hospital? If Roni survived, their friendship would be over, that much was for sure, and she might even tell the cops that Calista had attacked her when all she was trying to do was defend herself. And who knows, they might even believe her. And that would totally suck.

On the other hand, if she didn't call anyone and Veronica died, then she would have a body to get rid of and if she were somehow caught doing that, it would make her *seem* guilty even though she wasn't, not really, and it would not be easy at all to explain how she came to be disposing of her best friend's corpse.

So, really, what was she supposed to do?

She leaned over to get a closer look and smelled a strange mixture of coconut suntan lotion, fruity perfume, and fresh, tangy blood.

Veronica was just lying there breathing shallowly, maybe trying to speak, maybe not, it was hard to tell.

Calista didn't feel sorry for her, for someone who would get in her face like that. She took a deep breath, shook her head, and told her firmly, "I'm not gonna go to jail over you, Roni. Definitely not."

She stood again and waited until Veronica was still and stopped making those disgusting, wet gurgling sounds. Then she knelt beside her again. She'd watched tons of *CSI* reruns and knew cops could lift fingerprints—even from skin—so instead of feeling for a pulse, she put her cheek just above her friend's mouth, watched her chest to see if it would move, and waited to see if Veronica took a breath or exhaled.

Nope. Nothing.

Her friend's eyes had become dull and blank and it was kind of freaky seeing someone who'd been alive and arguing with her only a minute ago lying there dead.

Calista had never seen anyone die before, and the idea that Roni would never breathe again, never complain, never accuse anyone of sleeping with her boyfriend again was something that made Calista think about how thankful she should be to be alive.

Yeah, life was something you should enjoy as much as you can and take advantage of every moment you have.

Okay, so it was a little late for Roni to do that, but for the rest of us, you know?

So then there was this blood and a body and everything, and all Calista had wanted to do was spend the evening reading and listening to a little music and not having to deal with anything until Jared came over later to party.

At least Roni being dead made the decision about whether or not to call 911 a lot easier.

But how do you deal with all that blood? With all that *mess*?

She'd seen a movie once where the killer wrapped up a body in a shower curtain, so that was a possibility, but unless you had an extra shower curtain lying around, that wasn't really a good idea. If the police checked your place, they would be like, "Hmm . . . No shower curtain, huh? Guess what? We saw that movie too."

If she did use her curtain, what was she supposed to do then? Drive out to Walmart and pick up another one? Totally out of the way. Besides, they took advantage of kid workers in China or something like that—at least that's what she'd heard—and she wasn't into supporting places like that.

Besides, that wouldn't look suspicious at all, getting caught on a store's video camera buying a shower curtain the night her friend disappears.

Yeah. Right.

She decided to use plastic garbage bags instead.

Duct tape did the trick, holding them all tightly in place.

Loading Veronica into the trunk wasn't like she expected. Her body hadn't really been dead long and Calista could feel the warmth of her blood, even through the plastic garbage bags.

The corpse wasn't very cooperative. Roni hadn't kept herself in shape and Calista cursed more than once wrestling her into the car. Veronica could have made it a whole lot easier if only she hadn't eaten out so much over the last year and put on, like, twenty pounds.

The pig.

But at last Veronica was in there and Calista collected her friend's purse, her own bloody clothes, the knife, the roll of duct tape, and the towels she'd used to sop up the blood on the floor, then pulled onto the street and headed for the swamplands about ten miles from town.

As she did, something happened.

Something unexpected, but also rich and sweet and unforgettable.

Calista began to feel a small and secret pleasure. After all, she was driving around with a body in the trunk of the car and no one knew. No one had any idea.

It was like that feeling you get whenever you have something no one else knows about, when you know a secret and you get that quiet, private, tingling surge of excitement skip-scampering through you.

I know something you don't know.

A secret I won't share.

You'll never guess what it is.

I won't tell you unless I want to.

And you can't do anything about it.

Yes, it felt good.

Electrifying, actually.

Heart thumping, fingers tingling, Calista drove along the edge of the swamp until she found an isolated place where she could dump the body.

It was a lot easier getting Roni out of the trunk than it'd been stuffing her into it.

On the way back to her apartment, she dropped the knife into a garbage can beside a streetlamp on Vine Drive, then tossed the plastic bags, Roni's purse, her own ruined clothes, and the towels into a dumpster on the south side of the city.

She parked Roni's car in the long-term parking at the airport, took a taxi home, and then called Jared to see if he'd like to come over early since the night was still young and she didn't have any other plans.

The sex was especially good that night, and it made Calista think that maybe the secret that she knew about Roni was part of the reason why. It flavored the night with a buzz that was better than any drug she'd ever tried.

The police only questioned her once, but it wasn't as a suspect or anything. She told them she hadn't seen Veronica, had no idea where her friend might have gone—but all the while she was thinking about that secret that the cops didn't know about, that no one knew about, not even Jared. And it brought the sharp spark of exhilaration back all over again.

In her freshman English lit class they'd studied a story by Poe called *The Tell-Tale Heart*. When she was speaking to the cops it came to mind again. It was about this guy who went crazy because of the horror over what he'd done, the raw, unbearable guilt worming its way into his sanity until it literally drove him mad.

He'd killed this old man but heard the dead guy's heart continue to beat in his imagination. Calista had to admit, that would be pretty freaky.

But for her, the secret wasn't driving her mad. Roni's heartbeat didn't haunt her; guilt didn't scratch away at her conscience or invade her sanity or anything like that at all. Actually, thinking about what had happened was kind of thrilling and enticing and not really something she would want to have to ever give up.

The policemen just jotted a few things down and that was that. They never found the body, Veronica's car was probably still there in long-term parking, and life had gone on just like it does whenever a person dies and their body gets lowered into the ground and people go back home and flip on the football game or channel-surf their way to their favorite sitcom, pull out the munchies, and settle in for the evening.

Calista had killed two other people since the day she sliced open the belly of her best friend. Jared first, when he started to act suspicious, and then another guy when their relationship didn't really seem to be going anywhere.

But she had help with those two.

Help from this guy who called himself Akinsanya.

Man, it'd taken her forever to learn how to spell that. These days she pretty much stuck to calling him by his first name: Derek.

How he'd actually found her was still all a little fuzzy. He was friends with one of the cops who'd spoken with her, she knew that much. The cop hadn't said it in so many words, but she was pretty sure he knew she was turning tricks to make it through college. Maybe that's what it was, that's why he'd passed her name along to Derek. Because she was a call girl and Derek was attracted to her type.

An escort.

A courtesan.

She liked that last term. It wasn't so degrading and demeaning as *prostitute* or *hooker* or *whore*. None of those words brought any respectability to what she did. To who she was.

No one ever called her a courtesan, no one except Derek.

Anyway, after the cops talked with her, he contacted her because of this cop friend, and even though she said nothing about what happened with Veronica, she must have been pretty easy for Derek to read because he figured it out and brought it up one night when they were alone.

She denied it, of course she did, but somehow he could tell she was lying, and instead of accusing her of anything, he helped her get rid of Jared and made it look like he'd just taken off somewhere. As far as Calista knew, the cops were still looking for Jared as a suspect in Veronica's sudden disappearance.

The victim, now assumed to be the villain.

Dramatic irony.

She remembered that from her English lit class too.

And it was all another little secret that she and Derek shared.

Having someone know your secrets leaves you vulnerable to him, but also draws you close in a way nothing else ever can.

So, yeah, in a sense Derek had power over her, but she also had power over him. She knew what he was capable of, what he had done, so they were indebted and, in a very real sense, beholden to each other.

Yes, beholden. A word Derek had taught her and she'd always wanted to use.

Maybe that's what intimacy was really about—not so much trust and attraction like some people think, but about holding subtle degrees of power over your lover.

All because of the secrets you know.

And can use, when necessary, to your advantage.

Two weeks ago Calista had been there when they changed the role Thad Becker was going to play as the research progressed.

He hadn't picked up on using the exolimbs in a timely enough manner, and after three weeks Derek had announced that they were going to have to move things in a different direction.

While they could have terminated the test entirely, as they'd done with others in the past, at this point in the study Dr. Malhotra considered that to be a waste of resources, so they decided to change the exact nature of the tests they were doing on Thad.

She'd asked if she could be the one to give Thad the injection, and Derek had given her permission to do it.

Tomorrow morning she was scheduled to return and see how he was doing in his new role.

She wasn't sure about his condition, but from what she'd heard, he was not going to open his eyes again. Not ever again. But, connected up to the machines as he was, they would be able to keep him alive almost indefinitely.

It was sorta weird watching the guy just lay there like that. He looked like a total vegetable, but, at least from what she understood, he was still aware. That's the thing. His mind hadn't been affected at all. He knew what had happened to him. And he knew there was nothing he would ever be able to do about it.

Pretty wild.

Totally paralyzed.

Totally aware.

Forever, completely, irreversibly helpless.

Derek wanted one thing more than anything else—to live forever. That's not what Calista wanted. No, she didn't want to grow old at all.

He was looking forward to something he called The Singularity and would do whatever it took to "hasten its coming." Fine. Whatever. She was looking forward to tonight and tomorrow and taking every day one at a time as they came her way.

No, she was not a high-end escort. She made maybe a tenth of what some of them made. Totally unfair. She was just as good as any of them were—Derek told her so.

Well, she had something on her side.

Time.

They were going to age.

They were going to turn thirty and have wrinkles appear around their eyes and then turn forty and put on belly fat and sag in all the wrong places, and she was going to remain young and firm and desirable.

Derek had promised her this.

And one thing he'd never done was lie to her.

Now, she finished putting on her makeup and went downstairs to meet up with him in the living room.

She wore a tight, form-fitting dress that'd been designed with one purpose, made evident by the length of the slit up the side. And she was obviously well aware of what it was because, as she glided across the room, she made the most of every step.

"Are you ready for a memorable night, my love?" Derek asked her.

"Uh-huh."

He pulled out his car keys. "Well then, let's see how our dry run goes."

Sin City

Our flights go well, but still, by the time we land in Las Vegas it's nearly 11:30 p.m. and all of us are exhausted, travel weary, and ready to get acclimatized to our own time zone again.

Xavier has called ahead, and there's a limo waiting at the airport to take us back to my place.

Even more than most cities, Las Vegas has a different mood at night. During the day, Vegas looks like any other major US city—business going on as usual, the rush hour traffic pulsing through at regular intervals, Minivan Moms, kids waiting for school buses, late afternoon joggers.

But here, as dusk arrives, you can feel electricity begin to sizzle through the air. Whether you're downtown on Fremont Street watching five million lights put on a show above your head, or joining tens of thousands of other people walking the Strip, there's no place in the world like Las Vegas.

Walk the Strip on a Saturday night and you'll see all sorts of things: mimes, break-dancers gathering crowds around them and angling for money, musicians playing their instruments with their hats on the ground by their feet, people dressed up in outlandish costumes who'll get their pictures taken with you for a tip.

And of course, street magicians doing sleight of hand. Whenever I see them I always stay to see what they can do, and regardless of whether or not the magicians are any good, I leave a tip. I figure if they're good they need a boost to get onstage somewhere, and if they're not any good they need to pay the bills while they practice—and despite what you may have heard, the best place to practice sleight of hand is always in front of an audience instead of a mirror.

It's all part of what makes Vegas unforgettable.

During runs of my show, I've visited dozens of amazing cities all over the world, but it was only when I came to Las Vegas that I felt like I was finally coming home.

Sin City.

What happens in Vegas stays in Vegas.

That's what they say, and it makes a good marketing slogan. However, as attractive as the idea is, there aren't any places you can go where you're exempt from the consequences of your decisions. Obviously there aren't. A trip to Vegas isn't a journey away from accountability; it's actually a barometer of your character.

No, what happens here doesn't stay here. It's the wet dream of all hedonists to think there's a place you can go to fulfill all your fantasies and not have to carry any of the consequences of your choices with you back home.

Every city contains both a caricature of and an extension of itself. Here in Vegas, if you have the money, you can indulge in anything your heart desires.

Anything.

So that is my city.

And it is also a city of skateboarding and Little League games and strollers in the park.

That is my city as well.

There's a paradox to Vegas—so much of what you see on the Strip and downtown is facade, and yet the people you meet are showing you their true selves. Like the homeless person's sign I saw on one of the walking bridges over a side street off the Strip: "Will Smoke Your Weed for Food." No hiding anything there.

As one of my friends once told me, people in most cities wear masks all year round and only take them off when they visit Vegas. We live without any masks at all.

And that's one of the reasons I like to call this city my home.

The airport is nestled up right next to town, something that has concerned Las Vegans ever since 9/11. After all, if you were a terrorist concerned about the Great Satan spreading filth across the world, what better place to attack than Sin City itself? What better target that represents sexual indulgence and the capitalist vices of America than striking at downtown or the Strip? It looked like plans to relocate the airport were in place back in 2007, but the recession of 2008 and the lack of money flowing into the city put everything on hold.

The only person building anything major in the city at the time was Clive Fridell, who put up the Arête, where Charlene and I would be performing tomorrow night.

I've never verified this, but they say that during the day you can see the pilots' faces as they make their final approach if you're in the revolving restaurant on the top of the Stratosphere, the tallest observation tower in the United States. Who knows. It's something nice to tell the tourists.

Most people don't know it, but the Strip is not actually in Las Vegas but in a town called Paradise. Back in the forties there was a tax revenue dispute, and the casino owners established their own city to keep from paying taxes to Vegas. It's a lot easier, however, to just refer to the whole metro area as Las Vegas.

But it is interesting to note that I make a living by doing illusions in Paradise.

A lot of the other magicians and performers who've found some success in Vegas live in Summerlin or Spanish Trail, but my heart is closer to Paradise and that's where I wanted my home to be.

I'm not sure how many people can stay on the Strip. I've heard the number 125,000 tossed around. That sounds too high to me, but it's possible, when you consider that some of the resort hotels have six or seven thousand rooms all by themselves.

There are more than a hundred casinos in Las Vegas, including the ten-billion-dollar City Center, the most expensive building project in the history of the world, and the nearby Arête. With five thousand rooms the Arête isn't as big as the MGM Grand but at sixty-seven stories it's the tallest hotel in Vegas.

And, of course, at the Arête is the 920-seat auditorium where *Escape: The Jevin Banks Experience* is playing.

I'm actually glad we're bypassing the Strip tonight. Seeing billboard trucks and expansive digital screens with my face on them advertising my show always makes me feel a little odd, like I could never measure up to the hype.

Once you've lived in the public spotlight for any period of time, you know it's not all it's cracked up to be.

We drive past Industrial Boulevard and the contrast strikes me— Strip Club Row versus the Strip.

There are basically two kinds of prostitutes in Las Vegas: the high-end call girls and the lower-priced pimped girls. If anything, the police take more notice of the second group since they work mostly out near the seedier Strip Club Row rather than on the Strip in Paradise.

Human trafficking is a big problem in Vegas. Pimps will invite girls to town for supposed jobs as dancers or models, get them addicted to drugs, and then drag them into prostitution.

In Nevada, prostitution is legal, but decisions are made county by county about whether or not to permit it. In Clark County, the county that both Las Vegas and Paradise are in, it's illegal. So, as you cross the county line—especially out near Pahrump—you find a whole string of brothels.

However, the police have plenty of other things to deal with in metro Vegas, and they don't really bother with solicitation charges much, especially with the higher-priced escorts.

If you want to meet one of them, just take the last flight to Vegas from LA on a Friday afternoon. The girls are reasonably easy to pick out: they'll be gorgeous, dressed to kill, and traveling without a male companion.

On the Strip they'll hang out at the most expensive resorts and clubs, frequently checking their cell phones and always keeping an eye out for who's laying down the big money. Wherever you find the high rollers, you'll find the LA escorts.

They fly in, work the weekend, then head back to LA to their modeling jobs, acting careers, or whatever they do during the week.

Some of them have become good friends of Charlene's.

In fact, that's how we first met her body double Nikki Manocha, who has since moved to Vegas and now performs in our show.

I've always preferred a small house to a large one, but the place where I live now is a sprawling six-bedroom home that feels much too large for a single guy living by himself. It used to belong to my mentor Grayson DeVos, who performed exclusive magic shows here during the seventies and eighties before he retired from performing and took up mentoring upcoming illusionists and escape artists instead.

With secret rooms behind fake bookcases, hidden stairwells, and trapdoors that lead to passageways beneath the property, it's the perfect place for a magician to live.

For a while the property was in disrepair after a reclusive crime novelist named Alec Saule acquired it from Grayson, but when he died in a car accident last fall, the house went on auction and I was able to snap it up. It's still being renovated, with the thirty-two-seat parlor theater being replicated just as it was when Grayson held his shows there.

A couple weeks before we left for our trip to the Philippines, Xavier suggested I ask Fionna and her kids to house-sit for me while we were gone. "The kids will love exploring the place, and Fionna can keep tabs on the guys remodeling the theater."

Fionna went for the idea, and Xav was right, the kids were thrilled to come stay for a week at a historic magic mansion in Las Vegas. Actually, Xavier and Charlene are also staying with me for the time being, so it's like one big happy family.

We arrive at the end of the drive and I tap in the security code. The cast-iron gates part, and our limo driver eases up the palm tree–lined driveway.

He glances curiously into the rearview mirror at the three of us.

Xavier gestures toward me. "You're wondering who this is?"

Limo drivers aren't supposed to ask personal questions, but they can certainly reply when spoken to, and now he simply says, "Someone important, no doubt."

We snake along the drive to the house itself, and as it comes into view I can see the man's face in the rearview mirror again.

Xav leans forward. "You ever heard of Criss Angel?"

Oh, don't do this, Xav.

Our driver looks at Xavier then at me, his eyes widening. "You're Criss Angel?"

"No, I'm not Criss Angel."

Charlene gives me a glance but does nothing to help my cause. Xav leans forward and winks at the limo driver in the rearview mirror. "No. He's not Criss Angel."

That only serves to convince him more. "So you *are* Criss Angel."

"No. I'm not."

We arrive at the house, and as the driver is helping us with our bags he shakes his head. "Could you . . . um . . ."

"You want an autograph?"

"Oh, that'd be . . . Yeah, that would be amazing."

Maybe this would actually clear things up. I produce my business card case from my pocket, pull out one card, vanish the case, and sign the back of the card for him.

I sign it, as neatly as I can, *Jevin Banks*.

He cradles it admiringly in his hand. "Wait till I tell everyone I met Criss Angel."

Great.

As he drives away I tell Xavier, "I really wish you wouldn't do that."

"I know. That's what makes it so much fun."

Xavier's home—an RV complete with a twelve-thousand-dollar telescope for searching for UFOs, the plaster casts he's taken of supposed Bigfoot tracks, and the reams of paper and filing cabinets full of his "proof" that the Air Force is really doing tests on the next generation of autonomously flown unmanned aerial vehicles, or UAVs, in the desert near Groom Lake—sits to the side of my house, where he left it when we all went to the airport the other day.

Fionna and her two boys are waiting for us on the broad steps outside the house. By this time of night her two girls—nine and five—are undoubtedly asleep.

Donnie, who's thirteen, has a ponytail that's longer than his sister Maddie's. His skateboard is leaning against the side of the house, and I presume that his mom told him to leave it outside. I can imagine how much fun it would be to launch off the railing leading down the porch and can guess what he's been up to while we were gone. He's actually unplugged his earbuds and stopped texting long enough to smile a greeting to us.

"Your house is epic," he tells me.

"Thanks."

Lonnie, the oldest at seventeen, is already well on his way to becoming a man—and on his way to following in his mother's footsteps. He won a contest last year put on by Google to see who could hack into a root code that they established just for the event. It took him two hours and eighteen minutes—an hour faster than the second place finisher.

The guys welcome us and Donnie asks his mom if he can throw the pizzas in *now*. She tells him sure, go ahead, and I have to admit that even though I'm in that strange in-between place you get when traveling—exhausted and yet somehow wired, famished and yet somehow full—pizza sounds pretty good.

As the boys go inside, Fionna nods cordially to Xavier. "It's good to see you, Mr. Wray."

"And you as well, Ms. McClury. Have the children won any spelling bees while we were gone?" To put it mildly, Xavier is not a fan of homeschooling, and he and Fionna often go back and forth about it. I think it's friendly banter, but sometimes I'm not so sure.

"We're still in training, actually; thank you for asking. And do you know what time zone you're in now?"

"I think it's tomorrow."

"It's yesterday."

"Now you're just messing with me."

"Come on inside and have some pizza."

I round up some soda for everyone, and while we wait for the three pizzas to bake, Charlene and I catch up with Fionna.

Xavier heads into the other room to show the boys a new flaming bubbles effect he's been working on for my show.

When they're gone I ask Fionna, "Did you tell the kids what happened to Emilio?"

She nods. "Yes. We talked about it today. They know."

Charlene leans forward. "How are they doing with all that?"

"Well, thankfully, they didn't know him, I mean, apart from seeing him perform with you a few times last month when we were in town. I'm sure it'd be a lot harder on them if they were closer to him. Which reminds me . . ." She slips off to my library, which she's apparently been using as an office, and returns with her laptop computer. "Do you have that USB drive?"

"Xavier does," Charlene answers.

"Okay." Fionna hesitates, as if trying to figure out if this is the best time to go and ask him for it, then decides to just plop down again. She tries to stifle a yawn. "It's been a long day."

Charlene asks her, "You didn't find out anything else?"

"Not really." Fionna's frustration about her lack of progress is clear as she shakes her head. "I got a good look at Emilio's files. As far as I can tell there's nothing regarding RixoTray in any of his on-line backups. He did have a lot of articles he's downloaded recently, though, on a certain kind of jellyfish, *Turritopsis dohrnii*, and a disease called progeria."

I've done a number of benefit shows over the years for children's hospitals, one of them being Fuller Medical Center here in Vegas, where I ended up meeting a seven-year-old boy with progeria. It's an extremely rare disorder that causes children to age at seven times the normal rate. They usually don't live past the age of fourteen or fifteen before dying of old-age-related complications. It's tragic and sad, but the boy I met was more full of life and joy than most people I've met of any age.

Charlene stares at Fionna quizzically. "Articles on jellyfish and progeria?"

She nods. "I have Maddie doing an extra credit report on the jelly-fish. We can look at the progeria connection tomorrow."

The timer goes off, I check the pizzas and see that they're ready, so we call the boys and Xavier back into the room.

Fionna's sons fill their plates and are returning for seconds before Charlene and I have finished our firsts. Xavier manages to score a few extra pieces before the boys polish off the rest of the pies and head to bed.

When Donnie and Lonnie are gone, Xavier gives Fionna the USB drive, holding it on the edges to avoid leaving any more prints.

After only a few keystrokes she pauses. "Well, okay, right now I can tell you this is going to take awhile."

"Why is that?" I ask.

"DoD."

Xavier looks suddenly very interested. "Department of Defense?"

"I did a contract job for them a few months ago, and what you're looking at here are algorithms I've only seen on military servers."

"That's crazy," I say. "What on earth would Emilio have with Defense Department encrypted files? And what's the connection to RixoTray? None of this makes any sense."

"It doesn't make sense that Emilio was killed either," Charlene points out solemnly. "But somehow all of this fits together. We just can't see the big picture yet."

"In any case," Fionna goes on, "this USB drive didn't just come from RixoTray."

"No. Not if it has DoD encryption on it. Somehow it came from the military." Xavier downs one of the final slices.

"Or it passed through their hands, yes. I could work on it tonight, but . . ." Another yawn catches her off guard and stops her in midsentence. "This one could be a full day's work, even with Lonnie's help."

"Get some sleep," I tell her. "If we're going to do this, let's do it right. I want you to keep track of all the steps you go through to get in there, just in case we do need to go to the authorities about this later."

"So." Charlene is staring reflectively through the doorway at the fireplace. "Not only do we need to find out why Emilio might have this drive from RixoTray, and not only do we need to find out what files it contains, we need to find out who set up the security on it."

"And of course who killed him," Xavier mumbles introspectively. "And why . . ."

I can see his wheels turning. "What is it, Xav? Something else?"

"Just that Emilio went out to the road bordering Dreamland with me a few times. He was really interested in the place. If that's military-grade security on there, well . . ." He gestures toward the drive. "You never know."

Dreamland, otherwise known as Groom Lake, otherwise known as Area 51, is about eighty miles from here. It's the unofficial Mecca for conspiracy theorists and ufologists—even more so than Roswell, New Mexico.

Officially, Area 51 does not exist. Officially, no one works at the Groom Lake location.

It's not unusual to find Xavier parked as close as legally possible to the base so he can try to catch a glimpse of any aircraft—identified or unidentified, terrestrial or extraterrestrial—that might be entering or leaving the area.

"Xav, I'm sure this has nothing to do with Area 51," I tell him.

"Do you think he was killed because someone wanted the information on this drive?" Fionna asks me, and I'm grateful we're moving away from a UFO rabbit trail.

"Why not just steal it or question him about it? It doesn't seem like killing him would lead you any closer to these files, whatever they are."

"Tell you what . . ." Xavier offers Fionna the last piece of pizza, and when she declines, and then Charlene and I do as well, he goes for it himself. "Let's all get some sleep and get a fresh start in the morning. I think it's pretty safe to say we're all exhausted."

"You know," Charlene muses, "I really think we should talk with the FBI. Fionna, maybe you can copy the drive and I can give the original one to the Feds."

"They're not going to do anything," Xavier declares firmly, iterating his distrust of the federal government. "Except maybe get in the way."

"Well, we'll see. I can be rather persistent and strong-willed when I want to be."

"That's true," I agree.

A slight eyebrow raise. "Careful now."

"I'm just saying, you are a woman who knows how to get what she wants."

"Ah."

Our eyes linger over each other, she offers me a slight smile and it feels nice.

In truth, Charlene *is* a lot more diplomatic and patient than either me or Xavier, and I figure she really is the right choice to talk with the FBI.

"Good." I collect our plates and slip them into the dishwasher. "In the morning, Charlene, you can go to the federal building with what we know and see if they'll look into Emilio's death, Fionna and Lonnie can attack the USB drive, extract the files, work on decrypting them, and maybe Xavier and I can go to Emilio's house to have a look around."

"You're not a detective." Charlene's objection seems halfhearted, as if she realizes it's something she's supposed to say but doesn't really believe will convince me.

"No. But Fionna already tried the police and they're not doing anything. Emilio doesn't have any family here; we're the ones who had to put his funeral together. Besides, the police wouldn't know what to look for. Emilio was my friend. I've been over to his place dozens of times. If something's not right, even something small that the police would miss, I might be able to notice it."

When you're doing mentalism, you train yourself to notice things— the little things most people miss. So-called mediums and psychics are experts at picking up on nonverbal cues, clothing choices, subconscious habits, anything that's out of place on a person or in a specific setting. I've found that if you're going to debunk them, you have to think like them. It's taken me a few years, but I'm pretty good at noticing things that are easy to miss unless you're keeping an eye out for them.

"Alright." Xavier grabs his things to go to his RV. "I'll see you folks in the morning. Sleep tight."

"Good night, Mr. Wray."

"Good night, Ms. McClury."

I invite him to stay the night in the house, even though I suspect he'll decline the offer, which he does. "I sleep best in my own bed," he tells me. His bed is a thin mattress lying on a wooden platform in the RV.

After he leaves and Fionna heads down the hall, I walk Charlene to her room.

From the start she made it clear that if we were going to try to make things work between us, I had to respect her boundaries and her spiritual views about marriage and chastity.

Her deeply held convictions were part of what attracted me to her, though admittedly it wasn't going to be easy to live up to them. "I've made mistakes in the past," she told me when we started going out. "I don't want to make them with you. Do you know the odds of people who sleep together staying together long-term, versus those who get married first?"

"No," I answered honestly.

"Reams of research. We'd be shooting ourselves in the foot if we were intimate now. I really care about you and I want to see where this can lead, so let's do what we can on the front end to make sure the odds are in our favor." From anyone else it might have seemed prudish, but from her it seemed genuine and respectable.

One thing was for sure: it was definitely countercultural—especially in Vegas—but as long as it was the best route for us to take toward making this work, I was on board.

I had to hand it to her for setting down some ground rules, and I wanted her to know that I thought she was worth the wait, that I was in this for the long haul.

Outside her room I brush the back of my finger against her cheek. "How are you doing?"

"Good. I guess. Yeah. Considering everything."

"Come here." I hold her, and after a few minutes it feels as if we've given strength to each other—strength that neither of us had before.

It's a mystery to me how love can offer you more than you'd ever imagine and allow you to give away what you don't even realize you have—and somehow end up richer for it all in the end. The more you give, the more you have to give; the more you keep love to yourself, the less of it you have. It's the paradox at the heart of every relationship.

After a moment she steps back. "Everything that happened in the Philippines seems like it happened weeks ago instead of just during the last day or two."

"It feels that way to me too."

"It's strange how memory works."

I read somewhere that a philosopher had written, "We are the selves we remember." I mention that to Charlene and she considers it. "But what about the parts of our lives we forget?"

"Hmm . . ." Not a bad point. "That's all part of the equation too, I suppose. Maybe there's a reason we forget some things—the pain, you know? So we can move on."

I have the sense that she knows I'm thinking not just about Emilio but also about the loss of my family, but neither of us brings it up and that's okay with me.

A slight awkwardness edges in between us, for reasons I'm not even certain of, then we kiss, say good night, and I head to my room.

Even as tired as I am, I'm not expecting that I'll get the best night's sleep.

The idea of going to my dead friend's house to look around is troubling me as I change into a pair of shorts and a T-shirt and climb into bed.

Emilio.

My family.

Memories that will always be with me.

If we are the selves that we remember, then I expect I'll always have a self that's wrapped up in far too many layers of pain.

Calista took the hand of the man she'd been flirting with. He seemed like a nice enough guy, a little overweight, you know, but not too bad, and he was kinda cute in a middle-aged, balding guy sort of way.

They left the bar and walked together toward his hotel room.

A secret.

Yes.

He would not be getting what he expected tonight. Derek would be paying them a visit before they could get started, would drug him, and he would wake up tomorrow morning and not remember anything about the night.

Date rape drugs can come in handy. And Derek was an expert at using them.

She knew their mark for tomorrow night, but tonight had given her a chance to note the location of the security cameras so she could be sure to keep her back turned to them tomorrow.

The dry run had gone according to plan. She would be fine doing her job tomorrow evening when everything was on the line.

Not that she was concerned. After five years of doing this, she was confident in her abilities, but it was good to know that she could even work her magic in the Chimera Club, among the LA escorts and with the highest rollers in Vegas.

Tomás Agcaoili landed in San Francisco and took the shuttle to his hotel.

He would spend the rest of the night here and then fly to Las Vegas later in the afternoon to meet with the man who'd hired him to kill Emilio Benigno.

Tomás had gotten half of his money up front. Now that he'd done his part he was ready to get paid the rest, and then he could disappear forever.

But he'd failed to get the drive.

Amid the confusion beside the coffin following Emilio's death, he was supposed to have slipped away and gone through the man's things. But he hadn't gotten the chance before Banks and Wray chased him into the jungle and then took Emilio's luggage with them when they left.

It wouldn't be wise to appear before Akinsanya without the drive, but if he didn't meet with him he wouldn't get paid, so it was a catch-22. In the end, he decided that he would show up and explain that he had acquired the drive but lost it when he leapt off the waterfall, in the turmoil at the base of the falls.

It was destroyed, he would explain, lost for good.

However, he'd heard stories about what Akinsanya would do to you with the needle and suture thread if you disappointed him, and he couldn't even imagine going through that.

So, gather a little more information about the man before meeting with him. Maybe that would be a good idea.

Yes, tomorrow afternoon he was going to make sure that Akinsanya kept up his part of the deal, but first Tomás decided he would visit with Solomon in Vegas. If anyone could help him avoid problems with Akinsanya, Solomon could.

PART IV

Sealed In

Saturday, February 9
7:54 a.m.

During the night I dream that it is me instead of Emilio in the coffin.

I'm in total darkness and the snakes are active. I can feel them writhe across my body as I work at the handcuffs.

Somehow Charlene is sitting beside me, and despite the fact that it's obsidian black in the coffin, I can see her. But it's a dream and I know this, even as it's happening, and the believable and the impossible merge in dreams like they never do in the real world. So light and dark mean nothing. Senses blur. The unbelievable makes sense. The outlandish seems reasonable.

And so.

Charlene is warning me not to use the air tube, not to touch it, but nevertheless, I find it in the dark and bring it to my lips. I expect to feel the dry, leathery skin of one of the snakes gliding into my mouth or its fangs piercing my tongue, but instead, the air tube vanishes and suddenly I'm standing in the cemetery staring down at four open graves.

Emilio lies in one of them, Rachel and the boys in the others. Snakes curl across all four bodies, dozens of cobras on each of them in four winding, squirming masses. I rush over and try to clear off the

95

corpses, but I can't do it fast enough; every time I toss a snake aside, another appears.

Then my sons open their eyes and call for me to help them. They reach out their arms; I lean toward them, assuring them that I'm here for them, that I'll save them, that they don't need to worry because their daddy is here. But before I can lift the boys, the snakes slither one after another into their open mouths and I'm screaming and flinging snakes aside as the nightmare vanishes and I wake up alone in my bedroom.

I'm shaking, but it's not like in the movies where people sit bolt upright after waking from a nightmare. Instead, I just lie there listening to the harsh sound of my breathing as I try to untangle my waking thoughts from the dark ones of my dreams.

And in a strange way, I find it necessary to try to convince myself of something I already know, so I tell myself over and over, *It wasn't real, it wasn't real.*

A shiver, a residue of the nightmare, slides through me.

Just relax. It wasn't real.

None of that helps. Finally, I realize there's one thing I can do that might make it easier to move on.

Closing my eyes again, I attempt to reenter the dream so I can fulfill my promise to my boys, so that I can somehow rescue them. But I'm unable to pick up the nightmare where it left off. All I get is a nightmarish blur of images of snakes and corpses and cemeteries and tears.

After a few minutes, I open my eyes and keep them open, hoping to leave the dream world behind for good.

And thankfully, the dreams do begin to fade, as all dreams do, until they're nearly all gone, all except for the enduring impression of snakes slithering down the throats of my sons.

I rise, and during my shower I inspect my injured shin and snake-bitten arm. The bruise on my leg is deeply discolored. It aches, but I think I'll be able to get by without limping—which will be important for tonight's show.

Rest, ice, and a little vitamin I—ibuprofen—should help.

The arm is tender, but healing. Before getting dressed I put some antibiotic on it and gently bandage the wound.

I dress and slide my 1895 Morgan Dollar into my pocket.

Rings can get in the way of doing sleight of hand effects, so when Rachel and I married, we didn't exchange wedding rings. Instead, we exchanged coins, and this is the one she gave me. Though I have some in my collection that are worth more monetarily, this is the most valuable one to me, and I carry it with me nearly all the time.

I start filling the sink with water.

For the finale tonight I'll need to hold my breath for over two minutes while escaping from a straightjacket.

In a piranha-filled aquarium.

After being lit on fire.

And dropping thirty feet into the tank.

All Xavier's idea.

Of course.

We've been in rehearsal for this show for more than two months and I've managed to get out reasonably consistently, but still, I wish I could've had more time this week to put the final touches on the performance.

Well, it would have to happen at this afternoon's rehearsal.

And, of course, live at tonight's show.

I turn off the water, close my eyes, and take a couple deep breaths.

Then I start the timer on my phone and lower my face into the water.

I've drowned eight times in my career, and each time Charlene has brought me back. It's embarrassing when you drown while you're trying to entertain people. I always refund the money of audience members who come to shows where I die when I'm not trying to. Seems like the least I can do.

I come up for air.

Check the time: 1 minute 43 seconds.

Not very impressive.

I take a moment to regroup, catch my breath, and then I go under again.

After six tries my best effort is two minutes and ten seconds, but that's while I'm being still, without adrenaline, without struggling to get out of a straightjacket.

I'm way out of practice, but I tend to do well under pressure and I assure myself that I'll be okay tonight.

But I decide not to tell Charlene my time.

As I enter the hallway, I smell sausages sizzling downstairs in the kitchen and hear Xavier making funny noises and Mandie, Fionna's five-year-old daughter, giggling.

On the way past Charlene's room I notice her door is open. She's sitting on a stool in front of the mirror doing her hair. Having a slender, limber assistant is the key to a lot of effects, and she stays in remarkable shape for our show. And now, with black leather boots, fishnet stockings, and a stylish green skirt, she looks professional with a touch of sass.

"Hey, Jev, come on in."

I join her.

"You can close the door."

I do.

When I take a seat on her bed, I'm struck again by how attractive she is. It's the rare kind of natural beauty some women have that's simple and understated, where they don't need makeup at all, but when they use it they become unforgettable.

There's something intimate about watching a woman do her hair, and for a moment I'm entranced, then she asks me how I slept.

Charlene knows all too well how much my dreams have troubled

98

me over the past seventeen months, and I'm guessing she's not asking so much if I had nightmares as much as she is asking how well I've been able to move past them.

I'm at just that angle where I'm not sure if I should be addressing her reflection in the mirror or looking at her directly. I go with the reflection. "I dreamt of Emilio and Rachel and the boys. I couldn't save any of them. You were in my dream too. You tried to save me."

"Did I succeed?"

"I woke up before anyone could be saved."

She's quiet for a moment. "It was just a dream."

"Yeah." The moment brings an awkwardness that I don't like. "How about you? How'd you sleep?"

She brushes her hair quietly for another moment, and when she replies she doesn't address my question, but I can read an answer beneath her words. "I'm going to miss him, Jev. Emilio, I mean."

"Me too."

Then we're both silent, and time goes on until at last she gestures toward my arm. "How is that this morning?"

"Still stings, but it's getting better."

"And your leg?"

"How did you know I hurt my leg?"

"You were limping yesterday. You were trying to hide it, but I could tell."

"I must say, you are an astute woman, Charlene Antioch."

"Well, I work with an illusionist. We're experts at trafficking in deception. I need to be able to tell what's real and what's not."

"Now, see, I prefer the word *entertainment* to *deception*. Karl Germain liked to say, 'Magic is the only honest profession. A magician promises to deceive you and he does.'"

"Ah. Quoting the pioneers in your field now?"

"I need to rely on someone for credibility." Getting back to her original question, I rub my bruised shin gently. "Anyway, yeah. I bruised it when I landed in the water at the base of the falls. Smacked into a boulder. But it'll be okay. I've been knocked around a lot worse than this."

"So then you're going to be good for tonight? I mean, the straight-jacket escape?"

"I think so."

"You have to do more than *think* so, Jev. This effect is dangerous, you could—"

"I'll be alright. I'm sure I'll be alright."

"Have you been practicing your breath-holding?"

"Yes."

"What's your time?"

A beat. "It's sufficient."

"We could have Seth do it."

Seth Greene is my body double. When he's got his makeup on and the lighting is right, you really can't tell us apart. Well, truthfully, you could, if you were expecting to, but whenever he appears, it's in a situation where everyone anticipates that it will be me. And so that's what they see.

After all, people see what they expect to see. It's one of the three things illusionists rely on to make their effects work—sleight of hand, misdirection, and audience expectation.

I've trained Seth to do some escapes, but he's still learning, and I would never trust him to do the effect Xavier designed for me for tonight. I don't tell Charlene that, I simply reiterate that I'll be fine.

She sets her brush down and turns to me. Normally, she would have her cross necklace on, and the fact that it's missing just reminds me again of Emilio's death. "Did you think of me?"

"I'm sorry?"

"When you jumped off that cliff. Were you thinking of me—of us, I mean? Of how it would affect me if you drowned or landed on these boulders at the base of the falls?"

"I, well . . ." I want to tell her that I did, of course I did. After all, the last thing I would ever want to do is to hurt her in any way, but I sense that in this case the truth will hurt her feelings. However, in the end I go ahead, trusting that it would be better not to lie to her, so I just shake my head and tell her, "No. I was just thinking about stopping that guy. About catching him."

"I see."

"But that doesn't mean I don't care about you, or that I . . ." I'm really not sure where to go with this. I almost say, "Or that I don't love you," but hold back at the last second for some reason I can't put my finger on.

"I know you care about me."

"Sometimes I just make snap decisions."

She goes for her mascara and says softly and without any animus, "Yes. I know."

I search for the right words. On the one hand I have the sense that I should apologize for not hesitating at the top of that cliff, but on the other hand I can't understand how she would have expected me to be thinking about anything other than catching the guy who killed Emilio.

Besides, ever since I've known Charlene, I've been doing escapes that could have proven to be fatal.

She seems to be able to read my mind. "The more I think about us, the more I think about how hard it would be to go on without you."

Still unsure what to say, I finally just tell her that I'll see her downstairs, and as I head toward the kitchen, my thoughts circle around me like buzzards closing in on a corpse: *She knows what you're like, what you do for a living, so why did she bring this up now? Should you have chased Tomás at all or stayed with her and Emilio? If you were thinking about her feelings, would you have jumped off that cliff after all?*

And honestly, I'm not really sure about the answers.

Flapjacks

As I round the corner to the kitchen I can hear Fionna: "That's too many chocolate chips, Mr. Wray."

"You need an even ratio of chocolate chips to pancake batter, right, kids?"

Mandie chirps in her five-year-old agreement.

"At least a one-to-one ratio," Maddie agrees. "Minimum. Chipwise, that is."

Fionna lets out a motherly sigh.

I enter the kitchen and see that Xavier has a spatula and is leaning over the griddle. Fionna is brewing some coffee, and her two daughters are at the table watching Xav as he lifts one of his pancakes that's dripping melted chocolate and much too large for a single spatula, and flips it spectacularly into the air before it lands, incredibly enough, in the pan.

However, it ends up splattering chocolaty pancake batter onto the countertop and across his faded gray T-shirt, which has a picture of an alien and the words "If found, return to Area 51."

The girls love it. Fionna just shakes her head. "I'm not cleaning that up off the counter."

"That's okay, Jevin will. Hey, Jev."

"Hey." I greet Fionna and the girls, and they wish me good morning back.

Maddie, who turns ten next week, has a petite ponytail, studious glasses, and copies of *The Catcher in the Rye* and *Silas Marner* resting beside her plate, positioned just so next to her fork. She takes a moment to turn the syrup bottle so that it faces her directly, not angled forty-five degrees like it had been.

Mandie is sitting on a stool instead of a chair so she can reach the table easier. Her enormous stuffed dog, Furman, has his own chair beside her, his paws resting tranquilly on the table.

Keeping the girls' names straight has always been a bit of a problem for me, so I finally came up with a way to remember who was who—Maddie was born first, Mandie second, and *d* comes before *n* in the alphabet, just like Maddie came before Mandie. It's not much, but it usually does the trick.

"Okay," Xavier says. "Who's ready for a pancake?"

Mandie's hand shoots into the air. "Me!"

He passes his stack of pancakes around the table. After the girls have loaded their plates, I help myself to some as well. I find some ibuprofen and ice, explain simply that I bruised my leg on a rock in the Philippines, and take a seat at the breakfast counter. Holding the ice against my leg with one hand and eating pancakes with the other isn't easy, but I make do.

"Uncle Xavier?" It's Maddie.

"Yes?"

"Since you got here too late to tell us a story last night, can you do one now?"

Xavier has gotten into the habit of making up a story for the kids whenever he's around at bedtime. The girls love it, Lonnie seems impressed with Xavier's creativity, and Donnie, who acts like he isn't into it, is.

"I'm afraid not. Bedtime stories have to happen at night. It would break all kinds of rules if I told you a bedtime story at breakfast."

"There's rules?" Mandie asks, wide-eyed.

"Oh, yes. You have to be very careful about these kinds of things. For example, if I told you a bedtime story right now you might fall asleep, and your head would tip forward and your face would land right there on your plate, right in your pancakes. Melted chocolate chips and syrup would get all over your cheeks and maybe go *up your nose*, and that would not be a pretty sight."

"No it would not," Fionna agrees.

Mandie wrinkles up her face. "Up my nose?"

"And besides, the boys would miss out."

"We could wake them up?" she offers.

"Good luck." Maddie carefully lifts a precise little square of pancake to her mouth. She has a sausage link on her plate as well and is careful to not let the different types of food on her plate touch each other. "At this time of day that would be taking your life into your hands."

"Tonight." Xavier holds up his fork as if he's making a solemn pledge. "I promise."

"Pinky promise?" Mandie presses him.

He hooks his pinky finger around hers. "Pinky promise."

She smiles and, reassured, goes at her chocolate chip pancake with kindergartner gusto.

Xavier unscrews the top of a Nutella jar and smears a healthy glob of the spread onto his chocolate chip pancakes. "Ah, yes." He smiles. "Nutella is the new chicken."

Fionna looks at him blankly. "That doesn't even make sense."

He takes a Xavier-sized bite. "This is *good*."

"By the way, whatever happened with the cheese? You used to have this thing for eating cheese all the time."

"Moved on from that." He's speaking with his mouth full. "To nuts."

"Nuts."

"A different kind for every day of the week."

"And you're eating Nutella today."

"Yup." He swallows. "Made from hazelnuts."

"Ah, let me guess, tomorrow it's Reese's Peanut Butter Cups?"

"Actually, that's on Tuesday."

"And then what? Pistachio nut ice cream?"

His eyes light up. "Now see, that's good. I hadn't even thought of that one. I'm gonna go with that for tomorrow."

"Wonderful."

"Can I eat ice cream and candy bars every day too, Mommy?" Mandie asks.

"No."

I reposition the ice on my leg and work at finishing my breakfast.

Maddie looks up thoughtfully. "Uncle Xavier, I've been wondering, phonetically, why do we say a z sound for your name instead of an x?"

"You mean, why don't you say 'X-avier'? Pronounce the x separately?"

"Yes."

"Well, it would be like someone saying your name like this: 'M-addie,' or calling your mom 'F-ionna.'"

"Or 'M-ommy.'"

"That would be silly." Mandie giggles.

"Yes, it would."

Maddie considers that for a moment. "Or it would be like saying 'x-ylophone.'"

"That's right. You see, when an x appears at the beginning of a word—unless it's hyphenated, like X-Files—it makes the z sound, not the x sound. So when you say my name, it sounds like 'Zavier.'"

"Then why isn't it spelled that way?"

"Because then no one would ever have to ask me about it." The girls accept the mildly evasive answer, and Xavier puts down his fork. "So what are you two up to today?"

I hope he's not going to make some sort of smart comment about them being homeschooled, and thankfully he doesn't but just points to Maddie's copies of *The Catcher in the Rye* and *Silas Marner* and says good-naturedly, "Looks like a good day to tackle the classics."

"Oh," Maddie replies, "Mom doesn't like us to read the classics. I'm just doing a report on why you shouldn't read these two."

"She doesn't like you to read the classics?"

"Nope."

"That's right," Fionna agrees. "I don't want my children to read books that haven't stood the test of time."

"Wait. The classics *haven't* stood the test of time?"

"Well, not those two at least."

"Okay, that, you're going to have to walk me through."

"Sure, I'll pencil you in for tomorrow afternoon."

"Why not right now?"

"Builds more suspense this way." She flourishes her hand mysteriously. "Makes it all the more intriguing."

"You're just stalling."

"Uh-uh," Maddie cuts in. "She's got a bunch of reasons. Seriously."

Xavier pours a healthy dollop of syrup onto his Nutella-covered chocolate chip pancakes. "A homeschooling mom who doesn't want her kids reading the classics? I've never heard that one before."

"Mom's not your typical homeschooling mom," Maddie informs him.

"You know, I think I'm starting to catch hold of that." Then he nods respectfully toward Fionna. "Nice flourish, by the way, a moment ago when you said it builds suspense."

"Thank you."

"You need to teach that to Jevin."

We've been through this before. "Sorry," I tell him. "I don't flourish."

Xavier shakes his head. "I still can't believe you're a magician and you don't flourish. It's an unwritten rule. All magicians flourish."

"Grayson never trained me in the fine art of flourishing. Never flourished, never will."

A few minutes later Charlene joins us. We finish breakfast, and the girls head into the other room—Mandie to play with Furman, Maddie to finish the research she started yesterday on jellyfish. I put the melting ice away as we lay out our plan for this morning.

Even though I don't think Charlene is being chilly toward me, I sense that something has definitely wedged its way between us. Maybe it was my fault for chasing Tomás off that cliff, or maybe it was her unreasonable expectations, but in either case I don't want her to get the sense that I don't think about her feelings.

Well, maybe you don't—at least not as much as you should.

That thought ticks me off and troubles me at the same time.

"I checked online." She pours herself a cup of coffee. "The FBI office isn't open on weekends." When she goes on it's with a slight touch of sarcasm. "I guess they expect fewer crimes on Saturdays. Anyway, I'll see what I can do about setting up a meeting with an agent. In the meantime, I thought I'd do a little more research on cobras." She glances my way. "Try to figure out why that bite had such an effect on you the other day when we were in the Philippines—that is, if it didn't have its venom—and why it didn't hurt you worse if it did."

"Thanks."

Fionna flips open her laptop. "By the way, thank you for making breakfast for the girls, Xavier. I'm sure the boys will be sorry they missed it."

He pushes his chair back to stand. "I'll mix up a few more flapjacks."

She quickly waves that off. "No, no, I didn't mean it like that. It's fine." She checks the time on the clock above the sink—8:58—then addresses me and Xav. "So, like we talked about last night, while you two go take a look at Emilio's place I'll see what I can dig up here on this USB drive."

Charlene leaves to search the Internet for Sri Lankan cobra venom info, Fionna starts typing, I grab my lock pick set just in case I need it and then join Xavier in the hallway to the foyer.

"What's with the lock pick set?" he says. "Used to be you could use a safety pin, a needle, a paper clip, the prong of your belt buckle, a barrette . . . You must be out of practice."

I sigh, set it aside, and pick up a pen. "How about the spring from this?"

"Works for me." He holds the front door open for me. "We can take my RV?"

"Or we can take my Aston Martin."

"I was hoping you'd say that."

Disarray

We take my Skyfall Silver Aston Martin DB9.

I drive.

The streets are quiet.

A stark azure sky watches over my city, and it's as breathtaking as ever.

I'll never get tired of seeing the vast, cloudless Nevada skies. If you visit Vegas and spend all your time on the Strip and see only its lush palm trees lining the streets, you'd never guess that we only get four and a half inches of rain a year, that we're located in the middle of the Mojave Desert.

A stunning amount of water goes into creating the illusion that this is a tropical paradise. Gray water and Astroturf.

A mirage in the desert.

But the sky is not a mirage.

It is stunningly, marvelously real.

Out here in southern Nevada, it's clear nearly every day, which is one reason the Air Force has such a strong presence in the region. No hurricanes. No tornadoes. No blizzards. Just wide-open, endless blue skies, perfect for flying and, as Xavier has pointed out to me more than once, for testing experimental aircraft.

Although some people need to be at work early, nearly everyone in Vegas is involved somehow in the entertainment business, and the city doesn't really start stirring until nine or so, even later on a Saturday. Although the casinos are open twenty-four hours, quite a few businesses don't open until ten o'clock.

We keep different hours than most of America.

Actually, we keep the hours most of America would like to keep.

Before jumping onto I-15, our route takes us past 3650 West Russell Road, which is where Copperfield's "secret" magic museum is. He has semis parked beside it that say "The Magic of David Copperfield," so it's a tad obvious who owns the building. The place used to have a sign out front that read "Butchie's Bras and Girdles."

His semis with his name emblazoned on the side were parked in the lot the whole time then too, so I'm not sure how many people he was fooling with the lingerie sign.

Before continuing on to Emilio's house, I need to stop for gas. While I'm pumping, Xavier places both hands firmly against the metal support beam holding up the roof above the gas pumps, closes his eyes, and breathes in deeply.

"Um, what are you doing, Xav?"

"Discharging my static electricity. You can blow up or start on fire." He eyes me. "Haven't you ever read the warnings there next to the gas pumps? It can be fatal."

"You, of all people, are concerned about an explosion?"

"I like my explosions controlled."

"Xavier, how many times have you heard of anyone blowing up or starting on fire because he didn't discharge his static electricity at a gas pump? Or maybe, I've got it: keeping the deaths a secret is a Big Oil conspiracy so people won't be afraid to pump."

He nods at me knowingly. "Now you're actually starting to make sense."

"Uh-huh."

"Go ahead, discharge your static electricity, you'll feel better about it."

"I've never discharged my electricity in front of another guy before."

"I won't look." He turns away; I go ahead and discharge my static electricity. I'm not sure how long it should take. I count to five. "I don't really feel any safer," I tell him when I'm done.

"Well at least you won't blow me up. So, I was meaning to ask you, do you have anything special planned for Thursday?"

I join him by the car and wait for the tank to finish filling. "Thursday?"

"Valentine's Day. With Charlene."

"Oh. Right."

"So?"

I top off the tank, replace the nozzle into its slot at the pump. "Not really."

"So, not at all."

"Pretty much."

"You better come up with something special. You know how women can be about Valentine's Day."

I close the gas cover, snag the receipt. "Do *you* have anything special planned?"

"Why would I?"

"Just asking."

We climb into the car. "About who? With who?"

"Oh, I don't know. A red-haired hacker mom, maybe."

A blip of silence. "Nope. I don't have anything special planned."

"Well, you know how women can be about Valentine's Day."

"She's not expecting anything from me. I mean, why would she?"

I shrug. "Beats me."

"Mm-hmm." A pause. "You think I should get her something?"

"I think she wouldn't mind if you did."

I direct the DB9 toward Emilio's house, and after a little internal debate I decide to go ahead and bring up what's been on my mind.

"Xav, back at the house this morning, before Charlene came down-stairs, she asked me if I was thinking about her when I jumped off that cliff in the Philippines."

"What did you tell her?"

"The truth."

"Which was?"

"That I wasn't thinking about her. That I was just thinking about stopping that guy, Agcaoili."

He shakes his head disparagingly. "The truth can get you into seri-ous trouble, amigo."

"Yeah, no kidding."

"But"—now he points an admonishing finger at me—"it's always a lot less trouble than telling a lie."

"That might be debatable under certain circumstances, but I hear what you're saying."

"Buddy, if you're looking for relationship advice, I'm the wrong guy to come to. You know that."

Xavier never married but was left standing at the altar once when he was thirty-two, and as far as I know he never got close to propos-ing again in the two decades since. He rarely speaks about that day, and I know better than to bring it up. I'm not even sure Charlene and Fionna know about that part of his history.

"Well then," I press him, "maybe a little perspective at least."

I can tell he's carefully evaluating what to say. "Someone once told me that you can tell what's important to a person by looking at three things—his calendar, his checkbook, and his refrigerator door."

"Okay."

"Let's leave your calendar and checkbook out of this for a minute. Just take the fridge door. You still have photos of Rachel and your boys up there. From that trip to Disney World."

I still study that photo at least once a week, looking for hints of depression on Rachel's face, or threads of anger, or something, anything, hidden there that might serve as a clue to what she was about to do only two weeks later.

But all I ever see is a loving mother, a caring wife.

"Yeah." I'm not sure I want to be talking about my dead family right now. "I know."

"And you still have the picture up there that Andrew drew of your family."

Of course I know the one he's talking about: the drawing with stick figures of the four of us in the desert next to a tall cactus. In the picture, we're all smiling and holding hands. A happy yellow sun shines down from the top right corner of the page. Andrew's favorite animal was the turtle, and there are two green turtles walking toward us. Even the turtles are smiling in my son's picture.

"You know what else?" Xavier says. "What else is on your fridge?"

"Photos of you and Fionna's family and . . ."

Dad. Pictures of my dad . . .

My father and I have never really been close, not since Mom moved out when I was in middle school. Now that he comes to mind, I recall that he's supposed to be flying down Monday to visit—something that had slipped my mind earlier and just adds to the things on my already full plate.

But I know Xavier isn't talking about the photos of my dad.

"And of Charlene."

He nods. "Yeah. What, at least five or six of 'em? Then if I looked at your calendar and checkbook I'd see signs all over the place of how much she means to you. Don't read too much into this morning, dude. She's upset, we're all upset about what happened. She just cares about you. She wants to know you're thinking about her."

"I am."

"But you weren't. At the cliff."

"No, but I was trying to catch—"

"I know, I know, I'm just saying. You're a risk taker by nature, Jev.

You leap before you look. It's who you are. She needs to know that you're going to look in her direction before you leap next time—that she's important enough to make you think twice."

I'm quiet. "That was pretty well put, actually, for someone who's not good at relationship advice."

"It's based on something I read in a fortune cookie one time. A loose translation."

"Ah."

We're close now. Emilio's house lies just down the street.

"You know, Xav, I'm probably reading way more into this than I should, anyway. I'm sure it's nothing, just something for us to sort out."

He doesn't respond right away. "Yeah, I'm sure you're right."

I park by the curb in front of the house, which is brown, nondescript, and surrounded by scraggly cacti that don't look like they're handling the heat very well.

It's a humble home, unpretentious, and easily forgettable—exactly the kind of place my friend wanted so he could disappear into the fabric of everyday suburban life when he was in Vegas doing shows.

I unpocket the pen as we step out of the car. We start up the driveway, but even before I can get the top of the pen unscrewed to get to the spring, I notice that Emilio's front door is slightly ajar.

Xavier must see it too, because he pulls out a Taser.

"Since when do you carry a Taser?"

"Betty's been with me two weeks now."

"You named your Taser 'Betty'?"

"Yup. You think we should call the cops?"

"Let's have a peek inside first."

We walk to the house.

"Betty, huh?"

"I've always liked the name."

I press lightly against the door and it eases open. "Hello?"

No reply.

"The lock is shattered," Xavier points out unnecessarily.

"Yeah."

We both stand there for a moment, unsure what to do. "Well," he says at last, "it wouldn't be breaking and entering."

"Just entering."

"That's right."

"Which is what we were going to do anyway."

"Good point."

I put the pen away and he asks, "You scared?"

"Naw. I know TaeKwonDo."

He smiles. "Well, I know Betty. And she has a black belt in kicking butt."

"I think you've been watching too many Bruce Willis movies."

"That may be true."

Honestly, I don't think there's much of a chance that I'll need to do any TaeKwonDo or that Xavier will need to do any butt kicking with Betty. Yes, the door has been jimmied, but the neighborhood is quiet. No dogs barking, nothing out of the ordinary—except for the open door.

I step across the threshold.

The house is silent.

Tired sunlight passes blearily through the curtains, but even without the living room lights on I can see that the room is in terrible disarray.

The magic paraphernalia that normally lines Emilio's shelves lies scattered and broken throughout the room. The TV and its stand are knocked over.

The couch has been slit open and is spewing its contents onto the carpet. Emilio's bookshelves have been swept empty, and his collection of magic books is strewn all across the floor. One bookshelf has been pulled loose from the wall and lies sprawled across the books like a mother trying to protect her children from whoever had been in here rifling through everything.

"Hello?" I call again.

Still nothing.

Both of us are silent as we edge forward. I peer into Emilio's home office and see his computer's hard drive has been ripped out. The books on his desk have been knocked down, and several of them, *The Singularity Is Near*, *Singularity Rising*, and *Humanity 2.0*, lie flipped open on the floor. From what I can see, they're heavily highlighted and dog-eared.

A jumble of books on transhumanism, whatever that is, lies nearby. His checkbook and a Visa credit card rest in a clutter bowl on the edge of his desk.

I take it all in.

I'm near the fireplace, glancing up the stairway, when I hear the back door clack shut. It's impossible to tell if it was from someone entering or leaving.

"Who's there?" Xavier calls loudly as he flips Betty around in his hand. I'm not sure how to use a Taser, but I assume he's doing whatever he needs to in order to make sure she's ready to do her thing.

No reply.

I move toward the door to the patio. Out the window, I can see someone fleeing down the alley behind the house toward a white pickup truck parked near the intersection.

The guy is really moving and I can't make out much, but whoever it is, it isn't Tomás Agcaoili, the snake wrangler. Tomás is Filipino. This guy is Caucasian.

By the time I get outside, he has jumped into the truck, and when I run toward it to get the license plate number, he whips onto the street and tears off toward the intersection before I can read it.

"Get back to my car!" I shout to Xavier, who has emerged from the porch door.

We bolt to the Aston Martin. Jumping in, I fire up the engine and we peel away from the curb. Xavier grabs the armrest as I fly around the corner and accelerate toward the pickup.

"Just so you know." A shot of adrenaline rushes through me and it feels good. "This is my first car chase."

"I've been in a few."

"Must have been before my time."

"A lot happened before your time. Don't lose him."

I punch the gas. I've taken this car out in the desert a few times to see what she can do, and she can more than hold her own on the open road. I'm not sure how much I want to push her in town, but I also don't want this guy to slip away like Tomás did.

"Any idea what you're going to do when we catch up with him?" Xavier asks me.

"Whatever we need to in order to find out if he had anything to do with Emilio's death."

"That'll work."

I floor the gas pedal and let the DB9 do her thing.

Looking Twice

We gain quickly, and after two more turns, we're almost close enough to read the pickup's plates.

"I can make out an L," Xavier mutters, "and a seven. At least I think it's a seven."

"It is." Xavier eyes aren't as good as mine and I can read the rest of it. The driver we're following flares left through a red light. When I reach the intersection I slow to a stop. A moment later the light turns green but I don't stomp on the gas.

"I got it," I tell him softly.

"The plates?"

"Yes." I still don't pull forward. The pickup is heading toward the highway.

Xavier and I have known each other for a long time, and now when he speaks he reads my mind. "You're thinking about Charlene this time, aren't you?"

"Yeah. And what you said earlier, about her wanting to be important enough to make me think twice."

"To look before you leap."

"Exactly."

The pickup is gone.

I take a small breath. "And right now I'm looking."

"I'm proud of you, bro. You're teachable after all."

"Don't be too proud." I glide my fingers across the DB9's console. "I kinda leaped first. At least a little."

"I won't mention it." He has his phone poised in his hand. "So you got the plate number?"

I recite it to him but then hesitate. "I'm not great with make and model, though, so—" A woman putting on lipstick and driving a minivan pulls up behind me and lays on her horn. I roll around the corner and continue up the block. "It was a newish-looking white pickup, that's about all I know."

"It was a 2012 Chevy Silverado."

"You sure?"

"Pretty sure."

I look at him quizzically. "That's pretty specific. I've never known you to be a car geek."

"I'm not. But I know that vehicle all too well."

"How's that?"

"It's what the Cammo dudes drive out at Groom Lake—um, a private security firm. They guard the perimeter. I mean, sometimes they help with stuff on the base, resupplies, that sort of thing, but—well, that's what we call 'em. The dudes wear camouflage pants, sometimes they're called cami dudes instead."

"I get it."

"Anyway, remember when I mentioned just now that I was in car chases?"

"Yes. You never told me what side of the chases you were on."

"No, I didn't."

"But 2012 wasn't before my time."

"Neither were all the car chases."

"I see." I turn the car around.

The Groom Lake connection might be legit, but I'm not sure where that leaves us right now.

"So," I ask him, "you think it was a Cammo dude?"

"There's no way to tell for sure, but it would fit that whoever he was, he's at least with the same security firm."

"Well, for right now, we saw a male Caucasian fleeing the scene, we have the make, model, year, and plates of the vehicle. That gives us plenty to tell the cops. But you don't necessarily have to tell them that we were just in a high-speed chase with the suspect."

"Right on." He pulls out his phone again.

I aim the DB9 toward the next intersection, then turn left. "Why don't you call Fionna too, see what she can pull up on the plates."

"Where are we going?"

"Back to his house. I want to have another look around before the cops get there."

"It's a crime scene, we might leave DNA behind on the—wait. We already left DNA behind."

"Precisely. So what do we have to lose?"

"But Jev, that place was a mess. How'll you be able to tell what the guy was after?"

"I have a feeling I already know what he was after."

"What's that?"

"The USB drive."

A slight pause. "Gotcha."

He calls 911 and then phones Fionna while I guide the Aston Martin back toward Emilio's house.

• • ⸺ • • •

Colonel Byrne parked in the short-term lot at Las Vegas's McCarran International Airport.

After his forty-two-minute flight to Phoenix, he would be picked up by the associates of the person who came up with the idea for tomorrow night's transfer of merchandise. Perhaps he would be able to find out, at last, his—or her—true identity.

From the car's trunk, he retrieved the hard-cased suitcase containing the robotic arm and rolled it behind him as he headed for the terminal.

Harsh Mercy

Plyotech Cybernetics Research & Development Facility
Sublevel 4

Heston Dembski, RN, special assistant to Dr. Malhotra, had a problem.

He knew what was going on in the lower levels of Plyotech's R&D facility, and he was not sure what to do about it. He knew about the primate research, the gene therapy programs, the xenotransplantation initiatives, the neural implants. He had his theories about why things were taken care of in the way they were, but he couldn't be certain.

It was not his job to ask questions.

It was his job to assist Dr. Malhotra.

To do as he was told.

He'd just been transferred down here to work with the team two weeks ago. The prescreenings, background checks, and psych evals had all been intensive. At least two dozen other applicants who'd been interviewing with Heston hadn't made it. And so, he'd felt genuinely honored to get the job.

However, almost right away he was faced with a seemingly insurmountable ethical dilemma—assist with something you don't believe in to accomplish something you do, or betray those you work for just to calm your conscience.

From the start he'd felt a little uncomfortable with what they were doing but had tried to convince himself that it was all in the name of science, that the things he was seeing, the research he was finding himself a part of, were for the greater good. That it was necessary.

But then he came across the tests they were doing on patient 175-4, a man who Heston found out, through his own research, was named Thad Becker and had first volunteered for the program about forty days ago. Apparently, he'd come in as a quadriplegic and was outfitted with the experimental exolimbs, but had not been able to learn to use them yet.

And then, according to the charts, he'd slipped into a coma.

That's what Heston had been told, but that's not what he believed. No, if he was right, a coma, even death, would have been a better fate for Mr. Becker; Heston had no doubt about that.

This morning they were scheduled to do a brain scan on Thad in the specially designed fMRI machine, the one made for incapacitated patients.

Heston passed down the hallway to meet up with Calista Hendrix at the elevator bay.

He wasn't sure why she was granted access privileges that almost no one else was, but when she was around no one questioned it.

Throughout the rest of the facility, work was being done on reverse engineering the human brain to create smart machines and computers with strong AI, but down here the research focused mainly on direct machine-to-brain interfaces.

All of it was paving the way to using nanotechnology—that is, bioengineering at the molecular level—to scan the human brain and develop more advanced ways of interfacing humans with machines through electrode implants and, eventually, through implanted neural nanobots themselves.

Nanotechnology, bioengineering, and robotics were the three fields that held the most promise to help humans make the next great evolutionary leap—away from the limits of biological intelligence and cellular senescence and toward their destiny of technological immortality.

First, of course, it was essential to create a machine capable of not just recording information or processing at the computational level of the human brain, but also of capturing the essence of personality, dreams, aspirations, memory. In other words, consciousness—which science has shown must simply be an outgrowth of the complexity of an interplay of neural synapses.

So the goal: create machines capable of not just imitating human levels of consciousness, but of encapsulating it, and to eventually upload that consciousness onto a machine.

Colonel Byrne had made it clear that he was going to be the first one to be scanned, and even though Heston wasn't clear on the colonel's involvement with Plyotech, everyone in the division assumed he was part of the DARPA contract with Plyotech and they didn't question his involvement.

Heston found nothing objectionable or unethical about the colonel's goal, but the process of getting to that point was questionable. Whenever science is forging into new territory, things tend to get a little fuzzy around the moral edges. It's always been that way.

Heston told himself that over and over as his questions mounted and his reservations grew: it was just the nature of the business, the outgrowth of cutting-edge research. But that didn't serve well to quiet his questions or his reservations.

He met Calista Hendrix at the elevator.

"Good morning, ma'am."

"Mornin'." She flipped her hair back and joined him in the hall. He'd never seen her here in the morning before, but she looked as stunning as ever. "Did they do the scans on that guy yet?"

"Patient 175-4?"

She looked a little annoyed by the protocol of not referring to the patients by name. "Yeah."

"Dr. Malhotra is with him now. I don't believe he has gotten started with the fMRI. As far as I know he's still prepping the patient."

He led Calista to the room.

The paralyzed man was lying motionless on the gurney. His eyes were closed. Tubes ran into and out of his body.

Dr. Malhotra smiled broadly when he saw Miss Hendrix enter the room. "Good morning, Calista."

"Hey." She walked over and grazed a finger gently across Thad's cheek. "So, he's ready?"

"He is. I'm sure Colonel Byrne has explained to you that any movement gets in the way while we're doing the brain scans. It's much easier to work with patients when there's no extraneous movement."

She stated the obvious. "Easier than just asking him to lie still."

"From my experience, yes. Much easier."

"And so, he'll never wake up?"

"I'm afraid not."

"Technically then, so he's a vegetable?"

"Well"—he gave a small chuckle that made Heston uncomfortable—"it looks like that, but in his case he's perfectly aware of what's going on. We've simply induced a condition known as locked-in syndrome." A pause. "Actually, you did. With that injection you gave him last month."

Heston felt a terrible chill run through him.

Induced?

They induced locked-in syndrome?

No. This is not what you signed up for, this is—

"That what it sounds like?" Calista said.

Dr. Malhotra patted Thad Becker's arm. "The patient remains alert and aware but is unable to communicate in any way with the outside world. A few years ago there was study on persistent vegetative states, ones in which it was assumed the people had no cognitive awareness of their surroundings."

But he told you this patient was in a coma. Why is he telling you this now? Just because she's here? Could that be—

"And you're saying they do?" she asked.

"Yes, or at least those people in the study did. While doing fMRI brain scans of the patients, the doctors asked them to think of playing a tennis match, and the researchers found that the same areas of the brain lit up as when people typically think about, or play, tennis."

She considered that. "So how long had they been lying there like that? Longer than this guy?"

Heston already knew the answer to that; all of this had come up in his interview for the position.

Dr. Malhotra answered her. "Oh, yes. In one case the patient had been in that state for over twelve years."

"So that guy was aware of his condition but couldn't communicate in any way with the outside world, not in twelve years?"

Dr. Malhotra looked toward Heston and indicated for him to answer the question for him. "Yes," Heston said softly. "The researchers asked him yes or no questions to see which parts of his brain lit up."

"And they could tell by his brain activity what his reply was?"

Heston nodded. "They asked one patient if he was in pain. He said—well, thought—no." As he stared at the man lying before them, it struck him that this man was listening to everything they were saying.

"I'll bet they asked him if he wanted to die, if he wanted them to kill him."

"Actually," Dr. Malhotra responded, "asking that question would have put the researchers in a somewhat delicate situation. Wouldn't it, Mr. Dembski?"

"Yes."

"How's that?" Calista asked.

Once again the doctor looked toward Heston to answer her. "Well . . ." He really did not want to be talking about this. "If the patient expressed a desire to die, the doctors could not legally kill him, but if the patient was in a persistent vegetative state and unable to express any desires at all, they could remove his feeding tube, let him die a natural death."

"By starving him."

Heston was about to say, "Yes," when Dr. Malhotra cut in ahead of him: "Well, we typically don't put that fine a point on it. Under the law it's a legally acceptable treatment alternative."

Starving = a treatment alternative.

Talk about doublespeak. Orwell would have been proud of that one.

Calista bent and studied the patient's emotionless face. "So, let me get this straight. If they're not suffering you can let them die, and if they're trapped in, like, this mental prison for months or even years, you can't?"

"Well"—the trace of a smile flickered across Dr. Malhotra's face—"down *here* we can do as we deem necessary for the advancement of medical and scientific research. But yes. Life is valuable. The laws are in place to affirm that principle and protect that."

Is that how you affirm and protect life? By sentencing the innocent to the most terrifying sentence of solitary confinement imaginable?

"Huh," she muttered. "That's wild."

Heston couldn't even imagine what it would be like to be suffering from locked-in syndrome: trying to scream, listening to the nurses go about their job every day, lying for hours, weeks, years like that, left alone only with your thoughts, no way to move, to communicate, to show emotion, to show love. Every day waking only to find that you're not dead yet, that you're still unable to kill yourself and not even able to ask someone to do it for you.

It truly was the worst kind of prison he could think of.

"So." She rubbed her hand softly through Thad's hair. "How long are you going to keep him like this?"

"As long as it takes," Dr. Malhotra replied. "A month. A year. A decade. People have survived in this state for over twenty years."

And when Heston heard those words, he knew he was not going to let that happen. He made a decision that would undoubtedly cost him his job and, if the rumors were right about Colonel Byrne, might end up costing him even more than that.

But this wasn't right, it just wasn't right what they were doing here.

Dr. Malhotra leaned down toward Thad's ear and said to him, "I know you can hear me, Mr. Becker. I just want you to know that I'm going to do all I can to keep you alive. Be assured that every breath you take will be helping the advancement of science."

"Right now, though, there's no way to wake him up?" Calista asked.

"No."

"But he's heard everything we're talking about here?"

"Yes."

"That's sort of creepy. I'm glad I'm not in his shoes." She tapped his toe. "Or, well, whatever." She gave a girlish giggle as if all this was somehow funny.

Dr. Malhotra turned toward the door. "Heston, prepare the patient for the scan. I have a few things to discuss with Miss Hendrix. I'll be back in ten minutes."

After Dr. Malhotra left, Heston stared for a long time at the man lying there in front of him.

Patient 175-4.

Thad Becker.

He could see Thad breathing with the help of the ventilator, his eyes closed, his chest moving ever so slightly with the life that was pumping through him. The man was aware. He'd been aware the whole time and had heard the whole conversation about his condition.

Heston knew what he needed to do.

At the counter, he prepared a syringe with a very specific cocktail of drugs.

He had no idea what would happen to him if he did this, he didn't know if Colonel Byrne would do to him what he'd done to this man, but Heston couldn't bear to think about Thad lying here for months or years having his neural synapses studied in a sterile, objective way without any consideration for his desires.

There really was no reason to use an alcohol pad to clean off Thad's arm before inserting the syringe, but Heston did it out of habit—only realizing afterward how ludicrous it was, in this case, to take steps to eliminate or reduce potential infection.

He placed the tip of the needle against Thad's arm and hesitated for a moment. The machine beeped in a quiet, steady rhythm beside him.

Thad didn't move. Couldn't move. And Heston wasn't sure if he would have pulled away if he could, or if he would have reached over and pressed the needle in himself.

The patient couldn't make that decision, though, so Heston did it for him.

"I'm sorry," he said as he injected the cocktail of drugs into Thad's arm. He wasn't sure an apology was really necessary when you're releasing someone from a living hell. He wasn't sure it was necessary to apologize for killing someone who'd just been told he was going to be trapped there, in that locked-in state, for years or even decades, but still, Heston did apologize.

After a few more seconds the monitors stopped registering the signs of life and went blank. It was over.

As he was whispering a quiet prayer for this man, that he might find some peace in the afterlife, Heston heard a shuffling sound behind him near the door.

He turned, yes, he was aware of that—

And of seeing a gray blur of movement—

But that was the last thing he was aware of because someone swung a rod and struck him hard against the side of the head, and he crumpled, unconscious, to the floor.

Dr. Malhotra, who was holding one of the sturdy pipes used in the robotic research, stared down at Heston.

"It looks like you just found someone to replace Thad," Calista said.

"No. I've got something better in mind."

Billboards

Someone else must have called the police even before we did, because by the time we arrive at Emilio's house two officers are already there.

We tell them the truth: We'd come over to our murdered friend Emilio Benigno's house to see if we could notice anything out of the ordinary, we found the door open, stepped inside, saw that the place was a mess, and heard someone leaving through the back door. We followed him just long enough to get a plate number and a description of the pickup and then reported it to the authorities. We finish by explaining what happened in the Philippines.

"And what made you think there might be something out of the ordinary at your friend's house?" the beefy officer, whose name tag reads "A. Geisler," asks me in a somewhat accusing tone.

"Because he was murdered."

"In the Philippines."

"That's right."

"With cobras."

"Yes. So are you looking for the pickup? Did you put out an all-points bulletin or whatever you call it these days on the vehicle? Whoever was in this house might have been involved with planning Emilio's death."

His partner, Officer O'Nan, a slim man with a substantial mustache, answers instead. "I saw that on the news about Benigno. They said it was an accident. He was bitten by the snakes while trying to do a magic trick."

"It was not an accident," I tell them.

"I think that's something you should leave for the police to look into."

"We tried that." Xavier is getting frustrated. "Didn't get us anywhere. And if it was an accident, who was ransacking his home?"

"Burglars who watch the news and knew he was dead, that his house was empty, and that he was a successful international performer who would have money."

I gesture toward the house. "Burglars who leave his checkbook and credit card on his desk but tear all his books off the bookshelves? They were looking for something specific."

The two cops exchange glances.

"Uh-huh," Geisler mumbles. "Wait here for a minute."

They walk to the patrol car, and Geisler gets on the radio while O'Nan just watches Xavier and me.

"What are you thinking?" I ask Xav in a voice quiet enough to remain unheard by the two cops.

"I'm thinking, if someone was looking for that USB drive, we really need to find out what's on it." His words are as soft as mine were. "As soon as possible."

Before they find out we have it.

"I'm with you there."

Xavier calls Fionna, and while they're talking, he shakes his head and I get the message: *Nothing yet.*

The minutes stretch out, and when I glance at my watch I can see it's already nearly ten. The cops are still conferring with each other, taking turns on the radio. Maybe it's a good sign, maybe they're actually going to do something about all this.

Finally, they return and O'Nan tells us, "You can go. We'll take it from here."

"Take what from here? The murder investigation?"

He eyes me coolly. I don't look away. Finally, he clears his throat. "Look, like I said, I saw the news, okay? It's all over the Internet, what your friend was trying to do. It was an accident in another country. We don't have jurisdiction there."

"But if this person who was in the house was involved, you have jurisdiction over—"

"You're a magician, right? You got that show over at the Arête?"

I try to keep the exasperation out of my voice. "What gave me away?"

"The billboards. All over the city. I thought I recognized you."

"Good job."

This guy was a real Sherlock Holmes.

"Stick to doing magic tricks, Mr. Banks," Geisler says coolly.

He and his partner assure us that they'll take care of everything and exhort us to stop playing detective. As we're wrapping up the oh-so-productive conversation, Fionna phones and I excuse myself to take the call.

"Anything on the white pickup's plates?" I ask her.

"Nothing solid, although they are government-issued, which tells us something right there. If the truck is from this security firm Xavier was thinking of, I would think they'd be privately issued plates instead."

"Unless it was for Groom Lake."

"Maybe. I can't verify that either way. I'm still working on the USB drive—Lonnie's not up yet. I haven't heard from Charlene. When do you think you and Xavier will be getting back?"

"Maybe twenty minutes or so."

After I hang up, the officers ask us a few more questions, then Xavier and I climb back into the DB9. Both of us are quiet. I'm not sure what he's thinking, but I'm thinking of Emilio and all this mystery surrounding him.

And of how maybe I didn't know my friend as well as I thought I did.

⚬⚬ ⚬⚬⚬

10:03 a.m.

Charlene Antioch stepped through security at the FBI building for her meeting with Special Agent Clay Ratchford. Officially, the offices were closed, but he'd agreed to meet her and had suggested that his office would be the most appropriate place to talk.

⚬⚬ ⚬⚬⚬

Calista Hendrix left the Plyotech building and went home to plan for tonight, when she would be doing more than just a dry run.

According to Derek, everything depended on her getting the engineer to the hotel room this evening. Then tomorrow, Derek would get the information he needed from the man, and by Monday morning they would have the money to finish the research.

And she would be on her way to getting what she wanted more than anything else—the most advanced anti-aging program that medicine and science could offer her.

⚬⚬ ⚬⚬⚬

Dr. Malhotra made a call, and after he'd explained what had happened with Heston, he asked, "I have some thoughts, but I wanted to ask you. What do you suggest we do with him?"

"Keep him unconscious. We'll wait until the colonel returns to Las Vegas this afternoon before making any final decisions."

⚬⚬ ⚬⚬⚬

Neither Xavier nor I say much on the drive home.

I suppose we're both processing what happened. But now, as I park in my driveway, he breaks the silence. "Back there at Emilio's house, when we first walked in, I saw you looking around his study. I know the place was trashed, but did you see anything that struck you as unusual?"

"You mean besides the checkbook and credit card being left behind?"

"Yeah."

I mentally review our brief time in the house. "Maybe just his books. Emilio was a voracious reader, but it was almost always biographies, history, and magic. In this case it looked like he was recently researching something else."

"What's that?"

"Well, there were a number of books on transhumanism and The Singularity, whatever those are, but other—"

"What did you just say?"

"Transhumanism and The Singularity."

He looks past me at a spot in the distance that doesn't exist.

"What? What is it? You know what they are?"

His continued silence makes me a little uneasy.

"What's going on, Xav? What are they about?"

"It makes sense," he mutters, "with the progeria files . . . maybe . . ."

When he doesn't finish his thought, I press him, "Tell me what you're talking about."

"I'll do better than that." He turns and points at his RV. "I'll show you."

The Singularity

Xavier doesn't let too many people into his RV.

It contains decades' worth of his research into the paranormal, UFOs, cryptozoology, and government conspiracies. Overstuffed file cabinets fill every spare corner, star charts and posters of underwater sonar scans and a giant blow-up photo of George Edwards's 2012 photo of the Loch Ness Monster surfacing (which Xavier still claims is legit) cover the walls.

I pat a stack of papers. "What's up with you and manila folders, by the way? You never heard of computers?"

"Manila folders can't be hacked." He's bent over one of his filing cabinets. "Come here."

I join him at the far end of the RV.

"Who would hack into your files?"

"The government is everywhere."

"You're paranoid."

"*Prudent* is the term I prefer."

He's running his finger along the contents of his filing drawer, obviously looking for something in particular. "So, The Singularity . . ." He finds a folder, tosses it onto the table, and flips it open. "Here." He points to a printout of a 2004 article from *Christianity*

Today titled "The Techno Sapiens Are Coming," and a 2012 article from the *Smithsonian*: "How to Become the Engineers of Our Own Evolution."

"Let's see," he begins, "how to explain this . . . The word *singularity* relates to one thing in mathematics and in astrophysics—I'm not even exactly sure, something to do with event horizons, I think—but anyway, in relationship to transhumanism, it means something completely different, or, well, maybe the same, if you're talking about an event after which you cannot predict what is going to happen."

"Xav, you haven't even started yet and you're already losing me."

"Okay. I'm not even sure there's an agreed-upon definition, but basically it's the moment in the future, by maybe the midpoint in the century—some people say it's hypothetical, others inevitable—but the moment in history when several things converge: advancements in reverse engineering the human brain, nanotechnology, genetic research, information technology, and robotics . . . um . . ." He's really struggling here and that surprises me. It's just not like Xavier. Honestly, I find it somewhat unsettling.

"Focus, Xav."

"Right." He takes a breath. "The Singularity is really the moment when these converging technologies create a tipping point after which our understanding of what it means to be human will be irrevocably changed. It's when machines reach strong AI—that is, they're able to have emotional intelligence, language acquisition, and pattern recognition on the same level as human beings."

"So, when machines become self-aware? What? Skynet? A *Terminator* scenario?"

"Well, no one really knows what it would look like if machines were to become self-aware, or what might happen if they do. They could very well feel threatened by humans, and if they were allowed to make decisions, then an artilect war is not out of the question."

"An artilect war?"

"Artificial intellect. There's always the possibility that an artilect just wipes us out."

Now, that sounded more like the Xavier I know and love. "Okay, gotcha."

"No, it's not as far-fetched as you might think. When machines are able to do everything that we can do, but trillions of times faster and better than we can, we might become irrelevant."

"They won't make love better than we do."

A beat. "Okay, I'll give you that, but if machines decide we're getting in the way, they might just decide to eliminate us."

"When they become self-aware."

"Yes, or when they're given autonomy, the opportunity to make decisions without human involvement, especially when they have access to weapons systems."

My friend is able to angle almost any conversation back to his theories about the research going on at Groom Lake. "Like the Air Force tests out at Area 51?"

He taps a finger against the air to accentuate his agreement. "Precisely. Think about it. Today, if a drone identifies a target, a human operator needs to make the decision to fire. Well, what if we fed even more algorithms into the machine and gave it more parameters and data and so on, and then allowed it to fire when a certain level of certainty or verification was reached."

"You mean it makes the decision to fire."

He tilts his head back and forth as if he's having an internal debate about how to answer me. "That's probably looking at things more anthropocentrically than necessary. The point at which a machine can make a decision the way we understand making a decision is still a ways out, but for all practical purposes, yes. It makes the decision to fire."

"That could never happen. You'll always need humans to make the final decisions. Autonomous machines?" I shake my head. "It seems far-fetched."

"What about airplanes that can land on autopilot? Or the self-driving cars Google invented? They got the first driverless license in the country right here in Nevada a couple years ago. Or Israel's Iron Dome? Or other missile defense systems that identify missiles without humans in the loop? The only link in the chain that's missing is a weapons system that fires at a human target without human authorization. Besides, we already depend on autonomous decisions by machines for our livelihood."

"How's that?"

"On the stock market. We let them do our trading for us. It's all done through algorithms humans plug into computers. The firm with the best algorithms and the fastest computer wins. It's not even free trade, it's hardly capitalism since people aren't using capital to trade but are entrusting their money to computers. And it's impossible to regulate because you can tell everyone to only trade at a certain speed, but you can't regulate that. You can only encourage it. It's too late. You can't undo what we've done. The only hope would be to set up limits not at the source but at the destination."

"The actual stock exchange itself."

"Yes. Somehow find a way to regulate the speed at which transactions of any one computer or computer system can trade. But no one's even suggesting that. It's not a matter of if machines will have a meltdown sell-off like they did in 2008, it's when it'll happen again."

I'm not excited about the fact that he's making some pretty valid points. "I think we're getting a little off track here. Get back to transhumanism."

He digs through a file cabinet, and I'm not sure how he could possibly know what he's looking for, but he comes up with a file of papers and spreads it out on the table.

"How do you keep this stuff organized anyhow?"

He taps his head. "A steel trap."

"With a little rust. I mean, that comes naturally with age."

"A touch, perhaps."

He walks directly to a stack of papers beside his bed and shuffles through them. "Right now we're seeing exponential technological breakthroughs in bioengineering, gene therapy, synthetic biology, medicine, and nanotechnology. According to Moore's Law, which is a way of understanding the exponential growth in technology, the performance will continue to go up even as the price plummets—which has held true for the last forty years . . ."

He's flipping through the pages. "Even as some scientists are working at reverse engineering the human brain—which will happen within the next twenty years—other scientists are developing never-before-imagined nanotechnology applications and virtual reality interfaces. Within a few decades we'll be able to upload information directly to the human brain."

"Is that transhumanism?"

"Partly, yes. We're already merging more and more with nonbiological intelligence through neural implants and brain-to-machine interfaces. Eventually there'll be no going back."

"So we're going to become cyborgs?"

He's quiet for a moment.

"That's not seriously what you're telling me here."

"It's already happening—cochlear implants, bionic eyes, artificial limbs, synthetic organs, deep-brain stimulation, the next generation of brain-imaging technology—"

"Okay, okay." I hold up my hands. "I hear you. So, The Singularity is when humans are able to do what? Upload their consciousness onto a computer?"

"If desired."

"I'm still not sure I get the transhumanism part."

"The more we augment or enhance humans, at a certain point we may be more machine than biological entity, and even the biological part will be enhanced by gene therapy and genetic manipulation."

He reflects on that for a moment. "The big question at this point is really where you draw the line between augmentation and enhancement—or even if you should draw any line at all. For example, having glasses to augment your seeing, or wearing a hearing aid, or maybe having an artificial leg. That's all acceptable."

"And you're saying transhumanists want to take things further?"

"Exactly. From augmentation to enhancement. We use binoculars to see infrared, why not just give people the ability to do so? We use cars to travel at higher speeds than we can on our own, why not just merge people with Segways that let them do so themselves while preserving the planet's limited supply of fossil fuels? Through xenotransplantation we can—" He catches himself and explains before I have to ask him what that means: "The transfer of genetic or organic material between members of different species."

"Splicing genes of other species into humans?"

"Yeah, it's coming."

Though I don't doubt this aspect of what he's saying, it still unnerves me. It brings up images of the grisly experiments on the fictional island of Dr. Moreau.

Maybe it isn't so fictional after all.

He goes on, "There isn't even consensus today among biologists about what specifically constitutes *Homo sapiens*. Some scientists think we should drop the whole concept and see ourselves not as different or unique within the biological world, but simply a fluid moment in the ongoing evolutionary process. Xenotransplantation is going to blur the lines about what it means to be human even further—how much augmentation is acceptable. I mean, right now you've already got a debate going about cyberorganisms, synthetic biology, cloning, animal and android rights—so when computers reach strong AI, what kinds of rights should they have? Are they living, even though they're not biological? Do we have to redefine what it even means to be alive?"

"Android rights?"

"An android is a robot that looks human, a cyborg is a human that is part robot."

"Okay. And they have rights?"

"Well, that's what's being debated—if self-aware machines deserve the right to life, the right to never be unplugged or destroyed."

This is all a little more than I'm ready to process at the moment. I take out my Morgan Dollar and start flipping it through my fingers, something I tend to do when I'm deep in thought. "And you honestly think the government is doing this? Is developing these autonomous weapons, or is maybe wanting to enhance soldiers like this?"

"They've already admitted that they are."

"Not publicly, though, right?"

He scratches his chin as if he's trying to figure out where to start. "Okay," he mumbles. "'Technology Horizons.'"

He goes to the bottom drawer of his filing cabinet, yanks it open, and within seconds locates what he's looking for. He reads the title: "'Technology Horizons: A Vision for Air Force Science & Technology 2010–2030. Air Force document, AF/ST-TR-10-01-PR.' It was released back in May of 2010." He shoves the printout across the table toward me. It's several hundred pages thick. "You take this one. See what you can figure out."

I look at it unenthusiastically. "We need to be at the Arête by one."

He pulls up a report of his own, a printout called "Losing Humanity: The Case against Killer Robots" from a 2012 Human Rights Watch proposal, evidently to ban robots that could fire without humans in the loop.

"Well then"—he picks up a highlighter from a pencil holder on the countertop—"we better get started."

Lipstick

Roger Yarborough woke up in his hotel room, groggy and feeling a little heavy all over, as if he were on a planet where everything weighs twice what it does on earth. His sheets were a mess. He was dressed only in a pair of underwear.

He rubbed his hand against his forehead and took a long, deep, clear-your-head-in-the-morning breath.

Definitely too many cocktails last night.

Hungover, okay, yes. But there was something else, something vague that came back to him, like a memory on the edge of memories, as if he were trying to make out a shape encircled in mist but not quite being able to.

A figure walking with him. Foggy, but that much was clear.

A woman.

Yes.

The memory had to do with a woman, that much he could tell. He couldn't picture her face or even remember what she wore, but he did recall meeting her and coming back to the room with her and then . . .

Oh.

No.

Immediately, he went to his wallet to see if he might have been robbed after he passed out, but all his credit cards and even his cash were there. The cash surprised him since, had she been a hooker, he imagined he would have paid her before they got started, or at least she would have taken her payment with her when she left.

As all those thoughts rolled through his mind, he found himself staring blankly at his wedding ring.

He'd kept it on last night. He didn't always do that, but he hadn't been planning on picking anyone up when he left his hotel room.

Then again, it was Vegas.

Not quite subconsciously, he covered the ring with his other hand.

Roger traveled a lot, was gone on business nearly every week, so, sure, he'd had a few nights over the years that he hadn't spent alone in his hotel room. Maybe more than a few. Nobody could begrudge him that. He was just a normal guy with needs that had to be met.

But last night, whether or not he'd brought the woman whom he vaguely remembered back to his room—well, he couldn't be sure about that one way or the other.

Leaving the wallet on the dresser, he walked to the bathroom to splash some cold water on his face.

As soon as he flicked on the lights, he saw the sentence written in lipstick on the mirror: *Go home to your wife, Roger.*

For a long and unsteady moment he stood there staring at the words.

So he had brought a woman back here last night after all. And she hadn't robbed him, but instead she'd left this message for him.

How much did you tell her about Janice?

He didn't know, couldn't remember, wasn't sure he wanted to.

Roger had no idea what he might have done with the woman before she left, or how long she might have been here in the room with him, or who she was, and despite himself he felt a lump form in his throat.

He thought of his three children at home with Janice, his wife of nine years, what she would think if she saw these words, what his children would think if they knew what their daddy had done last

night and done all too often on those other nights on his business
trips. They didn't know about sex yet, but they did know that a
mommy and a daddy are supposed to be with each other. And only
each other.

Wetting a washcloth, he worked at removing the lipstick. It came off
easier than he thought it would, but even after it was gone, it wasn't
gone. He still saw the words as clearly as before, hovering in front of
him, written, as it were, across his reflection like scarlet letters etched
on his chest, and he wondered if he would see them every time he
looked into a mirror.

Go home to your wife, Roger.

His eyes went back to his wedding ring.

Go home.

To your wife.

He had a decision to make.

And he did. He kept the ring on, and he vowed he was going to
be able to stare into a mirror again and not be afraid to look himself
in the eye.

***

"What do you mean it wasn't there?" the voice on the phone said.

"It wasn't there. I tore that place apart, and the information isn't
on the hard drive. I've been scouring through it since I got it from
the house."

"You know how small a USB drive is. You can hide one just about
anywhere."

Silence. "He might have had it with him."

"I'm not ready to depend on what might have happened."

"Someone else showed up before I could finish."

"Who?"

"I don't know."

"You don't know."

"No. They must have called 911. By the time I circled back to the house, the cops were there."

"I know some people in the department. I should be able to find out the number they called in from. That'll lead us to the person who made the call."

"Yeah, they might have the drive, but—"

"You're going to have to pay them a visit to find out."

"This is out of my league. You just told me I needed to check the house."

"I told you that you needed to retrieve the files."

"I'm not the right guy to—"

"Remember the photos I sent you."

A pause. "Yes."

"Don't make the mistake of assuming that I will be reticent to post them online, as I spoke with you about earlier. I'm a resolute man."

This stretch of silence was the longest one so far. Finally the reply came: "How much latitude do I have in . . . obtaining the information?"

"Right now the only thing that matters is retrieving those files. I don't care how you go about doing it."

"Okay, I'll take care of it."

"Yes, I know you will."

Phoenix Sky Harbor International Airport

Two formidable Hispanic men met Colonel Byrne at the curb outside baggage claim. One of them was a medium-height, wide-bodied brute, thick and muscular. The other was at least six foot six and had a flat and pockmarked face that made it look like he'd run face-first into a brick wall at some point in his life and never quite recovered.

The colonel carefully set the suitcase in the back of the SUV, then took a seat inside the vehicle.

Each of the men wore jackets, but Derek could see tattoos on both of their left wrists. From his work in the military he recognized the Hezbollah insignias.

It didn't surprise him that the men were inked like they were. Over the last fifteen years Hezbollah, the Mujahideen, and Iran had developed a complex, mutual web of arms dealing, military tactics training, and intelligence sharing with the cartels of South and Central America.

The enemy of my enemy is my friend—it has been an operating principle of unlikely bedfellows for millennia. And the enemy of their enemy was America.

A driver sat quietly in the front.

The two tattooed thugs positioned themselves on each side of the colonel. One of them produced a blindfold and handed it to him.

"It's either this or drugs."

He accepted the blindfold, put it on, and the vehicle pulled away from the curb.

Autonomy

The only sound in the RV is the flipping of pages as Xavier and I make our way through the files and photocopied pages he has spread out before us on the table.

I have a pen in hand, and I'm taking notes from the "Technology Horizons" Air Force document as I move through it.

It states the priorities of Air Force research and development in the coming years:

> Two key areas in which significant advances are possible in the next decade with properly focused Air Force investment are: (i) increased use of autonomy and autonomous systems, and (ii) augmentation of human performance; both can achieve capability increases and cost savings via increased manpower efficiencies and reduced manpower needs.

Autonomous weapons and augmented human performance. Precisely what Xavier had been telling me about earlier.

As I read on I feel a squirm of discomfort in my chest when I consider the implications of what this document has to say.

> Closer human-machine coupling and augmentation of human performance will become possible and essential.

148

I peer across the table at my friend. "How did you get ahold of this, anyway?"

"It's in the public domain. Anyone can access it."

"So all this stuff you've told me over the years about the experimental aircraft out at Groom Lake . . ." I can hardly believe I'm saying this. "It's for real?"

He nods toward the report. "According to those Air Force documents—and other ones—the research is occurring as we speak. The military just doesn't announce where they're doing it. But one of the most secure military installations on the planet is Area 51. It's also where they test their most classified experimental aircraft and drones; we know that too."

I tap my finger against the pages. "So, it only makes sense that they would at least be doing some of these tests there."

"Yes."

Among conspiracy theorists, Area 51 is famously known as the place where the alien body, or spacecraft, or both, was taken after the supposed UFO crash in Roswell, New Mexico, back in 1947. According to Xavier and his friends, the Air Force has been studying the aircraft since that time, reverse engineering it, or at least trying to.

"How come you never showed me these documents before?" I ask him.

He shrugs. "You never took any of it seriously. I didn't think you'd accept them as legit."

"Okay, I'm taking you seriously now."

"Glad to hear it. Despite what they say, you're not an entirely lost cause."

"Thanks."

I go back to the Air Force document.

Augmentation may come from increased use of autonomous systems, interfaces for more intuitive and close coupling of humans and automated systems, and direct augmentation of humans via drugs or implants to improve memory, alertness, cognition, or visual/aural acuity, as well as screening for specialty codes based on brainwave patterns or genetic correlates.

Considering what Xavier has been telling me and what I'm now reading, I can actually see where he and his conspiracy theorist friends are coming from.

The military wants to augment humans with drugs and implants. A specific, direct, and purposeful move toward transhumanism.

Earlier, Xavier had mentioned that Emilio had shown interest in Groom Lake, we found a military-encrypted USB drive in his things, and he was murdered and his home ransacked. All of it is interwoven somehow, I just have no idea how.

When I consider the military's goal of augmenting people, my thoughts return to what Xavier and I were talking about earlier—enhancement and augmentation. It's clear that the more we merge with machines, or with other species, the blurrier the lines become about what makes us human.

"Xavier, the Air Force is looking for ways to augment and enhance its soldiers. Well, it doesn't take a rocket scientist to see the negative implications of all this. I can picture it now—you have unenhanced humans and you have augmented ones. How will they compete in sports contests? There won't be any way of evaluating them, comparing them, making things fair."

"And that's not all." He's flipping through manila folders looking for something. "Follow with me here. Machines follow protocol. In a sense, they would be better than human operators who might miss something, make decisions clouded by anger or feelings of revenge. Or even just weariness. Machines don't get tired in the afternoon and need a cup of coffee to stay alert."

"But what happens when a drone makes a mistake and kills innocent civilians? Who do you hold accountable? I mean, you're not going to court-martial the drone."

"The programmers. The ones who came up with the algorithms. Or maybe the manufacturer of the drone or its computer system. It's still a big question mark. Right now no one really knows. For the time being, killer robots are still on the drawing board." He taps the Human Rights Watch document. "But not for long."

That was a scary thought—that a computer programmer could be tried for war crimes for coming up with a certain algorithm.

Or what if he did it on purpose? Without human operators in the loop, all you'd need to do is hack into a drone—and that's already been done.

"Reprogram a machine with different parameters or rules of engagement." I'm thinking aloud. "And then if you started to get AI that could analyze data trillions of times faster than humans can . . ."

"Skynet."

"Autonomous weapons."

"A *Terminator* scenario."

"Exactly."

It's more than a little disconcerting how well the pieces fit together.

It's all just conspiracy theory stuff. They always find ways to "prove" their theories.

Yes, that might be true, but Emilio is dead.

But what did he have to do with any of all this? And how might he be connected to RixoTray?

Before I can reflect on that anymore, we hear from Charlene that she hasn't been able to get anywhere with the FBI. It's closing in on 11:30 now, and we need to be leaving soon if we're going to have time to grab lunch and make the one o'clock rehearsal at the Arête.

After the break-in at Emilio's house, and considering we have the USB drive that whoever was there was very likely looking for, I'm not keen on the idea of leaving Fionna and her kids alone here at the house.

I suggest to Charlene that we all meet at the Arête for lunch. Fionna can take her kids to the pool or to the rock climbing wall while we go to rehearsal.

I don't tell Charlene all of my reasoning, but she agrees with the idea of meeting at the hotel to eat, and while we finish up the conversation, Xavier goes to the house to see if Fionna is on board with the idea.

Since the Arête caters to the affluent twenty-something single crowd, there are more bars and nightclubs there than family-friendly sit-down restaurants. In fact, there's really only one choice.

"So, Jenny's Grille?" I suggest to Charlene. We've been there countless times, so I don't need to tell her where it is: just south of the main lobby, near the boutique shops.

"Sure," she tells me. "I'll meet you there."

Xavier returns and informs me that Fionna and the kids will be right out. We gather up our notes, and when the McClurys appear, I pack the kids into the Aston Martin so they can experience riding in the DB9, Xavier climbs into Fionna's minivan with her so he can fill her in on our transhumanism discussion, and we all take off for the Arête.

Dust of the Dead

Colonel Derek Byrne felt the SUV roll to a stop and heard a garage
door rattle shut behind the vehicle.

"Te lo puedes quitar," the man on his left said: *You can take it off.*

Derek untied the blindfold. They were in a dreary, abandoned
warehouse.

The men opened the doors and ushered Derek out of the vehicle.
The shorter of the men went for the suitcase and demanded that he,
rather than Derek, carry it.

"Of course."

Derek stood quietly with his arms outstretched, allowing the gi-
gantic man to pat him down. When he found the spool of thick
suture thread and the needle in Derek's pocket, he frowned. "What's
this for?"

"Sewing."

"Sewing?" He gave the colonel a scoff of disbelief.

"A hobby of mine. But if you don't trust me to have a needle and
thread, feel free to hang on to them. I'll just get them back from you
later."

"You know what?" He pocketed them. "I think I will."

Derek did not carry a gun. If he needed a weapon he would simply take one from the people attacking him and use it to kill them.

It was how he'd handled things in the past when he was on assignment in the Middle East working for the United States government. It was how he would handle things today, if necessary.

He noticed that the two thugs were both packing. That could work out well for him later.

The man frisking him pulled out the Ziploc bag of gray powder that Colonel Byrne had in his pocket. "What's this?"

"It's for my coffee."

The guy grunted. "Alright." He handed Derek back the plastic bag and announced to his associates, "He's clean."

The driver led the way, and the two brutes followed closely behind Derek. The warehouse smelled of long-accumulated dust and grease and was lit only by two narrow, grimy windows set in the wall nearly twenty feet above the oil-stained concrete floor. A thin fringe of dirty light crawled in beneath each of the three garage doors, but didn't offer much relief at all from the warehouse's consuming shadows.

Dead industrial machines languished in the center of the room. In the dingy light Derek wasn't able to make out what they might have been used for. Textiles, he thought, but he couldn't be sure.

The driver grabbed a sliding metal door and yanked it to the side to reveal a room illuminated only by several dozen candles. All the flames leaned to the side as the rush of air from the opening door swept over them, then flickered their way back to normal.

A statue of Christ nailed to the cross hung on the wall.

Three more men, all Hispanic, stood inside the room. Two had AK-47s in hand and slings of ammo draped across their chests. They flanked the third man, who was dressed in an immaculate, flawless white suit and carried no visible weapon.

A chair sat beside him. A small table with a carafe and two cups waited in the corner.

"Colonel," he said. *"Hola."*

"Hello, Jesús."

Jesús Garcia, head of the Los Zetas, one of the most powerful Mexican cartels operating here in the States, gestured toward the chair. Some of the cartels in El Salvador or Colombia are more established, but the ones in Mexico are quickly becoming one of the biggest threats to Americans, and Colonel Byrne knew better than to take this meeting lightly.

"Have a seat, my friend," Jesús said.

Derek knew it was a power play. There was only one chair. Sitting would put him at a lower level than the rest of the men, make it easier for them to loom over him.

He'd only met Jesús twice before, but said, "Let's both stand. That way we can look each other in the eye. Like friends do."

That brought a smile and a small laugh. *"Sí, sí, claro.* Of course."

For years, the US government has referred to its efforts against controlled substances as the War on Drugs. And now, the cartels have reached the levels of military sophistication to make that statement truer than ever.

They far outgun the police, even the SWAT teams, of nearly every major US city. They have better body armor, heavier artillery, and their communication systems are rivaled only by the US military.

When threatened, the cartels have gone as far as targeting US police officers and their families with sniper attacks. In some cities they have their own SWAT uniforms, they know the response times and routes, and they can respond before the actual SWAT team. They use high-capacity magazines and body armor and they're not going to quit or walk away until they have what they're after.

They also have high-explosive grenades and use standardized assault rifles and shotguns of the same design to make it easier to train and to exchange ammo and clips in gunfights. They're starting to use rounds designed to go through body armor and armored vehicles.

Some cartels even use small remote-controlled planes and submarines to transport their drugs to the states.

Hezbollah has been bringing people across the US border, in cooperation with the cartels, for the last decade. Derek knew this, knew that this connection was one that the US government was reluctant to publicly acknowledge but that existed nevertheless.

He also knew that in Mexico, law enforcement and the military were so infiltrated by the cartels that there really was no way of stopping them apart from US military intervention. But the US hasn't made a practice of deploying troops to Mexico because the cartels influence the judges, and if Americans are caught in that country, there's a law that they must be tried by a Mexican court rather than shipped back to the US for their trials, and US soldiers definitely did not want to be tried by a corrupt Mexican court.

Jesús asked Derek, "And how is Mr. Becker?"

"As far as I know he's hanging in there."

"But, as I understand, he hasn't served you as well as you'd hoped?"

"We're adapting."

"As you always do."

"As I always do."

Derek couldn't help but wonder if Jesús was the person masterminding the project. It would make sense—he had the money, the resources, the manpower, and the motivation to get behind it. But there was something about it that just didn't fit.

Maybe it was only a gut feeling, but whatever it was, it was there, and he held back from making too many assumptions.

Derek needed to feel things out, see where they led. As they say, discretion is the better part of valor, and he would do his best to discern the truth without being too blatant about it or coming across as unnecessarily intrusive.

On the other hand, there was something to be said about simply being direct, so he decided to play things by ear.

"I was told we were going to discuss the delivery of the merchandise."

Jesús gave him a half grin. "Right to the point. Yes, and that is one of the things I like about you. Coffee first?"

Decorum dictated that he accept the offer. "Certainly."

A few moments later the coffee was poured and Derek had mixed in the powder that he carried with him.

Jesús took a sip of his own coffee and watched the colonel curiously. "The first two times we met, you added that same powder to your coffee. It isn't creamer, is it?"

"No."

"And it's not some kind of drug."

"No, it's not."

"May I ask you, then, what it is you take in your coffee?"

The colonel dipped his spoon into the cup and gently swirled it. "Dust."

"Dust?"

"Yes. Ground up from a mummy."

The room was silent. Candles licked at the stale air. No one moved. At last Jesús laughed heartily. "Mummy dust?"

"Yes."

He looked at Derek slyly out of the corner of his eye. "I don't believe you."

"In the 1700s and 1800s it was quite common in Europe to eat mummies. They believed it served as a remedy for many common maladies, and also that it granted them long life. I do it as a tribute to them and as a reminder of the brevity and transient nature of our lives."

He took another sip and saw one of the men with the assault rifles swallow uneasily.

"In a way, this dust is a bit like rattlesnake venom."

"What are you talking about?"

"You can drink rattlesnake venom. Your stomach can digest it, but you wouldn't want an open sore in your mouth while you're drinking it. Or, let a snake pierce your skin with its fangs and inject the venom into your bloodstream, well, that's when you're in trouble. It's the same with the mummy dust."

"You can digest it but you wouldn't want to get it into your bloodstream."

"You absolutely would not. The chemicals they used to embalm the mummies. The germs. Not a pleasant way to go." He dabbed the coffee from his lips. "It took me years, actually, to find legitimate mummies that could be ground up, but finally I stumbled across a private collector in Germany who was able to supply me with what I needed."

Jesús shook his head. "I've seen some disagreeable things over the years, but even I find cannibalism a bit . . . excessive."

"Throughout history, humans have shown a distinct ability to find the practices of other cultures cannibalistic, even as they practice culturally-approved-of forms of it in their own."

A tiny smile. "Ah, but I'm afraid it's rather uncommon to eat people in Mexico these days. And we certainly don't grind up corpses and mix them into our coffee." His men snickered in agreement.

Derek pointed to the cross of Christ on the wall. "Jesús, your namesake told his followers to eat his flesh, to drink his blood. Mass, or the Eucharist, or the Lord's Supper, whatever term you wish to use, is a symbolic form of cannibalism that millions of Mexicans take part in every week. Catholics believe the body and blood of Christ are actually present. How is that not a cannibalistic ritual?"

Jesús clasped his hands together admiringly. "Well done. Very good, Colonel. Yet, despite that, I think I will pass on the mummy dust for today." He downed his own coffee. "So then, on to business?"

"Yes."

"The merchandise. It will be delivered tomorrow night?"

"At 8:46. Just as we agreed. That's when the training exercise begins."

"You're going to get the codes from the base's engineer?"

If Jesús wasn't the person orchestrating the project, he'd at least been well informed about the plans that had been put in place.

"Yes."

"Do you have him yet?"

"We will. Tonight."

"We?"

"I have an associate."

"The woman."

"Yes. That's right."

"You seem rather confident in her."

"She's quite good at what she does. And so am I."

Jesús took a moment to watch the candles flick and dance, throwing their strange and subtle shadows against the walls. "And you know where the airstrip is?"

"It's all been arranged."

They spoke for a few minutes about the details of who would be receiving the delivery, what to do if things didn't go as planned, and the transfer of money and of the essential information for using the device once it had changed hands.

Derek said, "I have a request of my own."

"Yes?"

"I'm planning to move our research out of the States. There's been more turnover in the department than I'm comfortable with. I'd like to relocate to a place with fewer liabilities and less possible exposure. Because of that, I'd like to renegotiate the terms of our agreement."

A small silence. "Renegotiate."

"Yes. I'd like to change the means of payment for my cut. I'm not interested in money."

SINGULARITY

"Drugs?"

"No. Volunteers."

"Go on."

"I need you to do what you specialize in."

"And which specialty would that be?"

"Kidnappings."

A mock scolding finger. "Ah, now, that's never been proven."

"Of course not. But I'll be needing more volunteers to continue my research. I think you can help me."

"From here in the States? Because, depending on the numbers we're talking about, it might attract undue attention."

"Mexico is fine."

"People disappear mysteriously from my country all the time."

"So I've heard."

"How many volunteers do you need?"

"Fifty."

Jesús didn't flinch at all when Derek mentioned the number. "And you're going to paralyze them all?"

"Locked-in syndrome. And we'll need all ages, both sexes, to study how neural impulses change over time and with the physical development of the body."

"Children too?"

"Yes."

Jesús walked to one of the candles, licked his fingers, closed them over the flame to extinguish it, then gazed at the colonel through the rising tendrils of smoke. "I choose the people."

"Certainly."

"But I need to know you're serious about this."

"What would convince you?"

His gaze went to the suitcase near the door. "A demonstration."

Out of the corner of his eye Derek saw the short, stocky man who'd met him at the airport grin and roll up his sleeves.

160

Ah. That kind of demonstration.

"Of course."

Derek removed the arm from the case and turned to the other man, the tallest one in the room. "Can you hold this for a moment?"

Somewhat taken off guard, he accepted the robotic arm. Derek was careful to hand it to him upright so that he was holding the base and the robotic hand was near his throat.

Then he turned toward the brutish man and prepared to defend himself.

To everyone in the room, it must have looked like Derek was just readying himself—and he was—but he was doing something else as well.

Derek was concentrating on sending the appropriate neural signals to the electronic array implanted in his left forearm.

As the stout man came at him, the fingers of the robotic arm twitched slightly, and then his associate who was holding the robotic arm said the last words he was ever going to say: "*¿Qué está pasando?*"

Derek's Spanish wasn't what it could have been, but he could at least make out that the guy was asking what was happening.

Well, he was about to find out.

The robotic arm twisted, the hand bent and clenched tightly around the giant's throat. He grabbed at it to try to pull it off, but since it had the grip strength of nearly twenty men, that was not going to prove very effective.

The bullish man who'd been coming at the colonel turned to look momentarily at his partner, and that was a mistake. Derek was on him and in two moves had disarmed him. He shot him through the left eye and then whipped around and placed a bullet in the foreheads of the two men holding the AKs before either of them could even raise their weapons to fire at him.

While the driver quivered in fright, the man on the floor who was choking writhed and tugged futilely at the robotic arm. With his throat completely closed off, he made no sound, but his face was getting red and his eyes were bulging out. It wouldn't be long now.

Derek faced the driver, who held up both hands and begged in Spanish for his life. Derek glanced at Jesús, who signaled for him to spare the driver, which he did.

Jesús scanned the room disapprovingly. "Good help is hard to find."

"If they were good, they wouldn't be lying dead on the floor."

"Indeed."

Both of them turned their attention to the choking man.

Derek decided to end things quickly and had the robotic hand close completely, driving its fingers through the man's throat and ripping out his jugular vein. A spray of hot blood shot through the air, the man convulsed, and then, as his body became still, the blood pooled profusely on the floor.

"That," said Jesús, "is very impressive."

"Thank you."

Derek retrieved his needle and thread from the man's pocket, then, through his thoughts, he released the robotic arm's grip on the corpse. "How far would you have let them go with me?"

"Just far enough."

"I understand."

Using the shirt of one of the dead soldiers, Derek wiped as much of the blood off the robotic hand and arm as he could.

The drug lord and the avenging hero gazed at each other. Neither appeared afraid. Neither was.

The driver stood nervously watching them, his eyes glued on the gun that Derek still held. Then his gaze shifted to one of the dead man's AKs and Derek said, "I wouldn't advise it."

That was all it took. The man nodded and actually took a step back.

At last Jesús said, "From what I understand, you have a plane to catch? Another meeting this afternoon?"

"At five. With Agcaoili."

"I hope it is productive."

"I'm confident it will be. And now, before I leave, just one question, if you don't mind."

"Of course."

Derek watched him carefully. "Are you the one behind all this? Orchestrating the project?"

"Hmm . . ." Jesús reflected. "And here I was about to ask you the same question."

For a moment they each studied the other man's eyes to discern if he was telling the truth.

Derek, for his part, was convinced that Jesús wasn't hiding anything.

"So we have a common friend then," Jesús said.

"If *friend* is the right word."

"If, indeed."

Then Derek and the driver headed back to the airport so he could return to Las Vegas.

When they were gone, Jesús Garcia made a phone call to have some cartel members come to clean up the warehouse and dispose of the bodies of the four men who had, apparently, not been as good as their salaries would have led someone to believe.

Then he made one more call to see if his contact at the Las Vegas Police Department had found out for him what he wanted to know.

The Arête

The Arête is something to behold.

Over the last couple decades, location-themed casinos have become popular in Vegas. On the Strip you'll find the Paris, the Venetian, and New York, New York. Off the Strip you have the Rio, the Gold Coast, and the Orleans.

But just as with any trend, when guests become too used to one thing they start to look for something that's new and different.

However, right about the time when Vegas was rethinking the location-based idea back in 2008, Lehman Brothers collapsed. The economy imploded, no one had money to come to Vegas, and real-estate values plummeted.

So, when billionaire Clive Fridell announced he was going to build an entertainment complex here two months after the stock market crashed, everyone thought he was crazy. However, he had cash in hand, plus properties in Singapore, Dubai, and his island resorts in the Caribbean that he could've sold if he needed to in order to get the capital necessary to build a multibillion-dollar resort casino.

Still, they told him he was crazy.

Still, he built.

And in the end, he had the last word, because if there was ever a time to buy property in Las Vegas, it was during the recession. Real estate was at decades-low prices, labor was cheap. It was almost as if Fridell had just won the jackpot at one of his own casinos.

Five years after construction began, the Arête opened.

The mirrored sides of the building might make you think of the Wynn or the Encore, but the sloping, asymmetrical mountain–inspired design for the top thirty stories puts it in a class by itself.

With the world's tallest indoor rock climbing wall on one end and one of the hottest, hippest nightclubs in North America on the other, it was clear that Mr. Fridell held nothing back when he delivered on his promise to bring Vegas a resort casino like nothing it had ever seen before.

I leave my car with the valet, and then Fionna's four children and I enter the Arête's lobby.

The kids have never been here before, and when they see the fountains and the enclosed courtyard next to the casino entrance with the indoor "mountain" and rock climbing wall that rises twenty stories, their jaws drop.

Donnie unplugs his earbuds. "This place is sick."

"I'll get you some passes," I tell them. "So you can climb it this afternoon while we're in rehearsal."

"Sweet."

"All the vegetation on the mountain is real, unlike at some of the resorts here on the Strip. And they don't pipe in the bird sounds. Those are actual real birds on the cliffs up there."

"An aviary," Maddie says knowingly.

"That's right."

People younger than twenty-one aren't allowed to linger in the gaming areas or go near the machines, so we take the long, circuitous route around the casino toward Jenny's Grille.

On our way, we pass the escalators leading down to the backstage area and dressing rooms for the theater where I'll be performing tonight.

The newer casinos aren't even typically called casinos, but rather resorts or entertainment complexes, and, truthfully, that's a better description of what they are.

Revenue from gaming has dropped to about 35 percent of most hotels' income—in contrast to the 95 percent it was a few decades ago. Television and the Internet have greatly affected the design of the newer casinos here in Vegas.

Now we have restaurants opening up with celebrity chefs, high-end shops selling designer sunglasses and purses, as well as jewelry that might easily cost hundreds of thousands of dollars. Shows now make up a major portion of the profit, when, in Vegas's early years, they used to be free.

Boxing is hot again, so is mixed martial arts and UFC fighting, which help boost gaming income.

Because of reality TV, spas and salons are popular and poker is making a huge comeback. But there are no reality shows about slot machines, and those are, at least to some degree, going by the wayside in modern Vegas.

To address the changing trends, the Arête has fewer slot machines per potential occupant than any other Las Vegas casino. The target demographic, young affluent Asians, don't play the slots nearly as much as middle-aged and older Americans. Instead, they prefer the gaming tables and video poker machines.

If you look around the Strip you'll see that the demographic is no longer rural cowboys like you find downtown at the casinos on Fremont, which is the more iconic 1950s Vegas with the casinos Frank Sinatra used to call *carpet joints*.

Now, it's the goal of luring in money from China that shapes the mood and feel of the Strip.

Fionna and Xavier are waiting for us by the overcrowded entrance to Jenny's Grille.

"I put my name in," Xavier tells us, "but there's a twenty-minute wait."

"Well . . ." I evaluate that. "We may need to order the food to go or get it delivered to the dressing rooms. Let's see how long it takes. Stay here, see if you can get a table and maybe order some appetizers. In the meantime, Fionna, I'm wondering if you can help me with something for a few minutes?"

"Sure."

Xavier and the children take a seat with the other people waiting for tables, and he starts telling them knock-knock jokes.

Fionna looks at me curiously. "What's up?"

"C'mon." I turn toward the marble hallway to the stores. "Let's go shopping."

The Black Card

"I need to get something for Charlene," I explain. "For Valentine's Day. Something stunning and memorable, something that really shows her how much she means to me."

"Jevin, she's going to be here any minute." We're walking side by side down the corridor lined with elite, designer stores. "I'm not sure we really have time to shop."

"What? We go into a store, choose something, buy it. In and out just like that. How long can it take?"

"Obviously you are not a woman." She sighs lightly. "Alright, let's go. I suppose if we hurry we might just make it back by the skin of our pants."

Now that's one I haven't heard before.

I pause and look at the line of shops ahead of us. "Did you find out anything from the drive yet?"

"I'm moving through it one file at a time. Slow but sure. So what are you thinking? Clothes? Jewelry? A car? Right here in this mall alone you have Gucci, Tiffany, Breitling, Louis Vuitton, Prada . . ."

"I'm pretty open."

"Well, we need to start somewhere, Jev."

I recall that Charlene left her cross necklace on Emilio's body in the Philippines. "A necklace. I think I want to get her a really nice necklace."

"Always a good choice. Where's the nearest jewelry store?"

"Just up ahead."

I've never been in this store before, but when we enter I find that the place looks just like I might picture a high-end jewelry store in New York City, London, or Paris looking.

A tall, angular man stands behind one of the glass counters. He appraises us as we enter, no doubt taking note of my jeans and tattered T-shirt, then he glances at his watch as if this has already been a waste of his time. Obviously, he doesn't recognize me from the billboards.

"May I help you?" he says. It sounds more like an accusation than a question.

"I'm looking for a necklace," I tell him. "Something really nice for a very special woman."

"I see." He looks at Fionna and nods stiffly.

"Oh, no. It's not her. She's here to help me choose the piece for my girlfriend."

"Well," he replies vaguely. "And do you have a price range in mind?" Once again he looks askance at my clothes.

"What kind of prices do you start at?"

"We have a few pieces for under twelve, but if you're looking for something more along those lines, there's a place across the street where—"

"What kind of prices do you *end* at?" Fionna asks.

"A quarter."

"Of a million?"

"Yes. Of a million."

"Let's start there," I suggest. "See if anything catches my fancy."

He doesn't reply right away. "Yes, well . . ." At last he turns to the glass case to his left, but doesn't remove the jewelry as he tells us about it. "Here we have a graduated necklace in platinum with 204 round brilliant and marquise diamonds. Twenty-five-point-eight carats. I have some smaller carat weights and different-length necklaces—"

Fionna shakes her head. "It's not Charlene. Too pretentious."

"Agreed."

He spends the next five minutes going through the pieces in front of him, but nothing seems right for Charlene, and at last, when I tell him we're just not interested in those necklaces, he doesn't look at all surprised.

My phone vibrates, and I see a text from Charlene that she has just parked and is on her way to the restaurant.

I thank the proprietor for his time. He grumbles a snippy reply, so I open my wallet and hand him one of my cards. "Call me if you get anything a little more expensive but not so showy in stock." Before I close my wallet I make sure he sees my black American Express Centurion Card. It's a card issued only by invitation. When I got mine, the holder needed to have at least twenty million dollars of assets. There's no limit to the card. I could buy this jewelry store and all that it contains with it.

His eyes widen and he gulps slightly. "Sir, I—"

I wink at him. "Right." I gesture toward the door. "Okay, Fionna. Let's go have lunch."

When we arrive at the restaurant again, we find that the wait time is still at fifteen minutes, which isn't going to work out for us at all. Headliners never need to wait in lines in Vegas, but I don't like skipping in front of people or drawing that kind of attention to myself.

As it is, there's no way we'll get seated and served and be able to finish our meal before we need to be downstairs at one o'clock.

Fionna suggests that she stay up here while Xavier, Charlene, and

I go to get ready for rehearsal. "We'll bring you something down," she offers. "Special delivery."

"But Mom," Maddie objects, "I didn't get a chance to tell everyone about the immortal jellyfish."

"Hmm . . ." Fionna is considering things when the pager goes off, indicating that our table is ready. "Well, that's a surprise. Okay, well, you three should probably head downstairs." Her gaze shifts back to Maddie. "How about we get seated, then Lonnie, Donnie, and Mandie can order while we go down to Mr. Banks's dressing room and you can fill us in."

Maddie nods. "Perfect," she says punctiliously.

Before they can leave, Mandie tugs on her mom's slacks. "Mommy, what's a gentleman's club?"

"Who told you about gentleman's clubs?"

"I saw a sign. On the way here." Her reading ability is another testimony to her mother's teaching ability.

They start to follow their server to the table. "Well, for starters it's a place where no true gentleman would ever go."

"Oh. Then why's it called that?"

But by then they're out of earshot, and even though I'm curious as to Fionna's detailed answer to her kindergartner, it's time for Xavier, Charlene, and me to take off for the escalator to the dressing rooms.

The receptionist at the Arête's front desk let Calista check in early, and the courtesan went up to the honeymoon suite on the top floor to make sure everything was ready for tonight.

It was soundproof.

She and Derek had checked that out earlier.

It would be important for what was going to happen in the room tomorrow.

Getting past the gaming area is like picking your way through a labyrinth.

There's no direct route to the theater entrance, and that's all part of the plan. Casinos are designed to keep you inside, not to give you a direct path to the exit door, because if you're outside walking the Strip you're not gambling, and if you're not gambling, the casino isn't making money.

Truthfully, Lady Luck has nothing to do with your winnings; Señor Computer does. He's the one who decides how much you're going to win at the slots. The best odds are always when you're playing the tables, and that's where the next generation wants to gamble. There's a saying around here that there are two types of people who leave Vegas—losers and liars. Not too many people figure out how to exit our city without becoming one or the other.

And almost always those are the ones who play blackjack.

On the way to the theater, Charlene fills Xavier and me in about her meeting with the FBI agent. "To put it bluntly, he wasn't very interested at all in what I had to say. I gave him the USB drive, but I'm not very hopeful."

She pauses, and I recall that Fionna was working with the copy she'd made, that Charlene had taken the original drive with her. "However, now with the break-in at Emilio's place, maybe the guy will change his tune."

"Unless," Xavier replies, "there are jurisdictional issues with the police department. You know how, in crime novels and TV shows, there's always an interagency rivalry between the Feds and local law enforcement. That could really slow us down here."

"Hopefully, life won't imitate art."

"There's only one way to find out."

She produces a business card from the federal agent she'd met with. "I'll follow up with him when we get downstairs."

We pass the sports betting area and find the escalator that leads down to the lower level where the green rooms are. Charlene tells me, "As far as the research on the cobras, you're not going to believe this, but there's a secondary venom in the Sri Lankan subspecies of cobra."

"A secondary venom?"

"It took a bit of searching—I actually had Donnie help me. As soon as I told him it was about snake venom, he was all about doing some extra credit work for his mom. Anyway, turns out there's hardly anything on the Internet, just one thing I came across. It's still undocumented, but I found one researcher's blog. He's a herpetologist and was bitten by a Sri Lankan cobra that had its venom glands removed. He describes a reaction similar to the one you had. The secondary venom is actually in the snake's saliva."

I can't imagine that too many people in the world have been bitten by Sri Lankan cobras that've had their venom glands removed, so it makes sense that the research isn't out there, but all of this just makes me feel worse about what happened to Emilio.

"So," Xavier says, "even if the cobras in the air tube hadn't killed him, if he were bitten by the other snakes and had a panic attack down there, he might very well have thrashed around, agitated them, and died from cardiac arrest."

We're all quiet.

Somebody wanted Emilio dead, and they did not want him to die well.

As we make our way to my dressing room, Xavier and I bring Charlene up to speed about the transhumanism angle.

"Genetics, biotechnology, nanotechnology, robotics, information technology, and cognitive science," Xav summarizes. "Advancements in those six areas are reshaping what it will mean to age and even what it means to be human. Watch the TED talk with Aubrey de Grey. He's a little out there, but he makes some good points. He talks you through it step by step, his process of eliminating aging. He believes it's immoral to keep children from staying young. He also thinks there are people living today who will live to be a thousand years old."

"What?"

"Based on the idea that if you can expand someone's life span for thirty years, then they'll be around to experience the advantages of life-extending technology that will be developed in the meantime and will have their lives extended again, and again."

"Until they're a thousand years old."

"In theory, yes."

"That's crazy."

"Some people think it's not so crazy at all."

Once we're inside, Xavier takes a seat on the countertop in front of the mirror and summarizes the issues involving The Singularity and autonomous weaponry.

Charlene looks impressed. "You two have been busy."

"Xavier had all of this in his files already," I explain. "I just finally gave him the chance to share it with me."

"After all these years."

"I might be a slow learner, but at least I'm teachable."

"Not completely a lost cause."

"Not completely."

Charlene takes a moment to process everything. "Let's say they do develop strong AI. How would they assure that the artilects don't attack humans?"

"We would have to assure that they reflect our values," I reply.

"Whose values?" scoffs Xavier. "I mean, whose morality do we stick the machines with? Which culture's? Which religion's? Protect the rights of women in Muslim countries? Protect the rights of unborn children in ours? If we really do make machines that reflect all of human nature, then we'll end up with greedy, self-possessed, violent machines that'll think nothing of genocide or even of annihilating humanity to achieve their goals. After all, that's how humans have acted all throughout history. If we make machines capable of thinking like us, you can be certain they'll turn on us eventually. No doubt about that."

Wow. Those are encouraging thoughts.

But the more I think about it, the more I have to admit that Xavier is right on the money.

I'm playing out the implications of all this when there's a light tap at the door. "Come in."

Fionna and Maddie join us, and Maddie repositions her glasses as she takes a seat. "Okay, I'm going to tell you what I found out about immortal jellyfish, the only animal on the planet that, left on its own, will never die."

Turritopsis Dohrnii

Okay, she has my attention now.

She dives right in.

"A fully grown *Turritopsis dohrnii* is tiny, not even the width of a dime. It doesn't have a specialized reproductive system like we do, but is capable of asexual reproduction. They're spreading almost uncontrollably in the oceans around the world, but that's not what makes them unique. It has to do with transdifferentiation. After the *Turritopsis dohrnii* reaches sexual maturity, the cells of the jellyfish change and it reverts back to a polyp colony again."

For a moment Fionna, Charlene, and I just stand there. Xavier doesn't move from where he's sitting on the counter near the mirror.

Maddie looks at us strangely, as if what she just said should have produced more of a reaction. "Don't you understand? Its cells change to an earlier stage in its life cycle."

Charlene speaks first, asking the obvious question. "It gets younger?"

"Yes. It gets younger."

"You're saying that this jellyfish ages *backward*?" I exclaim. "How?"

"Transdifferentiation."

"Which is . . . ?"

"It's when a non–stem cell transforms into a different type of cell. In this jellyfish, the cells in the umbrella of the medusa—the sexually mature jellyfish—invert, and the tentacles and the middle layer, called the mesoglea, are absorbed back in. It then reattaches to a rock and—"

"That's the polyp colony part?" Xav asks her.

"Yes. After the embryonic stage, young jellyfish separate themselves from the mother, and then the larvae sink or float through the water until they come to something like a rock or piece of coral or the hull of a boat or something, then they attach themselves and develop into polyps. The polyp feeds on plankton, eventually forming a small colony of polyps that are interconnected with tiny feeding tubes."

She takes a deep breath and then goes on. "Eventually, the colony forms horizontal grooves, and the uppermost one releases itself and becomes what we think of when we think of a jellyfish. At that stage it's called a medusa. After that, the jellyfish doesn't live long. It releases its gametes into the water, they form the fertilized egg, then the embryo or planula larva, and then another polyp colony begins."

Now she's starting to lose me.

Xavier too, apparently, because he looks a little bewildered. "Take us back to the jellyfish getting younger part."

"In times of stress, like when it's wounded or starving, the *Turritopsis dohrnii* is able to return to an earlier developmental stage and reproduce again. Like I was saying, it forms a polyp colony again, grows into a mature jellyfish, returns to a polyp colony."

"So . . ." I can hardly believe I'm saying this. "You weren't kidding when you said it will never die, that it lives forever?"

"Well, as long as it isn't eaten or killed, it has biological immortality, yes."

"You're not exaggerating this, Maddie?" her mother presses her. "It doesn't die?"

"In laboratory tests 100 percent of the *Turritopsis dohrnii* went through this process."

"Transdifferentiation."

"Yes, but"—she clarifies—"to be truly immortal, an organism would need to be immune to death, which isn't the case here."

We're all silent for a moment.

I'm looking at the poster child for homeschooling families. I don't care if she's only nine, this girl should apply for graduate school.

"That was a very good oral report," Xavier tells her.

"Thank you," Maddie replies politely.

"I'd give you an A."

"I will too," Fionna adds. "Now, Maddie, if you'd be kind enough to give us a moment, I'll be right with you and we can head back to the restaurant for lunch. Can you wait for me in the hall?"

Maddie steps out of the room and Fionna turns to us. "One of the files on the USB drive noted that RixoTray Pharmaceuticals is involved with transdifferentiation research. A Dr. Schatzing's heading up the program. I think it has something to do with an anti-aging drug they're trying to develop. Anyway, I'm not sure why any of this would have been copied onto a drive that has military-grade encryption, but at least it gives us our connection to RixoTray."

Xavier says, "Do we know where they're doing that?"

She shakes her head.

"Look into it," I suggest. "See what you can find out."

"We have threads here"—it's Charlene—"let's tie them together. The jellyfish research and the progeria research might tell us something."

Xavier folds his hands on his lap. "So, Emilio was trying to find a way to live longer?"

Progeria, aging prematurely, is the opposite of what happens with the jellyfish. I don't want to jump to any conclusions, but it's also hard not to acknowledge the obvious—especially when you consider the transhumanism research Emilio was doing.

"Or," I reply, "maybe to help someone else live longer. Think progeria for a second. The implications of studying it are profound. If people's genetic makeup can cause them to age at seven or eight times the natural rate—"

"Could the reverse be true?" Fionna interrupts, tracking right along with me. "Would it be possible, through some type of gene therapy or DNA manipulation, to program someone's genes to cause them to age that much *slower* than the rest of us? Or even to reverse the effects of aging, like with the jellyfish?"

I face Xavier. "Back at the RV you mentioned xenotransplantation, genetic splicing from one species to another . . ."

"It's all connected."

"I think"—Charlene flags her hand in the air—"we're getting ahead of ourselves a little here. We really need to find out what else is on that drive before we can figure out the next step."

Fionna picks up her purse. "That's my cue. It'll be easier to keep an eye on Maddie and Mandie if I head home after lunch."

I recall my earlier hesitancy to have them at the house by themselves. "Did you bring the USB drive with you?"

She produces it from her pocket. "I thought it might be best to bring it along. After all, someone broke into one house already looking for it—or at least we think he was looking for it."

Great minds.

"Work here," Xavier tells her. "I'll feel better about it. The kids can climb, swim—there are lifeguards at the pool."

But she shakes her head. "We didn't bring suits."

The suggestion that she could buy some at the hotel comes up, but she doesn't want to be "wasteful." He offers to ride back with her so she can pick up their suits from home, but she declines. "How about after lunch I drive back with Lonnie. He can run in and grab the swimsuits; we'll be fine. Then the two of us can work here while the younger kids hang out."

Xavier invites her to the box office so that he can get her family climbing wall passes and free tickets to the show tonight, she promises that she'll bring us some lunch, and they leave with Maddie.

Hoping that we might finally get somewhere with the Feds, Charlene calls the FBI agent's cell number from the business card he gave her earlier, but it goes directly to voicemail. She leaves a message summarizing what we've discovered and asks him to call her back.

At last she heads to her dressing room to get ready for rehearsal while I stand there for a moment, flipping the Morgan Dollar through my fingers processing what we've been talking about, trying to tie everything together.

And failing.

Eventually, I mentally shift into show mode and head to the theater.

•• •••

Tomás Agcaoili passed through security in San Francisco and maneuvered through the crowds toward his departure gate for his flight to Las Vegas.

His plan: upon arrival in Vegas he would briefly visit Solomon before going to meet with Akinsanya at five. As someone who had his finger on the pulse of everything that went on in the Vegas underground, Solomon was the one person in the city who would know how to deal with Akinsanya, if necessary.

Body Doubles

On one side of the stage is the mammoth piranha tank that was constructed specifically for tonight's climax. I'm not sure when the fish ate last. The crew is supposed to keep them well fed to make sure they don't attack me while I'm trying to escape the straightjacket, but the fish aren't predictable, and if they swarm in to attack, the divers we have stationed at the ready won't likely have time to unlock the shackles on my ankles and get to me in time.

As long as there's not blood in the water I should be fine.

The secret to magic these days is coming up with effects no one has ever seen before and doing them in a way no one could ever guess.

With the hundreds of Internet websites all sharing magic's secrets online, and the two dozen dedicated to revealing the secrets and illusions of the most successful magicians, you need to stay ahead of the curve. As soon as one person uses his cell phone to catch the glint of the cable you're using to help you "levitate" and posts that online, your career is over.

So we have to use something other than cable.

And tonight, in the same way, I have to pull off this effect without anyone figuring out how.

Thinking outside the box might be a cliché in the business world, but it's your bread and butter if you're trying to make up new effects to survive in the world of magic.

I remember one sleight of hand part of my show in the early days of my career that lasted three seconds. It took me a month practicing for nearly four hours a day before I could pull off those three seconds. But they were worth it. I got a standing ovation every time I did that effect, and it's the one that landed me my first gig on the Strip.

When we were considering this piranha tank escape, we went through the options carefully. Houdini would get himself shackled and locked in a trunk and then tipped off the edge of a pier or a bridge. He had to pick the locks and get out of the trunk before he drowned.

I've done that a few times, but I didn't want to repeat it. I wanted to push the envelope in a new direction.

Thurston would "hypnotize" a man in Indian garb, then he would lie in a clear box and they would sink that in water and put it on the side of the stage. The guy would stay there for twenty or twenty-five minutes in a state of "catalepsy."

It was an amazing effect, but it wasn't anything supernatural. The Indian man just knew how to take small, shallow breaths, something anyone can learn with practice, but few people are willing to put that kind of time into something they'll hardly ever use.

Houdini was an amazing escape artist, almost certainly the best ever, and he was a pro at self-promotion, but he wasn't a great magician. His close-up effects needed work, and when he would do shows the audience would often leave disappointed. But he was an excellent promoter. He would travel to a town and tell lies to the newspaper and they would print them, then he'd move on and do it again. Today, with the Internet, you can't get away with that.

Thurston, though. He was a master magician, and he was the inspiration of my mentor Grayson DeVos, the man I bought my house from.

Henning used to do Houdini's water torture escape, and he would struggle and appear to die, but they would raise a curtain over the tank so the audience didn't have to see his body. Then a man would rush out with an axe to break open the tank, they would drop the curtain, and Henning was gone from the tank. The man with the axe turns to the audience, and it's Henning.

"How did they do that?" I asked Xavier one time.

He just shook his head. "I have some ideas, but his effect designer was better than I am."

I wasn't sure about that, but regardless, we never did figure that one out.

Now, here at the Arête, there's a platform on the other side of the tank where we'll have two paramedics and divers in case we need them. In the tank there's a fake, sliding coral reef and a tube, just large enough for someone to swim through, that winds behind the reef and opens up at the back of the tank.

It's one of the most elaborate escapes I've ever tried, but it's impressive, especially with the prestige at the end when I appear, as Henning did, as someone you'd never expect.

Seth Greene, my body double, is waiting backstage.

I've never really thought he looks that much like me when he's not made up and isn't wearing an identical outfit, but that's actually a good thing. We need to keep his presence in the show under wraps. It wouldn't serve us very well if people saw someone who looks just like Jevin Banks going backstage or coming out of the green room after the show.

"Hey, Seth."

"Jev. Ready for tonight?"

"I think so."

"Been practicing that breath-holding while you were gone?"

"Yes."

Then his voice turns more serious. "Listen, I'm sorry about Emilio. Really."

"Me too."

"You alright?"

"I will be," I tell him, even though dealing with the death of those close to me has never been a strong suit of mine.

Neither of us knows what to say. Finally, he takes the conversation back to tonight's show. "So, you were cutting it close last week. The breath-holding. Seriously, you're good? I don't want you to drown tonight." He tries to make the next line sound good-natured, but I can hear a seriousness there, somewhere beneath the lightness. "It would ruin the show."

The fail is part of the effect. Escapes are always more interesting when they don't work, and in a sense I will drown, but I assume he means that I do so only as we've rehearsed.

"Yeah," I tell him, "it wouldn't be a great way to end this week either."

"But it might give me a new job, you know, if yours is open."

"Don't hold your breath."

"Ha. Touché."

Nikki Manocha and Charlene leave to warm up in the room at the end of the hall that's been set up for stretching, yoga, and dance rehearsal.

We have eight dancers in the show. They do a mixture of ballet, modern dance, and hip-hop during transitions to give us time to set up the next effect. Sometimes they dance during the effect as well, as distractions. When watching an illusionist it's helpful to remember three things: (1) explosions are diversions; (2) assistants are distractions; (3) unnecessary movement is misdirection.

Don't look at what the illusionist is showing you. The more time he spends proving there are no smoke and mirrors, the more you can be certain there are.

Charlene and Nikki have the same body type: pert, slim, flexible, and athletic. When I walk in, they're doing yoga. It looks synchronized, and that's key because they need to be able to do the same moves, at the same time, in the same way. They dye their hair the exact same color, and during the show they wear the same outfit, the same fishnet stockings, the same fingernail and toenail polish, the same earrings. Their hairstyle is identical.

All of the other magicians I've met who have big shows on the Strip use twins. It's almost a given for doing teleportation effects. When you see someone disappear and reappear across the stage almost simultaneously, it's almost always a body double or a twin.

Over the years there have been a few magicians who've even had a twin brother or sister and have kept it pretty well hidden, sort of like in the movie *The Prestige*. With the Internet it's a lot harder to keep secrets today, but it was possible in the past.

When watching a show you need to remember that nothing you see is real. You would swear that it is real, you would bet your life that what you think just happened, happened—but yet you know it did not. It couldn't have.

This is the game we play with the audience. A game they agree to. Audiences pay you to fool them, to play their expectations and concept of reality against them. And they'll be entertained just as long as they're fooled. But as soon as they know the effect, as soon as the mystery and the questions disappear, they'll move on to the next entertainment option. You're only as valuable to them as the secret you hold over them.

Just as always, Xavier is working with his team to make sure all the pyrotechnics are in place, that all the ropes we're going to set on fire as timers for my escapes have been coated with the right amount of the right kind of fuel and so on.

I used to do an escape with a blade about to sever a rope that's holding me above a bed of spikes, but then Xavier had the bright idea of lighting the rope on fire too. "That way if something goes wrong with the blades and you can't get out, you'd still die."

"Thanks for looking out for me."

"No problem. Besides, the show's more exciting when things are on fire."

"You think every effect is better if you light something on fire."

He eyed me. "Yeah. And?"

"Why don't you just set me on fire?"

"I like that." Xavier nodded. "That could work."

"I was kidding."

But it was too late.

And the seed for tonight's finale was planted.

Most people have no idea how much work goes into coordinating a major live stage show, let alone one with as many lighting, sound, and stage crew cues as a magic show.

Mime, music, and magic all work well with an international audience since they're visual art forms. You don't have to translate anything. I like explaining myself onstage as much as I like flourishing, so I typically go for the appeal of silent effects with overlaid music.

We use musical cues when you can't see your body double, your assistant, or the stage hands. Everything has to be as well timed as it would be for an orchestra. Only in this case, if someone misses her cue, I might end up impaled, drowned, or sawed in half.

So there's that.

After we all gather backstage, Xavier offers a few reminders about safety, and rehearsal begins.

Target Practice

Akio Takahashi, president and CEO of Plyotech Cybernetics, got the call from Undersecretary of Defense Oriana Williamson that she was on her way to Vegas to check on the progress of the DARPA funded research that Plyotech was involved with.

"Today?"

"Yes. This evening. Seven o'clock."

It was a Saturday. It was ridiculous to meet on a Saturday evening, especially with only a few hours' notice. He wet his lips nervously. "Why wasn't I told earlier?"

"I wanted this to be an impromptu visit."

Her reply didn't really feel right. What if he'd been out of town? What if she hadn't been able to contact him or he simply hadn't answered his cell?

Something else was up.

"Alright, I'll meet you at the facility. Seven, you said?"

"Yes. I'll see you there."

When Colonel Derek Byrne returned to Vegas, he was greeted with the news that Heston Dembski, Dr. Malhotra's special assistant, had killed Thad Becker.

"He's here at Plyotech," Dr. Malhotra said on the phone. "We were waiting for you to get back before deciding what to do with him."

"I'm on my way."

* * *

We spend the next few hours in rehearsal, working in the lunch that Fionna brings down in between acts.

It's four o'clock, and we're planning to run through a few parts of the show one more time when Fionna calls to tell us what she found out about RixoTray's research. "You're not going to believe this, but they're doing it at Fuller Medical Center. Right here in Vegas."

Actually, I do believe it. This is just more confirmation that everything here is somehow tied together.

I already know that Emilio performed several benefit shows there, just as I have. I don't know which charities he was raising money for, but I do know that he did events for the children's wing.

A thought strikes me. It might be a long shot. I lay it out there anyway. "There's a boy at the hospital with progeria; I've met him before. What if we set something up for tomorrow—a show for the kids. We can talk with the boy, see if he knew Emilio."

"You think you can get permission to go see the patients on this short of notice?"

"That's one of the assets I have," I remind her. "Fame."

I call the hospital administrator, and to say the least, she's excited to have one of Vegas's top magicians offer to perform a free event for the children's wing.

"When were you thinking?" she asks me.

"Tomorrow afternoon."

"Tomorrow."

"Yes."

A pause as she considers my offer. "We might be able to make it work. What time?"

"Noon or one. I need to be back here by four to get ready for the evening performance."

"How about one, then?"

"Sure. That should work."

"Some children won't be able to be moved from their rooms."

"I'll stop by to do some close-up magic for them, as long as visitors are allowed."

"Wonderful. I'll make all the arrangements. It'll be great to have you back, Mr. Banks. Everyone here is still saddened by the death of Mr. Benigno. Some of the children were rather close to him. It's such a terrible tragedy."

"Well, maybe I can bring a smile to some of their faces."

We talk for a few minutes to nail down the logistics, then Seth, Nikki, Charlene, and I meet to work on the timing and the musical cues for the opening sequence to make sure things will run without a hitch tonight.

Heston woke up in the desert to the ringing of a cell phone by his side.

It took him a moment to gather his wits about him.

The last thing he remembered was standing next to Thad Becker, administering the lethal dose of—

The phone continued to ring.

They brought you out here. They left you in the desert.

He finally answered it. "Hello?"

"I'd suggest you run."

"What?"

"Run. I need your help."

"Who is this? What's—"

"I'm zeroing in my rifle. I need you to run. It'll make it more realistic."

"No, listen, I—"

The dust less than a yard away from his foot exploded.

"Really, it'll help me a lot more if you run."

Heston scanned the desert but saw no one. There were scattered piles of rocks a few hundred yards away, but—

Another cloud of dirt burst to life beside him.

And Heston ran.

Colonel Byrne watched through his scope as Heston sprinted east.

He had the robotic hand with him, the base of it stationed next to the M4, the pointer finger of the hand pressed against the rifle's trigger.

He'd never used his thoughts to manipulate the arm and fire a rifle before, but it was just like using his own hand. The rifle was on a turret that the hand could manipulate, and now he practiced tilting and aiming the gun.

Targeting the back of Heston's head, Derek paused for a moment.

The brain does not die immediately. Even with a shot to a head, it takes up to eleven seconds for all of the synapses to stop firing, for everything inside someone's consciousness to grow still forever. What was it like in those moments, having the swift and certain knowledge that you're already dead but that your thoughts haven't quite caught up with your body? What kind of feeling would that be? Knowing that you were not about to die, but in a very real sense already had?

Akinsanya wondered these things sometimes when he killed someone.

And in his past he'd had the opportunity to wonder these things quite a bit.

He depressed the trigger and Heston dropped.

There.

One problem dealt with.

And it was useful to know that he could use the hand to aim and fire the rifle. After taking a few more shots to zero it in, he left for his meeting with Tomás Agcaoili, the man who would be delivering the USB drive to him.

＊＊＊

Tomás left the desolate building on the west side of town.

After meeting with Solomon, he decided it might be best not to face Akinsanya after all. The stories that Vegas's most connected drug dealer and pimp told him convinced him that he would be better off not chancing it with Akinsanya.

He would settle for half of the money—the cash he'd already received. Sure, that would work. He would disappear and trust that he'd be able to evade the mysterious man who'd hired him to kill Emilio Benigno.

＊＊＊

Jesús Garcia heard from his contacts in the Las Vegas Police Department and called the man he'd sent to Benigno's house earlier in the day. From a little research, he'd found out that Jevin Banks and Xavier Wray had been in touch with the ambassador in the Philippines about a USB drive that they had.

They'd been with Emilio when he died. It was obvious what had happened.

"There were two 911 calls this morning about the break-in," he said to Mr. Fred Anders, the gentleman he was blackmailing. "One from a neighbor, but the man you want is named Xavier Wray. He works on the crew of a show over at the Arête. You should be able to find him there."

"And you promise that you won't release the photos?"

"Get the drive from him and you'll have nothing to worry about. I'll call you later tonight."

"What time does the show start?"

"It runs from 8:00 until about 9:30. I'll call you at 10:15. I trust you'll have what I'm looking for by then."

"That's not a lot of time. It's not long enough."

"It'll have to be." There was no reply. "Well?"

"Alright. I'll talk to you at 10:15."

Jesús Garcia hung up the phone.

He was a careful man. He always planned for multiple contingencies, and he wasn't going to depend solely on Colonel Byrne to get him what he needed. What if the colonel didn't come through for him from his discussions with the base's engineer? Too much was riding on this for Jesús to chance a failure.

So, he'd put his own plan into play.

Everyone has secrets. Everyone has skeletons in their closet. The key is finding them and then making it clear that you're willing to expose them.

After all, there's nothing so powerful as a secret turned against the person who wants it kept quiet, and that's what he'd done with one of the security personnel at Groom Lake.

Or Cammo dudes, as people referred to them.

Conveniently, it was a skeleton Jesús's people had planted in his closet for him.

Somehow Emilio Benigno had managed to acquire the files, and now Mr. Fred Anders was going to get them for Jesús.

● ● ●●●

Calista Hendrix normally did not call her clients. It was almost an unwritten rule in her business. You wait for them to contact you. It was taking too much of a chance that their wife or girlfriend, or maybe even boyfriend, might answer the phone, and that would not be good for business.

But in this case, the guy only had an ex-wife, things were on a tight time frame, and she couldn't take the chance that he wasn't going to meet with her tonight.

She tapped in Dr. Turnisen's number and waited.

He was a regular client. Actually, she'd had to call him twice before and he'd picked up both times. She trusted that he would now as well, especially since they'd made plans last week to meet at 10:00 this evening at the Chimera Club.

He answered and must have recognized her number because he spoke her name before she had a chance to identify herself. "Calista?"

"Hey."

"Is something wrong?"

"I'm lonely. Can we meet earlier?"

"I won't be able to slip away. I'm not even sure I can make it tonight."

"No charge. This one's on the house."

A pause.

She thought that might do it, but she didn't want to wait for him to say no again, so she added, "I'm feeling naughty tonight."

"Really?"

"Oh, yes."

He hesitated, but finally agreed. "Okay, but I can't be there until at least 10:20, maybe 10:30."

"At the Chimera Club?" She had a thought. "Or do you want to just come to my room?"

"We'll meet at the club."

"I'll be waiting. I have some surprises planned for you tonight."

"Something memorable?"

"Very."

They agreed on 10:20. Then she hung up and called Derek, who had left to meet with someone—she didn't know who—to let him know everything was on schedule. "I'll have him back at the room by eleven."

"Perfect. I'll be waiting."

"You promise it's going to be quick?"

"Can't promise that, I'm afraid," he replied.

"And the needle and thread? You're going to use them?"

"Yes."

"Can I watch?"

"Yes."

"Well, I'll see you tonight."

"See you then."

Derek ended his call with Calista and waited at the rendezvous point for Tomás Agcaoili, but he didn't show.

When he tried Agcaoili's number, no one answered.

He gave it another half hour, but still there was no sign of him.

It looked like there was a little wrinkle in the plan after all.

He held his anger in check and processed where things were at.

Okay, he would find Agcaoili eventually and deal with him accordingly, but for now he would need to rely on the man Calista was meeting tonight.

As long as she delivered him, they should be able to make things work.

Yes.

With a little persuading, the engineer would tell them what they needed to know. And if there was one thing Colonel Derek Byrne was good at, it was persuading people to tell him things that they would normally have been unwilling to share with a stranger.

He received a call from Akio Takahashi, president and CEO of Plyotech's Cybernetics, about an upcoming, unplanned meeting with Undersecretary of Defense Williamson, and he told Takahashi exactly what to tell her and what not to.

End call.

Yes, it was definitely time to move the research out of the country.

Derek's goal was not just to hasten the coming of The Singularity, but to be present when it arrived. Whether that was in a biological body or a nonbiological one didn't matter so much to him. Those who control the machines that control our lives, control our lives. He wanted to be the one holding the reins when humanity galloped into its fast-approaching, inevitable evolutionary dawn.

• • ⟨• •⟩

We grab a late supper of subs and Cheetos at 6:45.

Charlene hears back from the FBI agent, but he seems to have not taken her as seriously as she hoped he would. He's not impressed with the RixoTray connection Fionna was able to discover on the USB drive. Only after Charlene presses him does he finally promise to have his team analyze the files on Monday.

Though Xavier's not usually one to say, "I told you so," when he finds out about that, he reminds us in no uncertain terms that the FBI's reluctance to get involved is just what he expected.

Now it's time to shift gears and put the final touches on the show.

All three of us try to slide thoughts of the search for Tomás Agcaoili out of our minds and focus on the upcoming performance.

Let's see how my breath-holding goes when it counts.

PART V

The Undersecretary

6:50 p.m.

Akio Takahashi waited anxiously in his office on the top floor of Plyotech's R&D facility northeast of Las Vegas.

The meeting with Undersecretary of Defense Oriana Williamson was scheduled to start in ten minutes, and he was hoping she would be late so he could have something, even if it was something small, to hold against her.

He was planning to say the things Colonel Byrne had told him to say—explain that the research has been going well but there haven't been any recent breakthroughs. He had the progress reports on his desk. They showed steady but not exponential progress on the program that the Department of Defense was paying for.

The reports weren't doctored, they just weren't complete. They didn't include information about what was going on in the building's unofficial lower levels. Akio was being paid very well to keep that under wraps. And he would be paid even better when they made the breakthroughs he'd been promised. He didn't know all that happened down there, and honestly, he didn't want to know.

He just hoped these reports would be enough to satisfy Williamson. He'd read over the files at least half a dozen times, trying to view them through her eyes, but he wasn't completely satisfied they were convincing.

And if she threatened to terminate the funding, he had no idea what he would do. Way too much was at stake.

"She's here, sir." His receptionist's voice came through on his iPad. When he was in the office, she was as well, no matter what time of day it was. It was in her contract. He tapped the screen and replied, "Kindly see her in."

A few moments later there was a light tap at the door as his receptionist, a diminutive thirty-year-old woman who was also from Akio's home country of Japan, politely eased it open, and Undersecretary of Defense Oriana Williamson strode into the room.

Chieko gently closed the door behind her as she seemed to dematerialize into midair.

Akio bowed respectfully to Undersecretary Williamson, and she gave him a perfunctory, militarily brisk bow.

"Good evening, Undersecretary Williamson."

"Mr. Takahashi." She stood ramrod straight and gave him a steady, if somewhat impatient, stare.

He gestured toward the leather chair facing his desk. "Shall we have a seat?"

"That won't be necessary. We won't be here in the office for long."

Of course he wanted to ask her why they would be leaving his office, but he had the sense that doing so might be considered impolite. And besides, he had something he wanted to do right away—assure her that things were on schedule.

But before he could, she said, "I'm here for one reason: I want to verify that you are making progress on the project."

"Yes, of course. Yes, we are."

"Let me make this clear. The oversight committee sent me here; it was not my choice. I do not like being called away from my family for this type of thing, especially on a Saturday. But the deadline is coming up, and we have not been impressed with the progress reports we've been receiving. The committee thought it best to have someone on-site."

His questions returned: *On a Saturday? Why on a Saturday evening?*

She seemed to read his thoughts. "They thought a little privacy would be in order, thus the weekend visit. And, I do admit that much more can be accomplished in person than over the phone or over the Internet. I'm sure you agree." It was clear by her tone that it wasn't a question but more of an exhortation for him to tell her that, yes, he did agree with her.

"Personal meetings are always most productive," he said as deferentially as he could.

A moment of unsettling silence followed his words as she let her eyes pass critically around the room.

"Well," he began, "I can assure you that the project is moving ahead." He directed her attention to the pile of folders on his desk.

"I would like a tour of your research facilities," she responded.

"A tour?"

"Yes. Show me around. I read copies of those reports on the flight here. I'm really not interested in going over them again. The US government is paying a lot of money—an exorbitant amount of money, in my opinion—to have you produce EEG helmets that can scan the brains of soldiers and transmit simple orders from one troop to another, and exolimbs that can be controlled by neural impulses. I want to see for myself what's being done, not read about it in a report."

It bothered him that she took the time to detail their contract with him like that. He knew all that, of course he did. Just the fact that she would run through it made him feel that she was somehow judging him.

"Well then." He gestured toward the door. "A tour it is."

The media is still reporting that Emilio's death was an accident, that a cobra with venom had mistakenly gotten enclosed with him in the coffin. That was partially true, only it hadn't been a mistake.

So, before the show I decide to put out a press release through my publicist detailing what actually happened.

Coming up with a statement isn't easy. After all, we don't have any specific evidence that Tomás had anything to do with the death of my friend. It's all circumstantial, and if we announce that Emilio's death was a homicide, we'll be called to account to provide evidence, which at the moment we still don't have.

So, in the end, I simply state that the authorities in the Philippines, in cooperation with the US ambassador in Manila, are still investigating the incident.

I hope that perhaps that might put a fire under Ambassador White-head to get something done.

Charlene and Nikki wear attractive, tight-fitting outfits that seem elegantly seductive, appropriate for the show but pretty mild by Las Vegas standards.

About five minutes before showtime as I'm talking with Charlene backstage, Mr. Fridell, the owner of the Arête, emerges from the hall-way that winds back to the steps to the sound booth. He doesn't dress anything like you might expect a billionaire to—jeans, a polo shirt, flip-flops, a ball cap. No bodyguards. No entourage. He looks more like someone who's visiting the casino than the man who owns it.

I've only spoken with him in person a few times. The last time that he came to the show he told me how much he enjoyed it and offered to extend my contract indefinitely. It was an attractive offer, but life is uncertain and I don't like to sign up for anything long-term, so we settled on a six-month extension.

He shakes my hand. "Jevin, I wanted to offer my condolences. I understand that you and Mr. Benigno were quite close."

"Yes. Thank you."

"If you need some time, we can black out some dates next week. I was thinking tomorrow in particular. You know Sunday night can be slow anyway."

That's quite an offer. It would cost him tens or even hundreds of thousands of dollars, plus the hassle of refunding money to those who've already purchased tickets.

"No. That won't be necessary."

"Well then, let me know if there's anything you need."

I'm not sure he's the right guy to clear this with, but I decide to bring it up so it wouldn't be out of the blue. "I'd like to take a few moments before the show tonight to speak about Emilio. Offer a moment of silence."

"Of course. I'll let the show manager know."

And then he excuses himself to do a walk-around and make sure his guests are having a good time. Unlike some of the other casino owners in Vegas, he takes as much time catering to the casual gamblers as he does to the high rollers.

I don't know him well enough to be able to tell if that's all just a public relations ploy or if he really does care about everyone's experience, but it does impress me.

And then, at 7:57 our cue music begins, we all wish each other luck, and three short minutes later the curtain rises.

Prions

I step onstage and begin the show by speaking directly to the audience. "I'd like to dedicate this evening to Emilio Benigno. He was killed in the Philippines this week. He would have wanted this show to go on. It's the kind of performer he was. He was a great magician and a close friend."

I invite them to join me for a moment of silence, and then I leave the stage so the dancers can come on while I get set for the first escape.

In one sense each show gets easier, and in another, they never get easier at all. If you're attentive to the details, every performance becomes more refined, shaping effects by the millisecond. Just like an Olympic sprinter, you're measuring your progress in hundredths of a second on escapes and quick changes, and refining the accuracy of stage marks to make sure you're in the right place at the right time.

You can get by with just doing a series of effects, but I've always believed you need an emotional connection with the audience, otherwise it's just eye candy. You have to tell a story, just like in writing a screenplay or a novel. An effective magician is always a storyteller. And what is a story? It's the introduction of a character who faces a conflict that escalates into a climactic conclusion that provides the audience with a satisfying resolution.

And of course you need emotion. It does no good if the audience doesn't feel. And a good twist at the end always makes for a better story.

But tonight pulling everything together is harder than ever.

From the start of the show, I'm distracted.

The lights come up and I go through the first sequence, a series of vanishes and metamorphosis illusions with Seth, Nikki, and Charlene. To set up the effect, Charlene and four of the dancers step out of a cloud of Xavier-manufactured smoke and approach a glass wall on the middle of the stage.

By passing around the wall and pressing against it, they prove to the audience that it's solid. Then the dancers exit, the music builds, and I come onstage and approach the wall and press my hands against it.

The smoke that's trapped on one side of the glass barrier makes it clear that there are no holes in it.

The dancers reemerge, swirling crimson clothes. As they dance and twirl around the glass, curling the smoke around them, I step through the glass, then hold my hands to the side and levitate into the rising smoke, where I vanish.

It's all passable, but I can't stop thinking about everything that's been going on this week.

I do my best to hide my limp, and at least that goes reasonably well.

Charlene does an escape from a cage that's swinging toward a wall bristling with swords. It's an idea she came up with herself and Xavier designed for her at the warehouse where he does all of his research and brainstorming, not far from the Strip.

Tonight the effect goes flawlessly.

Well, at least one of us is in top form.

When you've done as many shows as I have, you can tell when things are clicking and when they aren't. Tonight it feels like a night of work for me instead of a show that's cruising along on all cylinders. I'm not focused like I need to be, and during one escape with a spinning blade I almost don't make it out of the handcuffs in time.

It makes the effect more dramatic, and I'm guessing that the audience has no idea how close I am to losing my fingers, but Xavier does, and after the effect he corners me backstage.

"You okay?"

"I'm fine."

"You're thinking about Emilio, aren't you?"

"Trying not to."

"Well, stop trying and succeed. You need to be present, in the moment."

I know this, of course. "Yeah."

"Don't give me a mess to clean up here tonight, bro."

"I won't. Thanks for the reminder."

"And this is where we're doing research on self-replicating nano-bots." Akio Takahashi swept the door open dramatically, and Under-secretary Williamson stepped into the room.

"So the reverse engineering of the prions is going well?"

So, she had been reading the reports.

"Yes. It's coming along fine."

Prions are proteins that self-replicate. By reverse engineering them, Plyotech's researchers should theoretically be able to create nanobots that do the same thing.

"And you've put adequate safeguards in place?"

"Of course." But, in truth, no one really knew what kinds of safe-guards were necessary or even how to implement enough of them. But Plyotech's safety measures were on par with what other companies in a similar line of research were doing.

Nanotechnology was changing the landscape of science and medi-cine forever. Already Plyotech's scientists were working on ways to have nanobots rearrange atoms to develop new life-forms, to help heal diseases, to create stronger metals. And all of this was just the beginning.

"And the gray goo scenario?" she asked.

Akio was surprised she would even bring that up. It had been addressed numerous times in their reports, and she should have been well versed in Plyotech's containment protocols.

"We've taken measures to reduce the chances of it."

"To reduce them?"

"There's no way to eliminate them entirely, but the nanobots we're proposing on developing will be programmed to stop at very specific times, in very specific ways."

The gray goo scenario was basically the result of nanobots gone berserk. Anything that's self-replicating needs control measures so it'll eventually stop.

Cancer cells, for example, multiply without any mechanism to stop replicating. And they don't, until they kill the organism they're living in.

If nanobots self-replicate and create more nanobots that also self-replicate and create more nanobots, well . . . eventually you would have a planet devoid of carbon life-forms, simply made up of nanobots replicating themselves indefinitely into more self-replicating nanobots.

The first order of business when developing a new virus or bacteria is to form an antidote. It was proving to be the same with nanobots.

Theoretically, scientists would find a way to stop them before anything reached a cataclysmic scale, but in reality, even though there was an international moratorium on actually producing self-replicating nanobots, they were being researched in dozens of countries. After all, you can't slip behind other companies in the technological race toward a brighter future.

It's just that none of the nanobots under question had been created yet.

Or at least, unleashed yet.

But malicious ones were coming. Human nature being what it was, it would only be a matter of time.

"What else?" she asked.

"That wraps up the tour. Unless you have any other questions?"

"I would like to see the research areas whose findings are not recorded in the reports."

"Excuse me?"

"I said the findings not recorded in the reports."

He tried to look her in the eye while he lied. "I don't know what you're talking about."

"There are gaps. I'd like you to fill them in."

"The reports cover all of our progress relative to the defense contract."

She eyed him for a long time. "My flight leaves tomorrow evening at six o'clock. At noon—and I don't care if it's Sunday or not—I will be returning here to your facility. That should give you enough time to collect the information you need to fill in the gaps for me. If I'm not satisfied, we will pull the funding for this research and initiate a probe that, I can guarantee you, will be thorough enough to tell us everything we want to know about those holes. Good night, Mr. Takahashi. I hope you are able to collect the pertinent data for me. I do not appreciate having my time wasted."

"Of course." He tried to sound as nonplussed as possible.

She spun on her heels. The sound of her stiff shoes clacking against the floor echoed sharply down the hallway as she left.

And Akio Takahashi went back to his office to try to figure out what to do.

All he could think of was calling Colonel Byrne to see what he would suggest.

⸺ ⸺⸺

Fred Anders planned to corner Xavier Wray after the show.

For now, he sat in the third row watching Jevin Banks do some of the most incredible escapes and illusions he'd ever seen.

The theater was packed, and in the mist that curled out from the stage and the spotlights filtering through it, he felt almost like he had entered another world.

He'd heard of Banks before but had never been to one of his performances. Now, he could hardly believe what this guy could pull off.

Fred had been counting on the fact that there would be no metal detector to get into the show, and so he had his handgun with him, the one he carried at work at Area 51, where he served as one of the perimeter sweepers.

He was a security specialist.

Otherwise known, at least to all conspiracy theorists in the area, as a Cammo dude.

Before I know it, it's time for the piranha tank escape.

Chaos will make the switch easier.

We always try to use it to our advantage.

I always want an element of danger.

The dancers come out so we can prep for the effect.

In four minutes I'm going to drown.

In a sense.

There are three ways to hold your breath longer—four if you count inhaling pure oxygen before you go onstage, which I'm not a fan of. First, fill your lungs completely, usually through buccal pumping, a way of rhythmically opening and closing your mouth in a certain way to draw in more air. But you risk arterial gas embolisms, which is not a good thing.

I avoid that.

Second, hyperventilate right before you go under water, and third, slow your metabolism. This can be done by fasting and relaxation techniques. In some cases, you can actually double or even triple your time by doing both techniques. With practice most people can learn to hold their breath up to three minutes.

There's always the unexpected to deal with, however.

Once I was performing in Quito, Ecuador, and didn't take the elevation into consideration. The city is located at more than nine thousand feet above sea level, and the difference in altitude cut more than thirty seconds off my time. I hadn't been planning on that when I did the escape, and it almost cost me in a big way.

Fred watched as Banks appeared on the platform high above the water tank on the side of the stage.

Tight spotlights narrowed in on him as a video appeared on a screen being lowered to the left of the stage. It showed piranhas in a jungle river circling in on a monkey and attacking it ruthlessly, until, moments later, nothing but a churning of blood and fur and bones was left.

Banks invited two audience members up to strap him into a straight-jacket. His feet were shackled together, and he wore a weight belt to keep him at the bottom of the aquarium.

An announcer explained that the average person can hold his breath for forty to forty-five seconds. He encouraged the audience members to hold their breath with Banks as he disappeared into the water.

The platform would drop away and he would plunge into the aquarium. He needed to get out of the straightjacket, get the weight belt off, and get out of the shackles before drowning or being attacked by the piranhas.

But first two of his assistants doused him with some sort of flammable liquid.

And set him on fire.

Breathless

The flames rage up my body.

My face is covered with a gel that protects your skin when your clothes are lit on fire, but still, the heat is intense and severe.

The key to getting out of a straightjacket is flexibility, practice, and the way you position your arms when they're strapping you in. Everything seemed alright a few moments ago, but now my right arm, the one that was injured by the snakebite, is much more cramped than it should be.

As far as I know, no other magician has attempted an escape while in a flaming straightjacket, and I can tell why.

The heat is almost unbearable.

And it's terrifically hard to breathe.

The water will put the fire out, but I'm counting off the seconds in my head, and I have at least ten more before the platform I'm standing on is going to drop away.

I struggle with the straightjacket more than normal, and that's not good because once I hit the water it'll be even harder to escape—moisture makes the fabric cling to your skin, and it becomes like a wrestling match with yourself. The toughest straightjacket escapes are underwater ones.

Six seconds.

I get my right arm loose and close to bringing it over my head, but

I wait. I'll do that as soon as I hit the water, otherwise I'd be brushing the flaming straightjacket right across my face.

Four seconds.

The waterproof, fire-resistant gel on my face is almost melted away. I'm trying to draw in deep breaths, but it's nearly impossible since the fire is swallowing the oxygen all around me, I only have a couple—

Two seconds.

I snatch in a final, strangled breath that's going to have to last me two minutes.

And then the platform gives way.

• • ⬭ • • •

The platform split apart beneath his feet and Banks dropped nearly three stories into the tank. It was filled only enough to displace the water without splashing piranhas all over the stage or onto the audience.

A cloud of smoke and an audible hissing sound followed him as he hit the water and sank immediately to the bottom, the weight belt dragging him down.

Fred took a deep breath to see how his breath-holding compared to the magician's.

Banks appeared to be having a rough time getting out of the straightjacket, but Fred figured it was all part of the act, that it was all carefully rehearsed to make things look more dangerous than they were in order to make for a more exciting escape.

A giant digital stop-clock hanging above the stage ticked off the seconds, marking how long he'd been underwater.

So far, twenty-five.

Fred was still able to hold his breath along with Banks. When he looked around the audience, he saw a few people nearby let out whatever air was remaining in their lungs and draw in several gasping breaths.

A circle of bubbles escaped from the bottom of the aquarium, obscuring Banks for a few seconds. It was undoubtedly part of the trick, but when the bubbles disappeared he was still in the straightjacket.

By now the time read fifty-four seconds.

And Fred ran out of breath.

***

I lose track of how long I'm underwater, but before I dropped I hadn't gotten nearly as much air in my lungs as I should have and already I can tell.

It's a tight squeeze, but I manage to slide my right arm up over my head, and from there I work at the left arm.

Then I have the straps to deal with.

And the weight belt.

And the manacles on my ankles.

We'd talked about using spring-loaded shackles, but I'm an escape artist and I like doing the picks myself. I have a hairpin in my left hand. After I get out of the straightjacket, I'll use it on the manacles.

But now, the way I'm feeling, I'm not sure that insisting to pick the locks had been such a good idea.

***

One minute, nineteen seconds.

By now, most of the people surrounding Fred had started breathing again. Everyone looked tense. The breath-holding challenge had worked. The audience was gripped, nervous, and staring with rapt attention at the stage.

Another blast of bubbles engulfed Banks, and when they cleared away he was still in the straightjacket but had made some progress and was close to getting out.

***

It happens as I'm tugging the jacket off.

The bite on my right arm rips open and a streak of fresh blood slithers into the water, then expands into smokelike crimson streaks that curl all around me.

And that's when the piranhas move in.

A collective gasp rose from the crowd as the fish swarmed en masse on Banks. No matter how much you practice a trick, this couldn't possibly be part of the plan.

The water seemed to boil with fish and blood and bubbles, and then two divers leapt in from the platform on the other side of the tank and their flippers kicked up sand from the bottom of the pool, further obscuring everything.

Finally, one of them surfaced, looked around, and then went under again.

It appeared that the audience members were holding their breath again, but this time in worried anticipation. Some of the women stared wide-eyed at the stage with their hands over their mouths.

Then both divers were at the surface, shaking their heads and getting out of the water. The bubbles stopped, the fish dispersed, the sand began settling and there was no sign of Jevin Banks.

Until one of the paramedics turned toward the audience, took off his cap.

And it was Banks.

He waved to the crowd, flourished with his hand, everyone went crazy and the curtains fell.

Then the music started again, and the dancers came out to take a bow as the curtains rose once again. The assistants and then Banks appeared, bowed, and then the show was over.

A pretty amazing climax.

Fred decided he would wait until the crowd had cleared out and then find a way backstage to locate Xavier Wray.

The man who was blackmailing him was going to call at 10:15, and he needed to find out the location of the USB drive from Wray before the call.

As long as he could corner Wray alone somewhere, it should be enough time.

While he waited for the auditorium to clear, Fred glanced his hand across the gun that he carried and ran through what he was going to say to Wray to convince him to give up those files.

I was backstage getting treated for the bites on my arm when Seth took a bow for me, just a few minutes ago.

To put it mildly, the effect had not gone well at all.

I was supposed to have been working at the shackles when the bubbles rose a third time, then, while I was hidden, free myself and duck behind the fake reef as Seth slipped in to take my place. Then I would go up the secret tunnel to the trapdoor and pull on the paramedic clothes as Seth pretended to drown and the divers leapt in to rescue him, kicking up sand that obscures him enough for the audience to not notice that he's not me.

They would bring him to the surface, lay him on a stretcher, and the paramedics would work on him, then cover him with a sheet with a body form on it so that as he slips down into a secret compartment below the gurney, it looks like he's still on the stretcher. Then, when the taller of the two paramedics pulls the sheet back, the body has vanished, and when the paramedic looks up at the crowd and pulls back his cap, the audience sees that it's me.

A bow.

Applause.

Curtain.

But not tonight.

The fish went after the wound on my arm with a frenzy, and I knew I needed to get out of the water. So, I got out of the manacles and weight belt, went through the passageway early, got Seth to do a quick change in my place to appear as the paramedic, and then, after the curtain rose, take my place bowing to the audience.

At least with him here we'd salvaged the show, but my arm was a mess. I had a few bites on my hands and neck, but those weren't serious. The fish had targeted the location of the wound, and my arm was not looking pretty. Those fish just do not like to let go after they dig in their greedy little teeth.

Thankfully, my clothes and the gel on my face, which didn't attract the fish at all, protected the rest of me.

However, now I feel like I was slow, sloppy, and that everyone on the team knows it.

The real paramedic frets over me, and after I get my arm bandaged, I assure him that I'm fine, even though I'm not feeling fine at all. I have no idea how I'll perform tomorrow night with my arm in this condition, but I don't tell anyone that. In the morning I'll see how it's doing and make a decision then.

I thank Seth for covering for me and then meet up with Charlene and Xavier to debrief what happened.

All around us, thick cables snake along the floor, and stagehands work at replacing props, resetting effects for tomorrow.

"We shouldn't have let you attempt the escape." Charlene seems more upset with herself than with me. "We knew you weren't feeling 100 percent, that your arm was injured."

"It was my choice. I thought it would be okay."

She shakes her head, and her tone turns to one of concern. "Are you alright? Be honest with me."

"Yes."

Xavier scratches at his goatee. "We're not finishing with this escape tomorrow night unless Seth does it."

"I can do it."

"No." His tone is firm. "I don't want to chance it."

"Seth isn't ready to do the straightjacket escape yet."

Tension that I don't like bristles through the air.

Neither of them looks convinced that I'll be okay doing the effect tomorrow, and at last I tell them, "I'm going to get changed." They don't respond, and I leave for my dressing room.

I can hear them discussing something between themselves as I walk away.

While I'm pulling on my dry clothes, my dad calls and explains that something came up and he won't be able to fly down after all to visit on Monday. He doesn't tell me what it was, and that doesn't necessarily surprise me.

When he asks me about tonight's show, I don't bring up the incident in the piranha tank or my wounded arm, but rather highlight some parts of the performance that went well.

It's not easy to know what to say. On the one hand it eases my stress level a little that he's not coming, but on the other hand I know spending time together, even if it's awkward, is good for us.

Ever since my mom left us when I was in sixth grade, my father and I have been struggling to find our place in each other's lives. Sometimes the past has the power to send ripples forward through time, affecting the trajectory of a relationship forever, and that's what happened with us.

"I heard about Emilio," he tells me, "what happened overseas. I'm sorry. I should have called earlier."

"It's okay." I don't specify if I'm referring to how I'm handling the loss or the fact that he didn't call earlier. "When do you think you might be able to make it down to Vegas?"

"Not sure. The airline said I can take up to six months to use the ticket."

"Okay."

The conversation dies off. Maybe both of us are waiting for the other one to speak, maybe we both just can't think of anything to say.

"So, I'll talk to you soon," I say at last, because that's the kind of thing you're supposed to say, although I doubt we'll connect for another couple weeks.

"Okay. Have a good week."

"You too."

"Goodbye, Jevin."

"Bye, Dad."

I hang up. Only when I look up do I see Charlene standing in the doorway.

"You heard that?"

"Part of it."

"He can't make it. My dad, that is."

"Is everything alright?"

"I didn't ask." I hesitate as I realize how odd that might sound. "But he sounded okay."

"Well, that's good."

"Yes."

"How did it go, talking with him?"

"Pretty much the same as usual."

"Awkward."

"Yeah. Awkward."

She takes a step into the room. "Listen, back there, a minute ago, when I was . . . well, you just . . . you need to take care of yourself. You always try to push things and it worries me."

I pocket my cell phone and join her at the door. "Have you ever heard of Alex Honnold?"

"Who's Alex Honnold?"

"He might be the greatest free soloist to ever live."

"Free soloist? You mean at some sort of musical instrument?"

We start down the hallway.

"At rock climbing. Free soloing is where you climb without a rope. Alex has free soloed some of the hardest climbs in the world, some more than three thousand feet high, without a rope."

"He scales these cliffs with no safety system?"

"That's right."

"Three thousand feet?"

"Yes."

"And what if he falls?"

"He doesn't fall."

"But what if he did?"

"He doesn't, Charlene. That's my point."

"But if he did. He would—"

"He would die. Yes. But he doesn't fall."

She backs up and gives me a look that speaks volumes. "Jevin, I don't even understand what you're talking about here. You have a death wish?"

"No, of course not." It seems too cliché to say that I have a life wish, so I hold back. "I have too much to live for. But if we don't risk, we don't live. Alex doesn't want to die, neither do I. But I've always gambled—"

"For more than you can afford to lose. Yes. I know."

"We all talk about taking risks, but what does that really mean? It means taking the chance that you won't come out unscathed. Life without risk is just sanitized death. I can't play it safe. I'm not designed to."

"I think it's something you might want to learn."

"Charlene, this is—"

"I'm not saying you can't take risks, but you can't be risking everything. Alex could fall. He could. Sometimes I think you're more addicted to adrenaline than you are to . . ."

"To you."

"To us."

Her words leave me with nothing to say. Regardless of what I should have done at the cliff in the Philippines, I have the disquieting feeling that she's right.

"Play it safer for me," she says softly. "If you get hurt, you're not the only one who would get hurt. If you were to die, I would too. Inside."

I don't want to make a promise that I can't keep, and I really have no idea what to say.

For a long moment neither of us speaks.

Finally, when she does, she changes the subject and her voice takes on a more detached, objective tone. "Fionna and the kids are waiting up by the ticket booth. Xavier is going to tell them a bedtime story, and then there's something for us to look into."

"What's that?"

"Fionna got a notification. She'd set up some sort of tracking program, and her computer found a record of Tomás Agcaoili landing in Vegas."

That got my attention. "He's in the city?"

"It looks like it."

"So they're heading back to the house?"

"Xav wasn't sure about your plans, so he offered to do the story here instead of at home."

"Where is 'here'?"

"The last I heard they were going to head to the parking garage."

"That seems like an odd place to tell a bedtime story."

"Xavier's idea."

"That explains it."

We hurry to meet up with them.

As we go, I'm thinking of how in the world we might find Tomás, and also about Charlene's concern for me and if I can change who I am enough to satisfy her, if I can learn not to climb so high without a rope.

It would mean giving up a big part of who I am, and I'm not sure that's something I'm ready to do.

Or something I'll ever want to.

＊＊　◇＊◇　＊

Fred needed to find a way to get Wray alone to speak with him.

It wasn't going to work to approach him while he was with a group.

Keeping his distance, he followed Wray, the woman, and the four kids to the parking garage and watched as the children gathered around him, the two girls sitting on the rear bumper of a minivan.

Fred struggled with what to do. His car was two levels up, but if he left to get it, Wray might slip away.

However, when he saw the kids settle in, he ended his internal debate and went for the elevator.

There were open parking spaces nearby. He could get his car, park on this level, and wait for Wray to leave. Then he could confront him and find out what he needed to in order to keep his blackmailer from releasing the photos.

Seruvian Trolls

Charlene and I arrive as Xavier is beginning his story.

"It happened on the year when Halloween fell on Friday the thirteenth . . ."

Mandie's eyes grow large, but Donnie looks at Xavier curiously. "That doesn't even make sense. Besides, it has to be continued from the last time you told us one."

"You remember where we were?"

"Of course."

Mandie slides close to Xavier and takes his hand. Maddie sits ladylike on the edge of the bumper. The boys stand attentively nearby.

"Well, let's see . . . So, you remember what was happening?"

Mandie raises her hand.

"Yes?"

"The princess was on her way to the castle, and there was this really big monster on the edge of the Tangled Forest waiting for her."

"It was a Seruvian Troll," Donnie clarifies. "A poisonous one."

"Ah, yes." Xavier acts like he doesn't remember any of this, but I'm sure he does. "So, a Seruvian Troll. Now, anyone who knows anything about trolls knows the worst kind you can ever meet are the ones from

Seruvia. They have hair growing all over their bodies. They have a wart on the end of every hair."

Maddie wrinkles her nose. "Ew."

"They have ears on the bottoms of their feet so they can hear people who are—"

"Trip-trapping across their bridge?" Mandie offers.

"That's right. Trip-trapping across their bridge. They have eyeballs in their bellybuttons so they can see people trip-trapping across the bridge. And they have noses growing out of their armpits. And as you can guess, that's a very bad place to have a nose grow."

"Yeah," Donnie agrees. "No kidding."

"So anyway, as you already know, this story happens in a faraway land where kings rule and princesses attend lavish balls and dragons dwell in the hills. It's a land of ancient magic and talking animals and a terrifying wizard."

"Do the animals know magic too?" The question comes from Mandie. I'm surprised it hasn't been addressed before in their story times.

"Only two of them do. A squirrel named Travis and a spider named Alexander."

She nods as if that clarification makes all the sense in the world. "What's the princess's name?"

"Maddie."

"No it isn't." Maddie shakes her head. "Last month you told us that other princess had my name, the one from Pruellia."

"Oh, yes, that's right. This one was named Donnie."

"Was not," he objects. "She was a *princess*!"

"Okay, sure, I was just kidding. Anyway, for real, she was named Mandie . . ."

When he says that, the real Mandie's eyes light up with satisfaction.

"And she was the daughter of a lovely queen named—"

"Fionna!" Mandie says enthusiastically.

"Yes. Fionna. And she was the most captivating queen in that land or any land anyone had ever heard of before."

Fionna looks pleased and nods to him. "Thank you, Mr. Wray."

"You're welcome, Ms. McClury."

As Xavier goes on, Fionna receives a text and frowns slightly as she reads it. She gives me a quiet glance, and I get the sense that something is up. However, she holds back from saying anything and lets Xavier continue his story.

"Well, Mandie had a magic wand with her that she could use to cast a spell that would knock down any monster that came after her . . . She'd named her wand 'Betty' and she'd never had to use it, but now, when she faced the troll, she had no choice. She raised it, and as he came at her, she aimed the wand at him and said the spell and knocked him down when he was only five paces away from her. She had Travis and Alexander with her—"

"The squirrel and the spider," Mandie reminds everyone.

"That's right. And Travis knew a freezing spell he tried to cast on the troll, but just at the last moment the troll jumped up and raised a mirror—"

"I didn't know he had a mirror." Donnie's tone seems to indicate that he thinks he has caught Xavier making a mistake.

"And neither did Travis," Xav says without missing a beat. "And the spell bounced off the mirror and reflected back to hit him, and he immediately froze solid. When Mandie tried to unfreeze him, Betty froze as well and then cracked in half. The troll laughed and said, 'Now you're all mine!' He rushed at her and just as he grabbed her, Alexander leapt off her back and the troll escaped with her before Alexander could save them."

"Uh-oh." Maddie looks genuinely concerned.

"The troll took her back to his lair beneath the bridge, where it was so dark you couldn't even see the chin on your face."

All four of the children stare down trying to see their own chins.

"And I'll tell you more tomorrow."

"Tell more now!" Mandie pleads. "Pleeeeeeeeeease?"

"Nope. I'll tell you the next chapter the next time we get together, hopefully tomorrow night. You know the rules."

"There's rules about this too?"

"We need to save some of the story for tomorrow. We can't use it all up tonight or we won't have any left."

"There's too many rules." She folds her arms grumpily.

"Okay, kids." Fionna rounds up her children. "We need to get home. Tell Uncle Xavier good night and thank him for the story."

They all do. Mandie gives him a big good-night hug.

As the kids begin to climb into the minivan, Fionna says to Xav, "Thanks for not making it too scary. You know how Donnie can be." She makes sure that's loud enough for him to hear, and he rolls his eyes at her.

"I don't get scared of his stories."

"Oh dear. I didn't know you were listening."

"Uh-huh."

When the kids are settled, Fionna discreetly shows us the text she'd received, a message that apparently came from her computer, and I can see why she'd given me an anxious look a few moments ago.

Agcaoili had just bought a ticket for a red-eye later tonight, a flight that leaves in three hours.

"I thought you should know."

"Thanks."

"I need to get my kids home."

"Sure. I'll call you later if we need anything."

Fionna opens her door and Donnie asks from the backseat, "Mom, can we get some butane and hydrogen tomorrow?"

"For what?"

"You add them to soapy water and have someone, like Maddie, hold out her hand and you just light it and—"

"I don't want you lighting your sister on fire, Donnie."

"Again," Maddie adds.

"Again," Fionna reiterates.

Again?

"But Mom, this morning Xavier showed us how to do it *safely*."

"Uh-huh."

And then she swings the door shut and I can't make out the rest of the conversation.

Charlene, Xavier, and I discuss the news Fionna just shared with us. I ask if they have any idea how we can find Tomás in the brief window of time we have.

"We could show up at the airport?" Xavier notes the obvious.

"And do what?"

"Hmm . . . Not sure. Contact security?" But then he argues against his own suggestion before we can. "No, what are they going to do? The guy is legally here, he's not under investigation by anyone. There's no reason for them to detain him."

"I think the airport should be our last resort. In the meantime, we need to talk to someone who might know him before he ever goes there."

"Who might know a snake wrangler who murdered a man halfway around the world?"

"Exactly."

"Exactly what?"

"That's the key."

He looks at me quizzically. "What is?"

"That he murdered a man halfway around the world and then ended up here in Vegas. He doesn't live here, we know that already. He came here for a reason."

"To see someone," Charlene interjects. "To get paid."

"That's what I'm thinking, yes."

"But how in the world are we going to figure out who he came here to see?"

"We're not."

They share a glance, and Charlene says, "Okay, now you're starting to lose me."

"You have Nikki's number?"

"Sure."

"Let's call her. I think she might be able to help us."

The Hideaway

On the phone with Nikki, I summarize what's going on and then ask her, "Do you know of anyone who might . . . well, we're looking for someone who a murderer might have come to Vegas to meet with."

Someone from the criminal underworld, I think, but I don't say that.

Before joining our show, Nikki was a high-end call girl, but you can't be in that business for long and not make at least some contacts with the girls on the other end of the spectrum.

"I really couldn't say."

"Think about it, Nikki. Someone, anyone, who would be well enough connected to know a hired killer. A pimp? A dealer? A bookie?"

She considers that for a long time before replying. "There's one man, but you wouldn't want to meet him. I've heard stories."

"Stories?"

"About the things he does to people. I met some girls who worked for him. One of them tried to keep some of the money that a client gave her and that she was supposed to hand over." Nikki hesitates, and when she goes on there's a thin tremor in her voice. "She showed me the scars, Jevin. Believe me, you don't want to meet with this man. He's hard-core."

Vegas has a spotted history. People don't typically like to admit it, but organized crime built this city. It used to be that the mob ran most

228

of the gambling here, but as revenues from gambling have decreased, it's pretty much common knowledge that the mob has moved on to drugs and prostitution, so when Nikki says this guy is hard-core, I assume he's connected to organized crime.

While we don't know for sure that someone hired Tomás to kill Emilio, based on all we've been able to uncover since we returned to the States, it seems pretty likely. It's impossible to know if this man has any connection to Emilio's death, but it's at least a place to start.

"Nikki, we know that Agcaoili killed Emilio. From what you're telling me, this guy you're thinking of might be our best bet in locating him. Even if he doesn't have the information himself, he might know someone who knows someone."

She's slow in replying. "They call him Solomon. That's really all I know."

"Solomon."

"Yes, but I don't think—"

"Where can we find him?"

I don't give up, and after one more objection she finally sighs. "Over on Industrial Boulevard. Try a bar called the Hideaway. I've heard some girls mention it a few times. That's all I know. But I really don't think you should do this."

"Duly noted. Don't worry, if anyone asks who told us about Solomon, we never talked to you."

I don't get to that part of town much and I don't know where the Hideaway is, but she gives me directions.

After the call, I update Charlene and Xavier on what Nikki told me, and Charlene asks, "What are you suggesting we do?"

"Not *we*, me. I'm going alone."

"No you're not. Remember what we talked about earlier? About you thinking about me—about the two of us—before jumping into things? If you're going to talk with this man, I'm coming with you."

"Charlene, no."

"I know some girls who might have heard of him. I might be able to smooth the waters. If anyone should talk to him, it's me."

"I can't let you come. Not if there's any chance you might be put in danger."

"Well," she insists, "I'm at least going to come to the bar with you. If you need to go and talk to this man alone, alright. Fine. But I'm not going to sit at the house worrying about you. I'm coming along."

"So am I," Xavier informs me firmly.

I try to dissuade them, but they're as determined as I was with Nikki, and in the end I give in.

I'm guessing that it might not be best to park my $183,000 Aston Martin outside a bar in that part of town, so I suggest we take Charlene's Ford Focus instead.

The FBI isn't taking any of this seriously, the police aren't being helpful, so at least for now it's up to us to find out some answers. This could very well be our only chance. If we don't find Tomás in the next couple hours, he might slip away and we would likely never solve the mystery of Emilio's death.

A thought strikes me: Solomon might be involved in all this, might be the one who hired Tomás.

Keep that in mind. See how it goes. Feel him out.

For a moment I consider contacting Fionna and letting her know what we're up to, just in case something goes wrong, but then I decide it would only make her worry.

As we're taking our seats in the car, Xavier looks deep in thought. "If we somehow do manage to find this guy Solomon, and he actually does know something that can help us, he's not just going to tell us what we want to know. He'll want something in return." He turns to me. "What are you willing to offer him?"

"Money."

Charlene starts the engine. "How much?"

"As much as I need to."

Fred cruised behind the Ford Focus as it left the parking garage. As he was pulling onto the street, the man who was blackmailing him called.

"I'm following Wray now," Fred told him. "I'll find out what you want to know. I just need to get him alone first."

"I've given you enough time. I told you who he was, where he would be—"

"No, listen, just give me another hour. I'll get the files. Trust me."

The line was silent, and Fred began to wonder if the man was still there.

"One hour," the voice said. "And then I'm posting the pictures online. You know what's going to happen if those photos are made public."

Fred felt his temperature rising. "Yes, I know. I'll get the information you want. I'll talk to you in an hour."

"One hour."

The call ended.

Fred was motivated. He was not going to let those photos go public. He would do whatever it took to find out the information from Wray.

Whatever.

It.

Took.

Calista Hendrix sipped at her drink and gazed around the Chimera Club, the swankiest club on the Strip, but she didn't see Dr. Jeremy Turnisen anywhere.

She checked the time again.

Yes. 10:20. He was a very punctual man and was not in the habit of being late, but he had mentioned on the phone that he wouldn't be able to meet her earlier, so maybe he'd had a hard time slipping away from whatever he was doing.

Techno music pumped through the air and the dance floor thrummed with people losing themselves in the beat. Sweaty bodies sliding against each other in ways that would have been considered inappropriate twenty years ago but that were the norm today. Especially in Vegas.

A melee of madness, she thought. A phrase from some book they'd studied in her lit class back in college.

Man, it was weird how she remembered stuff from that class at the strangest times.

Jeremy wasn't the kind of man to dance in a club like this, more the kind to play blackjack at the tables on the next level up, but nevertheless she searched the crowd carefully.

Typically, they met here by the bar, but perhaps he'd gone to the blackjack tables to look for her.

After paying off her tab, she navigated through the crowd toward the escalator.

Driving down the Strip is easier emotionally on me than walking it because when you do that, you're faced with the people on the street corners handing out full-color business cards of escorts and strippers.

The folks hawking the cards have stacks of hundreds of them and snap them with their hands—a sound you get to know all too well when you live here in Vegas—then offer them to you as you pass.

All along the Strip, you'll find newspaper boxes with flyers promoting strippers, exotic dancers, and other "entertainers" with the promise that they'll make it to your hotel room within twenty minutes.

When you've worked in Vegas as long as I have, you can't help but end up meeting some strippers. One of Charlene's best friends is an exotic dancer. She doesn't do full service calls, but according to the ad she takes out in the circulars that are distributed so freely on the Strip, she will "shower in your room or watch you shower! Can't sleep? Let's get together! Independent girl, no agency!"

I once asked Charlene about her friendship with her and some of the other prostitutes we know. Considering Charlene's faith, her reply both surprised me and didn't surprise me: "Jesus was a lot more willing to attend a party with prostitutes than to shun them."

"But how do you think Jesus feels about those girls?"

"I think he loves them so much he was willing to die for them. The least I can do is love them enough not to judge them."

Full service means just what it says.

On the cards and flyers, there are photos of the girls without their clothes on, with small boxes, stars, or flowers covering their nipples and carefully positioned between their legs.

The circulars are split into categories: exotic dancers, massage, college coeds, naughty nurses, Asians . . . and some categories that are best not to mention.

You can close your eyes and pretend this isn't our world, but it is. You can look away, but the flyers and business cards are everywhere, and whenever I catch a glimpse of one of those pictures of a young woman who should be at the mall hanging out with her friends or making plans for college, baring her breasts and advertising her services, it's heartbreaking.

But it's all part of Vegas, and you can't understand our city unless you accept that it's part of our everyday reality.

Here, you can become an "exotic entertainer" when you turn eighteen. One of the saddest ads I've seen was in a flyer that someone discarded on the sidewalk in front of me recently. It contained the photo of a young girl in pigtails and the words: "Just outta high school! Barely legal! Anxious to meet you!"

I never had a daughter, so I can only imagine what it would be like to be that girl's father. Especially if I happened to stumble across that flyer.

She's someone's daughter.

That's what I think of whenever the people at the street corners try to hand me another card with a photo of a topless girl—she's someone's daughter. In Vegas she isn't old enough to have a beer or slide a bill into a slot machine, but she is old enough to get a job dancing nude in front of strangers.

She's someone's daughter.

I love my city, but it's one of the things I would change if I had the chance.

So now we leave the Strip and all that it is—the good and the bad—and head for Industrial Boulevard.

Dr. Jeremy Turnisen did not work for the United States Air Force. If you asked him what he did, he would say that he has a job in research and development.

Every day except Wednesday, when he takes his day off, he leaves his home on the outskirts of Las Vegas, drives to the airport, boards a small private jet, and is flown to an undisclosed location. At the end of his workday he returns, drives to his home in the suburbs, and either lifts weights in his garage or watches reruns of *NCIS* on television.

If you see him, he'll be dressed as a civilian.

Research and development.

That's what he'd tell you he does for a living.

And he would be telling you the truth. He does work in research and development.

His name does not appear on any official USAF personnel rosters. If he were ever to be interrogated, he would only be able to give his name because he has no rank and serial number.

His specialty is strong AI and autonomous weaponry algorithms.

After his pioneering work at MIT and twenty-two patents in robotics, the military recruited him.

Well, not officially.

Because he doesn't officially work for them.

But if things were official, he would have been recognized as one of the world's experts on unmanned aerial vehicles and would have pioneered the research into the next generation of autonomous drones that could also be controlled, when necessary, by the thoughts of pilots on the ground.

But since that program didn't technically exist, none of those things did either.

Tonight he was scheduled to meet Calista at the Chimera Club. Traffic had slowed him down, but now he pulled into the parking garage, entered the Arête's lobby, and found his way through the gaming area to the club.

I'd Like You to Meet Betty

When *CSI* was in its heyday, some scenes were filmed downtown with just B-roll of the Strip. There's one bar in particular that they used in a number of their episodes. It's a dirty, angry little place that fit in with some of the sleazier, grislier crimes of the series.

Not a weed in the parking lot.

No weeds without rain.

The air in the bar seems to be stained darker than the night air outside. The close-quarters smell of sweat and spilled beer permeates the neon sign–lit room.

A dance stage with a pole waits at the far end of the bar. Right now there aren't any women dancing, but I can't imagine that at a place like this it'll be a long time between dancers. Most people think exotic dancers get paid to dance, but they don't—at least not at most places in Vegas. Instead, they pay the owner from the tips they get. Depends on the bar, of course, but I'm guessing that here, the girls don't go home with a whole lot of cash in their pockets.

Many of the bars in this part of the city have topless servers. Here, the women serving drinks wear scant bikini tops. It isn't much, but it's enough to make Charlene at least somewhat comfortable having them around me.

"Well?" she says. "Where do you want to start?"

I study the place, looking for someone who might be Solomon, but don't see anyone who fits the bill or looks like a pimp or a seedy, underworld drug lord.

A group of ten bikers is gathered on the south end of the bar. Scattered throughout the place, people sit alone or in small groups, talking in the booths and at the tables.

"I don't think he's here."

"Why do you say that?" Xavier asks.

"From what Nikki told me, I'm guessing he's not a biker, and if he's as well connected as she led me to believe, I don't think he would be sitting by himself or with a date. I'm guessing bodyguards close by, probably a few girls on his arm."

"I'll go ask around."

"Um, I'm not sure that's the best idea."

"Naw." He pats his coat pocket. "I've got Betty with me."

Charlene eyes him. "Betty?"

He opens his pocket to show her his Taser. "We go way back, Betty and I."

"Two weeks," I remind him.

"Two weeks."

And then, before I can try to convince him to stay with Charlene and me, he leaves for the group of bikers.

Some of the guys in the nearby booths eye Charlene. For a moment I'm tempted to tell her to wait for me in the car, but I'm not sure I want her sitting out there alone.

"Stick close to me," I tell her. And we head to the bar.

We find empty stools next to each other, I order two beers, and when the bartender brings them, I tell him I'm looking for someone.

"You a cop?"

"No."

"Reporter?"

"No."

"Movie producer?"

"Sorry, no."

He studies my face, peers at Charlene and then back to me. "You look familiar."

"I have a show, over at the Arête. I'm an illusionist."

A look of recognition. "You're Jevin Banks."

"Yes."

"I've seen your picture around town."

"Billboards."

"Yeah."

"I get that a lot."

"Who are you looking for?"

"Solomon."

He shakes his head. "I don't know anyone named Solomon." I'm pretty good at reading people, but he has an air of practiced indifference about him, so I can't tell whether or not he's telling me the truth.

"I was told I could find him here."

Xavier seems to have been accepted by the bikers—he's standing in their midst and they're all laughing together. I can't help but wonder how he made friends so quickly.

A hulking man sitting beside Charlene looks like he's had too much to drink, and I'm not happy about the way he's ogling her.

"Sorry." The bartender passes a bar towel unnecessarily across the counter. "Can't help you."

I lay a hundred-dollar bill in front of him. "It's important."

He pauses momentarily. "How important?"

I place another Franklin on the bar. "Pretty important."

He accepts the money and nods toward the end of the bar, where a somewhat dumpy-looking fortyish guy with a comb-over is sitting by himself.

From a corner booth, Fred Anders watched as the bartender directed Banks to a middle-aged guy sitting by himself, then Fred shifted his attention back to Wray, who was talking with some bikers on the other side of the room.

I look at the man the bartender pointed out. "That's him?" But my gaze quickly drifts to the gorilla who's checking out Charlene. His muscle T-shirt looks like it might have been painted across his chiseled chest. He has me by at least fifty pounds. He would not be easy to put down if I needed to, but I figure I could do it.

Martial arts versus brawn?

Brawn is going down every time.

Unless he knows martial arts too.

That wouldn't play out so well for me.

In answer to my question the bartender says, "That's the guy who can lead you to him. But if I were you, I wouldn't go. You really don't want to meet Solomon."

Before I can reply, the man who can't keep his eyes off Charlene licks his lips. "Honey, why don't you pull your stool a little closer?" A couple of the guys nearby him grin.

"No thank you," she tells him, then lowers her voice and turns to me. "Jevin, I think—"

"What, you too good for me? I won't bite." He glances toward his buddies. "Unless you're into that." They chuckle and give more of their attention to the interchange.

"No thank you." She stands.

He goes on, "I think I could—"

But I cut in, "The lady said no."

It's obvious by now that he's not simply coming on to her but also putting on a show for his buddies, and that means he'll probably be less willing to accept no for an answer than if he were alone and simply looking for someone to take home. Whenever a guy has an audience he's much more motivated to want to save face.

He appraises me coldly. "You might best keep out of this."

"I'm having a conversation over here," I tell him, "and neither my friend nor I are interested in being interrupted by you anymore."

"Jevin." Charlene puts her hand on my shoulder. "It's okay."

He leers at her. "I can show you what a real man is—"

"She made it clear," I tell him firmly, "that she doesn't want to chat. A gentleman respects a woman's wishes."

Charlene closes her eyes and shakes her head slightly: *Oh, Jevin. Why did you have to go and say that?*

"Are you trying to start something? Boy."

"I don't start fights," I say. "I end them."

By now, all the people on this side of the room have turned their heads and are facing us. I don't take my eyes off the man who was disrespecting Charlene.

"Well." He grins and holds his hands out to the side, inviting me to push him or throw a punch. "What are you going to do about it?"

"Whatever I have to."

Two of his friends push back their bar stools and stand. The guy glares at me. "Who exactly do you think you are?"

"A man who doesn't like to see people get hurt."

"Then stay out of this."

I stand up. "But I don't always get what I want."

He follows suit, rising, and then straightening up to his full height. He peers menacingly down at me and cracks his neck.

Okay, this guy is really big.

I lower myself to get into a stance for TaeKwonDo. He swings at me and I duck, evade the punch, and get ready to do a knife hand strike to the back of his neck to put him down, but suddenly there's a slither of electricity and the man jerks and drops, writhing, to the floor.

Tasered.

Xavier is standing by my side with Betty in hand.

The downed man's friends help him to his feet and gather around him, but the bikers form a tight-knit cluster around Xavier.

"I think we should go," Xav tells me. He begins to ease toward the door. I take Charlene's arm and follow closely behind.

I hear threats and shouts behind me, and even though I'd been geared up for a fight, I'm glad to get out of there before things explode.

"Why did you have to Taser him?" I ask Xavier. We're almost to the exit. "I was about to take him down. I've spent three years studying TaeKwonDo."

"Yeah." He holds Betty up. "And I watched a five-minute You-Tube video on how to use these suckers. Who's the king of time management?"

I hate it when he's right.

"Next time, at least let me hit him once."

Outside the bar, we're getting into Charlene's car when I hear someone yell. "Hey!"

I spin, expecting a man—or men—from the bar to rush me. But it's not someone looking for a fight, it's the man the bartender had told me could take us to Solomon.

"I hear you're looking for Solomon."

"We are."

"How did you hear about him?"

Charlene answers for me. "A friend of one of his colleagues."

I doubt that'll be enough, and I debate what to tell him to convince him to help us, but surprisingly he accepts what Charlene said and heads toward a blue sedan parked nearby. "Follow me."

With the fight erupting in the bar, Fred didn't have an easy time getting to the door, and by the time he made it outside, Wray and the two people with him were climbing into the Ford Focus.

Okay, he was running out of time here.

They took off after a sedan and, trying not to be too conspicuous, he followed after them.

⸺

Calista found Dr. Jeremy Turnisen at one of the blackjack tables.

Everyone who plays blackjack uses some sort of counting system. If you don't, you're just letting the odds get the best of you, and you're throwing your money away.

Most systems are based on keeping track of the number of cards that count ten. When the tens are rich in the deck, you want to increase your bet. The dealer has to hit on a soft seventeen, but typically, depending on what cards have been laid, players will want to hold at a sixteen, maybe at a seventeen, almost always at an eighteen.

Whatever Jeremy had, he was increasing his bet when she approached.

He was focused on the table and didn't see her at first, so she eased in beside him, close enough for him to smell her perfume, to feel her presence.

She brushed a hand ever so slightly against his arm and indicated toward his pile of chips. "It looks like luck is on your side tonight."

He put his hand on hers. "It looks like it is."

She wanted to get him alone, back to the room, to Derek, who was waiting in the closet with the Dalpotol and the cloth to cover Jeremy's mouth, but she also didn't want to press Jeremy too much or make him suspicious.

Before she could think of what exactly to tell him, he said, "I'm on a streak."

She kissed his cheek. "Well then, play for keeps. Remember, tonight, winner takes all."

"Sounds good to me."

Down the Rabbit Hole

We follow the man in the blue car through a winding series of back-streets until we come to a deserted alley on the east side of town.

As Charlene is parking, she asks Xavier how he connected so quickly with the motorcyclists. "They sure warmed up to you fast."

"I'm an expert at winning friends and influencing people."

"Uh-huh."

"That, and we share mutual feelings toward the intrusiveness of the federal government."

Now that, I believe.

"And respect for vets."

"Gotcha."

Charlene turns off the car, and we all step into the cool night.

A dumpster rests nearby, and the stench of filth and rot fills the alley.

The man we'd followed shambles toward us and introduces himself simply as Martin. "Solomon doesn't like it when people waste his time. You better have a good reason to be here."

"We do."

"And that is? I need something to tell him."

I decide it might help us get an audience if I tell Martin the truth. "I'm looking for information that might lead us to a man who murdered my friend. I'm willing to negotiate for the information. I have resources at my disposal."

"Resources."

"Yes."

After spending a moment mulling that over, he indicates toward a rusted door on the other side of the alley. "This way."

Of course I'm curious about Martin's connection with Solomon—if he works for him, if he's just a stooge who brings people here, if we should be afraid of him despite his mild demeanor. Or if, possibly, he's actually Solomon himself.

I'm also wondering why he tracked us down outside the Hideaway in the first place.

Together, the four of us stand outside the door. Martin raps on it. I'm expecting it to open slightly, or for a small panel to open and for him to whisper a password or something along those lines, but the door swings wide and an African American man who looks the size of an NFL lineman blocks the entrance. His head is shaven, and the occasional light from the streetlights at the end of the alley reflects dully off it.

Martin speaks first. "I have some people who want to see Solomon."

The guy assesses us and then leans down and whispers something incomprehensible to Martin, who whispers something back. Then the bodyguard or bouncer, or whoever he is, disappears into the building, closing the door with a thick metallic clang behind him.

Martin turns to us. "He's checking. He'll be right back."

It doesn't take long before the man returns and points to me and then Charlene. "You two can come in." His voice reminds me of the sound a sledgehammer might make smacking against concrete. He points a thick finger at Xavier. "You stay here."

I glance at my friends, and both seem to accept the terms. While I like the idea of Charlene being close to me where I can keep a protective eye on her, I'm committed to shielding her from a potentially dangerous situation, and I sense she'd be safer out here with Xavier and Betty.

"She stays here," I tell the sentry. "I come in alone."

He folds his massive arms. "I'd advise you to accept this gracious offer."

Martin looks at me urgently. "Go on in. Both of you." His tone makes it clear that he thinks it would be safer to follow the instructions than to upset Solomon.

Charlene puts a hand on my arm. "I'll be fine. Let's go."

"No. This is—"

"I don't think that we want to make him angry."

"Listen, I've already had a friend murdered. I can't take the—"

"I trust you. That you won't let anything happen to me."

I process that. "I won't."

"I know."

I mentally prepare to do whatever's necessary to protect her, if it comes down to that.

The guard pats me down to make sure I'm not carrying any weapon. All I have with me is my car keys, my Morgan Dollar, and the deck of cards I typically carry after my shows in case I run into fans in the lobby.

I'm not comfortable with the idea of this guy frisking Charlene, but he doesn't even attempt to. He just scans her detachedly and must find no reason to suspect that she's armed, because he nods. "Alright."

Xavier steps back, and I keep Charlene by my side as we follow the mammoth guy, with Martin bringing up the rear. Behind me I can hear him pull the door shut and slam a deadbolt into place.

Charlene doesn't seem afraid as we pass through the dimly lit hallway. A series of doors about twenty feet apart lines the sides of the hall.

Standing beside maybe half of the doors are women dressed in cheap, skimpy lingerie, waiting expectantly. One at a time, as we pass, they eye us. A couple of them smile alluringly. One woman points to Charlene and then to me, motioning for us to join her.

"No thanks," I reply.

The walls are dingy and covered with crude graffiti. The sounds coming from the rooms that don't have a woman standing by their door are the sounds I expect to hear.

We reach the end of the hall, and the guard who's leading us pulls out a key and unlocks the scratched steel door in front of him. It opens with an abrasive scraping sound.

Inside the room, half a dozen women—three Asian, two Hispanic, and one Caucasian, and all dressed in the same style of seductive lingerie as the women in the hall—lounge on pillows surrounding a bone-thin Caucasian man who looks about twenty-five or thirty years old.

He's shirtless and has an intricate tattoo with a Chinese inscription wrapping in a serpentine circle around his neck and ending with a red drop, which I assume is supposed to be blood, falling into a vial tattooed onto his chest.

The smell of marijuana lingers fresh and ripe in the air, and all the women except for one of the Asians, who's seated near the man and has a length of chain fastened around her neck, look high. The man, who I'm assuming must be Solomon, holds the other end of the chain, and as we step into the room, he tugs it softly, drawing her closer to him.

Martin and the sentry leave us alone, locking the door behind them.

"I'm Solomon."

"Jevin."

His gaze shifts to my right. "And you are?"

"I'm Charlene."

He studies us for a moment, then folds his hands placidly on his lap. "You're not part of the law enforcement community, are you? Recent Nevada law. I'm asking this directly. You need to inform me if you are."

"We're not," I tell him.

Most of the women appear uninterested in our conversation. The one with the chain around her neck looks demurely in my direction, then Solomon pulls lightly on it again, and she nestles in closer to him and gently kisses his fingers one at a time. I see a series of fresh scars on her thigh. One looks like it was branded on there.

"I understand you wanted to see me."

"I'm trying to find a man named Tomás Agcaoili. He murdered my friend and I want him to pay for it. He flew into Las Vegas earlier today. I think someone hired him to kill my friend, and I think that person might be here in Las Vegas."

Solomon has sharp, incisive eyes, and when he lets his gaze pass from me to Charlene, I sense that he's carefully evaluating what to say. "Tomás Agcaoili."

"Yes. I'm willing to pay for information."

"I don't want your money. There's something else you can give me if you really want me to tell you what you came here to learn."

The guy who'd been driving the blue car backed out of the alley and took off, and Fred Anders, who'd been watching from the shadows near the street, took a deep breath and then drew his gun.

Wray was finally alone, standing in the alley, staring at the door that Banks and the woman had disappeared into.

Fred eased forward, shaded by the darkness draping across this side of the alley. When he was just far enough away to be safe from the Taser that he knew Wray carried, he called out to him.

"Xavier." Wray turned and Fred leveled the gun at his chest. "Throw your Taser to me."

Wray reached toward his pocket.

"Slowly."

Without a word he produced the Taser and tossed it toward Fred's feet. He kicked it back behind him and it slid under the reeking dumpster, then he closed the space between himself and Wray.

"I need to talk to you."

"Well." Wray didn't look afraid, but he was eyeing the gun cautiously. "I'm all ears."

"You were at Benigno's house this morning."

"Yes." A pause. "Ah. And so were you."

"Do you have the drive?" Fred asked.

"The drive?"

"The files." He raised the gun. "Do you have them?"

Wray raised his hands. "Easy now, bro. Yes."

"What's on it?"

"I'm not sure. Something about a pharmaceutical firm's research, that's all we know."

"I need that drive."

"I don't have it with me."

"Then you're going to take me to it."

"No, I need to stay—"

"You're coming with me." He waved the gun to signal Wray to go with him to his car. "Let's go."

Solomon's Dilemma

"What was your friend's name?" Solomon asks me.

"Emilio Benigno."

"He was killed in the Philippines."

I'm a little surprised he knows that, but it could just be from watching the news. "Yes."

"Why?"

"Why was he killed?"

"That's right."

"I don't know. If it's not money, what do you want from me?"

"I know you can pay. I know who you are, Mr. Banks."

In this case I'm not sure if fame is an asset or a liability. "Billboards?"

"Tomás."

"So you do know him."

"I do." A light breath and then a warning: "This is a dangerous world you're poking your nose into, Mr. Banks. I would suggest that you leave it alone, but I'm guessing that since you've come this far, that's not going to be enough to convince you."

"No, it's not. Where is Tomás?"

It takes him a moment to reply. "Do you remember the story of King Solomon and the baby?"

Charlene speaks up. "Two women came to him. They told him that they lived together in the same house, that they'd both recently had babies only a few days apart, but no one else was there to see the babies. One of them died in the night."

A nod. "Very good. And do you know how?"

"The first woman claimed that the other had rolled over in her sleep onto her own baby and it died. Then, according to her story, the other woman switched the children so that she would have the living baby. But the woman she was blaming claimed the first woman was lying—that the living child was hers and the dead boy was the son of the first woman. And so it went—back and forth."

"Exactly. And so Solomon was faced with a dilemma." He holds his hands in the air as if he's balancing the truth in them. "What was he to do? The women argued bitterly in front of him, each claiming that the dead baby was the other woman's."

"Solomon ordered that the living child be cut in two," Charlene answers, "with half of the boy going to each of the women. One of the women told the soldier to go ahead, while the other cried out, 'No! Give the boy to her! It's her son!' And Solomon, knowing that the child's true mother would do anything, say anything, to save the boy's life—even if that meant letting the other woman raise him as her own—judged that the baby was hers and stopped the guard before he could harm the child. He gave the boy to her."

Solomon taps a finger against the air. "You see, sometimes we have to take chances to find out the truth. Something must be at stake. Unfortunately, in this world, the way it is, honesty is in short supply. Did you know psychologists say that men tell six lies every day." A small laugh. "Twice as many as women, interestingly enough."

Some of the women in the room like that and smile or snicker.

I'm not sure where he's going with all this, but I get the sense that things are not moving in the direction I would like them to move in.

"What is it you want?" I ask him.

"One magic trick."

Apart from close-up work with cards, I prefer the word *effect*, but I'm not about to correct him. "One trick?"

"Yes. That I haven't seen before, and that I can't figure out. You give me that, and I'll give you Tomás."

"Why?"

"Why would I give you Tomás?"

"Yes."

"I'm not sure he told me the truth," he says pointedly. "Maybe he did. Maybe you did. Can you do it?"

"Okay." I pull out my deck of cards. "I'll do it."

Charlene looks at me somewhat uneasily.

Solomon steeples his fingers. "I used to do a little sleight of hand myself. Close-up effects, back when I was growing up. It's like that for most magicians, I suppose, huh? They start with the walk-around and street magic tricks, but to ever make it big you need to do the stage stunts. That's why Blaine doesn't have a show here in Vegas, right?"

"I really couldn't say."

He gives me a head tilt and a faint smile. "I've lived in Vegas my whole life. I've seen a lot of tricks."

"You haven't seen this one." I riffle through the deck but keep the cards in order. I do an overhand shuffle, a strip and a weave, cut the deck one-handed, and then pause. The secret to card tricks, to so many things, is not in what cards you're dealt but in what you do with the ones in your hand.

He can tell I'm just getting set up for the effect. "Do you need a table?"

"That would be best. Yes."

He gestures to one of the women, and she crawls forward and positions herself in front of him. He pats her back, but I'm not going to demean her like that.

"The floor will be fine."

He catches my drift. "I understand." He pats her butt and she scrambles out of the way.

I hand Solomon the deck so he can inspect it.

When working with control cards, you need to be able to know exactly where they are in the deck and be able to shuffle off any card that you want to, when you want to. Some people are able to shuffle off the second card or the bottom card, but the best sleight of hand magicians in the world can do any card they choose.

I can do any card I choose.

But first you have to memorize the deck to know where the cards are that you're working with. That's the hard part.

I'm not nearly as good as Lennart Green, but I can memorize a deck as I shuffle through them, noting the cards, the order, the orientation. He can do it in mere seconds, but it takes me about fifteen to twenty, which might be too many in this case.

I hand Solomon the cards. "Shuffle the deck as much as you'd like."

Playing cards are always packaged in the same order so whenever you open a deck, you already know where every card in the deck will be. If you're careful enough and practice shuffling enough, you'll know where each card is, even after you cut or reshuffle them. If I ask you to cut the cards, it doesn't change the order of the cards, it doesn't shuffle them, it just simply changes which cards are on the top of the deck.

One magician in the thirties knew half a dozen ways to do the same card trick. He invited people to try to guess how he did it, but he would shake his head. "No." And then he'd prove it by doing the effect again, but this time he would change his technique. He cycled through things that way, always staying one step ahead of them, and no one ever pinned him down or figured out what he was doing until he explained it all in a book he wrote late in his life.

I kneel while Charlene waits nearby. "I'll deal five poker hands. Tell me one card you'd like in each of the hands and which hand you'd like to be dealt if you were in the game."

It's close to an effect Green does, but as far as I know he's never done it quite like this, and I have the sense that this way will be harder because I'm allowing Solomon to choose one of the cards in each of the hands and not a single control card.

And I'm going to allow him to shuffle the cards himself before I deal them.

While I'm not looking.

Holding the cards facedown, he passes his way through the deck. "They're still in order, aren't they?"

"Yes."

He checks them, flipping through the cards faceup. "Alright. Let's go with the five of diamonds, the nine of hearts, the three of spades, the king of clubs, and the queen of hearts."

"And which hand would you like to be yours, if we were playing poker?"

"The second hand you deal out. The one with the nine of hearts."

I think of Emilio and how much is at stake here. It takes me a second to calculate what each of the hands is going to have to be, then I close my eyes. "Shuffle the cards."

He seems to guess what I'm going to do. "You're kidding."

"Shuffle them and I'll show you the trick."

After a few moments he tells me that I can open my eyes, and he hands me the deck.

Tonight I'm going to have to do this nearly as fast as Green does, and I've never even attempted that before. I turn over the deck so I can see the cards, then finger my way through the deck, noting the location of the cards Solomon chose, memorizing their position and the position of all the other cards I'll need in order to deal the hands I'm planning on dealing.

I give myself eight or ten seconds—it's hard to say since I'm not really paying attention to the passage of time, just committing the deck to memory.

Then I turn the cards over, riffle through them twice, and glance at Solomon. He's watching me attentively.

Man, this would be a lot easier if I had another deck and I could just switch them without him seeing.

I focus on the cards.

Okay, if I'm right, I know the location of each of the twenty-five cards. Now, I just need to shuffle them out of the deck in the right order into the five poker hands.

As I do it, I banter slightly to keep from focusing too much on what I'm doing and let instinct take over instead. "You met with Agcaoili today, didn't you?"

"I did."

I finish with the first card in each hand and start going around again. "Did you hire him to kill my friend?"

"No, I did not."

"But you know who did?"

I finish with the second, move to the third card in each hand, then the fourth.

"I don't know his name. He calls himself 'the hero avenges.'"

That brings me up short. Distracts me. And that is not good. I think of the man we stumbled onto last fall, the assassin the FBI still hasn't been able to locate. "Akinsanya?"

"So you've heard of him. That surprises me."

Studying Solomon's eyes, I see no deceit there, and I can tell that everything he's been sharing with me is true.

Akinsanya is involved? How? And why? Because of the RixoTray connection?

I do my best to return my attention to the deck, but I still have one more card to deal into each hand and I've lost my place.

Bad, bad, bad.

I take a small breath.

The five steps Arno Ilgner outlines in his book on mental training for rock climbers to deal with the fear of death, *The Rock Warrior's Way*, come to mind. They're the same five steps I use to deal with fear in my escapes: observe, accept, focus, intend, commit.

Quickly, I go through them, observing what I've done, accepting where I am, focusing on what's happening, intending to succeed, and committing myself fully to what I'm doing.

I finish dealing the cards.

Set down the deck.

For a moment I stare at the five hands I've dealt on the floor.

Okay, let's see if I was able to pull this off.

I turn over the second pile, the one that Solomon chose for his own hand, the one containing the nine of hearts. "This is your hand. A flush with a two, four, five, eight, and nine of hearts."

"Impressive."

Next, I turn to the fourth pile. "But you might have been dealt a full house." I show him the three kings and two sevens that I'd dealt into that hand.

"A better hand," he says.

"Or this one." I flip over the third deck. "Four threes beats a full house." I move on to the first hand, a straight flush of the four, five, six, seven, and eight of diamonds.

"But I wouldn't have wanted that hand either." He's staring at the fifth and final hand. "Right?"

"Right." I reach for it. "And this is my hand."

He guesses even before I have the chance to turn them over—the only hand that could beat a straight flush. "A royal flush."

I flip over the cards in order, the ten, jack, queen, king, and ace of hearts.

"Bravo, Mr. Banks."

"Thank you."

"You memorized the deck that quickly?"

"I did." I'm not sure he'll count that as figuring out the effect.

Technically, he might, but it's the best I can come up with on the spot, and it's really the only possible way I can think of to even attempt this effect.

"How did you do it so fast?"

"I didn't think about it too much. I suspected it would distract me if I didn't trust my instincts. I pictured something else instead."

"And that was?"

"The face of my friend Emilio lying dead in his coffin."

Without any hesitation he tells me, "Tomás Agcaoili is at the Nite Owl Motel out on the edge of town."

"I know where it is."

"Room 214."

"He's there now?"

"Yes. Waiting by the phone in case I should call to warn him that Akinsanya is on his way to find him. He's scheduled to fly out later tonight."

"So I've heard."

He doesn't ask me how I know that.

"But he's going to take a bus out of town instead. He knows people will be looking for him. I suggested he book the flight. Misdirection. I'm sure you, of all people, understand the importance of that."

"When? When does the bus leave?"

"Within the hour."

"Will you warn him that I'm on my way to find him?"

"No."

"Why not?"

"You're just looking for justice, something King Solomon himself would have helped you find. And Agcaoili didn't tell me the truth." He leaves it at that, and I decide not to ask him to elaborate. I just want to get to the Nite Owl Motel as quickly as I can.

The colossal guy who'd led us into the room with Solomon leads us past the women in the hallway and back outside.

Neither Xavier nor Martin is in the alley. Charlene's car is there, Martin's sedan is gone.

When we try Xavier's cell, he doesn't answer. Charlene and I both check our phones and don't find any texts or voicemails from him. When we call Fionna at the house, she tells us she hasn't heard from him.

Charlene asks me if I think Xavier might have gone somewhere with Martin.

"That's the only thing I can think of."

"What do you suggest we do?"

Actually, that's a good question. "Well, Xavier can take care of himself. He has Betty with him, and obviously, he's well versed in how to use her. I say we keep trying his phone, go to the Nite Owl Motel and see if Agcaoili is still there, then worry about finding Xavier."

Charlene takes her place in the driver's seat and starts the engine. "Jevin, how did you know Solomon had never seen that effect before?"

"Because I haven't seen it. At least not done like that."

"But it's possible that he had."

"I doubt it. I was making it up as I went along."

I give her directions to the Nite Owl. "Tomás is obviously dangerous," she tells me somewhat apprehensively. "I think we should call the police, have them take him in."

"For what?"

"Murder."

"That hasn't been proven. The police in the Philippines officially recorded Emilio's death as accidental, remember? Not even the FBI is willing to look into it. Just because Tomás is here—if he's even at the motel at all—doesn't mean anyone in law enforcement is going to take our accusations against him seriously."

Only as I'm explaining all of this does it strike me that I have no real plan for what to do when I find Tomás. I've been so focused on just locating him that I haven't thought through where to take things from there.

I'm not sure what else to say, and apparently Charlene is at a loss as well, because we're both quiet as we make our way through traffic to the Nite Owl Motel.

◦•⸺•◦◦

In order to keep his gun trained on Wray, Fred had him take the wheel.

Now they pulled into a parking lot outside a warehouse southwest of the Strip.

"What's this?"

"This is where I design the effects for the show I work on."

"Banks."

"That's right."

"And the USB drive is in here?"

"Yes."

Fred gestured for him to turn off the engine. "Alright, then. Let's go."

◦•⸺•◦◦

We pull up to the Nite Owl Motel.

Charlene parks. "It reminds me of the motel from *Psycho*."

She's nearly as much of a movie addict as I am, and honestly, I have to agree that Norman Bates's motel does come to mind, except this place is two stories instead of just one.

"What are you thinking, Jev?"

"I'm reevaluating what I said earlier about calling the cops. Maybe we should."

"What'll we tell them?"

"We'll tell them there's been a murder, and the man who did it is in this motel room."

"But we don't know yet if he's really there."

True. "No, we don't."

Regardless, after a little more discussion I go ahead and make the call, telling the 911 operator what we know.

Then we wait.

Minutes pass by.

The clock in the car tells me it's just six, but it seems like sixty.

Finally, I get out of the car.

"What are you doing?"

"I'm going up to the room."

"Why?"

"To stand near the door and make sure he doesn't run away before the police arrive. We'll adapt, come up with something to tell them if he's not there."

Considering our conversations earlier today about how she doesn't want me risking too much, I prepare for a disagreement. However, this time she doesn't argue but instead just exhorts me, "Be careful."

"I will."

I head to the stairs that lead to the walkway encircling the second story. I have no idea what the response time for the police will be. I'm hoping it won't be much longer.

But what then? What'll happen after they arrive?

They certainly won't arrest Agcaoili without good reason, and when they find out that he's not even considered a suspect by the Philippine National Police—if anyone'll get arrested, it'll be Charlene and me for accusing him of murder.

Maybe I hadn't thought this through so well after all.

I reach the second level and walk toward room 214.

So wait for the police or go after him yourself?

Knock on his door or wait?

I pass room 208.

But what would happen if I did knock on his door? If I did confront him? He fled once and left a writhing pile of cobras behind to block my path. He's obviously dangerous—

Room 210.

But if the police just release him, he'll get on that bus and he'll be gone—

212.

And he'll undoubtedly take steps to make sure we never find him again.

I arrive at room 214.

And stare at that door.

No police sirens yet, but that doesn't exactly surprise me. I doubt they would come in with their lights flashing and sirens blaring, especially if they were coming to apprehend a murder suspect, as I'd told them Tomás was. After all, making that much of a scene would only warn a suspect and give him a chance to flee.

The muted sound of a television in the room seeps through the thin walls, but I can't see inside because of the heavy curtain that's pulled across the window.

Is he even here? Was Solomon telling the truth?

A phone rings inside the room.

I lean close to listen. The ringing stops, but I can't pick up any of the conversation.

Now I'm really not sure what to do.

I glance back toward the parking lot and see that a police cruiser has crawled into the far end over near the motel office.

Okay, now the police are here, now I can—

The door in front of me bursts open and Tomás appears.

After three years of sparring, instinct takes over, and I raise my hands to fight back or block if he comes at me.

But rather than run like he did in the Philippines, he immediately flicks out an automatic knife.

"Señor, retrocedes."

"No. I'm not getting out of the way."

Not until the police get up here.

With his other hand he flicks out another knife, then cries out something in indistinguishable Spanish and lunges through the doorway at me.

The Warehouse

I like sparring in the gym, but I've only had to use TaeKwonDo twice in real life. Both times were against the same man and both times he had a knife. The first time, he managed to slash Charlene's arm; the second time, he didn't fare so well. I knocked him down, he landed on the blade, and he never rose.

One knife that time.

Two tonight.

Agcaoili swipes one blade toward my abdomen, but I step to the side and knock his arm out of the way with an outer forearm block. Out of instinct I use my right one, which is also my wounded one, and a rush of pain shoots through it, cutting across my shoulder and burying itself in my chest.

Okay, that arm's out of commission.

Not good.

Although the walkway runs the length of the building, it's only about five or six feet wide—not a lot of room to maneuver, so when he comes at me with the knives again, I end up with my back against the railing.

I land a kick to the side of his knee and it buckles but doesn't break,

261

and he manages to still rush me, slashing a knife wickedly through the air at my left arm.

I slide to the side just in time and do a jump front kick to his sternum to push him back. I manage to land a spinning side kick against his ribs. I don't know if I broke any or not, but I know he felt that.

His expression becomes fierce, barbarous, and he flips the knife in his left hand around and goes for my throat, but I duck and land a punch to his rib cage where I kicked him.

All at once, the police siren cuts through the night and the flash of blue lights flicks across the side of the building. Out of the corner of my eye I see an officer sprinting toward the stairwell.

Hold Tomás off. Just for a few more seconds.

I've retreated a step and my back is against the railing again.

He comes at me fast, just as the officer makes it to the top of the stairs about fifty feet away. "Drop the knives!"

I knock Agcaoili's right hand out of the way, and the blade in his left skims across my chest. Snagging his elbow, I spin backward to get out of the way. He smacks hard against the railing and the momentum tips him forward, he flails for a moment and then falls two stories and lands on his back with a harsh crunch on the roof of a car parked below.

The police officer has his gun drawn on me. "Put your hands to the sides!"

I do.

"Down! Get down!"

As I kneel and then lie down on my stomach, I peer through the railing. Amazingly, Tomás pushes himself to his feet and scuttles off the car. A female officer is dashing toward him.

The cop by my side cuffs me.

My attention is on what's unfolding in the parking lot. Tomás still has one of the knives in his hand and is facing down the cop who's standing about fifteen feet from him. She has her gun aimed at Tomás's chest and is shouting for him to drop the knife *now!*

Rather than pull me to my feet, the cop here on the walkway tells me to stay down, then aims his gun at Tomás to help his partner.

More sirens blare through the night.

Backup.

It's over. They're going to get him.

Part of me wants the officers to shoot him, to end this, to deliver swift and certain justice. A life for a life.

The police officer in the parking lot orders Tomás to drop the knife and finally he must realize that the gig is up, because he tosses the knife aside. A moment later he's on the ground and cuffed.

Well, at least with him in custody, maybe we'll be able to find out some answers about how Akinsanya is involved in all this and why he wanted Emilio dead.

As the cop pulls me to my feet and hustles me toward the stairs, I expect him to read me my rights like they always do in movies, but instead he just says, "What happened here?"

"I was standing outside his door waiting for you to arrive. He came at me with the knives. I was trying to defend myself."

"I saw what you did," he says somewhat cryptically, and I'm not sure how to take that—if he's accepting my version of things or not. "We got a call that there was a murder."

"It was overseas. I think if you offer him something in exchange for information, he can tell you who paid him to kill my friend. I think it's a fugitive wanted by the FBI who goes by the code name Akinsanya."

The officer stares at me blankly. "What?" I run through it again as succinctly as I can, and then we reach the bottom of the stairs and Charlene rushes toward me.

"Stand back, ma'am."

From here I have no idea how things are going to play out.

The officer walks me toward one of the police cars as his partner and two other officers who've just arrived manhandle Tomás into another squad car.

Just how much trouble I'm in, I don't really know.

But right now at least I'm happy about one thing.

Tomás Agcaoili is in custody.

And he is going to face justice for what he did to Emilio.

• • — • • •

"So where is it?" Fred demanded. He was running out of both patience and time.

"This way." Wray led him past a series of water torture chambers, spinning blade machines, and other strange apparatuses that Fred couldn't even identify but that Banks evidently used for his escapes.

A set of fluorescent lights high above them lit the room brightly, and Fred was glad because in a place this cluttered with hiding places, he did not want Wray to slip off somehow into any shadows.

An extensive collection of handcuffs, shackles, straightjackets, ropes, and manacles lay on a wide counter attached to one wall. Swords and daggers hung on a vast pegboard. Handguns, throwing knives, targets, and walkie-talkies in various need of repair were scattered across the countertop. Fred had no way to know if the guns were genuine or just props for the show.

"Don't try anything."

Wray didn't answer.

"I said, don't try anything."

His only response was to point toward a set of drawers on a rolling stand twenty feet away. "It's over there."

"Why there? Why is it even in this warehouse?"

"To keep it safe," Wray answered vaguely. "Here, I'll go get it."

"I'll get it." They were ten feet from the drawer, and Fred motioned for him to stop walking. "Which drawer?"

"Second from the top."

Fred waved him away. "Get back."

Wray retreated four steps until he was standing between a steel water

264

tank and one of the cluttered workbenches. He had his hands raised slightly in the air to reassure Fred that he wasn't a threat.

Fred's phone rang.

The ringtone told him it was the man who was blackmailing him. He was going to demand the files.

Which Fred did not yet have.

He opened the drawer, kept his eyes on Wray, but when he felt around inside there was only a jumble of hand tools.

The phone rang again.

In desperation, Fred glanced into the drawer, and that must have been what Wray was waiting for, because he snatched something off the counter and threw it toward Fred.

Even in the large room the explosion was deafening. A burst of smoke poofed into the air and Fred struggled to grab a breath, and by the time the air had cleared Wray had already ducked out of sight.

The phone continued to ring.

Answer it!

No, don't. Get Wray.

Fred didn't know what to do. On the one hand he didn't want to upset the guy by not picking up, but on the other hand he had nothing to tell him.

He'll release the pictures.

No, not if you get the files in the next couple minutes. You can call him back. Find Wray!

Fred did not answer the phone.

At last it stopped ringing and he called out, "I will shoot you if you don't give me the files!"

No reply, apart from the blunt echo of his words bouncing off the walls.

The warehouse was so full of magic equipment that Wray could be just about anywhere.

Fred cautiously glanced toward the pegboard to see if Wray had gone for a weapon, but it didn't appear that any were missing. He crossed the room toward the warehouse's entrance to block it off so Wray couldn't sneak away.

"Who sent you?" It was Wray's voice, but with the echo Fred couldn't tell where it was coming from.

"I'm telling you—"

"Don't move. I have a crossbow aimed at your back."

Fred felt a cold clamp of fear.

"Get rid of the gun," Wray called.

No, no, no, don't.

"Listen to me," Fred replied hastily. "I don't want to hurt you, but—"

A crossbow bolt whizzed past him and embedded into a wooden crate about ten feet in front of him.

"Get rid of the gun."

Fred's heart was hammering.

You can't let those photos go public. You'll lose your job, you might go to jail.

But the fear of getting a crossbow bolt in the back overrode the fear of what might or might not happen in the future.

You were never going to shoot him. Not really. This isn't you. You're not a killer.

He threw the gun away, and it clattered against the concrete and slid fifteen feet away.

"Who sent you?" Wray's voice sounded closer, and Fred could only imagine that he'd stepped out of hiding to get a better shot.

Fred really didn't know what to say, but before he could make up something threatening or intimidating, the truth slipped out. "I don't know. He has photos. Damaging ones. Of me. He said if I didn't recover the drive he would release them."

There, he'd laid it out. Now he would have to face the consequences, but at least he wouldn't be caught up in doing anything violent, anything that went against his deepest convictions.

He might end up in jail, but at least he wouldn't end up a killer.

"You drive a 2012 white Chevy Silverado." Wray's voice sounded like it was coming from maybe ten feet behind him.

"Yes."

"You're a Cammo dude."

Fred hesitated. "Yes."

"Turn around."

Fred did.

Wray was only a few steps away and had the crossbow aimed directly at his chest. What he said completely took Fred by surprise: "I won't press charges for kidnapping if you help us."

"Help you do what?"

"Find out what we need to from Area 51."

The pictures will get released!

But then again, if Wray knew what the files contained and if he helped him with this deal with Area 51, maybe something would lead back to the guy who was blackmailing him.

There was no way to tell, but what was worse, having the photos released or being charged with armed kidnapping?

"Alright. What do you need to know?"

Access Codes

The police arrest Tomás and take him away.

The officers interview me, but Charlene and two other people who have stepped out of their motel rooms as witnesses confirm my account of what happened—that Tomás came at me with the knives, and I was forced to defend myself. Even the officer who cuffed me agrees that things played out that way.

While he doesn't sound too convinced that Emilio was murdered, he promises that he'll follow up on it.

Although I suspect that I might be in deep trouble, thankfully the officers don't hassle me much. However, they do tell me that they want me to come with them to the station.

When I ask if we could take care of it in the morning, they inform me in no uncertain terms that it will be best to take care of it tonight.

"We'll give you a ride back home when we're done." The officer is filling out paperwork already, even as she's speaking with me.

"I can come along, take you home?" Charlene offers, but I encourage her to head back to the house and fill Fionna in on what's been going on.

"Just to the Arête parking garage will be fine," I tell the officer. "My car is still there."

268

After explaining to Charlene that I'll see her back at home, I ride with the police to the Las Vegas Police Department.

It doesn't take long to answer the officers' questions, and in the end they have me sign some forms and I give my official statement. Thankfully, it doesn't look like they're going to take me to task any more about the fight.

I overhear them talking about their arrival at the motel. Apparently, after they caught Tomás they figured out that the phone call to his room had come from the front desk, and when they questioned the guy working there, he gave up that Agcaoili had paid him fifty dollars to call in case any cops showed up at the motel.

So, Solomon *had* kept his word and had refrained from warning Agcaoili. Regardless of what criminal activities he might be involved in, telling the truth really did seem to matter to him.

After we leave the interrogation room and they return my phone to me, I notice a text from Xavier that I should call him ASAP.

There's also a text from Fionna that she finished decoding the USB drive: "You're not going to believe what I found."

As they shuttle me to my car they finally let me make some calls to my friends, and I reach Xavier, who's made it home and is with Fionna and Charlene.

"What's going on?" I ask.

"It'd be better if we explained it all in person."

"Don't leave me hanging here, Xav."

"It's Area 51. I think we can get inside."

"What? What are you talking about?"

"I'll tell you everything when you get here."

"Fionna texted me that she found out something."

"I'll let her explain that in person. How long till you arrive?"

"Fifteen minutes, maybe twenty."

"We'll explain it all then."

On the way home I process everything.

The police officer witnessed Tomás attack me with the knives, so I figure they'll charge him with aggravated assault, at least, if not attempted murder. Even though Ambassador Whitehead and the FBI, and even the officers from this morning after the break-in at Emilio's, promised to look into things, none of them was very convincing.

Even if they don't follow through like we'd been hoping they would, I imagine that at this point Tomás will be facing serious jail time. And at least now all the information about what happened in the Philippines would come out.

We also know something we didn't know this afternoon.

Akinsanya is somehow a part of all this.

But how? With the connection to RixoTray, it does seem to make sense, but what does it have to do with Emilio? And how does Area 51 work into the equation?

All those things are intimately tied in with my friend's death, and I can't imagine that I'm going to feel any real closure on this until I get a few more answers.

Certainly that USB drive figured into everything as well. Whatever information it held might just untangle some of what was going on.

Last year Akinsanya, a skilled sniper, faked an accident that took the lives of several suicide bombers in order to help set up an assassination attempt. From all we know about him, he is a master of misdirection.

Right before he died, a contract killer had warned me that Akinsanya would find me. I had no way of telling if that was an idle threat, if Akinsanya was still interested in finding me or not, but now I can't put those words out of my mind.

There's a car I don't recognize in my driveway.

Inside the dining room I find Fionna, Charlene, and Xavier waiting for me.

There's also a man I don't know sitting at the table drinking a

Sprite. He's wiry and scruffy, with dirty blond hair and anxious eyes. There's sweat on his forehead even though it's not unreasonably hot in here. I take a seat. "And you are?"

"This is my new friend, Fred Anders," Xavier answers for him. "He's a Cammo dude. And he's on our side."

Fred nods. His hand is shaking slightly as he takes a drink from his soda.

Apparently, Xavier has already shared the story of his night with Fionna and Charlene, but they patiently sit through it again as he fills me in. Fred fidgets nervously the whole time.

The crossbow is from an effect Xavier designed where Charlene shoots it at me and I catch the bolt in my hand—well, at least it looks to the audience like I do.

"You shot a crossbow bolt at him? Seriously?"

"Not at him," Xavier clarifies. "Near him."

Fred speaks for the first time. "Sure seemed like it was at me to me."

"I could have shot it closer. I have pretty good aim."

"Everyone does from ten feet," he grumbles.

Xavier reaches down and picks up the crossbow.

"Whoa," I say. "You brought it with you?"

"You never know when you might need a crossbow on hand."

"Put that thing down," Fionna exhorts him with a motherly scold. "Before someone gets hurt. Right now you're treading on thin water."

He obeys.

Fred adds some details to Xavier's account, telling us about the blackmailer. He asks pointedly if we can help find out who the person is.

I can't help but suspect that Akinsanya might very well be behind all this. "What is he threatening to release?"

"I can't tell you that."

"Look, if we're going to help you, we need to know what this is all about. We can't get tangled up in something that's going to put anyone else in danger."

"Or us in jail," Fionna interjects.

At last Fred gives in. "Photos."

"Of what?" I ask.

"Of . . ." I can tell this is really hard for him. "A hotel room. What happened there."

"And that was?"

"There were drugs."

He pauses. I sense he's not done. "And?"

"And a photo of a driver's license."

"Go on."

"Of a girl."

I can guess where this is going. "Underage?"

He shakes his head in exasperation. "I swear I don't even re-member her coming back to the room with me. I met a woman at the bar, yes. We talked, but I'm telling you, I went back to my room alone. And she looked old enough to be there. She was drinking, for goodness' sake."

"And when you woke up the next day?"

"Everything was there in the room. Cocaine, meth, a pair of ny-lons, and some panties. I got rid of everything, but then this morning printouts of the photos were waiting for me in my mailbox." He stares at us one at a time, gauging how much we're buying his story. "You have to believe me."

"Actually," Fionna says, "no we don't."

"All a setup?" It's Xavier.

"Well, all I know," answers Fred, "is that those photos can't get released. I'd lose my job for sure, maybe even go to prison if the girl comes forward to testify."

"Your word against hers," I note.

"But she's got the pictures on her side."

"True." I sort things through. "When did all this happen?"

"I was at the hotel last night."

That was fast. This blackmailer didn't mess around.

"The day after Emilio was killed," Charlene says softly.

"Who's Emilio?" he asks.

There isn't time to get into all that right now, so I wave off his question. "Later. For now, it sure looks like you were set up, and the timing fits in with the rest of what's going on. So, for now I'll tell you what—we'll do what we can to keep those photos private, and by the way all of this is interconnected, I'd say there's at least a chance we can help in that regard." I think again of Solomon, that he might have information about this blackmailer, but I don't want to visit him again. I have the sense that it would be pushing our luck.

Solomon?

Akinsanya?

Another criminal who's even more connected?

My mind is buzzing with way too many questions that have way too few answers.

We turn our attention to Fionna.

Again, this seems like a review for everyone else, but they bear with her as she says to me, "While you were chasing Agcaoili and Xavier was shooting crossbow bolts near Fred—"

"At Fred," interjects Fred.

"Near," Xavier replies.

"At."

"Enough, boys," Fionna chides them. "Anyway, while you two were at the warehouse, I figured out what's on the USB drive: work schedules, access codes, and shift change information for a private security firm. The one that takes care of the security at—"

"Groom Lake," Xavier interrupts excitedly. He nods toward our guest. "Fred's already confirmed it. The info is legit."

They seem to have granted the guy who abducted Xavier at gunpoint an awful lot of trust already.

"Hang on." Something isn't quite clicking here. "Fred, if you can

273

confirm the codes and so on, why would this blackmailer need the drive? Why couldn't he just get those details from you?"

He shakes his head. "I don't have access to all that information. Maybe I should have said it all *looks* legit—but you'd actually have to enter the security codes to be sure. There's lots of security around the perimeter, but access to the buildings is usually gained by swiping an ID card or entering a passcode. I haven't been in too many of them, but the passwords on that drive are the right format."

Xav goes on, "And you know what all this means?"

"What's that?"

"It means we can get on the property."

"Why would we want to do that?"

"To find out what the Holy Grail is that everyone is after. To untangle everything. Especially in Building A-13."

"A-13?"

"It's on the drive," Fionna explains. "It seems like that's where the main program, or research, or whatever, is being housed."

I glance toward Charlene, anticipating that she'll object to anything along the lines of traveling to Groom Lake and rescue me from having to argue with Xavier, but she doesn't. "I've had some time to think about this," she says. "I'm warming up to the idea. I think I need to sleep on it, though." Then she abruptly switches topics and explains that about half an hour ago she got a call from the FBI agent she met with this morning.

It seems that suddenly Agent Ratchford was very interested in what we had to say about Tomás Agcaoili and this connection with Akinsanya, the man the Bureau has been tracking for the last four months. "He wants to meet with me tomorrow morning," she explains. "Apparently, he's going to talk with Agcaoili first in jail. We're meeting at eleven."

But that still leaves us with the question of what to do with our new friend Fred.

Despite the trust Xavier has put in him, I'm not comfortable with him staying in the house, but I'm also not sure I want him leaving. By kidnapping Xavier at gunpoint, he's already proven himself to be dangerous.

"Fionna, did you download everything from the drive?"

"Yes."

"Can you make the encryption on it even tougher to get through?"

"Sure. I suppose."

"It took you an entire day to get through—and that was with Lonnie helping you. How many people could get through those files faster than you did?"

She ponders that. "I can only think of half a dozen people I know. Some nation states could, and of course, if it's someone who has access to the military encryption codes they were using, they could certainly get in a lot quicker."

By itself, the drive might be enough to buy us enough time to explore this connection with Akinsanya and how Emilio ended up with the drive in the first place. People were willing to kill over this information, so there is obviously something huge at stake. And now that we're entangled in it all, I'm not going to wait around for the FBI or the ambassador in the Philippines to finally look into things. Not if this poses any danger to my friends.

Which it does.

Also, by adding the firewalls, we can buy Fred some time before those photos are released to the media or posted online.

Whoever this blackmailer is, he put Fred up to kidnapping, and even to the point of threatening murder, in the hopes of acquiring this drive. Who's to say that he's going to stop at that? If he doesn't get what he wants, he might just send someone else, very likely someone even more motivated than Fred was, to get the drive.

"Is it too late to call back this guy who was blackmailing you?" I ask him.

He shrugs uneasily. "I don't know."

"You say he was going to post the photos online?" Fionna says.

"Yeah."

"Well, let me check to see if he has."

"How?"

"I just need a head shot of you. I'll do an image search. Trust me."

She takes his picture and sets to work at her keyboard. After ten minutes she's convinced that whoever the guy is who was blackmailing him hasn't posted the photos.

"But are you sure?" Fred asks.

"No, of course not. I can't be positive. But if he was going to post them to any public site, at least any of the most popular thousand or so, he hasn't done it yet. And if his point was to expose you, wouldn't he post them somewhere where people would easily see them?"

"I don't know. I mean, it doesn't make sense that he hasn't. He was very vehement that I get that drive by the time he called. I can't believe that he wouldn't have posted them."

"If he did, he didn't put them anywhere very public."

"Maybe he still wants something to hold over you, and he knows that as soon as he releases them he loses his bargaining chip," I tell him.

"Maybe."

"Whatever his reasons, let's do what we can to move forward here. Call him. We'll give you the drive. Deliver it to him. But there's just one thing I'm going to ask in return."

"What's that?"

"Help us find out what's in Building A-13."

He looks like he's about to say something, but holds back.

"Well?"

"I'll see what I can do."

Trusting Anders not to tell the blackmailer the truth is a risk. I don't know how we can assure that he won't do it, except that Xavier could go to the police and explain that Fred had kidnapped him at gunpoint.

"Give me your number," I say. "I have a feeling I'll be calling you tomorrow."

"I work tomorrow."

"That's even better."

I turn to Fionna. "Listen, the more I think about it, the more I think we shouldn't give the information on this drive to anyone other than the authorities. Can you set up the drive so that, after they get through your firewalls or security measures or whatever, that the drive erases itself?"

"It'd be my pleasure. I'll even drop a little Trojan in there to have the drive notify me when the firewalls are cracked. That way we'll know when the bad guys know they've been had."

"Groovy." Xavier gives her an approving nod.

She takes some time to reinstate the security measures on the drive, adds firewalls of her own, we give Fred the drive, and he leaves to call his blackmailer and deliver the drive to him.

As we're on our way back to our rooms, Charlene sidles close to me. "I'm proud of you, Jevin."

"For what?"

"For everything tonight. For standing up to that guy at the bar, for coming up with a card trick on the spot for Solomon, for taking down Tomás. I'm proud of you."

"You're not mad that I'm still sort of a leaps-before-he-looks-er?"

"Maybe. A little. But I'm more thankful that you're a do-anything-for-the-people-he-cares-about-er."

"Works for me."

And then we say good night with more than just words.

Calista kissed Dr. Jeremy Turnisen.

They were back in her soundproof suite.

She had her arms around him, and she could feel his heart drumming wildly in his chest.

She drew out the kiss, then pulled away, looked at him devilishly, and pushed him back onto the bed.

He grinned. "You said on the phone you were feeling naughty tonight."

"Close your eyes."

Without any objection, he did as he was told. He was hers and she knew it. They both did.

When Jeremy's eyes were shut, Derek slipped quietly out of the closet. He sprinkled a little liquid onto a handkerchief he held in his hand.

Jeremy lay back and Calista straddled him. "Keep 'em closed, or do I have to get out a blindfold?"

"Promises, promises."

"Mmm." She positioned herself on top of him so that he couldn't roll away and then placed her hand over his eyes.

"I'll keep them closed," he said obediently.

She licked his lips seductively, then took his hands and pressed them down against the bed and brought them together above his head.

"You *are* feeling naughty tonight." His voice was breathless.

Derek crossed the room and leaned over the bed, pressed his left hand against Calista's to hold Jeremy's hands firmly in place, then slid the cloth over Jeremy's nose and mouth.

He struggled, but Derek and Calista held him down securely.

"Yes, Jeremy, my dear." As he faded into unconsciousness she gently stroked his cheek. "You have no idea how naughty I'm feeling."

PART VI

The Three Laws

Sunday, February 10

I wake up refreshed.

It's been an incredibly eventful week, and I think all the stress, jet lag, and lack of sleep have finally caught up with me. When I check the clock I see it's closing in on nine o'clock.

Though I suspect that by this time everyone, except for maybe Donnie and Lonnie, will be up, the house is quiet.

As I get dressed, everything from the last couple days revolves in a confusing swirl of memories and emotions through my mind: Emilio's death, the hectic flights back home, chasing the pickup, the incident in the piranha tank, visiting the Hideaway, making up a card trick for Solomon.

Then, of course, meeting the Sprite-drinking Cammo dude, Fred Anders, here at my house.

Quite a week.

Though I feel pretty well recuperated, my boulder-smacked leg is still sore and my arm really stings—this has been the worst couple days of my life for being attacked by exotic animals. Cobras. Piranhas. Enough with all that.

After smearing some antibiotic on the bites, I make my way downstairs and find Xavier in the kitchen finishing a large bowl of pistachio nut ice cream. A box of Captain Crunch cereal and a gallon jug of 2% milk sit beside it on the table.

"Morning, Xav."

"Hey, Jev."

"Pistachios today, huh?"

He holds up a spoonful of ice cream. "Fionna bought it for me yesterday. Nothing but the finest."

"She's taking good care of you."

"Yeah, well, I know who butters my cake."

I blink. "I think she's rubbing off on you."

"Hmm," he says noncommittally.

"Where is everybody?"

"Sleeping in, I guess." He points to the percolating coffeepot. "Charlene was down a few minutes ago, though. Put some java on. She mentioned she's heading out in a bit to catch church before meeting with Agent Ratchford at eleven. I haven't seen Fionna, but I think I heard the girls moving around. They may have been down already, I'm not sure. I just came in."

I join him for a bowl of cereal. "Any word from Fred this morning?"

"Not since I got up, but last night around two he swung by my RV to return Betty to me. She was under a dumpster—that must have been nasty retrieving her, means a lot. Anyway, he told me he'd just dropped off the drive at the location the blackmailer arranged. At least up until that time the pictures weren't posted yet. That's all I know."

"You two really hit it off."

He shrugs. "First Cammo dude I ever met who wasn't trying to arrest me."

"No, he was trying to kidnap you—actually, he did."

"True. But I'm a forgiving kind of guy. You never know what kind of strange people you're gonna end up being friends with. Heck, I'm even friends with you."

"I'm not going to make any smart comment about which one of us is the strange one."

"Strange is in the eye of the beholder."

"I won't argue with that. Getting back to Fred, I suppose you picked his brain pretty thoroughly about Groom Lake."

"Tried to, but apparently the military keeps its secrets pretty well hidden even from the Cammo dudes. He wasn't able to tell me a whole lot that I didn't already know." He finishes the ice cream, licks off his spoon. "Did describe the road layout of the base, though."

He pours himself a heaping bowl of Captain Crunch and has to use his hand to hold all the cereal in when he adds the milk.

We both eat in silence for a few minutes. I debate whether I should join Charlene for church. She goes at 9:30 nearly every week and hasn't been pressuring me to join her, but I've definitely sensed that she's pleased when I do.

It's not that I'm purposely avoiding it, but ever since the death of my family, God and I have had an on-and-off relationship—or at least I have with him.

You can't go through the trauma of having your wife murder your two boys and take her own life and not end up mired in questions about good and evil, about meaning, about whether God exists—and if he does, if he really cares.

Go through something like that and you'll see how well trite answers and clichés really work out for you. And how hard it is to find solutions that actually do.

And now this week.

Tragedy, eternity, injustice—an awful lot has landed here in my lap. Maybe it wouldn't be such a bad idea to join Charlene and see if it would help me sort through things, at least a little bit.

Besides, if I go along today, I can join her for the meeting with Agent Ratchford.

An ulterior motive?

Maybe.

I'll just call it an added incentive.

While Xavier and I wait for Charlene to return downstairs and for Fionna and the kids to appear, we get talking about what happened last night with Tomás, Solomon, and Fred, and eventually the conversation circles around to the transhumanism research that seems to be at the heart of everything that's going on.

He goes for some grape juice from the fridge. "So. Artificial intelligence. What would it really mean for a machine to become self-aware? Think about the implications. If we don't have a soul—let's say for argument's sake that we don't—if all we are is a collection of biological systems and we can reverse engineer those, create them, maybe even improve on them nonbiologically through nanotechnology and synthetic biology, what essentially would be the difference between us and machines? Metaphysically speaking, that is."

"Well, the key would be if we don't have a soul."

"But if you could upload someone's consciousness onto a machine, would their soul live there too?"

"I have no idea."

"We upload our consciousness and we can theoretically live as long as there's electricity or batteries to keep the computer running. Continue learning, never grow any older, live forever, even survive a zombie apocalypse."

"I like how you threw in the zombie survival perk."

"Always a nice little side benefit of nonbiological existence."

Strange scenarios come to mind—not so much about zombies, but about human consciousness being uploaded onto a computer. Do that, then place it in a robot. Make the robot look realistic. Destroy the computer or unplug it—would you be guilty of murder?

Is the essence of what makes us human found in our consciousness, or is it somehow tied to having an impermanent, transient body?

I finish my cereal, slide the bowl back. "So, just for argument's sake, let's say we have hundreds of millions of people's consciousness existing on some sort of highly evolved Internet. What if someone sends a virus, wipes them all out? Is he the worst mass murderer in history or just a computer hacker?"

"It wouldn't have to be a hacker. It could be a mistake. All of humanity—if society chooses to still use that word to describe what we are—could be wiped out in one tragic programming blunder, computer glitch, or inappropriate application of the machine's protocol."

"And AI, how would you even keep it under control?"

Donnie comes down the stairs, and he must have heard us talking because he says, "Asimov."

"Asimov?" Xavier says.

"Isaac Asimov. The Three Laws of Robotics."

Xavier stares at him blankly. I'm at just as much of a loss as my friend is.

Donnie looks more than just a little shocked. "You never read Asimov?"

Xavier shakes his head.

"I mean, maybe in school. I don't really recall," I tell him. "The Three Laws of Robotics. Is that one of his books?"

Now it's his turn to shake his head, but he's doing so out of exasperation. "Okay, listen, these are really famous, anyone who knows anything about robots knows them—or at least they should. Seriously, you guys never heard of 'em?" He helps himself to some coffee, and even though he's only thirteen, it doesn't really surprise me.

"You know, now that I think about it, I might have," Xavier acknowledges. "But I'm not sure what they are." For all he knows about killer robots and doomsday scenarios, I'm surprised he's not more familiar with these three robot laws, whatever they are.

Donnie takes a deep breath and shuffles off to the other room, obviously still more than just a little sleepy. A moment later he returns carrying a book. "I don't know 'em by heart," he explains.

"That a classic?" Xavier asks.

He's paging through the novel. I can't see the title, but it must be one of Asimov's. "Depends on your definition," he mumbles. "Let's see . . . Okay. Sure. Here it is: '(1) A robot may not injure a human being or, through inaction, allow a human being to come to harm. (2) A robot must obey the orders given to it by human beings, except where such orders would conflict with the First Law. (3) A robot must protect its own existence as long as such protection does not conflict with the First or Second Laws.'"

Donnie goes back to flipping through the book. "He added one more later, but instead of calling it the fourth one it was like a prequel. He called it the zeroth law." Finally, Donnie finds what he's looking for. "'Zero: A robot may not harm humanity, or, by inaction, allow humanity to come to harm.' So it broadens it to relating to the human race."

"Can you read through them again?" Xavier asks.

"Sure." He does. "These laws appeared throughout Asimov's stories with some variations, you know, but the general meaning never changed." But then he qualifies that. "Well, at least not in the stories I've read."

To me, the laws seem like a pretty good place to start in this whole discussion about robotics and autonomous machines. "They sound like they might not be that bad a set of laws for *people* to follow."

"No kidding," agrees Xavier.

Donnie sips at his coffee, then joins us at the table. "Ever think about what would happen when a computer passes the Turing test and Searle's Chinese room scenario?"

"What are those?" I ask.

Another look of surprise. This boy is obviously more well versed in killer robot theory than either Xavier or me.

"Different tests for artificial intelligence." He leaves it at that, and I get the sense that he isn't really interested in elaborating to a couple of neophytes like us.

"You seem to know a lot about all of this."

"I like science fiction, and this stuff comes up all the time. I mean, think about it, what happens when strong AI appears and a machine says it's alive, and that it deserves to be granted the same rights as we have—you know, the rights to life, liberty, the pursuit of happiness, all that? How'll we argue with it without undermining our very premise that it's not alive? After all, you don't argue with something that isn't alive, trying to convince it that it isn't."

Not a bad point. "I hadn't thought of it quite like that."

Our conversation shifts back to what makes humans unique, and I hear light footsteps descending the stairs. A moment later Mandie appears, carrying Furman. "What are you talking about?"

"How robots are different from people," Donnie answers.

"Oh." She positions Furman on a chair so he can watch her eat breakfast. "That's easy."

Xavier looks at her questioningly. "Really?"

"Mm-hmm. They can't smile and mean it. Can you make some more chocolate chip pancakes today?"

"Um . . . Let me clear that with your mom first."

That satisfies her for the time being.

Robots can't smile and mean it. That's a better answer than I could have come up with, and that from a five-year-old.

Maybe someday in the future they will be able to smile and mean it. What would be the essential difference then?

That's definitely more than I'm ready to process at this time of day.

Over the next few minutes Fionna and the rest of her family join us, and Charlene comes down and pours coffee into a travel mug.

"I think I'll come along today." I grab a to-go cup of my own. "To church. Jeans okay?"

"Jeans are fine."

She grabs a Bible, we hop into the DB9 and take off.

Roses and Thorns

The auditorium at Charlene's church is larger than the theater at the Arête. I'm guessing there are maybe twelve hundred people here.

We sing four songs—I wouldn't call them hymns exactly. They have more of a college rock feel to them, and there's no organ, just a band on the stage. The guy on lead guitar isn't bad. They jam a little bit and it's nice, definitely not your grandmother's church service.

There are some announcements, and then the head pastor comes onstage to introduce the guest speaker for today, a missionary doctor on furlough from his work in the slums and leprosy colonies of India. He's white-haired and slow to take the stage and looks like he's in his late sixties.

After some opening comments, he tells us the story of his first visit to India.

"It was about fifteen years ago, and I was doing some work in an AIDS clinic. The man who organized my trip worked with a number of ministries and programs to help societal outcasts. He invited me to visit with some street workers—prostitutes—who were being trained as peer counselors to other prostitutes. They would teach them how to avoid AIDS, what to do if someone got violent, and so on."

It seems like this man knows his audience. There's no way to be sure, but I can guess that most of the people in the auditorium who've lived in Vegas for any length of time have met prostitutes.

"We arrived in a dingy building that served as an AIDS hospital for them. The women greeted us joyfully, handing us roses to welcome us. It was tragic and beautiful. While talking with them we asked if any of them had hope that they could do something different, and in that small room packed with fifty street workers, not a single hand went up. All at once my host stood and offered to buy sewing machines for the center and to hire someone to come in and teach sewing. 'If you'll come for three months once a week and can make me a shirt when it's over, I'll buy you your own sewing machine and you can start a business as a seamstress.' You should have seen the smiles and nods in the room."

His story grips me, and when I glance around I can see that I'm not the only one. Hardly anyone around me is stirring.

"Well, afterward I asked my friend, who wasn't by any means rich, how he would pay for it. 'The money will come in,' he said simply. 'God will provide.' I didn't know what to say. I didn't have a lot of money with me, but I offered him a hundred dollars. 'Here,' I said, 'use this to help with the expenses.' And he took my hand and looked me directly in the eye and said, 'You just bought two sewing machines. You just saved two women's lives.'"

The missionary pauses, but just for a moment. "I'll never forget that day. And I've never looked at the impact of spending fifty dollars the same again. I still have the roses on my shelf that the women handed me as I entered that room."

I have the sense that he might move to asking for donations to the ministry he works with, but he doesn't go there. Instead, he dives into the heart of his message. "We live in a fallen, broken, stunning, and breathtaking world. We can tell we're from here but don't belong here. We're meant for more than this. We are dust and bones and blood and dreams, skin-covered spirits with hungry souls. We are nurses and terrorists, lovers and liars, suicide bombers and little grinning children with milk mustaches. We are both the thorns and the roses, the harlots and the children of the king."

The paradox of life on this planet.

The paradox at the heart of human nature.

A woman can be a loving mother of her two sons and then one day decide to murder them and kill herself.

An angel and a devil wrapped up into one.

He goes on, "Chesterton called us 'broken gods.' Pascal called us 'fallen princes.' Philosophers have long wondered how we fit into this world, somewhere between the apes and the angels. To make us into one or the other is to deny the full reality of who we are, because we have both animal instincts and divine desires."

Charlene has often told me that it's no coincidence when a sermon touches us where we're at in our lives, that it's evidence of a bigger plan at work. And now, this missionary's words naturally make me think of the discussions I've had over the last couple days with my friends about people merging with machines, about souls and life and what makes us human after all.

Then the missionary concludes his brief message. "A friend of mine told me that followers of Christ are each Cinderella in the moment of transformation—half dressed in ashes and rags, half clothed in a royal gown ready to meet the prince. We are far worse than we would ever on our own admit, and loved by God more deeply than we would ever dare to dream. We are both worthless and priceless, terrorists and saints, lost and homeward bound. Without the love of Christ we are lost, mired in our past, in our selfish choices, in our ruthless pride. With faith in him, the Bible tells us that we will share eternity with God in a place of complete joy and glory. We want to love and be loved, and we ache for the eternal. We hunger for the things that the physical world doesn't offer. And we wither and die inside when we don't find them."

When he ends his talk, silence pervades the auditorium. From attending here with Charlene before, I know the sermons are typically much longer than this. There's an awkward moment while he gathers his notes, and I get the sense that the band and the lead pastor don't really know what to do.

The missionary turns hastily to leave the stage, and finally the minister hurries up to take his place. He leads a prayer and the band must be taking their position while he's praying, because as he finishes the music begins again.

We sing a few more songs, and the service draws to a close twenty-five minutes early.

Afterward, I want to talk to the missionary about some of the things he said, but there's a substantial line at the front of the church. I linger for a few minutes, but in the end I decide we should probably be leaving for our meeting with the FBI agent.

At the car, Charlene asks me, "Well, what did you think of that?"

"Honestly?"

"Honestly."

"I thought it was no coincidence that we were here today."

Colonel Derek Byrne and Calista were in their room at the Arête, and now their captive sat in a chair, still drugged from the night before.

While Calista stroked the man's hair, Derek contacted Jesús Garcia to notify him that Tomás Agcaoili had been arrested the night before, but Jesús had already heard the news.

"He doesn't know enough to be a threat to either of us," the cartel leader told him.

"I would still prefer that he doesn't remain a loose end. I'll take care of it."

"No. I know some people in the department. I'll deal with it. Let me make a few calls."

After hanging up, Derek watched Calista gently caress Jeremy Turnisen's cheek.

"When is he gonna wake up?" she asked.

"Not for another hour or so, not with what I gave him last night. A syringe full of that drug will put someone out for at least six or seven hours. I'll let you know when we can start trying to rouse him."

He was secured to the chair, his wrists and ankles duct-taped to it.

Derek had some very specific things to ask this man, but he wanted him to be fully awake and coherent when he spoke to him. So, for now he let him sleep until the drugs wore off completely.

They had all day. For the moment at least, there was no rush.

Together, he and Calista spread out the plastic sheet around the base of the chair.

Then Derek made sure he had enough black thread to last through the afternoon.

Timeline

Vegas resorts and casinos are famous for elaborate buffets, but on Sunday mornings there are almost always long lines, so Charlene chooses Hash House a Go Go, a favorite local restaurant, for the meeting.

However, when she calls Special Agent Clay Ratchford, he tells her that he's changed his mind and doesn't want to meet in a public place after all. "We'll meet in the lobby of the federal building."

He's waiting for us when we arrive.

After unlocking the door, he ushers us to a semicircle of leather chairs.

Ratchford is a studious-looking man who immediately gives me the impression of someone who might be more comfortable sitting behind a desk than chasing down criminals on the street. Stylish glasses. Hair carefully parted on the side. Small, pebble-like, inset eyes.

"Good morning, Miss Antioch."

"Good morning, Agent Ratchford."

He doesn't look especially happy to see me, but Charlene informs him that I'll be able to help answer his questions. "Jevin knows more about everything that's going on than anyone else does."

Agent Ratchford's handshake is less than firm.

When he doesn't take a seat, neither do we, and the three of us end up all standing somewhat uncomfortably in the middle of the lobby.

No guards.

No one else around.

The lobby smells vaguely of the overripe lemon scent of a hospital. From where we're standing, the sunlight that angles in through the tinted windows misses us completely, and Agent Ratchford is standing in a shadow, backlit by the breezeless day outside.

The air conditioner isn't on, making it warm and stuffy in here, and I find myself wishing we'd been able to meet for some food in Hash House a Go Go after all.

Instead of bringing up the USB drive, Ratchford jumps right in and asks us about our past experiences with Akinsanya.

We summarize the crazy events that happened in Philadelphia in October, when we ended up averting an assassination attempt against the president that Akinsanya was apparently behind.

Agent Ratchford shakes his head slightly. "Last evening I did some checking. There's no official record that the president was ever in any danger."

"I know," I tell him. "The administration denied any of this happened." That was something that only served to confirm Xavier's views of the government. "But still, ever since then the Bureau—your Bureau—has been following up with us to see if we know anything about Akinsanya, or if he's contacted us."

"And he hasn't?"

"No."

"Still?"

"No."

Charlene asks if his team has made any progress getting through that USB drive she gave them yesterday.

"At the time, it wasn't placed on the top of our priority list," he answers. "But we're getting started on it this morning."

"You mean, *you* didn't place it at the top of the priority list." Charlene is obviously not happy that they didn't take her seriously yesterday.

He looks at her severely. "Correct. *I* didn't place it at the top of the priority list. But I am now."

"It may take you awhile to get through the security on it."

He scoffs at that. "I'm sure our technicians won't have any trouble."

"It took Fionna all day, and that was with Lonnie's help," Charlene tells him.

He eyes her with a touch of suspicion. "Who are Fionna and Lonnie? And what do you mean it took her all day?"

"Friends of ours. They're good with computers. They made a copy of the drive to work on."

"They made a copy of the drive?"

I cut in, "We weren't confident you and your team were going to look into it promptly."

And as it turns out, you weren't, I think, but keep that to myself.

I debate whether to tell him what Fionna found in the files and finally decide that giving him as much info as possible will be the best bet in seeing any serious progress, so I fill him in about the Groom Lake shift schedules and access codes.

"Groom Lake," he says skeptically.

"That's right."

He doesn't seem too impressed. "Well, we'll look into that."

"Did you hear what I said? These are codes that would allow someone to—"

"I heard what you said. We'll look into it."

"Do you want us to send you the files?" Charlene asks.

"That won't be necessary. As I said before, I'm sure our technicians won't be needing any help. Let's focus for a moment on Akinsanya. How did you find out about him again? That he was involved in this?"

It's not impressing me that this guy is refusing our help when it comes to information about the drive that he and his team decided not to make a priority. I have the sense that something more is going on here, but at the moment I can't guess what that might be.

Since Solomon took a risk and was willing to help us last night, I don't really want to give his name to Ratchford. However, if I don't explain where we got the information, it might hinder the Bureau's efforts to sort out who Akinsanya really is or where he might be.

Last night Solomon had asked us straight out if we were with the law enforcement community, so I doubt he'll talk to the FBI even if they do locate him.

Charlene speaks up before I can. "Our source would rather remain anonymous."

"Miss Antioch, I would advise you not to get in the way of this investigation."

"We're not getting in the way," I tell him. "Everything you have so far came from us. You weren't even going to expedite this until you started to take us seriously last night. And we just offered to give you what's on the drive, but you weren't interested."

He takes off his glasses and polishes them with his shirt. "Is there anything else you know that you aren't telling me?"

Okay, this guy is officially starting to annoy me.

"No," Charlene answers. "Obviously, Tomás knows more than we do. You have him in custody, ask him."

"I did. This morning."

"He can lead you to Akinsanya."

"Yes," he says, and I can't tell the extent of what that answer is supposed to mean. "Did your source, the one who would prefer to remain anonymous, mention anything about a timeline?"

The lemony scent in here is getting to me. I wish we were at least walking around outside. "A timeline?"

"We intercepted a communiqué. We have reason to believe that this man, Akinsanya, might be in the area. Something is going down."

Why on earth is he sharing this with you?

"No." I feel a surge of suspicion, and suddenly I don't like the idea that we are in this building alone with him. I glance toward the door. "We don't know anything about a timeline."

"And you still refuse to tell me the name of the person who told you that Akinsanya was involved?"

"He's not a fan of talking to law enforcement personnel," Charlene notes, almost certainly understating things.

For a moment the air in the room seems to stiffen, and then Ratchford glances at his watch. "Yes, well, I have an appointment. If you find out anything more about Akinsanya, I want you to tell me about it immediately."

And that's that.

Even though it's warmer outside than it was inside the building, it seems less oppressive.

On our way to the car Charlene says, "Well, that was even shorter than the abbreviated church service."

"No kidding. And didn't that whole conversation just seem weird to you from start to finish?"

"Yes." She pauses. "Are you thinking we should go back to Solomon? Maybe follow up to see if he'll give us more info on Akinsanya?"

Actually, I haven't been.

The idea of appearing before Solomon again doesn't exactly thrill me. "I think we should pursue some other avenues first."

I click my key fob's unlock button.

"Like what?"

"I'm not sure." I climb into the driver's seat. Charlene slides in beside me. "But I have the sense that if Solomon found out that we've been talking with the Feds, and then we suddenly show up again and ask him for more information about one of the Bureau's most wanted terrorists, he might not be as . . . well, as . . ."

"Beneficent?"

"Sounds like a word Maddie might use."

"I think that's where I heard it."

"Well, yes. Not as beneficent."

"So what are you suggesting?"

"As far as Akinsanya, I'll need to think about that. But I do know two things I'd like to do."

"Yes?"

"Grab a burger, then head on to the Arête. I think we'll have just enough time before the show at the children's ward of Fuller Medical Center."

"Just enough time for what?"

"There's something I need you to help me pick out."

"What's that?"

"A gift for someone special."

A Girl's Best Friend

Undersecretary Williamson arrived at the Plyotech Cybernetics research and development building.

Yesterday, she'd made it clear to Takahashi that today when she returned she wanted to see the research areas that would clear up the gaps she'd noticed in the reports. Also, based on information she'd been given, she had a strong reason to believe that Akio had not been completely up-front with her.

He was standing beside the security checkpoint near the front entrance when she arrived.

Though it was Sunday, two security guards were on duty and requested that she pass through the metal detector.

"You have got to be kidding me. I'm the Undersecretary of Defense for the United States of America."

"It's our policy," Takahashi explained awkwardly. "Even I have to walk through there."

"Even you do."

"Yes."

"Well then." Though she was tempted to say more and had some choice words already in mind, she chose to hold back and instead clomped her purse onto the conveyor belt, dropped her keys, watch, and cell phone into the tray, and walked briskly through the metal detector.

The buzzer went off.

"There's metal in my left knee from a knee replacement."

The two guards looked at each other, and finally one of them said to her reluctantly, "I'm going to have to wand you."

She glared at him, then held her hands out to the sides. "Fine."

When that was finally over, she collected her things and Takahashi pointed to the stairs. "I'd like to take you to the lower level."

She recalled the elevator buttons from her trip up to his office yesterday. "I didn't know there was a lower level."

"Most people don't."

The proprietor of the jewelry store is standing behind one of the cases polishing the glass cover when we enter. He immediately recognizes me from when I came in with Fionna yesterday. "Sir! It's good to see you again. So, you were looking at necklaces? Yes, as I remember, you are a man of impeccable taste. May I—"

"I'll be with you in just a moment," I tell him, lifting the line that merchants typically use on customers, and he looks momentarily disoriented, which is what I always go for when I say that. Sometimes it's just fun to mess with people.

"Yes. Um . . . Of course."

"Come here, Charlene."

She follows me toward the women's necklaces. "So we're looking for something for a woman?"

"Let's say I was. That I was looking for a necklace for a woman."

"For just any woman?"

"No. As I said before, it's for someone special."

"Hmm . . . And do I know her?"

"I think you two are fairly well acquainted."

"I see. And what does she like? Diamonds? Platinum? Silver? Cubic zirconia?"

"Not that last one."

"No?"

"No. It has to be the real thing. Diamonds, I'd say. I think she would like diamonds."

"Well, you know what they say about diamonds. That sounds safe."

"I'm not shooting for safe, exactly." I point to an extraordinarily brilliant diamond necklace displayed behind the glass. "I'm really looking for something unforgettable. Something that would pretty much wow her. Blow her away."

"You must really like this mystery woman a lot."

"*Like* might not be the right word."

"Really?"

"Nope. And I want this necklace to let her know that."

"The right piece of jewelry can speak volumes." Her gaze wisps across the engagement rings, but only briefly. "So, a necklace."

"Yes."

"Diamonds?"

"That's what I'm thinking."

"Well. These are all certainly nice, but you don't need to spend a lot of money to express this sentiment you have in mind."

"Is that so."

"You could just tell her. Three words is usually enough."

"Three words? That's all you need?"

"Usually. Yes."

"Well. I'll take that under consideration."

"Uh-huh . . ." She taps a finger against the glass case, then brushes her hand across the case that holds the engagement rings and looks at me demurely. "I'll have to think more about what would be ideal as far as jewelry goes, but for right now I don't think any of those necklaces are quite right for a woman that special to you."

I flag the man behind the counter. "Not today. Maybe another time."

He opens his mouth partway as if he's going to reply, but decides against it and goes back to needlessly polishing his already spotless display cases.

I catch up with Charlene outside the store, and we leave for the hospital to do the children's show.

•　•　•••

Derek decided it was time to wake up Dr. Jeremy Turnisen.

"Can I do it?" Calista asked.

"Sure."

She did it with a kiss.

Well, more than one.

As he regained consciousness, she stepped back.

Derek stood beside her, fingering the needle and suture thread. "We'll give him a little time to recover. Then we'll get started."

Eyelids

Xavier meets us in the parking lot near the main entrance. He has a duffel bag full of props with him. We tell him about our rather truncated meeting with Agent Ratchford.

"So he didn't want to see Fionna's findings?"

"No," I reply. "To be frank, it was all very odd. I couldn't quite put my finger on what he wanted—it seemed like he wanted information about Akinsanya, but . . . Well, all I can say is that I got the impression something more is going on here with Ratchford's interest in the case."

"So did I," Charlene adds.

Xavier takes a moment to reflect on that. "Well, let's do the show and then figure out where to take things from there."

For the performance, I plan on card tricks and small effects, and I figure there'll be plenty to choose from in the voluminous bag Xavier is toting.

We're on our way to the front door when I get a call from Mr. Fridell that tonight's show has been blacked out.

I imagine this must be related to what happened last night during the finale. "Is it because of the accident involving the piranha tank? I don't think the audience even knew it wasn't part of the effect. Seth's prestige salvaged things. We can still make that effect work."

"The show manager and I talked it over. There are other factors to consider. Legal matters. And public relations. I know the audience members weren't supposed to be filming your escape, but someone took cell phone footage of it and posted it online. The media got ahold of it and has been running with it this morning. Our lawyers think it would be best to take a day off so we can respond appropriately to the news stories and the queries we're getting."

I blame myself, and I hate the feeling it gives me.

"I'm not upset with you or your team," Fridell assures me. "I'm just glad you weren't hurt any worse. We'll have to consider the possibility that our lawyers will want that trick out of your show."

Though I can understand where he's coming from, I'm not sold on the idea. "I'd like to be in on that conversation."

"I understand. I'll keep you in the loop."

"And there's no way we can still go on tonight?"

"The box office is already in the process of refunding tickets. For now, tomorrow's show is still on. I'll pass your views on to our lawyers, but I can't promise anything. We'll talk as soon as I know anything more."

After we end the call, the hospital's receptionist directs Charlene, Xavier, and me to the administrator's office, where Ms. Sage-Turner enthusiastically leads us up to the third floor's conference room/lounge in the children's wing where we'll be performing.

Akio Takahashi did not take the undersecretary down to sublevel 4.

He thought that by showing her some of the research that happened on the level directly above, he might quell her curiosity. So, he led her to sublevel 3 instead and began explaining the company's findings on swarm technology using insect-sized reconnaissance robots.

It'd better be enough for her.

Because if it wasn't, he didn't know what he was going to do.

⚬⚬ ⚬⚬⚬

Putting the thoughts of tonight's cancelled performance out of my mind, I focus on entertaining the children. Though my arm is aching, thankfully the show goes by without a hitch.

I do a series of street magic effects and mentalism, and the kids love it.

Although some hospital staff are present, most of the audience of three dozen or so is made up of children who are cancer patients. Some kids are recovering from operations, injuries, or broken bones.

It's great to see smiles on their faces as I rip up oversized playing cards and then restore them, pull a chain through my neck, and toss my Morgan Dollar up and vanish it in midair.

Charlene helps me with some of the illusions, and even Xavier gets in on the act, doing a cups and balls routine and then showing the children how it's done so they can perform it for their friends. He wants to do his new flaming bubbles effect, but as he's pulling out the necessary chemicals, Ms. Sage-Turner quickly but politely puts a nix on that.

⚬⚬ ⚬⚬⚬

Derek sat on the edge of the bed and told Jeremy Turnisen what lay in store for him if he was not cooperative.

His eyes were wide with fear, his voice quavering. "If I can help you, yes, yes, I'll do anything. Just please, don't hurt me."

In response, Derek freed the man's hands, but left his feet bound to the chair.

"I want to show you something." Derek nodded to Calista, who went to retrieve a tablet computer from the desk. "I'm going to ask you a series of questions. I want you to be as forthcoming in your answers as you can be. It'll save us both a lot of time and effort."

"I'm telling you," Turnisen pleaded, "whatever it is you want, I'll help you, but you have the wrong man. I'm just an engineer—"

"Where?"

"Where?"

"Where do you work? Where do you do your research?"

"I'm self-employed. I can give you my files, my client list, everything."

"I'm sure you can."

Calista returned and stood expectantly beside Derek. "Show him," he said.

She swiped her finger across the screen to pull up the photos she'd taken for Derek out in the desert, the pictures of Heston Dembski, RN, former special assistant to Dr. Malhotra. There were a dozen photos of the man after Derek had finished his target practice on him.

Turnisen gulped, almost imperceptibly. "What is it you want from me?"

"The launch codes."

"What?"

"The launch codes. For the test flight scheduled tonight at 8:46."

"I don't know what you're talking about."

"I know where you work, Jeremy."

"I told you, I'm—"

"Please. No lies."

Calista scrolled through the photos again, to make sure Jeremy got a good look at all of them, but he closed his eyes and turned away halfway through.

"Why did you kill that man?" he whispered.

"To make clear to you how serious I am about getting what I want." Derek patted Calista's arm, and she bent and straightened out the plastic sheet that was spread out beneath the chair.

"What's that for?" Turnisen's voice trembled as he spoke.

"Easier cleanup." The colonel removed the needle and heavy, black thread from his pocket. "Hold out your wrists."

"No. Listen, I'm telling you, I—"

"Hold them out or I'll start with your eyelids."

The French Drop

The boy with progeria, who I find out is named Tim, isn't there in the conference room, which is okay by me because I was actually hoping to talk with him privately.

Some of the children who couldn't come are asleep, a few are contagious, one is in a coma. One burn patient, who tipped a deep-fat fryer of hot grease onto her head, was so easily prone to infection that she was isolated in a section of a room partitioned off with a plastic tent.

Since our performance tonight at the Arête was cancelled, I call off our afternoon rehearsal. That means we aren't under any time constraints, so after the show, Xavier, Charlene, and I split up the remaining rooms and do some walk-around effects for the kids we're allowed to see. I'm even able to do some card tricks for the girl with the burns, from the other side of the plastic sheet where the nurses do most of their work.

The last room I visit is Tim's.

Children with progeria don't need to stay in hospitals, but they often have recurring health issues that cause them to spend more time

308

there than other children, and the nurse who's leading me to Tim's room informs me that that's been the case with him.

We arrive and she knocks gently on the door. "There's someone to see you, Tim." We wait for him to invite us in, then we enter.

It's hard to describe how a child with progeria looks.

Tim has lost nearly all of his hair. His face gives you the impression of an old man and a young boy mixed together into the same body. He has a high forehead and a sharper than average nose. A movie I once saw about Benjamin Button comes to mind, but even that doesn't do justice to portraying someone who has progeria in real life.

Tim remembers me from the time I was here doing a show before, and his eyes light up. I join him by his bed and the nurse gives us some privacy, closing the door quietly behind her.

Tim is seven. Unless there are unforeseen complications or unexpected treatment breakthroughs, he'll likely die of old age within seven or eight years.

My boys were five when they died, and even though Tim looks nothing like them, I end up thinking of them when I see him.

I do a few vanishes with the cards and then offer to teach him how to do a French Drop for coin tricks, but he tells me he already knows how to do it.

Sure enough, when I hand him my Morgan Dollar, he goes through the proper mechanics of the move. His technique is good, and even though I can follow the coin, to an untrained eye he would have likely pulled it off.

I'm impressed. "Who taught you how to do that?"

"Emilio."

"Emilio Benigno?"

Tim nods. "He was my friend. He went to heaven."

"Yes." I fumble for how to reply. "He did."

"We'd go and watch the fountains sometimes. You know, at the

Bellagio. My parents are divorced. My dad can't see me anymore. Emilio was nice to me."

Emilio's friendship with Tim is news to me. I knew about my friend's shows here at the hospital, but I didn't know about his personal connection with any of the patients. However, from all I do know about Emilio and his sense of compassion, the extra time he spent with Tim doesn't surprise me.

Tim didn't seem sad a moment ago when he said that Emilio went to heaven, but his mood has shifted and he becomes more melancholy. "He said he was gonna help me."

"How was Emilio going to help you?"

"To not get old so fast."

Immediately, Emilio's transhumanism books and his research on the jellyfish and progeria come to mind.

"Do you know how he was going to do that? To help you not get old so fast?"

"The drug people."

"The drug people?"

"From RixoTray. The doctor who asks me all the questions and gives me the medicines. Dr. Schatzing."

Tim looks past me out the window. The whole idea of coming in here to cheer him up seems to have backfired, and it looks like the conversation is only serving to make him somber.

I'm trying to figure out the best way to turn things around again when he offers to show me another trick.

"That'd be great."

He picks up the straw from his lunch tray, tears off one end of the paper wrapper covering it, and slides the part that's still around the plastic up and down five or six times. Finally, he removes it, then slides the miniature pepper shaker to the center of the tray.

After carefully balancing the straw on the pepper shaker's lid, he passes his hands close to the straw and it begins to spin.

"I'm not blowing it," Tim tells me proudly. "It's magic."

I know it's the static electricity that builds up from the paper rubbing against the plastic straw, but who's to say there's nothing mysterious or magical about that? An invisible force that seems to come from nowhere and that most people couldn't explain if given the chance? Sounds like magic to me.

"Yes," I tell him. "It is."

At last the nurse appears in the doorway and it's time to leave. I promise Tim that I'll be back. He puts his frail arm around me, and it both breaks my heart and lightens it when he gives me a hug. "And maybe I can teach you some more tricks," he says.

"I'd like that."

In the hallway, I meet up with Charlene and Xavier. We thank Ms. Sage-Turner for scheduling the show on such short notice, but she tells us that she's the one who should be thankful.

"We'll be back," Charlene promises her.

"We'll look forward to it."

I venture a guess. "I understand there's some progress being made on the progeria research front."

"It looks like a sizable anonymous donation is coming in." She looks very pleased. "We're working with RixoTray Pharmaceuticals on a joint project."

"That's fantastic."

A nurse flags her down, she excuses herself and steps away.

As my friends and I head for the elevator bay, I tell them about my encounter with Tim. "Emilio promised he would help him to not grow old so fast. How could he make a promise like that?"

"He wouldn't have," replies Xavier, "unless he knew for sure something was on the horizon. Some sort of breakthrough."

"Maybe he learned something from the RixoTray researcher?" Charlene says. "This Dr. Schatzing?"

Is he the one who gave Emilio the RixoTray USB drive?

What about the DoD encrypted files? Why would Schatzing have those?

Well, either he has a connection to Groom Lake, or Emilio did.

It was a lot to chew on.

As we ride the elevator down to the first floor, Charlene continues, "Remember how we were talking about why Emilio might have been interested in all this, and we were thinking it might be because he wanted to find a way to live longer, or he might have wanted someone else to live longer?"

"It looks like we just found that person," Xavier answers.

"Yes," I agree. "I think we did."

Outside the hospital, Charlene surprises me by saying she really does think we should talk with Solomon again.

"About Akinsanya?"

"Yes. I mean, think about it, he's really the key behind all this, isn't he? If we can find him and turn him in to the FBI, they'll be able to dig through all the layers and find out what's really going on. Besides, as far as we know, he's the one who hired Tomás to kill Emilio. And somehow, Solomon knows about him. He might be able to lead us to him."

Even though I'm more than a little hesitant to contact Solomon again, at this point I have to admit that it might actually be worth it.

"If we go this route, I'm talking to him alone this time."

"Betty and I are coming along," Xavier says unequivocally. "And no, that's not up for discussion."

Rather than argue or ask to come along, Charlene just nods. "I can accept that. As long as you three are careful."

"Three?"

"Two guys plus one Betty."

"Gotcha."

"Call me. Keep me up to speed."

"I will." I hand her my keys and she takes the DB9 back home while

I ride with Xavier in his RV toward the Hideaway. A very low-profile vehicle. Perfect for searching for clandestine crime lords.

We don't see Martin when we walk into the bar. There's a different bartender working today, and when we ask her about Solomon, she tells us she has no idea who that is. She doesn't know any Martins either.

Even laying a hundred-dollar bill on the table doesn't jog her memory, and I believe her.

At last we go back to the RV and Xavier says, "Okay. Let's swing by the alley."

I have the feeling that we won't be granted access to see Solomon without Martin's help, but it's worth a shot.

Between the two of us we're able to find the alley without too much trouble. Xavier parks the RV along the street beside it.

No one answers the rusted door when we knock. I try opening it but find that it's firmly bolted shut. There's no lock for me to pick on this side of it.

"Well," Xavier says, "at least we gave it a shot."

"Back to square one."

"Do not pass Go. Do not collect $200."

On the way back to the house, Fionna calls. I put her on speaker-phone so Xavier, who's driving, can hear what she has to say.

She tells us that when Charlene was at the front gates of my house waiting for them to open, she saw a sedan with two men sitting in it across the street. "They're still there," she informs us. "I can see them from the window in the library."

"It might not be anything." But I don't exactly believe that.

"I had Lonnie and Donnie go outside to play some catch. Football. They got a closer look. One of the men is watching the house through binoculars."

"Feds," mumbles Xavier.

"Or cops," she suggests.

If we're going to keep looking into all this, I don't want anyone—not cops or FBI agents—staking out my place.

I think things through and come up with something that should be able to free us up from being watched by whoever's outside those gates.

"Okay, listen, Fionna. Have everyone stay in the house. I have an idea."

After ending the call I tell Xavier to turn around. "We need to head to the Strip."

"Why?"

"There are a couple stops I need you to make on the way to my house."

Misdirection

2:46 p.m.
6 hours left

We take care of the errands I had in mind and then arrive at the gates to the drive leading to my home.

Sure enough, the black sedan is parked nearby.

Xavier's driving, so I get out and walk around the RV, punch in the security code, making sure that I'm visible to the men in the car as I do, then climb back in.

I pretend I don't notice them watching me.

The gates swing open, we drive in, and I put things into play.

Undersecretary Oriana Williamson waited as patiently as she could for Akio Takahashi to finish telling her about the miniature flying robots.

Finally, she just cut in. "Look. We've been walking around here since noon and I've had enough of this. Here's what I'm wondering: Have there been any breakthroughs on the bionic forefront?"

"Nothing we haven't already reported to the oversight committee."

"That's not what I heard."

A pause. "From whom?"

"A friend. I want to see the blueprints for this building."

"Excuse me?"

"You heard me. I want to see the schematics. And I want to see them now so I can make my six o'clock flight."

⚫⚫ ⚫⚫⚫

Officer Gordon Shepard peered through his binoculars and watched Charlene Antioch and Jevin Banks leave the house and slip into the Aston Martin parked out front.

"Man, we are in the wrong profession," he said to his partner, Ron Ledger. "Wait till you see this car."

When it came into view, Ron grunted. "You're not kidding. That just ain't right."

The gates swung open and the Aston Martin turned south, toward the Strip.

"Call Garcia." Gordon started the engine. "Tell him they're on the move."

⚫⚫ ⚫⚫⚫

Derek got the call from Jesús Garcia while he was tying off the sutures closing up one of the longer slits he'd made in Dr. Jeremy Turnisen's abdomen.

The man tried to protest but the gag swallowed most of the sound.

"*Buenos días*, my friend," Jesús said.

"Hello, Jesús. To what can I attribute the honor of this call?"

"Well, there are three matters to discuss."

"Go on." He snipped off the end of the thread.

"First, a certain performer has been looking into his friend's death. I believe you know him? From last fall?"

"Banks."

"Yes. I thought it'd be best to keep tabs on him, so I have two men

316

tailing him. I'll let you know if anything comes up that might be of interest to you."

"Thank you."

"Second. The time frame. Are we still on schedule for tonight?"

"We're still looking at a launch time of 8:46."

"You're confident that you'll have what you need by then?"

"Yes."

"Perfect. Alright, finally, then, Tomás has been taken care of."

"Is that so."

"Yes."

"Well, that's good to hear."

"Focus on the engineer."

"Don't worry." He let his eyes travel to the blood dripping onto the plastic sheet beneath the chair. "I am."

***

Officer Shepard followed Banks's sports car down the Strip. Eventually, it stopped at the Arête.

He watched as Banks handed his keys to the valet parking attendant, went around the side, and opened the door for Antioch. Then the two of them swept off into the resort.

"I guess we're gonna have valet parking today too," he said to his partner, stepping out of the car and handing over the keys to the sedan. "Let's go."

***

I glance at Charlene. "Okay. There's no sign of them. I think we're good."

I'm standing beside my library window, scrutinizing the neighborhood.

Fifteen minutes ago we'd watched as Seth and Nikki left the house dressed in our clothes.

Without a show tonight, the two of them had some free time, and since I'm paying them anyway, I decided they could hang out at the Arête as long as we needed them to.

On our way back to the house from the alley, Xav and I had picked them up and hid them in the back of the RV.

Body doubles can come in very handy.

Everybody should have one.

Now it's time to get some answers without anyone peeking over our shoulders.

Though the kids are upstairs—Lonnie doing homework, Donnie playing video games, the girls making Valentine's Day cards—I close the library door to give us a little added privacy.

Xavier is on his laptop surfing the Internet, and suddenly he exclaims, "Oh, this is not good."

"What?"

"Tomás Agcaoili is dead. He was found in his cell about an hour ago."

"You're kidding."

He surfs to another site, scrolls down, then taps the screen. "Hung himself with a belt."

"What cop in his right mind would leave a belt in a cell with a prisoner?" I say, thinking aloud. "Wouldn't they guess that he could use it for a noose?"

Fionna looks at us intensely. "The clot thickens."

Close enough.

"Yes, it does," I agree.

So, Tomás is dead.

A life for a life.

In a sense, justice for Emilio's death has been meted out, but on another level it hasn't been.

Someone hired Tomás to kill Emilio.

And that person is still out there.

Akinsanya?

It seems possible, likely even, but—

From out of nowhere another possibility comes to mind: *What about Solomon? Could he have mentioned Akinsanya just to start you looking in the wrong direction?*

He gave you both Akinsanya and Tomás. What if he's playing both sides? He knew who you were, had to know the Feds are after Akinsanya. Is this all just window dressing to keep you away from the truth?

I find myself trying to piece everything together, but at least for the moment, it seems like a maze that I'm going through backward, looking for the start but running into dead ends with every turn I venture down.

You don't have a show tonight.

Fred is working today.

You probably still have time before the blackmailer's people are able to crack the security measures Fionna put on the drive.

"Any word yet on if that drive has been hacked into?" I ask her.

She shakes her head. "Good so far. I'll be notified as soon as someone gets through the firewalls and attempts to access the files. Could be soon. Could be never."

We have shift information and passcodes for accessing Building A-13 at Groom Lake.

If you're going to do this, today is the day.

Now is the time.

Somehow all of this ties back to whatever lies in that building.

I turn to Xavier. "I think it's time to call Fred."

"And?"

"And see if he'll help us get into Area 51."

"Now you're talking." He draws out his cell and starts punching in numbers.

"Hang on," Fionna says in her mom tone. "I've been thinking about this since you brought it up last night. Do you have any idea how absurd this plan is? Groom Lake is one of the most secure military installations on the planet."

"True," Xav acknowledges. "But we do have the security firm's shift rotations and access codes. And we have a man on the inside."

She doesn't look convinced.

"Let's at least see what Fred says, see if he found out what's in this mysterious Building A-13."

He puts the call through. We can only hear his side of the conversation; unfortunately, it doesn't sound like he's finding out what he was hoping to.

Finally, he hangs up. "Well, there's some good news and some bad news. Actually, a couple pieces of both."

"Start with some of the bad news," Charlene says.

"He doesn't know what's in A-13. That's bad, but it's attached to a hangar, which means—"

"Experimental aircraft."

"Most likely. Yes."

"I'm confused"—it's Fionna—"is that good news or bad news?"

"I call it good. But back to bad news: we'll be needing a white 2012 Chevy Silverado or we're never going to make it onto the property."

"And the good news?" I ask.

"You have an American Express black card."

Silverado

Jesús Garcia watched the news report about Tomás Agcaoili's untimely death, then checked in with his associates in Las Vegas and found out that they had not made any progress in deciphering the USB drive yet.

The level of security convinced Jesús that the drive was authentic.

Well, the computer technicians who worked for the Los Zetas cartel knew what they were doing. They would get through the firewalls by tonight, and even if Colonel Byrne wasn't successful in getting the information from the engineer, Jesús would still get the drone.

For years the cartels had been trying to get their hands on one of the US government's drones. And now they would have one that was not only armed and able to autonomously target and fire on whoever the cartel decided were its enemies, it was also able to be controlled by the mere thoughts of a pilot on the ground.

And once they had it in hand, they would be able to reverse engineer it and develop their own fleet of drones to patrol the borders, the crops, the farms that they were hoping to control.

The drones would provide not just an eye in the sky but a finger on the trigger.

Or at least, the *thought* of a finger on the trigger.

Which, in the wars of the future, was going to be more than enough.

As far as dealing with Fred, Jesús wasn't petty and he wasn't interested in ruining the man's life unnecessarily, so he held back from posting the photos online.

Instead, he took some time to confirm the arrangements with his people to make sure they would be on hand tonight when the drone landed in Mexico.

Before leaving to go truck shopping, we make some calls.

We can't find any dealers with white 2012 Silverados, but we do find a new 2013, and the guy on the phone assures us that it's not that much different than the previous year's model. "She's a beaut and I can fix you up with her today. She's just sittin' right here on the lot waitin' for someone to drive her home."

On our tight time frame I decide it's best if we just go for it.

But before we leave, Xavier checks his texts and tells us, "Looks like a tad bit more bad news. We're gonna need radios. That's how the Cammo dudes communicate between trucks. If we don't have one we'll stick out like a sore thumb."

"Any good news related to that?"

"What about the walkie-talkies at the warehouse?" he suggests. "You know how we used to use them to talk to the stagehands and the guys in the lighting booth in the back of the auditorium? You still have 'em stored over there."

"Do any of them still work?"

"They do. But I don't know if they'll be the right frequency, or the right model, that sort of thing. I'd say I doubt we'll be that lucky, but it's worth a shot. We can take 'em along."

We have radio patches that we use now. They're nearly transparent and you wear them behind your ear, but that was obviously not what we were looking for in this case.

"While you guys go buy the truck, I'll go grab the walkie-talkies," Charlene says. "Save some time."

"Okay, one more thing." Xavier is looking at his cell phone screen. "Fred says we'll need to have our paperwork in order."

This is just getting better and better.

"What paperwork?"

"He's sending a link to some online forms we'll need from their security firm. And if we're going to show up, that means someone else needs to *not* show up."

Fionna offers to take care of that while we're gone. "Once I'm on the website I'll send a message to the two guys who're supposed to be showing up for work this afternoon, tell them there's been a scheduling change."

"Great," Xavier says.

"Don't be too long getting that truck." She's studying the files she pulled up from the USB drive. "It looks like if we're going to make this work, you'll need to be entering Groom Lake by 5:15. That's when the shift change occurs."

From there, things move quickly.

I put the truck on my AMEX Centurion Card, and we zip back home to get the walkie-talkies from Charlene and the completed paperwork from Fionna. She has also printed out the access codes and passwords from the USB drive.

"You think we should bring the drive along with us?" Xavier asks.

"I'd rather leave it here." *Just in case we get arrested*, I think, but say, "Just to be safe."

Fionna slips it into her purse.

The pickup only has dealer plates on it. My "BANKS1" plates won't work, Xavier's "UFOHNTR" probably wouldn't be a good choice, and Fionna's minivan plates are from Chicago, so we end up using the plates from Charlene's car.

"This might be a problem," Xav notes. "They're not government-issued like the ones on Fred's truck. Remember? When Fionna ran his plates?"

"I have a friend at the DMV," she informs us. "I'll see if we can get this pickup registered under the right name for those plates, at least temporarily, in case they run them at the base."

"It's Sunday afternoon," I remind her. "The DMV's not open."

"My friend works flexible hours."

I have the sense that her "friend" might actually be her computer and that she's going to do a little work that might not be best to mention to us, but either way I trust she knows what she's doing. "Alright. Great."

She checks the names on the staff rotation. "Jevin, we'll make you Colin McIntyre. Xavier, you're Aurelio Gonzalez."

"*Sí,*" Xavier replies.

I promise Charlene that I'll look before I leap, if it comes to that.

"Just don't do anything stupid."

"And how does sneaking onto Area 51 with Xavier *not* fall into that category."

"Well. Good point."

"Listen, how about you and Fionna look into the RixoTray researcher Dr. Schatzing, see what you can find out about him and his connection with Emilio. Now that we know what we're looking for, maybe you can pull something up from Emilio's computer files, something that'll give us an in for talking with him."

"Sounds like a plan."

She gives me a kiss. In the other room Fionna is passing a folded-up clump of papers to Xavier. "I didn't have time to tell you this earlier," she explains softly. "Read it on the way."

Then we call upstairs to tell the kids we'll see them later, say goodbye to the women, and take off in the Silverado. Though I'm curious, I don't ask Xav about the papers that I saw Fionna slip to him.

"Can you think of anything else we might need?" I ask him.

"Just one thing."

"What's that?"

"Camo. We can't forget our camo."

"I don't think we have time to go camo shopping, Xav."

"We're going to have to make time. We can't imitate Cammo dudes dressed like this."

The second sporting goods store we call has what we need, and thankfully, it's on the way out of town.

We touch base with Fionna and confirm that the other two Cammo dudes who were scheduled to show up for work this afternoon won't be coming.

"Don't forget, you need to check in at 5:15," she reminds me. "And don't be late."

"Gotcha. 5:15." I check the clock in the car. "We should be fine."

At last we're on our way to the west entrance to Groom Lake to see if we can really get into Area 51 without being arrested.

I drive while Xavier unfolds the papers Fionna handed him and begins to read.

Outside the Box

3:46 p.m.
5 hours left

Akio Takahashi watched the undersecretary study the blueprints he'd dug up.

She was taking her time, and he didn't know if that was a good sign or not.

They did not contain any information about the secret fourth sublevel, but she might be suspicious.

She'd mentioned that a friend of hers had told her about recent undisclosed research findings on the "bionic forefront."

But who? Could it be someone on the project? They were all thoroughly vetted, so that seemed unlikely. But if not, who could have found out about that?

Obviously, someone had access to the information, or she wouldn't have heard about it.

As he was sorting things through, the undersecretary straightened up but said nothing, just stared at him.

He smiled. "Satisfied?"

She took a deep breath.

Akio waited anxiously.

"Yes."

He barely managed to hold back a sigh of relief. "Well. That's good, then. So, alright. And will there be anything else I can help you with?"

"No." She gathered her things. "The oversight committee will be in touch." She gave no indication if they would be giving him good news or bad.

"Of course," he managed to say. "Would you like me to walk you to the—"

"I've just spent how long studying your building's blueprints? I think I can find my way to the front door on my own."

"Certainly. Of course."

She gave him a clipped goodbye and headed for the door.

When it'd closed behind her, Akio finally let out that sigh and slumped into his chair.

It looked like he'd dodged a bullet. He decided to wait until she was past security, just to be sure, before placing a call to Colonel Byrne to update him.

And to let him know that someone had been in touch with the undersecretary, sharing details that should have—without a doubt—remained under wraps.

<hr />

Curiosity gets the best of me.

"Hey, Xav, can I ask you what you're reading? What Fionna gave you back at the house?"

"Her answer to my question yesterday."

"And that was?"

"Why she doesn't want her kids reading the classics."

Ah.

Yes, that's right.

I almost forgot about that.

"What does she say?"

"Let's see . . ." He shows me that there are three pages of meticulously written notes. "Read it or summarize it for you?"

"A summary is good."

"Give me a sec."

As Undersecretary Williamson drove away from the Plyotech Cybernetics R&D facility, she put a call through.

A voice answered. "Yes?"

"Reschedule my flight. I'm going to be staying the night in Vegas."

"Yes, ma'am."

"It's here. They're hiding it. I'm not sure where, maybe another level that doesn't appear on the schematics."

"What do you propose we do?"

"I'll call you later. In the meantime, I'm going to pay a visit to a friend of mine to find out what's really going on here."

"Well, she actually makes some good points," Xavier tells me.

"I'm all ears."

"For starters, does anyone cry today when they read—or watch— *Hamlet*?"

"I'd have to say probably not too many, no."

"That's what she says too. But people will cry watching a Hallmark commercial. Why?"

"Hmm. I guess because we have to mentally translate Shakespeare, and the story becomes an intellectual exercise rather than an emotionally engaging experience."

"Exactly. And, as Fionna says, 'By forcing students to read stories that don't emotionally resonate with them, we systematically teach them to hate reading. It's happened to a lot of kids.'"

I can't argue with that. I hated some of the "classics" I had to read in high school and college.

"And," he continues, "she believes that the classics weren't as well written as stories are today. The authors simply didn't have the ability to edit and word process like we do today, so they were forced to settle for manuscripts that were *good enough* rather than the *best possible*. A good author today might edit a scene twenty or thirty times. Can you imagine retyping *War and Peace* or *Moby-Dick* thirty times?"

"That's not really how I'd like to spend an afternoon. Or every afternoon. For a year."

"Me neither. She points out that writers a couple hundred years ago didn't have as much competition as writers do today, so they didn't need to be as good to get an audience. They could . . . let's see . . ."

He flips to the next page. "I'll just read this part. 'Writers in the past relied on gimmicks that are too puerile for today's narratively astute and discerning readers. For example, Charles Dickens often used coincidence to solve his plot problems. It's lazy writing, and contemporary readers know that and expect better stories. You just can't make that fly today. You can't introduce characters, develop them, and then just discard them (i.e., *Les Misérables*). Or be heavy-handed and didactic (*Pilgrim's Progress*) or all but incomprehensible (*Ulysses*). Marketable stories today (that is, stories people read because they want to, not because they were told they're supposed to) have to be, and are, better crafted.'"

"Wow. And this from a homeschooling mom."

He considers that. "Maybe homeschooling isn't a lost cause after all." He peruses the sheets. "There's one last section here. The competition part. 'Today hundreds of thousands of titles are published every year. Obviously that wasn't the case a couple hundred years ago. Today's writers are competing for people's attention against millions of other writers, billions of websites and blogs, not to mention video games, television, Facebook updates, tweets, movies, and so on. They have to be better just to survive.'"

"What about the test of time? Remember how she told us that *The Catcher in the Rye* and *Silas Marner* hadn't stood the test of time?"

"Well, she says that the test of time is if people in the future still want to read a book and don't just do so under threat of punishment."

"A bad grade."

"Exactly. A book you're forced to read but would never read if you had the choice hasn't stood the test. So, Poe's stories have stood the test of time, *The Lord of the Rings* has stood the test of time; *Silas Marner* has not."

"Fionna sure thinks outside the box."

"Yes." Xavier seems deep in thought. "She does."

Undersecretary Williamson found out that her friend wouldn't be able to meet until seven.

It wasn't what she'd been hoping to hear, but she went ahead and set up the meeting at the Arête.

Which was, as it turned out, the most natural place for the two of them to have their chat.

Charlene helped Fionna look through Emilio's files, following up on any references to Dr. Schatzing, RixoTray's progeria researcher.

As she did, she told herself not to worry about Jevin and Xavier. They were big boys. They could take care of themselves.

No, she didn't want to be clingy or overprotective. No, no, of course not. She didn't want Jevin to change for her. The very fact that he was a bold, adventurous adrenaline junkie was one of the things that had attracted her to him in the first place.

And, yet, in a way she did want him to change.

It was all very confusing, as if something was getting lost between her head and her heart.

She didn't think it was fair of her to ask him to give up something essential about who he was just to be with her, but if he didn't, she was afraid she might lose him for good.

You have to let go of someone to let him fly free, but if you don't hold on to him you might lose what you care about the most.

The house phone rang, and Fionna looked at her strangely. "I didn't even know that was connected. The whole time we were house-sitting here it hasn't rung."

Charlene eyed it.

"So you'll text, no problem," Fionna said, "but you really don't like talking on the phone."

"No I do not."

"Why is that?"

"Call it a quirk."

The phone continued to ring.

"Should I answer it?" Fionna asked.

"Not too many people have this number," Charlene muttered.

Another ring.

Maddie's voice floated down from upstairs. "Should I get that, Mom?"

"We got it," Fionna called back, then asked Charlene, "Well?"

Charlene finally picked up. "Hello?"

"Yes, this is Clive Fridell. I was looking for Jevin Banks. I tried his cell but he's not picking up."

"Mr. Fridell? This is Charlene Antioch, his assistant. We've met a few times."

"Yes, yes, of course, Miss Antioch. I didn't recognize your voice. Good to speak with you." She got the impression that he really did remember her and really was glad to be talking with her. "Is Jevin there?"

"He's out, I'm afraid. Running errands." She decided not to elaborate: *He's currently sneaking into a top-secret military installation. May I take a message?*

"And how is he? I mean, after last night? Be honest, now."

"He's alright. He's a pretty resilient guy."

"That he is. I'm glad to hear he's recovering. And how have you been through all of this?"

"I'm good. Thank you for asking."

"Well, I told him I'd call back when I knew more about the status of tomorrow evening's show. I've been talking with our lawyers and it looks like we're a go. But the piranha tank is out, I'm afraid. We'll be removing it in the morning."

That was going to be a chore. She had no idea how they were going to get it off the stage before the evening show.

"Jevin won't be happy to hear that." Actually, she wasn't either. It was going to be hard to top that for their finale.

"I understand, but some matters are out of my hands. Oh, one other thing. Emilio had a locker that he used when he performed here. As I understand it, he didn't have any family in the area?"

"That's right. We're taking care of his estate."

"Perhaps you or Jevin would like to pick up his things. There are a few notebooks and some paraphernalia for a couple tricks. It's not much, but I don't want the box to get lost or misplaced."

"Are you there now?"

"We have the items in the security office."

"I should be able to come by tonight. If that'll work."

"No rush. Give me a call when you get here."

"I will."

"See you soon."

He told her his cell number and they ended the call.

Then Charlene went back to helping Fionna with her research.

But, honestly, it was hard to concentrate.

Her thoughts of Jevin just wouldn't leave her alone.

And now, her curiosity about what might be in Emilio's notebooks was edging in, a close second.

Groom Lake

4:46 p.m.
4 hours left

In the late afternoon sunlight, desolate mountains rise in the distance.

As we approach the base, we review the information from the files Fionna pulled up. I can't help but think of our discussions regarding the essence of human nature, and that sends my thoughts back to the sermon from this morning, to the paradox of terror and beauty that the missionary pointed out lies at the heart of this imperfect world.

I summarize the message as concisely as I can for Xav—the incongruity between who we are and who we aspire to be, what we dream of and the nightmares we have to live through.

"I wonder if that's what makes us different from machines," he reflects.

"What's that? Being incongruous?"

"In a way, yes. Or free will, the ability to choose. We're not programmed to do it."

I think of equivoque, or the magician's choice, when the person we're doing an effect for appears to have free will but doesn't. We force him to choose a specific card or we don't tell the audience what we're going to do, so we still have control over the outcome. Then we can

333

adapt to what they choose to make things end the way we want. It's one of the keys to mentalism. "Like a psychological force."

"But the deal is, in real life we have freedom, the ability to do otherwise, and no one is out there stacking the deck against us. If free will didn't exist, all societies would have to abandon their justice systems because behavior would simply be hardwired in our brains."

"And you can't hold someone accountable for an action if he can't do otherwise, if he has no actual freedom to resist that act."

"Right. A world without a belief in free will would be one without accountability. And, I guess when you think about it, it'd also be one without punishment for criminals. In fact, no concept of crime or morality or right and wrong at all—that's our turn up ahead. About a quarter mile from here."

I slow down and look for the turn, but all I see is an unmarked, dusty road off to the left up ahead. "That's it?"

"Yup. It goes a couple of miles across public land. They use dust, not gravel. It's so the Cammo dudes can see any vehicles approaching."

"They can probably see us from a mile out."

"At least."

I turn onto the vacant road, sending a cloud of dust trailing in the pickup's wake. "So you're saying that we can create machines that respond to algorithms, make decisions based on complex protocols and vast amounts of data, but the machines can't choose to go against them. You can have all sorts of robot laws, but as long as they have to follow them, they're not free."

"Right. Machines don't choose to go against protocol, but we do. Humans do. We're incongruous, like you said a minute ago. We go against our nature. That's why we hold people responsible for their actions. We wouldn't condemn a drone to be destroyed—the same as a death sentence for a human—because of firing a missile at a civilian or for following its protocol or being true to its mission. No, we would hold the human designers or software producers responsible."

My thoughts float back to what we were talking about yesterday: computer technicians being held accountable for war crimes when all they did was program in a certain algorithm.

Our conversation trails off and silence takes over. I have the sense that, for both of us, it's a lot to think about. Especially considering the autonomous weaponry and unmanned aircraft we know—or at least highly suspect—is being tested and manufactured here at Groom Lake.

Aircraft that can, for all intents and purposes, choose on its own when to fire and who to target.

⁘ ⸺ •••

Calista was impressed with how well Jeremy Turnisen was holding out keeping the launch code sequences from Derek.

She couldn't tell if Derek was getting frustrated or not. He was not an easy person to read.

"I know you've been developing drones that can fly autonomously," Derek told Jeremy. "Unmanned aerial vehicles that can be flown using the neural impulses of pilots in remote locations."

"Thought-controlled drones?" Jeremy gasped. "This is crazy. I'm telling you, I'm not the man you're looking for. Please, you have to—"

Derek went on unfazed. "I want one of the drones you've developed. I have someone waiting across the border in Mexico to take delivery of it. All I need from you is the updated launch codes for tonight's test flight, and we can both be done with this unpleasant business."

He removed the robotic arm from the suitcase in the corner of the room. He placed the needle between its thumb and forefinger, set the arm on the floor next to Jeremy's leg, and removed the man's left shoe.

Apparently he was going to use it to do some of the stitching.

Calista had been sitting on the bed doing her nails. Now she stood and entered the conversation. "Just tell him, Jeremy. I'm serious. I have stuff to do, and things are just gonna get worse for you if you don't."

"You should listen to her," Derek said. "She knows what she's talking about."

Jeremy took a deep, painful breath. "I don't know any launch codes. Please, just let me go. I won't press charges. I swear, I just—"

Calista rolled her eyes. "Derek, maybe he's telling the truth."

"Dear, perhaps you'd like to watch some TV. Leave the two of us alone."

"Whatever." She left for the other room of the suite.

Condescension. No, she wasn't stupid. And feeling talked down to was not something she liked.

Yeah, sometimes Derek was sweet to her, but sometimes, like right now, she didn't like the way he talked to her.

Not at all.

"Try the walkie-talkies," I tell Xavier.

He goes through the channels and can't find any signal from another unit. "Strike one. Let me check the cells."

He pulls them out while I drive. "Looks like we have a couple of bars out here. Surprises me a little—we're in the middle of nowhere. Not great for conversations, but we should be able to text. I'll give it a provisional strike two."

Eventually, we come to a small parking area and a sign prohibiting photography. The road continues to the west. There's no gate, but there is another prominent sign, this one warning that deadly force can be used on anyone caught on the property.

"That's gotta count as strike three," I say.

"Don't worry, they don't usually shoot people. They just detain you and then turn you over to the sheriff's department for trespassing."

"And you know this from firsthand experience?"

"Yeah, a couple of them. But I only had to spend a few nights in jail. Nothing serious."

"Ah. But they could shoot us."

"Theoretically."

"The sign doesn't say anything about *theoretical* deadly force."

"I've never heard of anyone actually getting shot."

"Have you ever heard of someone impersonating Cammo dudes and driving all the way to the research area of the base?"

He hesitates. "Not recently."

"Remind me once again why we're here?"

"To find out why Emilio was murdered. And to find out who was ultimately behind it."

I let the truck idle and consider what Charlene told me, the look in her eyes when I mentioned that I hadn't thought of her before leaping off the cliff in the Philippines.

Finally, Xav breaks the silence. "We could turn back."

"Yes, we could."

"If we drive any farther we'll officially be in deep—well, I think you probably know—if we get caught."

"You mean *when*," I say. "You don't think we're actually going to be able to pull this off without getting caught, do you?"

"Well, we can at least hope we will—get caught, that is."

"You're hoping we'll get caught?"

"Yeah. Instead of shot."

"Oh."

"Theoretically."

"Right."

I look at him. "We still have eight miles to go?"

"It's a couple more miles from there to where we're supposed to be meeting Fred. But yeah, eight miles to the front gate."

"You mean to the security guards at the front gate. The ones authorized to use deadly force on trespassers."

"Pretty much. Remember last night when Fred said that the codes looked legit?"

"Yes."

"Let's hope he was right."

For a long moment neither of us speaks.

Then I pull forward off the public land onto the outer fringes of Area 51.

PART VII

Secrets

We arrive at the first security checkpoint at 5:21 p.m.

Six minutes late.

Fionna had warned us to make sure we were here by 5:15 and I'd assured her that we would be, but the drive along the dirt road had taken longer than either Xavier or I anticipated.

Now, I wonder if our little venture into Area 51 is going to be cut short before it has a chance to really begin.

We have the wrong-year vehicle.

The truck has Charlene's plates.

And it's brand-new.

However, thankfully, after driving along the dust-covered road, the vehicle doesn't look new at all but rather like it's already seen better days.

Parked beside the guard shack are two white pickups similar to the one I'm driving. The one closest to us has two men in the front seat, and when they see us drive up, they take off in the direction we just came from, obviously confident we're their shift change replacements.

Two more Cammo dudes are standing guard by the other truck. I wave to them as if I know them, hoping it'll be enough to get us through, but it's not.

One of the guys steps in front of our truck and holds up a hand, palm facing us: *Stop.*

The other man studies us coolly from the side of the road.

I brake and let the engine idle.

The guard has a semiautomatic machine gun slung across his shoulder. He approaches my door, and when I roll down my window he asks us for our paperwork.

I hand him the papers Fionna printed out for us at my house.

He stares at the top page, then at us. "Gonzalez and McIntyre?"

"Sí." Xavier goes for a Spanish accent but he sounds about as Hispanic as Arnold Schwarzenegger does.

"And you're McIntyre?" the guy asks me.

"Yes."

"Hmm." He studies my face, then eyes Xavier. "You two new?"

"We've been working on the other side of the base," Xavier explains with his distinctive accent. "First shift over here."

"So you guys know Redmond, then?"

I try to read his expression, his inflection, try to tell if he's testing us or not. He might just be making up the name to see if we're legit or not.

He waits.

"Redmond." Xavier shakes his head and says cryptically, "I shoulda known."

"So you do know her?"

"We worked on the other side of the base." Xavier manages to make it sound like a subtle rebuke. "What do you think?"

It looks like the guy's not quite sure how to take that. He glances at his watch. "You know how they can be when we don't show up on time."

"Don't we ever," I agree.

"Why didn't you radio in?"

I show him one of our walkie-talkies and then toss it to the floor. "Broken."

342

"That's not even the right model."

"No kidding," I grumble.

Again he looks a little unsure how to respond. "Hang on a sec. Let me call in the plates."

"It's a new truck," I explain. "They told me to use my personal plates until they could issue the official ones."

Without giving any indication of what he thinks of that, he leaves for the guard shack.

"Well," Xavier says softly, "let's see if Fionna's friend came through for us."

"Do you think the guy was just testing us with the whole Redmond deal?"

"Hard to say."

We wait.

Maybe he isn't calling in the plates. Maybe he's calling in for backup.

At last the Cammo dude stops tapping at the keyboard and approaches us again.

Alright.

Here we go.

He walks up to my window without saying a word, then hands the papers back to me. "Have a good one out there. Watch out for UFO nuts."

"We will," Xavier says.

"There are a lot of weirdos out there."

"Yes, there are." His accent is getting worse each time he speaks. Reminds me of Kevin Costner in his Robin Hood movie.

Before the guy has a chance to change his mind, I pull forward. "And Fionna comes through again."

"She deserves a raise."

"Buy her something nice for Valentine's Day and I'm sure she'll call us even."

"I'll do my best to come up with something memorable."

Derek was in the bathroom washing the blood off his hands when he suggested they go down and grab some dinner. Calista offered to get the food and bring it back up for them.

"No. I'll come with you."

She eyed the engineer. "Leave him here?"

"He's not going anywhere."

He confirmed that Turnisen was bound and securely gagged. As they exited the room he placed the "Shh. Do not disturb" sign on the door handle.

The engineer still hadn't shared anything helpful with them. For his sake, Calista wished he would just tell them what they were trying to find out.

She couldn't help it: she was beginning to wonder if maybe he didn't know the information Derek was looking for.

It was possible.

If that was the case, she didn't know how she was going to get what she wanted, what Derek had promised her—the secret to lasting youth.

They took the elevator down to one of the Arête's four-star restaurants.

But how is this guy Turnisen connected to any of that anyway?

She really didn't know.

They ordered.

Something was on her mind. She'd spoken with Derek about it before but had never gotten a satisfactory answer.

After their server was gone, Calista said, "I need you to be honest with me."

"Of course."

"Why did you choose the name Akinsanya—'the hero avenges'? Are you the hero?"

"I aspire to be."

"Who are you trying to avenge?"

"The ultimate enemy. The enemy of us all."

She pondered that. "Death."

He looked impressed. "Exactly."

"That's why you want to upload your consciousness onto a computer. To live forever."

"Yes."

No one lives forever.

Especially not when they cross the avenging hero.

It was one secret she knew.

Yes, they were beholden to each other.

Beholden.

For a moment she thought about secrets, about all that they mean, about the power that they have.

When she first met Derek, she had a secret and he had found it out—she'd killed her best friend.

And he had taught her to kill again.

I know something you don't know.

A secret I won't share.

All of that had brought them together in a way that was powerful and intriguing on so many levels.

It reminded her again of that story by Poe, *The Tell-Tale Heart.* A guilty conscience will drive you mad.

As her teacher had told her when they were studying the tale, "A secret held too close will try to climb to the surface, even if it has to scratch through your sanity to do it."

Now she said to Derek, "We all want someone to tell our secrets to, but we want one secret, always at least one secret, to keep to ourselves. Because when we are fully known—"

"We are fully vulnerable."

"Yes. Which is why those who know us best can hurt us the most."

"That's a keen observation."

She watched him sip his water. "Have you been keeping any secrets from me?"

He set down the glass. "Why do you ask?"

"Curiosity."

"And control?"

"Maybe."

He evaluated that. "Well, yes, I have kept some things from you."

"Like?"

He scratched at the side of his chin. "Why are you asking me this now, Calista? As you said a few minutes ago, we all have the desire to keep at least one secret to ourselves, to be known but not fully known."

"I want to know you fully."

So that you can control him?

Is that all this is to you?

No.

It suddenly struck her.

Love, intimacy, was not just about the power that you hold over your lover, but about the power that you give up to be loved.

Okay, are you saying you want him to love you?

And then the answer came, blunt and clear and surprising: *I want someone to.*

Like with Roger Yarborough, the guy she'd picked up the other night for the dry run with Derek. She'd left a message on his mirror for him to go back to his wife. Whether or not he did, she had no idea. But that he would do so, that he would stop lying to her, stop deceiving her—that would be the way for him to show her real love.

No, Calista did not like it that Derek had just admitted that he'd kept things from her.

"What about you?" he asked her. "Have you kept anything from me? Any secrets you haven't been willing to share? Anything that would help me to know you fully?"

She hesitated slightly. It was kind of weird getting into all this now, but things were coming to a head this week and she was going to get what she wanted—the ability to stay young, desirable, attractive.

"Well?" he said.

"I am more afraid of growing old than I am of dying."

He was quiet.

"Your turn. Your secret. Is there another woman?"

"No."

"A man?"

"No."

"Then what have you been keeping from me?"

He tilted his head slightly, stared at her as if she were a curiosity, a specimen rather than the woman he had been sleeping with for nearly four years.

"I drug you sometimes."

"What?"

"At night. Before you go to sleep, I drug your drinks so you won't wake up in the mornings until I'm done with you."

A flush of uneasiness. "What do you mean, until you're done with me?"

"Doing as I please with you. While you sleep."

She stared at him for a long moment.

"There. Now we have everything out in the open." He reached across the table and offered her his hand. "No more secrets. We can enjoy our meal and no more—"

She pushed her chair back from the table.

"Oh, don't be like that." There was that condescension in his voice again, and she hated, *hated* when people talked to her like that.

She walked around the table.

And slapped him.

He just directed his gaze back at her, the blood already seeping from his lip. He used a finger to dab some away and rubbed it between his fingers but didn't say a word.

Calista turned and strode away amid the gasps of the people sitting nearby.

He betrayed you! He took advantage of you! He lied to you and he thought it was no big deal!

Oh, she could tell he wasn't sorry, he wasn't sorry at all. He thought it was all some sort of game.

All he cared about was himself—about getting these codes from this man up in their room.

Now, that's where she headed: to Jeremy, who waited helplessly for her, and the one who was avenging death, to return.

The Green Door

There are two more security checkpoints.

The first one goes smoothly.

At the final guard station, a fifteen-foot-high metal fence rimmed with razor wire stretches out of sight in both directions. Jagged, tire-piercing spikes like rental car places use to keep you from stealing cars off their lots rise from a section of paved road in front of us.

Apparently, no one has radioed in that we're on our way because they're not expecting us when we arrive.

Unlike the other two checkpoints, which were staffed by Cammo dudes, this station is manned by Air Force Security Forces Specialists, and they're taking their job very seriously. While one of them inspects the paperwork, two others bring out bomb-sniffing dogs and a mirror sweep to check under the pickup for explosives.

No banter. No joking around. No conversation at all.

Xavier and I wait anxiously for them to finish their inspection.

∙◦═◦∙

Charlene's thoughts were drifting toward what might be contained in Emilio's notebooks, and she was about to suggest that they go and pick them up when Fionna said softly, "I might have something on Dr. Schatzing."

"What is it?"

"So I was doing some checking on his phone records, right? And—"

"Wait, Fionna. Is that even legal?"

"It is when you have a contract with Verizon to see if you can break into their system. Landed it last month. You wouldn't believe how often it's already come in handy."

"I can only imagine."

"Anyway, our friend here makes a lot of calls to a certain escort agency. High-end girls." She pulled up a file and highlighted the appropriate data on the screen. "It looks like he enjoys the company of a female companion two nights a week."

Charlene pointed to another recurring number, this time on his incoming calls. "What's this?"

"Let's find out."

After a few seconds of typing, Fionna said, "Looks like that's from the security guard station at the entrance to his gated community."

"They ring him when the girls arrive."

"Yup."

For a moment it seemed like neither one of them was sure where to take things from there. Finally, Fionna suggested, "I think we should call him and ask about Emilio, how he knew him, if he might know who could have been behind his death. Just be up-front about it. Why not? What do we have to lose?"

Charlene stared at the phone.

"Oh. Right." Fionna picked it up. "I'll do it."

She punched in a number and started with her name, but was quickly cut short. Fionna listened for a few seconds, and before she could get out a full explanation, whoever had answered hung up.

Finally, she did as well. "I think I actually found someone who likes talking on the phone less than you do."

"No easy task."

"No it's not. But if I repeated what he told me to do to myself for disturbing him, I think you'd agree with me."

"I'll take your word for it."

Fionna screwed up her mouth. "So where does that leave us?"

The incoming calls from the subdivision's security entrance came like clockwork at eight o'clock nearly every Saturday and Sunday night.

A plan was forming in Charlene's mind.

It was ludicrous.

But maybe it wasn't so ludicrous after all.

"I'm not sure," she replied, caught up in her thoughts.

Fionna stretched, then cracked her neck. "I should probably spend some time with my kids. They'll be wanting supper pretty soon, and I'm not sure what else to do on this front. If Schatzing won't talk to us, we'll just have to wait until Jevin and Xavier get back from Groom Lake and figure out a plan then."

But Charlene was already figuring one out.

What are you even thinking? Go get the box of Emilio's things, look through them. Decide then. You should still have time.

"Tell you what, why don't we take the kids out, get a bite to eat at Jenny's Grille at the Arête. We can pick up Emilio's things from Clive Fridell while we're there. Who knows, maybe there's something in them that can give us a clue as to how to move forward."

"Hmm . . . We *are* kind of in vacation mode. I suppose eating out one more time this week would be alright. I'll round 'em up."

"I'll make the arrangements with Fridell."

Officer Gordon Shepard cussed, then called Jesús Garcia. "It wasn't them."

"What?"

"Banks and Antioch. It wasn't them. We were following lookalikes.

They were gambling and signing autographs here, but then I heard one of the security guards mutter something to his buddy about 'em. I showed him my badge, asked him about it. Turns out he knows Banks and Antioch, works their shows. These two are their body doubles."

"Clever." Garcia sounded more impressed than upset. "And so you have no idea where Antioch and Banks really are?"

"No. Unless they're still at the house."

"Where are you?"

"Still at the Arête."

"Stay there until I contact you. I have a couple calls to make."

"We need to check in at the station, put on our blues, get the patrol car."

"When?"

"Within the hour."

"I should be able to get back to you by then."

It takes nearly fifteen minutes, but at last the Air Force personnel clear us and return the clipboard to me. "Alright. You're clear to Gate 11. You know the routine."

"Sure," I tell him. "Thanks."

He presses a button and the spikes in the road retract, allowing us to drive forward. Then he steps aside and waves us through.

I ease past the razor-wire fence, over the retracted spikes, and onto the military installation itself.

"We did it." My voice is soft. Almost reverent. "We're here."

A nod. Xavier looks like he's in a daze. He's dreamed of coming here for years, and I can see it's a little overwhelming to him to finally be on the installation.

"Now we just need to find Building A-13," I say.

"Stay on this road for now. I'll give you the directions."

"I wonder if it's where they keep the Ark of the Covenant hidden. You know, like from the *Indiana Jones* movies?"

Xavier is quiet.

"I was kidding, Xav."

"I know. The Ark of the Covenant is really in Ethiopia. In Aksum. It's guarded by virgin Coptic Christian monks who aren't allowed to ever leave the chapel's property, where it rests, after they've been anointed to be its protectors."

I can't tell if he's being serious or not. "Really?"

"If you believe the stories."

"And do you?"

He gives me an answer that's not quite an answer. "You know me."

"Oh. Right."

I performed a show at Nellis AFB right near Vegas, and Groom Lake reminds me of it.

Landing strips, yes. Aircraft hangars, yes. Administration and research buildings, yes, all of that.

The base is extensive, and I'm not too excited about the idea of driving around looking for the right hangar, especially in the waning sunlight. I don't expect that we're going to find any placards with a "You are here!" arrow on them, so I'm glad Xav spoke with Fred earlier about the base layout. I trust he'll be able to direct me.

There are a few military vehicles, some civilian cars, and other white pickups around, but there's not a lot of traffic on the roads, and having never been here before, I'm not sure if that's normal or just a result of being here on a Sunday evening.

Now that we're on the base itself there doesn't appear to be as much of a security presence.

Which actually does make sense. Just like in airports after you pass through the TSA checkpoints: if you make it that far everyone assumes you're not a threat.

Xavier points. "Turn left up ahead."

"Fred's going to meet us there?"

"Last I heard, yeah."

The intersection, just like all the ones we've come to so far on the base, has no road signs.

"You're sure this is the way?"

"Pretty sure."

"Pretty sure."

"It should be a building with a green door. I'm not certain if it'll be labeled or not."

"A green door? That's all you have?"

"Green Door Tour. It goes back to Vietnam. They would mark the color of the door by the level of security clearance."

"And a green door was a high one?"

"The highest one."

We make two more turns and then come to a building with a Cammo dude truck parked out front.

A simple sign by the side of the structure reads: A-13.

As we pull up beside the other truck, I get a good look at the front of the building.

It has a green door.

Building A-13

Fred exits the other truck and hurries toward us. "You two are late."

"That last security checkpoint slowed us down," I explain.

"Well, this is as far as I go. We aren't allowed in any of the actual research buildings."

"But do you know what goes on in there?"

He's slow to answer. "I did some asking around. See that hangar over there?"

It was attached to the far end of the building. There was no way to miss it. "Yes."

"They're doing work on drones. That's all I know. Something with autonomously flown drones. Only a skeleton crew of people assigned to the project."

He scans the area. "I don't see any other vehicles around, so that's a good sign, but it's possible there are still some people inside. Personnel get dropped off, picked up around here all the time. From what I hear there's a test scheduled for later tonight. I'm not sure when people will start to arrive."

"Okay," Xavier tells him. "Thanks for your help. We'll be careful."

"I really don't think you should go in there." There's more than a little uneasiness in Fred's voice. "It's a miracle you've made it this far. I think you oughtta get out of here, go back home."

"We're here to see what all this has to do with the murder of our friend," I remind him. "And we're not turning around until we have some answers."

He bites his lip, looks around nervously, then leads us to the building and pulls out a security-coded swipe card.

"I managed to get this, but I need it back in thirty minutes. Got it? If I don't return it, we're all going down."

"That doesn't give us a lot of time," Xavier says. "Are you sure you can't—"

"Positive. Get in there, get what you need, and get out. But before you do anything, you need to move your truck." He points to a nearby maintenance building. "Park it behind there."

We hide the pickup, and when we return, he swipes the security card and points to the keypad. "Type in the code Fionna pulled up. That should get you in. From there, you're on your own."

I check the papers she gave us, punch in the number, the light beside the keypad turns green, and there's a click as the front door unlocks.

Fred hands me the card. "Thirty minutes."

"6:45. Gotcha."

"I'll meet you behind the maintenance building where you parked your truck. Don't be late."

Xavier thanks him one more time. We tell him goodbye, he leaves, and Xavier and I step inside Building A-13.

I close the door behind us.

A lobby. Beige. Spartan furniture. Lit by stark fluorescents overhead. Concrete block walls. The air in the building smells stale and musty. The AC is blasting through a vent right above our heads.

No one is here.

"What if we do meet someone?" Xavier asks me quietly. "How are we gonna explain what we're doing in here?"

That sign on the edge of the property warning about the use of deadly force pops to mind.

"I'm working on that." I pull out my phone.

"We checked on that earlier," Xav reminds me. "Remember? Only a couple bars."

"They have to communicate with each other somehow. And there were no landlines leading to this building."

"How do you know?"

"I was looking for them."

"Buried wires?"

I show him my phone. "Maybe. But I've got good reception here. It looks like they must have a cell tower here on this side of the base."

"That'll be good if we need to call for help." Then he adds reflectively, "Except most everyone around here would rather shoot us or arrest us."

"Thanks for that reminder there."

"No problem."

Hallways branch off from both sides. "So, split up or stick together?" I ask.

"Splitting up might save us time, but I vote we stick together."

"I'm good with that." I gesture toward the hallway on the right. "Let's start over here."

"And what exactly are we looking for again?"

"We need to find out what the research that's going on in this building has to do with Emilio's death."

Calista stood in the honeymoon suite staring at Jeremy Turnisen. Unconscious, gagged, legs still bound to the chair, hands drooped limply on his lap.

He was breathing weakly.

Derek had sewed the man's wrists together, piercing all the way through them with the needle and heavy suture thread before tugging it tight and wrapping it around several times, then tying it off.

Jeremy was missing three fingers, all severed cleanly from his left hand by one of the knives on the desk. The gruesome sewed-up incisions on his stomach and face defied description.

He was helpless. Vulnerable.

Just like Thad after they paralyzed him.

Just like you in the mornings when Derek has his way with you.

He betrayed you.

Drugged you.

Took advantage of you.

Derek wanted information from this man, but he hadn't been able to get it, even after spending the majority of the day interrogating him.

If that's what you want to call it.

Calista had no idea how long she might have before Derek decided to return to the room. Maybe he would finish eating, maybe he was already on his way up.

Through the open bathroom door she saw the drugs he'd used on Jeremy last night lying on the counter. *They're probably the same ones he uses on you.*

Anger sliced through her. What had he said earlier? That they usually put someone out for at least six or seven hours?

How much time did he spend with you in the mornings after he drugged you?

Despite herself she felt a chill.

She picked up one of the knives and approached the man in front of her.

There was a ton of blood on the plastic sheet, so she kicked off her shoes before stepping onto it.

The knife was brutally sharp. She already knew that from watching Derek work.

Derek.

The man who drugged her.

Just like he drugged this guy.

A squirm of disgust ran through her.

She remembered that first time she killed someone, the time when it was a mistake, when her friend was coming at her and she swiped that blade toward her stomach and it ended up cutting her open. It was disgusting. Disturbing. Messy.

No plastic sheet that time.

She watched Jeremy breathe, the gentle, somewhat uneven, rise and fall of his chest.

How much pain would he be in if he were awake?

Calista leaned forward.

If she did this, things would never be the same between her and Derek again.

They're already different.

Yes, yes they were.

And it was his fault, not hers.

If she did this, she might never get what she wanted, might never get the treatments he'd promised her.

But right now she wanted to punish Derek, the man who'd called her his courtesan and then treated her like his whore—punish him by not letting him find out what he'd been trying so hard all day to discover.

He'd taken advantage of her, and he admitted it right to her face and showed no remorse.

No. Of course not. She'd never seen him show remorse over anything.

Well, that was about to change.

She placed the blade carefully against the man's right wrist.

Steadied it.

Pressed down.

Drew it back sharply.

And cut through the black thread that was binding his wrists to-gether.

All we find down the first hallway is a series of a dozen sparsely furnished, crypt-like classrooms. The chairs and tables all look left over from the fifties. If this is a top-secret research facility, the government was obviously pouring its resources into something other than creating high-tech, twenty-first-century classrooms.

Chalkboards in two of the rooms contain indecipherable formulas. I take photos of them with my cell. Trying to figure them out might be a good school project for Lonnie.

Satisfied there's nothing more here for us to see, we venture back to the lobby to explore the other half of the building.

Apart from the humming rattle of the overtaxed air conditioner, everything is quiet and still.

If they are doing top-secret drone research here, then where are the computer labs? The control centers? This can't be the right place.

The other hallway has a number of classrooms similar to the ones we found earlier, but it also has a door at the end that requires us to swipe the security card again.

I pass the card through the reader, the door opens, and we get our first glimpse into the hangar attached to the back of Building A-13.

Descent

The hangar is dark, but the hallway light that seeps in from behind us is enough for me to see what's in here.

Three drones sit before us, sleek, stealthy, menacing. They almost look like living creatures lined up, ready and waiting here in their lair.

It's eerie.

I've seen drones before in movies, of course, and on the news, and they look stark and intimidating, but when you see them in person they're even more impressive.

Xavier walks over as if in a trance and reaches out to touch the one closest to us, but I grab his arm and hold him back. "What if they're wired like car alarms? That would not be a good thing."

"Yeah," he mutters, then points at two narrow missiles hanging from the bottom of it. "This puppy is armed."

I gaze around the hangar.

All of them are.

Suddenly, I really do not want to be here.

Glancing at my watch I see that we've already used up six of our precious minutes. Twenty-four left before we need to return the security pass card to Fred.

"You're the expert on Groom Lake. Any idea where we go from here?"

Xavier's eyes are still on the dimly lit drone. "No one's really an expert except the people who actually work here. But, from what I've read, most of the high-level research takes place underground. Bombproof command centers, that sort of thing. I say we look for an elevator."

In the faint light I study the wall of the building. It looks like there's a set of sliding doors at the far end near an exit door to the runway.

He's following my gaze. "You think that's it?"

I tap my phone's screen to use it as a flashlight. "Only one way to find out."

Calista was not able to wake up Jeremy Turnisen.

She realized she'd better hurry if she was really going to let him go free because Derek might be returning to the room any minute.

Or he might just be sitting down there taking his good old time enjoying his steak. Just remembering what it was like when he had his way with you.

Yeah, she could picture him doing that alright.

Either way, if she was going to free Jeremy she needed to wake him up.

"Hey." She slapped his face. "Jeremy, open your eyes."

His only reply was a soft groan.

She slapped him again, harder, and blood began to ooze out of one of the wounds Derek had given him and then sewed back up again.

Jeremy didn't awaken.

She cut the duct tape from his legs and wondered if she should just stop there, just take off, just leave the guy on his own to see if he could get away.

No.

He'd never make it out of the hotel.

And what message would that give Derek? That she was just act-

ing out and cut him free but didn't have the guts or the brains to see
things all the way through?

Okay, but how to get him out of the room?

She dead-bolted the door while she debated what to do.

⁂

Yes.

It's an elevator.

Next to it is a glass door that leads outside, and about a hundred
feet beyond the tarmac I can see the outline of the maintenance building we hid the truck behind.

Before stepping onto the elevator, I feel my cell phone vibrate and
find a text from Charlene that she's going to pick up some of Emilio's
notebooks that were found at the Arête.

Hmm.

Notebooks are good.

Notebooks might just mean answers.

Pocketing my phone, I swipe the key card, the elevator doors glide
open, and Xavier and I step inside.

There's only one button. Xavier presses it. "Well, here we go."

The doors close and we descend into the earth.

⁂

When Jesús Garcia's cell rang, he thought maybe it was his people
calling back about the two phone traces that he'd put into play, but
it was not.

"Sir, we made it through the USB drive, but it's empty."

"What do you mean, it's empty?"

"I mean, someone set this up so it would erase the files if you got
past the security measures."

"So recover them."

"We can't. The files are gone."

SINGULARITY

"They're not gone. They're—"

"I'm afraid they are, sir."

"Keep working on it."

A pause. "Yes, sir."

Garcia laid the phone down slowly.

The USB drive was a dead end.

Really? Was it really?

Well, if so, Colonel Byrne had better come through with the engineer or else that drone was not going to get delivered.

And if that was the case, there were definitely going to be consequences.

Fionna was in her minivan with her children en route to the Arête when her phone buzzed with a notification.

Charlene had mentioned that she had another errand to run later, so she'd driven separately, and now, not wanting to check her texts while driving, Fionna asked Lonnie, who was in the front passenger seat, to read it for her.

"It says the files were deleted."

Ah.

So, the blackmailer's people had finally managed to get through the security codes she'd put on the USB drive.

Now they had nothing.

But they also *knew* they had nothing.

She had Lonnie text Jevin, Xavier, and Charlene to update them. It might just affect the trajectory of things for the rest of the night.

The elevator stops and the doors slide open.

At last it looks like we've reached the high-tech area of the base.

The overheads are off, but sporadic emergency lights allow us to see well enough to make out at least some of what lies in the expansive room.

Work stations, extensive computer servers, filing cabinets. Off to the left, an area with drone parts, even what look like EEG helmets attached to elaborate virtual reality computer modules and looming high-def screens.

"What now?" Xav asks.

"We see if we can find anything that might have to do with Emilio."

Derek Byrne was still at the table when he got the call from Jesús Garcia. "How is it going with the engineer?" Garcia asked.

"I assure you things are still on schedule."

"Remember I told you that I would notify you if I learned anything about Antioch and Banks that might be of interest to you."

"Yes."

"They used their body doubles to slip away from my men. I found Banks. His signal cut off just a couple minutes ago, but you aren't going to believe where he is."

"Where's that?"

"Groom Lake."

A pause. "Really."

"Yes. And Antioch is at the Arête. How did Banks get access to the base?"

"He must have gotten the drive from Agcaoili before he was killed," Derek said reflectively. "That does explain a few things. What do we know about Banks and Antioch? Are they more than just co-workers?"

"I'll have my people check into that. You take care of the engineer. Make him give you the information. I'll take care of Banks and Antioch."

"How?"

"I have a few ideas."

Derek hung up, settled his bill, and as he took the elevator back toward his room he contemplated what to do.

Banks and Antioch. Yes, he remembered them from last fall. Now here they were, getting entangled in things once again.

RixoTray.

Plyotech Cybernetics.

First Emilio getting mixed in.

Now Banks and his friend, all wrapped up in this drone exchange.

Once again Derek found himself wondering who was behind everything. Was it Garcia after all? What about Akio Takahashi? That seemed unlikely.

But if not him, who?

Who knew about everything that was going on? Earlier Akio had informed him that Undersecretary of Defense Williamson mentioned that someone had confided in her about some undisclosed research.

But who? Who knew about that, and why would they report it?

Derek reached the sixty-seventh floor, left the elevator, and started down the hall.

The only other people who were informed about what was going on in sublevel 4 were the orderlies who worked there, and Calista. But he doubted they were involved and he couldn't imagine that it was her.

The only one left was Dr. Malhotra.

Derek reached the room.

Yes.

Dr. Malhotra. He had the contacts, but what did he have to gain? More money for his research?

Possibly.

Derek unlocked the door.

The bloodied plastic sheet was there. The chair was there. But both Calista and the engineer were gone.

"Calista?"

No reply.

He searched the suite, the bathroom, the closets, under the beds.

No one.

Nothing.

Yes, Calista had acted out before. Yes, she'd been upset when she left the table, but he never would have suspected she would do something like this.

He phoned Dr. Malhotra.

"Yes, sir?"

"I need you to come to the Arête. There's a small problem that needs to be taken care of."

"Of course."

"And my rifle. It's in my office. Bring it along."

Charlene left Fionna and her kids at the table with their chips and salsa appetizer and went to meet with Clive Fridell to pick up the things that had been found in Emilio's locker.

She found him at the front desk waiting for her.

"Miss Antioch. Good to see you."

"You too, Mr. Fridell."

"Clive. Please."

"Clive, then." She glanced around but didn't see any box of supplies or notebooks. "The items from Emilio's locker?"

He gestured for her to join him down a hallway marked SECURITY PERSONNEL ONLY. "Come right this way and I'll get you all taken care of."

The lights in the room must be attached to motion sensors, because a few minutes ago when Xavier and I began our search they flicked on automatically.

Now, I glance at my phone and see that we only have twelve more minutes before we need to return the security clearance card to Fred.

There has to be something here.

The status lights on the computer monitors indicate that they're powered on. I tap a couple of space bars to wake them up, but the only thing that comes on the screen is an official-looking insignia for the base and a password prompt. None of the passcodes Fionna gave me do any good when I enter them in.

I notice a check-in sheet hanging from a clipboard near a hallway that leads to the restrooms. When I flip through the last few weeks, I see that there are apparently regular tests on Sunday nights. Staff started signing in beginning a few minutes after seven for the tests that were scheduled later in the evening.

It's 6:35 now.

Man, I do not want to be here when the research personnel start showing up.

You have to return the key card by 6:45 anyway. You'll be good.

At a security console in the back of the room, an array of screens displays security camera footage of the hangar, the outside of the building, the front lobby.

All quiet.

Without having access to the computers, we're left with scouring the substantial file cabinets that line one of the walls.

"Xav, they have almost as many manila folders as you do in your RV."

"I told you. They can't be hacked. Writing stuff down. It's a good idea."

"They also can't be searched in ten minutes."

"Well, let's find out."

He yanks open another file drawer, flips to the Bs, and begins scouring the files for Emilio's last name while I look under the Rs and then the Ts for any connection with RixoTray or the transdifferentiation research at Fuller Medical Center.

Charlene accepted the rather substantial cardboard box from Clive Fridell.

"I'm planning to catch the show tomorrow night," he told her.

"I hope you enjoy it."

"I'm certain I will."

She was anxious to look through the items but knew she needed to wait until she was alone before paging through the notebooks or sorting through the illusions and effects.

He reached out his hand. "Good night, Miss Antioch. I'll see you tomorrow."

She set the box on the desk while she shook his hand. "Goodbye, Clive. And thanks again."

"Of course."

He led her back down the hallway, and she took the box to her green room where she would have the privacy she needed while she examed Emilio's things.

Five minutes left.

Still nothing.

I don't know what might happen if we're late getting the card back to Fred, and I really don't want to find out.

"Xav, we need to go."

"Yeah. I know. You find anything?"

"No."

"I can't believe we made it all this way, only to come up short."

He finishes flipping through one of the manila folders he'd laid open on the file cabinet, then folds it up frustratedly, jams it back in place, and slides the drawer closed.

Four minutes.

I'm leading him through the winding path between the work spaces on the way to the elevator when I see it.

A photo on one of the desks.

And when I realize who it's a picture of, I stop abruptly. "Wait, Xav. Look."

I pick up the photo and show it to him.

It's a picture of Emilio standing next to Tim, the boy with progeria. They're in front of the Bellagio fountains, and Emilio apparently took the photo himself by holding the camera out in front of him.

Tim has a grip on Emilio's other hand.

A nameplate on the desk tells us that it's Project Director Dr. Turnisen's work space. It's the only photo on the desk.

So, he knew Emilio.

Is he the one who got him the files?

The RixoTray drive came from Dr. Schatzing. The files on it came from Dr. Turnisen? Is that it? Is that—

When Xavier speaks, it's almost like he's reading my mind. "He must be the one who provided Emilio with the access codes to this building."

"But why?"

He shakes my head. "I don't know. But I think we might have found what we were looking for. We need to go."

"Hang on." I flip out my phone and take a picture of the photograph. A thought comes to me. "Xavier, get some footage of the room."

"We need to get moving, bro."

"I know." There are no bars on my phone, but that's no surprise considering how far underground we probably are. "Just, quick. Get what you can. Maybe Fionna can analyze some of this stuff if we have images for her to search online with."

He fishes out his phone, and the two of us set to work getting as much footage as we can in the next minute or two.

I whip open the drawers in Turnisen's desk and find a number of USB drives with the RixoTray emblem on them and a small notepad that contains sets of alphanumeric sequences corresponding to dates. It only takes me a moment to realize all the dates are Sunday nights.

Manila folders can't be hacked.

And neither can handwritten notes.

The digits and letters under all the dates are in pencil, but tonight's had been erased before being rewritten in pen. It's the only entry written in pen.

I photograph the pages, return the notebook to its place, and when I look up to see where Xavier is, I notice movement on the security camera monitor pointed at the front of the building.

Two vehicles have pulled up, and three men and a woman dressed in military fatigues are on their way to the front door.

Tarmac

6:46 p.m.
2 hours left

"Xav!" I exclaim. "We gotta go. Now." On the screen I see another vehicle trundling up the road toward the building.

We hurry to the elevator.

Hop inside.

As the doors close, I realize something. "The lights in the room were movement activated. Those people are going to find the lights on. They'll know someone was down here."

"Maybe no one will notice."

"Yeah. Maybe." But that's a wish, not a prediction.

We reach the ground level. The elevator doors sweep open, and I hear voices and footsteps coming from the hallway that leads to the front lobby.

"Come on," I whisper urgently. "We need to hide."

We make it only five or six steps into the hangar before the lights blink on.

We dive down behind the nearest drone and hold our breath.

Across the hangar, the four Air Force personnel emerge from the hallway. They're laughing and talking about one of their friends and how drunk he was last night.

372

Heart pounding, I wait for them to pass. From where we're crouched beside the drone, I can see their legs as they cross the hangar toward the elevator.

As they come our way, we slide incrementally to the side to stay hidden.

They gather around the elevator no more than twenty feet from where Xavier and I are hiding.

There's no reason for them to think someone might be in here. No reason for them to investigate the hangar.

Still, it's possible.

All they have to do is look in our direction and—

The elevator doors open, they disappear inside, and then the doors close again.

"Let's go." I'm already on my feet. "Out the back, toward tarmac."

Xavier and I emerge into the night and sprint across the tarmac toward the maintenance building that hides our truck.

⋅⋅ •••

Charlene set the magic effects aside for the time being and focused on Emilio's notebooks.

As she lifted one of them, a security pass card with an insignia for Groom Lake on it slipped out. The name on the card: Dr. J. Turnisen.

How did he get that?

Well, regardless, it definitely connected Emilio to the base.

She flipped open the notebook that it'd come from.

Emilio's artistic bent came through in the sketches, doodles, graphs, and notes he'd left behind.

What caught her attention was the last entry, which Emilio had jotted down on the day before leaving for the Philippines. "8:46 Sunday night. The Schatzing grant?"

She stared at the words.

Cryptic, but they tied things back to Dr. Schatzing again.

That's what he discovered.

Is that why he was killed?

Earlier this morning when Ratchford had met with her and Jevin, he'd asked if they knew anything about a timeline.

So.

She had to do this now. Tonight. Find out whatever she could from Dr. Schatzing.

Jevin wouldn't want you to do this.

No, but she didn't have to tell him. She could just head over, get the information she needed, and come back before he returned from Groom Lake.

For the show, she had plenty of alluring outfits here at the Arête that she could choose from. Some were obviously designed only for stage work, but some would work perfectly for passing as a high-end escort.

She could get an audience with Dr. Schatzing tonight, and she could ask him in person what he knew about Emilio and the promise he'd made to Tim at the hospital when he gave the boy his word that he was going to help him not grow old so fast.

Schatzing expected his escorts to arrive at eight, which meant she needed to get there early if she was going to talk with him before the real escort arrived.

Using her phone, she looked up his address online. If she hurried, there should be just enough time to get changed and drive over to Summerlin to his subdivision.

Laying the notebook aside, Charlene went to her wardrobe to find just the right clothes.

"Where were you two?" Fred gasps as we round the corner.

"Long story," I tell him. The desert is cooler than when we'd entered the building. A scattering of distant stars glance down at us detachedly through the night.

He checks the time. "I need to go. Did you find what you were looking—"

His radio blares to life, asking for all security units near Gate 11 to take their stations. "Possible Roswell."

"Roswell?" Xavier says.

"It means intruder, someone who's not supposed to be here."

"The lights," I mutter.

"What?"

"Motion sensors in the—never mind."

"You guys gotta go. Now."

Xavier and I jump into my truck.

Fred hands Xavier his walkie-talkie. "Take this in case you need it."

"What about you?"

"I'll be alright. Keep an ear on what's going on. Take it slow, stay on the main roads, keep heading east. Call me when you get home."

"Can we leave before the shift change?"

"If anyone asks you for a clearance code, tell them you're in a forty-twenty-two. It means there's a family emergency and you need to leave. Now, go on, get moving before someone sees us back here."

He gets into his truck and peels off south. I head east. While I do, Xavier checks his phone and notifies me that there's a message from Fionna that the USB drive Fred handed over to the blackmailer was accessed and has now subsequently been erased.

"Send her and Charlene the video footage of the research room and the photo of Emilio and Tim that was on Dr. Turnisen's desk."

"Gotcha."

I aim the truck toward the dust-covered access road that leads out of Area 51.

Undersecretary Williamson dropped her car off with one of the Arête's valet parking attendants and went inside the hotel for her seven o'clock meeting with the person who'd informed her about the undocumented research going on at Plyotech Cybernetics.

Charlene was pulling on a pair of stockings when a text came through from Jevin with an attached photo of Emilio with Tim. There was also some video they'd taken of one of the rooms at the base.

She could watch that later.

For now, she focused on the photo.

It confirmed that Emilio knew Turnisen.

And the words in Emilio's notebook sure seemed to indicate that he knew Schatzing.

Did Turnisen know Schatzing too?

Her mind buzzed with the connections, the possibilities, the myriad of facts that were somehow related.

The USB drive came from RixoTray, yet it had the Groom Lake access codes on it—codes that allowed someone to get all the way to Turnisen's research room in Groom Lake.

That, and the security clearance card.

8:46 p.m.

Yes, she needed to do this.

She needed to see Schatzing tonight.

She was wriggling into her dress when her phone rang. This time Agent Ratchford's number came up.

If nothing else, she was being forced to confront her quirk of not liking talking on the phone.

"Hello, this is Charlene."

"Miss Antioch, Agent Ratchford. I feel a little strange asking this, but you told me that two of your associates had been able to open the files from your copy of the USB drive?"

She guessed where this was going. "You'd like the information we offered you earlier today."

"Yes, well, it seems our people haven't been able to access the drive as quickly as I thought they would. You mentioned Fionna and Lonnie?"

"They're here now. At the Arête. I'll give you Fionna's cell number."

After hanging up, she texted Fionna that Ratchford was going to call her and that she would see them later.

Then she finished getting dressed and headed to her car to go visit Dr. Schatzing.

Still in the hotel room, Derek Byrne tried to sort through where Calista could have gone with Dr. Turnisen.

With his injuries, the man wouldn't have been able to walk out on his own. She wasn't strong enough to support him.

A wheelchair?

Derek went to the room phone and called the front desk. The woman on the other end referred to him by the alias Calista had rented the room under: "How may I help you, Mr. Brantner?"

"Yes, the wheelchair my wife requested hasn't arrived yet."

A moment passed as she typed. "I apologize, sir. It should have been sent up already. I'll make sure it's on its way."

"Thank you."

"Clive."

"Oriana."

"It's good to see you again."

"And you as well." The undersecretary was not the hugging type, so she gave Clive Fridell a brisk handshake instead.

"It was a surprise to hear from you earlier," Clive said. "I assume you're in town to check up on what's happening over at Plyotech?"

"I am. You told me they were doing some unofficial research there regarding bionic technology."

"That's what my people have heard."

Though she was tempted to do so, she didn't ask who his people were. He was a billionaire many times over, one of the richest people in America. When you have money and power like that, it's not hard to find out people's secrets.

He was also on the board at Plyotech. He might have heard about it from someone there. The puzzle might not be any more complicated than that.

He pulled up a chair for her. "Please, have a seat."

She did.

He sat beside her.

"Now, Clive," she said, "tell me what your people have heard. I'm very curious where this research is taking place if it's not in any of the rooms on the building's blueprints."

"Alright, here's what I know."

⁘ ⦁⦁⦁

Fionna received a call from FBI Special Agent Ratchford that he was on his way to the Arête.

"How long until you get here?"

"Fifteen minutes or so. And the USB drive, do you . . . ?"

"I have it with me."

"Perfect."

"Text me when you arrive."

"I will. And your associate Lonnie, Miss Antioch noted that he's there with you?"

"Yes, he is. I'm sure he'll be glad to talk with you as well."

"I'll see you soon."

She hung up.

"Well, Lonnie, it looks like the FBI needs our help."

"Cool."

"Kids, let's get some dessert. I'm thinking the Chocolate Fountain. A business meeting—dessert compliments of the Federal Bureau of Investigation."

"That's what I'm talking about." Donnie nodded. "Taxes actually being put to good use."

* * *

Derek Byrne ran everything through in his mind.

So Calista had called for a wheelchair, but where did she go? And how would he find her? With Turnisen in the shape he was in, it seemed unlikely that she would just be able to wheel him out of the hotel without drawing undue attention to herself.

It was possible, but . . .

He made his way through the casino to the parking garage and found her car still there.

A taxi? A limo?

After confirming that his own car was in its spot as well, Derek returned to her car, made sure no one else was there watching him, then knelt and punctured her tires.

That would keep her from driving off.

He needed a way to narrow things down.

He knew her credit card number.

That was a start.

* * *

I take it easy on the roads. After having our plates run and our paperwork verified, we make it past the first two security checkpoints without any trouble, and at last we approach the final one.

"This is it, Xav."

"Third time's a charm."

In my headlights I see the Cammo dude who checked us in earlier step into the middle of the road.

He raises his hand as an order for us to stop, which I do.

Tension tightens in my gut.

I roll my window down.

You're still on the property and you're not supposed to be. They could still arrest you.

Or shoot you.

"Clearing out?" he asks me with a touch of disbelief.

"Yeah."

"You know what time it is?"

"We're in a forty-twenty-two." I point to Xav. "His wife was in a car accident. We just got the word."

The guard leans a flashlight in, studies Xavier for a moment. "What's your wife's name?"

"My wife?"

"In the car accident."

"Fionna."

It takes him a long time to reply. "Well, I hope she's alright."

"Me too."

"Radio in when you're off the property."

"Gotcha."

We pull forward and almost simultaneously let out deep breaths.

"I had to think of a name off the top of my head," he explains.

"Sure."

"It was either her or Betty."

"I think you made the right choice."

"When we tell this story, we can leave that part out."

"Right."

Then he's quiet.

We'd actually been on the base. We'd actually explored one of Area

51's research facilities. Any number of Xavier's friends would have given their right arm to have done what we just did.

Nothing on UFOs, but the unmanned aerial vehicle research sure did seem legit.

Xavier's explanations of things over the last couple days run through my head, and I ask him about one of the things he brought up but we never really examined in-depth. "Hey, yesterday when you were filling in Charlene on transhumanism, you mentioned someone named de Grey. I don't remember reading about him. What's his deal, exactly?"

"What?" I must've caught him deep in thought.

"De Grey. I was wondering what you knew about him."

"Oh. Yeah. Well, he points out a bunch of ways—six or seven, I'm not sure—that our metabolism eventually causes pathology, and that's what causes us to age and eventually to die. I haven't memorized his list, but he goes through things that could stop that like cell therapy, removing toxic cells, halting the degradation of cells as they reproduce. I'm no expert on any of it, but he claims that we've been able to do all those things on mice and should be able to do them all on humans within the next decade."

"So this guy, he thinks he can cure aging?"

"He calls it *engineered negligible senescence*—um, senescence is when cells deteriorate as they age—but yes. From the things he says, it sure seems like he believes it. In science fiction movies you might have someone growing a clone to use their organs to stay alive, but it's much easier to replace yourself with yourself."

"What do you mean?"

"Growing an organ from your own cells. Create a scaffolding to support the cells, say with a 3-D printer, build the organ on it. If you need a replacement you won't need to wait for someone else to donate an organ or fear that your body will reject it. It's already been done with bladders, skin, muscle tissue, ears."

"You're kidding me."

"No. Any organ can be grown in a laboratory—kidney, lungs, hearts. There's that famous case of Claudia Castillo back in 2008, when scientists used her own cells and the windpipe from a cadaver to create a lab-grown windpipe for her."

It's a lot to think about.

Is death really negotiable?

"In all of this bioengineering, don't you think we're playing God?"

"If there is a God, a good God—and I believe there is—then wouldn't he want us to remove the most possible suffering from the most amount of people? I mean, to remove suffering, to show love and compassion, is the highest ideal, the core characteristic of God, the one he would want us most to emulate."

"Maybe removing suffering isn't the best way to show love?"

We both have to think about that.

"And, I suppose, if there's no God, then we're masters of our own domain, and why not help evolution along in welcoming in a new era of immortality."

The field of transhumanism and the coming Singularity really do raise a lot of ethical questions, some of the most basic questions of existence: Who am I? How am I unique? What is the meaning of life? When does life begin? And at an even more fundamental level, what is life anyway?

All of these thoughts about living forever only serve to bring back memories of my wife and my two boys.

And Emilio.

All lost far too soon.

Death might someday be negotiable, but it isn't yet.

Not by a long shot.

The stars stare down across the lonely desert. Xavier calls Fred to tell him we're safe, and I drive through the bleak night toward home.

Derek stepped up to the Arête's front desk and put on a worried face. "My wife is with my brother, and he has a very serious medical condition. I know she checked in earlier, and I need to find out what room she's in. I was supposed to meet them here in the lobby, but my flight was late. I assume she had to take him up to the room."

The clerk didn't even look up from the keyboard. "And what's her name?"

To use her credit card she would have had to use her real name.

"Calista Hendrix."

She typed, then shook her head. "I'm sorry. No rooms to a Calista Hendrix."

He let that sink in.

Brantner? Would she have used your alias?

That was doubtful.

"Is there another name it might be under?" the woman asked.

Jeremy had his wallet with him last night when she brought him up to the room.

"Yes, actually. My brother's. Jeremy Turnisen. Try that."

After a moment of working on her computer, she smiled. "There it is—6743." She gulped slightly, perhaps realizing she probably shouldn't have said the room number aloud. "Would you like me to ring them?"

"As I said, my brother is ill. I'd rather just slip in if I could without disturbing them. Can you give me a key?"

She bit her lip. "I'm not supposed to."

"Yes, I know, I understand." He reached for his wallet, bluffing that he was going to show her his real name. "Do you need to see an ID? Is that it?"

"Um . . ." She looked around uneasily. "You know, no, that's okay."

She processed a key card and handed it to him. "I hope your brother starts feeling better."

"That's kind of you. I'll pass along the sentiment. Thank you."

⁘

Charlene drove toward Summerlin, piecing together the connection between Emilio, Groom Lake, and RixoTray.

The key card.

The jellyfish research.

Building A-13.

She didn't know why Emilio had landed in the middle of all this, but his relationship with Dr. Turnisen and his promise to Tim that he would help him to not grow old so fast were all related somehow.

Everything was interrelated.

Maybe the man she was on her way to see would help her figure out how.

⁘

Derek stood for a moment outside room 6743 and considered what he was going to do to Calista and Jeremy.

He still needed those launch codes.

The test flight was going to happen in just under ninety minutes.

That should still be plenty of time. He'd get the information, call it in to the number his contact person had provided him, and the drone would be delivered to Garcia's people in Mexico.

If he was going to continue his research he needed to move the program out of the country, and if he didn't deliver the drone tonight, that was going to severely hamper his working relationship with Garcia, whom he was now depending on for his new test subjects.

He mentally prepared himself to take whatever measures proved to be necessary to assure that things happened tonight on schedule.

As he was fishing the room key out of his pocket, he got a call from Dr. Malhotra that he had arrived at the Arête.

"Come up to 6743. I'll be waiting for you inside the room."

"What about your rifle?"

"Leave it in your car for now."

Then he hung up, slid the key through the card reader, and swung the door open.

The Syringe

Derek stepped into the room.

Ten feet away, Turnisen sat in a wheelchair staring at him coolly. Calista stood beside him, a syringe in her hand, the tip pressed against the side of Turnisen's neck.

"Close the door," she said.

Derek did.

"So you drug me in the mornings."

"Easy now, Calista." His eyes were on the hypodermic needle. "You don't want to do anything you're going to regret."

"I already did."

"What's that?" He took a step toward her.

"Trusting you—and don't come any closer or I inject this, do you understand?"

Derek paused. "What do you want?"

"What do I want?" she scoffed. "To stay young! I already told you that! But you, you're trying to *cheat death*." Sarcasm shot through the last two words.

"I'm not trying to cheat death; death is trying to cheat me. It's trying to take away all that I've ever accomplished, all that I've learned, all the memories and dreams and joys I've experienced in my life. You can understand that, can't you, Calista? Death is trying to cheat me. And it's trying to cheat you too, take your youth, your beauty—"

"Stop! Quiet!" She repositioned the needle. "You don't care about anyone else. Just yourself. It's all about you. You don't care that death is cheating anyone but you. You kill and you don't care as long as you get what you want."

He held up his hands, palms toward her as if to show her that he was not a threat.

"So," she said, "you need these codes for tonight? Or else you won't be able to send them to your people?"

"That's right."

"Well then, this time I guess you're not gonna get what you want."

And then she injected the contents of the syringe into Dr. Jeremy Turnisen's neck.

Derek sprang toward her, snatched at the needle, and pried it from Jeremy's neck as the engineer began slumping in his chair, then turned to Calista. "What was it?" he roared. "What did you give him?"

"Wouldn't you like to—"

He backhanded her violently and sent her spinning around, slamming face-first against the wall.

He grabbed her by the throat, heaved her to her feet. "I asked what you gave him."

She spit in his face and tried to kick him in the crotch, but he was able to deflect her leg.

He slammed her to the floor and went to check Jeremy's pulse.

The man was still alive.

Good, yes, good.

But what did she give him?

And where did she get it?

A knock at the door.

Dr. Malhotra had arrived.

The Escort

7:46 p.m.
1 hour left

Charlene drove up to the guard station at the entrance to Dr. Schatzing's gated community in Summerlin.

"May I help you?" The man in a security uniform who was standing there paused flipping through his *Sports Illustrated* swimsuit edition just long enough to gaze over his glasses at her.

"I'm here to see Dr. Schatzing."

"And your name?"

"Just tell him I'm the girl from the agency."

"Ah." He appraised her. Based on Dr. Schatzing's phone records, Charlene expected him to call the doctor to announce that she was there, but the guy didn't even bother. Instead, he just raised the bar for her, Charlene thanked him and drove through.

●● ●●●

While Dr. Malhotra tried to awaken Turnisen, Derek Byrne mixed a saline solution in with the gray powder that he carried with him for his coffee.

Then he filled a syringe with it.

388

"Now, Calista." He bent over her and brushed a strand of hair away from her bruised and swollen face. She lay bound on the floor. He'd wound the suture thread tightly around her wrists and ankles; she wasn't going anywhere.

He held the hypodermic needle close to her face. "Do you know what's in here? Dust from a mummy. The chemicals in it make it fatal if it's injected into someone. And I can almost guarantee you that it would not be an enviable way to die."

"You're sick, you know that? You are one sick son of a—"

"None of us are well, Calista. That's part of the problem."

"I know you won't kill me. You need me to tell you what I gave him. If he doesn't wake up, you don't get your precious little launch codes. So how does it feel to be the one who's helpless?"

What drug could she have gotten on short notice? What did she inject him with?

It wasn't like she was planning any of this. And he didn't have a lot of medications or drugs around, in fact—

Oh.

Yes.

"You used the drug that was there on the counter, didn't you?"

She gave him a satisfied grin. "The same one you used on me. Oh yeah. He'll be out for at least six or seven hours. Remember? That's what you—"

He hit her in the face again, this time with a closed fist. She cried out, but then he was tired of hearing her talk and he used duct tape to gag her.

They could try an injection of adrenaline on Turnisen, but the syringe she'd given him had been full, and it wasn't going to be easy to revive the engineer. And even if they did manage to, he'd be so groggy and incoherent he might not be able to help them at all.

You need those launch codes!

Where could he get them? Where could—

Banks.

He's at Area 51, or at least he was.

He has the USB drive.

Garcia's people were investigating Banks's relationship with Antioch. There might be something there they could leverage to their advantage.

He pressed the side of Calista's face hard against the carpet. "You told me you were more afraid of growing old than of dying. So in that case, this is going to be my way of showing you mercy."

Her eyes grew large with terror.

"I'm not going to make you face your greatest fear."

He jabbed the syringe into her neck and injected the mummy dust into her jugular vein.

Calista felt a terrible fire burst apart inside of her.

She screamed into her gag, but it was clear even to her that no one outside the room would ever be able to hear her calling for help.

"So," Oriana Williamson said to Clive Fridell, "you're saying that this man, Thad Becker, was working for you?"

"Not exactly, but he was under the employ of some people I know. I'm afraid that's all I can really say at this time."

"And he disappeared?"

"He did."

And then Clive told her everything that Becker had told him before he went to visit Plyotech last month.

"You're Lonnie?" Agent Ratchford said.

"Yes."

"You're . . . but you—you're . . ."

"I'm seventeen."

Fionna's other children were all standing in line to order their fudge, truffles, and chocolate cake, watching the restaurant's giant chocolate fountain flow down as they did.

"Ah, well, I wasn't implying that you weren't good at what you do, it's just . . . Well, all I can say is, I'm impressed. So now, can you two tell me what you found out when you managed to open the DoD files?"

"We can show you if you have your laptop," Fionna said.

He lifted his briefcase. "I do."

"Good." She pulled the USB drive out of her purse. "Let's get started."

* * *

Charlene walked up the path to Dr. Schatzing's house, repositioned the strap on her dress, then knocked and waited for him to answer.

She could hear movement on the other side of the door. At last it swung open and a man faced her. Early fifties, a little overweight. An overly serious face. "Hello?"

"Hi." She smiled flirtatiously. "I'm the girl you called for."

He let his gaze slide all the way down her body and then slowly make its way back up until he was looking her in the eye again.

"You're early."

"Bonus time. For being a faithful client."

"I asked for Jewel."

"Jewel's not feeling well." She shifted her weight, swiveling her hips. "If you don't like what you see, I can always . . ."

"What's your name?"

She went with a shortened version of her real name. "Charli."

"Is that your real name?"

She bit her lip shyly. "We're not supposed to give our real names."

"Ah."

"And your name?"

"Donald."

"Real name?"

He hesitated, let his eyes crawl down her again. Though she'd expected him to look at her like this, it still made her feel used by him.

The doctor stepped aside. "Come on in."

She joined him in the living room, and he shut the door behind her.

Okay, now that she was inside she needed to offer him the truth—that she wasn't really from the agency but was here to find out what he might know about her friend's murder.

Tell him, Charlene. Just explain it; tell him what you really want.

But she felt nervous, uneasy, unsure how to shift to the topic of Emilio.

Collect your thoughts, Charlene. You need to—

"May I use your bathroom? Freshen up for a moment?"

"Of course." He pointed down the hall to a door near the base of the stairs leading to the second floor. "Would you like a drink?"

"What are you having?"

"Bourbon."

"Bourbon, then."

Derek stood beside Calista, whose face was twisted in pain.

It might take awhile for her to die; he didn't know, he'd never killed anyone this way before.

He nudged her with his toe as he phoned Garcia. "The engineer is a no-go."

"What? You led me to believe that—"

"I know. And you said you'd take care of Banks and Antioch. What did you have in mind, exactly?"

Garcia told him.

"Do it," Derek said. "We can still make this happen tonight."

•• •••

Charlene stared at her reflection in the mirror.

You should have just told him at the door who you are. What are you doing? The longer you wait, the harder this is going to be!

She took a deep breath, tried to center herself, then left the bathroom, rehearsing in her mind what she was going to say: "There's a friend of mine that you knew. Emilio Benigno. He's . . ."

No, you need to start out telling him who you are. The worst he can do is kick you out of the house.

"Listen, I'm not really who I said I was. I'm not really from the agency . . ."

That's what you need to say.

Charlene was at the base of the stairs when she heard the dull thud of something heavy landing on the floor in the kitchen and the simultaneous shattering of glass. As she was about to call out to see if Dr. Schatzing was okay, she heard a voice that was not his. "Find her. Go."

Oh.

Not good.

It's the people who had Emilio killed! The ones behind everything! It has to be!

You can't let them catch you. You can't—

If there were people in the kitchen, she would never be able to sneak past them to the front door. The only other choice was running up the stairs beside her.

She peeled off her high heels and, holding them, bolted up the staircase, trying to be as silent as possible.

If Jevin were here he would probably fight whoever was down there. But that was Jevin. Most of the time she could take care of herself, but she couldn't imagine fighting off more than one person.

However, she did have another gift, a well-practiced skill that she'd honed over the years—fitting in trunks, small cages, and hidden compartments. She could hide in spaces people would swear no woman could ever fit inside.

"I got the upstairs," another voice said.

Go, hurry!

As soundlessly as possible she started down the hall, then stopped in midstride.

Above her was the trapdoor to the attic. A string that would trigger the release mechanism was tucked up in the crack beside it.

Gun in hand, the first man edged up the stairs. As he moved in to cover the hallway, he saw a string hanging down from the door to the attic.

It was swinging.

Charlene scrunched up as small as she could in the dark. This wasn't ideal, not ideal at all, but it would have to work. She just needed to wait long enough until they were distracted and she could slip away.

A ladder unfolded when he pulled the string.

Leveling his gun in front of him, he ascended the steps.

Before emerging through the hole at the top, he took a small breath to steady himself, then eased up and peered around the attic.

In the light that snuck up around him from the hallway and that crept in through the small window on the wall in front of him, he could make out shapes in the darkness.

The place was filled with boxes and crates.

He turned in a slow circle, trying to take everything in.

No movement.

He climbed all the way up and began checking every hiding place he could find.

⋅•⋅ ⋅•••⋅

Fionna explained what was on the drive as Lonnie navigated through the files using Agent Ratchford's computer.

The agent paid close attention, then finally said, "I'm primarily interested in Akinsanya. We have reason to believe that he might be in the greater Las Vegas area. Are you sure there isn't anything else you can tell me that might help us track him down?"

Fionna wasn't sure she should reveal any information about Jevin and Xavier being at Area 51, but she did connect the dots for Ratchford between RixoTray and Dr. Turnisen by showing him the photo of Emilio and Tim that Jevin had sent to her.

That seemed to spark his curiosity. "And do we know where this Dr. Turnisen is?"

Fionna shook her head. "I'm not sure. We haven't tried to contact him."

Agent Ratchford produced his phone. "Give me a minute. I'll find him. At least my people are good at one thing."

⋅•⋅ ⋅•••⋅

Nothing in the attic.

He'd searched the entire place and was on his way to the steps that led back to the hallway when he paused.

One of the trunks was large enough.

Yeah, it was possible.

He turned toward it, unlatched the clasp, and flipped open the lid.

Empty.

⋅•⋅ ⋅•••⋅

When Charlene had grabbed the string for the attic door and swung it, then hurried to the bedroom at the end of the hall, she'd been hoping that both men would go up there looking for her.

But that's not how things had played out.

There was just one set of footsteps above her in the attic.

One set.

He found the swinging string. Once he sees you're not in the attic, they're going to know you're up here somewhere. They will find you.

She peered out the window.

It was a two-story drop.

There was a pool filled with water and covered with a plastic tarp. However, it wasn't directly below the window, and even if she jumped out as far she could, she didn't think she'd make it to the water's edge.

The only other choice was the hallway, but if she went out there they'd catch her immediately.

Hide. You have to hide.

She scanned the room.

In the closet? Under the bed? Behind the dresser?

All too obvious.

If she could duck into another room, maybe she could fit under the sink in the bathroom, maybe—

Heavy steps on the staircase told her that the second guy was on his way up.

No, please, no!

"She's up here somewhere!" one of the men cried. "We got her."

Jump. You have to jump.

She went back to the window and threw it open.

The cool air swirled in around her.

No, the pool's too far; you'll never make it.

The door behind her crashed open. "Do not move! I will shoot you!"

She gripped the windowsill. Didn't turn around to look at him.

You have to get out of here. They'll kill you!
"Step away from the window."
She eyed the pool, calculated if it was possible to—
"I said, get back from the window."
But she didn't step back.
Instead, she leapt into the night.

The Fear of Dying

Charlene smacked onto the plastic tarp but wrenched her ankle against the side of the pool as she did.

The tarp swallowed her up, wrapping tightly around her, sucking her under.

From the water escapes she'd done over the years, she knew she just needed to relax, focus, move slowly. But as she tried to free her arms, her legs, kick to the surface, the plastic held her fast.

Easy, Charlene. Don't panic!

For certain effects, she needed to be able to hold her breath for two and a half minutes, but tonight the issue was getting untangled from the plastic that was keeping her from the surface. And she hadn't gotten much air before plunging under the water.

She tried to be still to let the plastic float away from her, but that did nothing to free her.

Easy.

Take it easy.

You need to get out of here.

Calming herself and shutting out the panic, she extended her arms slowly and rotated to the left, toward the top of the pool.

She sensed that the plastic was parting. By gently spinning a little more, she was finally able to ease the plastic aside and make it to the water's surface.

She grabbed a breath and headed for the side of the pool. Heaving herself out, she stood and almost toppled backward as she put pressure on her injured ankle.

No! You have to run!

A police car was sitting next to the curb.

Awkwardly, painfully, she hobbled toward it but found it empty.

"Ma'am?" a voice behind her called. "Are you alright?"

Heart hammering in her chest, she turned and saw a police officer walking her way.

"There are two men," she gasped, "they're trying to—"

And then she saw the second officer leave the house.

No, they were the—

The officer who was closest to her spoke softly. "I'm going to need you to climb inside the car now, Miss Antioch. I know it's no Aston Martin, but it's gonna have to do for tonight."

The two men converged on her, and though she desperately tried to fight them off, it was only a matter of seconds before they had her cuffed and locked in the back of their patrol car.

Officers Gordon Shepard and Ron Ledger climbed into the squad, and Gordon made the call. "We've got her. We're bringing her in."

"Good."

"What about Schatzing? Do you want us to take care of him too?"

"Is he dead?"

"Naw. But he was bleeding pretty bad there on the floor."

"Leave him. All we really need right now is the woman."

Calista thought only of death.

Derek had left her tied up on the floor with Dr. Malhotra watching over her and the unconscious engineer, who was lying on the bed on the other end of the honeymoon suite.

Thoughts of growing old, something she would never do now, filled her head. Images of sunsets and oceans, of mountains and beaches, of children laughing, of herself in the mirror, wrinkled and spent with the years, but smiling. She would never experience any of that.

Never experience anything except this room.

Maybe she didn't fear growing old more than dying.

Maybe she did fear dying most of all.

Hearing footsteps, she turned and saw the doctor on his way toward her.

He leaned close enough for her to smell his stale breath. "Don't worry. If you survive I'll make sure what's left of you goes to good use. I've been looking for a new volunteer to take Thad's place. You're already familiar with the program, you'll be perfect."

She prayed she would die quickly, before Malhotra could sever her spinal column and paralyze her from the neck down.

But she was not confident that this prayer was one that was going to be answered.

The Offer

8:06 p.m.
40 minutes left

My phone rings. Charlene's photo comes up on the screen. "Charlene, hey, what's—"

"Mr. Banks?" It's a man's voice. "Jevin Banks?"

"Who is this?"

"Akinsanya."

It feels like a clamp is squeezing around my heart.

He's calling on Charlene's phone!

He—

"We have Miss Antioch. She's right here with me now. Would you like to speak with her?"

I feel my left hand form a white-knuckled grip around the steering wheel. "Yes."

A moment, and then, "Jevin! I'm at the Arête. Call the—"

Her voice becomes faint as she cries out "police!" and Akinsanya's voice comes back on the line again. "You have something I want."

"What?"

"The launch codes."

"What are you talking about?"

401

"I know you were at the base."

"I don't know anything about any launch codes."

"You have the USB drive."

"Yes, but it didn't have any launch codes."

"I hope, for Miss Antioch's sake, that it did."

Play this right, Jevin. Buy some time!

"Okay. Alright. I'll give them to you. But not over the phone. I need to see her, we do it in person."

Silence. "I'll call you back and give you a location. Until then, do not contact the authorities. I'll know if you do. And I will not hesitate to hurt Miss Antioch in even worse ways than you can imagine."

The line goes dead.

Xavier only heard my side of the conversation, but that's enough for him to piece things together. "They got Charlene and they want the launch codes?"

"It was Akinsanya."

"What?"

"With Turnisen's involvement and the test schedule, I can only guess the codes are for those drones, for tonight."

"They're armed."

"Yes, they are."

"Jev, even if you had the codes you can't give them to him. You know that, right?"

I'm quiet.

"Buddy, there's no telling what he might use that drone for. If there's even a chance that he could fire one of the—"

"This is Charlene we're talking about."

"I know. But you could also be talking about the lives of hundreds or even thousands of people."

I don't know what to say. I have nothing to say. "What if it was Fionna and her kids who were in danger?"

"It might be. We don't know."

He's right. We don't know. Before you make any decision, you need to find out where that drone is heading, what they're planning to do with it.

Xavier puts a hand on my arm. "Hey, we're gonna get her back, alright?"

"Yeah."

"Should I call Ratchford?"

"No. We can't contact the authorities. Akinsanya said he'd know if we did, and I believe him. We need to figure out what the launch codes are—so at least we have something to negotiate with."

"How?"

"Let's start with Fred, see what he can find out. Maybe he can get back in the building. Maybe his people can locate the codes."

"Jevin, I don't think that—"

"We have to come up with something, Xav—before we get to Vegas. This is Akinsanya we're talking about. He will kill her. You know that. If we don't get him what he wants."

He quietly taps the dashboard, thinking, then lifts his cell and puts the call through.

Fred doesn't answer.

As Xavier leaves a voicemail for him to call us back, I try to think of a way to bluff my way through saving Charlene's life.

While Agent Clay Ratchford waited for his people to contact him with the trace on Turnisen's phone location and credit card usage, he watched Lonnie work his magic on the laptop.

Obscure computer code scrolled across the screen, and Clay couldn't help but think of *The Matrix*.

This kid was amazing.

He couldn't help but wonder how good the person was who'd taught him—his mom.

When his phone rang he picked up.

And got the news: Turnisen was staying here at the Arête. His Visa card had been used to reserve a room earlier this evening.

Clay stood.

"What is it?" Fionna asked.

"Turnisen. You stay here with your kids. I'll be back."

And he strode briskly toward the reception desk to get Turnisen's room number.

We hear from Fred.

No, he can't get back into the building.

No, he has no idea what the launch codes might be.

And no, his contacts would never be able to find them out, at least not tonight before the test flight.

I try to keep the speed down on the drive back to Vegas, but it's not easy. Still no word from Akinsanya about a meeting place.

He has Charlene.

The woman I love.

And you've never told her so, not in so many words, not by using the three words that matter most.

No.

No, I haven't.

"Xav, I took video of a notebook in Turnisen's desk. I want you to pull it up on my phone."

He does.

"Hit play, then pause it and read me the numbers listed for tonight."

"Why?"

"I need to know what they are."

"You think it's the launch sequence?"

"I'm not sure. But if nothing else, maybe it's something I can use to stall with."

He looks at the screen. "Jevin, this code is at least, I don't know, thirty or forty characters long."

"I can memorize a deck of fifty-two cards; I can memorize a list of numbers and letters. Read them off."

He makes it through the list twice before my phone rings.

He studies the screen. "Unknown number."

"Let me have it."

I accept the phone, and as soon as I tap the screen Akinsanya's voice comes on. "Leave your car in the Arête's parking garage. Take the elevator to the first floor of the casino. Go past the gaming tables to the escalator that leads down to the green rooms. Someone will meet you there."

"Who?"

"Be here in fifteen minutes."

"Let me talk to Charlene."

But the line is already dead.

I hand Xavier the phone.

"What do we know?"

"We go to the Arête, near the green rooms. He wants me there in fifteen minutes. But I don't know if they're aware that you're with me. He didn't say anything about you being there, or about what you're supposed to do."

We're less than five minutes from the hotel.

"That could work to our advantage."

"Yes." I'm deep in thought. "It could."

Backstage

8:31 p.m.
15 minutes left

Xavier's warehouse is on the way, and it only takes a couple moments to swing by and pick up the things I have in mind: a radio transmitter patch and receiver, a crossbow, and an indiscreet case for him to carry them in so he can get it into the Arête without being stopped by security.

My conspiracy theorist friend really is a good shot with a crossbow.

I place one of the transparent radio transmitters behind my left ear. It looks like a small piece of thick, clear tape. Hopefully, they won't find it if they search me.

Using this, Xavier will be able to hear everything I say.

Back on the road, Xavier changes out of his camo clothes as I drive, then he fits the radio receiver into his ear.

"Xav, you need to promise me you won't make any move or tell anyone where we are until I give you the go-ahead."

"How are you gonna let me know when you want me to call the cops?"

"I'll ask to see Charlene before I give them any information. I need to make sure she's still alive. If I say, 'What have you done!' it means she's dead. We have nothing to lose. Call the cops."

"Jev, she's going to be alright. Don't even—"

"I'm just saying, just in case."

He's quiet.

"If I tell her, 'It's going to be okay,' that means I need you to come in alone. I'll try to give you any other info I can about what we're dealing with."

"What about if you want me to call hotel security?"

"I'll just ask Akinsanya, 'How did you get past the Arête's security?'"

"Got it."

I take a moment to review the random alphanumeric list. With everything that's going on, I'm having a hard time remembering the last ten digits and letters.

"Review the code for me."

He reads through it again, and I concentrate on the end sequence.

"Jevin, you can't give them this code. No matter what happens in there. You understand that, right?"

I glance at him. "You told me the right one, didn't you? You didn't change any of it?"

"No. It was the right one. I'm just saying—"

"I got you." I stop at that, avoiding making a promise I won't be able to keep.

After dropping Xavier off halfway down the block, I cruise into the Arête's parking garage.

Before leaving the pickup, I change out of the camouflage and into my street clothes.

As instructed, I ride the elevator to the first floor of the hotel's casino and walk past the gaming tables, keeping my eyes focused straight ahead, trying not to attract any attention from people who might have seen the billboards of me out front.

I get a few looks of recognition, but thankfully no autograph requests.

I make it to the escalator that leads down to the green rooms. Typically, there are hotel security personnel down here to keep people out of the stage area, but tonight there's just a police officer.

"Follow me," he tells me brusquely.

An LVPD officer? So, Akinsanya really would have found out if you called the cops.

I wonder if he's one of the two men who were staking out my house, but it was impossible to know since I hadn't been able to get a good look at their faces.

We walk around the corner and through the doorway to the hall that leads to the backstage area. He locks the door behind us, quickly frisks me, takes my cell phone, and smashes it to pieces beneath his heel.

I'm nervous he'll find the radio patch that's behind my ear, but he's not looking for anything like that and he doesn't check for it.

People see what they expect to see.

The secret to misdirection.

He points to the hallway that leads past the dance rehearsal room. "This way."

"Where's Charlene?"

"Just walk."

His name badge reads "G. Shepard." I take it as a bad sign that he's willing to let me see him in his uniform and let me read his name tag.

He wouldn't let you see that if he was planning on letting you walk out of here alive.

"Why are we meeting backstage?" I ask, to give Xavier our location.

The cop doesn't reply, just orders me to keep walking, so with him right on my heels, I cross down the hallway toward the stage.

Calista heard a knock, then heard the door to the room bang open. Then shouting.

A gunshot.

Another.

The loud thunk of a body hitting the floor.

She wasn't sure what was real. Maybe she was imagining this, hearing things.

The sounds came from the other side of the suite. She was weak and tried to roll over to see what was happening, but couldn't make it.

There was a scuffle of movement, the harsh sound of male voices, and then a man was kneeling over her, removing her gag.

"Ma'am? Are you okay?"

She shook her head feebly. "I'm . . ." But she couldn't get any other words out.

"My name is Agent Ratchford." He was freeing her wrists and ankles. "I'm with the FBI. What's your name?"

"Calista," she managed to say.

"Calista, who did this to you?"

"He injected it . . . into me." She gestured toward the bag of gray powder that he'd left on the counter in the bathroom. "I need help."

"What did he give you?"

"Dust. Poison." She was finally able to speak, but every word was a chore. Leaning on one elbow, she could see a couple security guards bent over Turnisen, who was on the bed at the other end of the suite. "I don't know."

But then she toppled back to the floor.

"Who? Who injected you?" Agent Ratchford pointed toward Dr. Malhotra's body, which lay near the bed. The pistol he carried was beside him, where he'd dropped it when he was shot. "That man?"

She shook her head, starting to lose focus. "Derek."

Ratchford called to one of the other men, who she now saw was from hotel security, "Get an ambulance here, stat! And contact poison control!"

He turned to her again. "Where is this Derek?"

"He left. I don't know."

"Do you know his last name?"

"Byrne. But he likes to be called . . ."

"He likes to be called what?"

She tried to catch her breath.

"Who is this man?" he asked her.

"Akinsanya."

Antidote

"What?" Clay gasped. "Did you just say Akinsanya?"

"Yes."

"And you don't know where he went?"

"He took . . . a wheelchair . . . "

A wheelchair, huh?

This is a casino, he thought. *They'll have surveillance footage of all the hallways.*

•ᴗ •••

The officer leads me through the backstage area.

I notice the props for our show—the cages and swords, the glass panels and trunks with hidden panels and sliding doors. If I could lose the cop I might be able to use something back here against Akinsanya.

Before you do anything, make sure Charlene is okay.

As we cross onto the stage itself, I see that the auditorium's house lights are off, but one of the spotlights is on and is directed at center stage.

"Go up there," Officer Shepard commands. "Stand in the light."

I walk onstage.

The piranha tank on my left looms in the darkness. The platform high above it that broke away and dropped me into the tank is out of sight. The larger platform on the other side—the one where the gurney was, where the divers were stationed, and where Seth took his bow—is also engulfed in shadows.

I enter the circle of light. "Alright," I call. "I'm here."

The words echo eerily through the vast, empty auditorium. The acoustics are good, and I'm confident that anyone in here would be able to hear me.

"Where is she? I want to see her."

No reply.

When you're a Las Vegas performer you get used to not seeing the audience. Instead, you spend most of the show with spotlights glaring in your eyes. Now, I use one hand to shield my eyes from looking directly into the spot so I won't be blinded by it.

"I said I'm here," I repeat, louder this time. "Where's Charlene?"

A voice drifts down from the platform where the divers sat. "I've been looking forward to meeting you, Mr. Banks."

It sounds like the same person who was on the phone with me earlier, the one who identified himself as Akinsanya.

When I turn, I can't tell who's up there. "Where's Charlene?"

"Tell me the launch codes."

"Let me talk to her."

"You're going to have to trust me."

"I'm not going to give you anything until I see her."

He ignores that. "I propose an even trade."

"Yes, I get it," I say impatiently. "I know: the launch codes for Charlene. Now where is—"

"No."

"No?"

"No: the launch codes for the antidote."

My heart stops. "What?"

"Wheel her out."

Another spotlight flicks on, illuminating the far side of the stage. It might mean someone is in the lighting booth controlling the lights, or it just might be Akinsanya using the booth's iPad with all the controls.

The police officer who led me here appears from the darkness. He's pushing a wheelchair.

Charlene is sitting in it. Her wrists are cuffed to the chair. She's gagged but conscious.

"Charlene!" I start toward her, but the sharp blast of a gunshot ricochets through the theater and the stage splinters to pieces beside my left foot.

I stop.

"Don't go any closer"—it's Akinsanya—"I want you to tell me the launch codes, but you don't have to be able to walk to do that. The next bullet goes through your left thigh."

The shot seemed to come from the back of the auditorium near the lighting booth rather than from the platform above the tank.

Another person? How many people do they have here?

Choosing to confront us here in the theater really isn't a bad idea. Keeping the effects of one of Vegas's most famous performers secret is a priority for the Arête, so this place is secure. To keep our music from distracting people in the gaming area, the theater is soundproof as well.

"Take off her gag."

Akinsanya's voice: "Go ahead."

The officer obeys him.

"Jev," she gulps in a breath, "don't give them what they want. I heard 'em talking; they want a drone. They want—"

"That's enough," the cop tells her.

"It's for a drug cartel. They're delivering—"

"I said that's enough." He grabs her hair with his right hand and yanks her head back.

I feel my hands tighten into fists. "Let go of her now, or you will never use that hand again."

"Do it," Akinsanya orders.

The cop untangles his hand, shoving her head roughly to the side as he does.

"Did they poison you? Drug you?" I ask Charlene urgently.

"They gave me something." She's coherent at least, not out of it. At least not yet. Her eyes go to her arm where I assume they must have injected her. "I don't know what."

This isn't happening, this can't be happening!

"It's going to be okay," I tell her, using the phrase that will give Xavier the signal to come in alone. "Everything's going to be fine."

My friend would hear that through the radio.

They might have some surprises on their side, but we have at least one on ours.

Xavier was waiting at the base of the escalator, phone ready to call the police, when he heard Jevin's words through the radio receiver assuring Charlene that she would be alright.

That meant he was to come in alone.

The door in front of him was locked.

But Jevin wasn't the only one who knew how to pick a lock.

I face Akinsanya. "What did you mean, the codes for the antidote? What did you give her?"

He's still in the dark. I can't see his face.

"Dalpotol, for what it's worth. She's a slim woman. Based on her body size and the dosage, I'd say she has maybe four minutes left, maybe less. Now, tell me what I want to know."

You need to get that antidote.

If you tell him the codes, any number of people might die!

But if I say nothing, Charlene will.

The stage lights come on and I see a man sitting on the scuba divers' platform. Short-cropped, dark hair. Stocky. Late fifties. He's holding a syringe. Akinsanya. "You don't have a lot of time to deliberate this decision. Don't make a choice you're going to regret."

The drones are armed.

Charlene's life.

Or handing over a drone to a terrorist.

Suddenly I wish I hadn't memorized that code, then I wouldn't have to decide.

But I had.

And I remember it.

"How do I know that's really the antidote?"

"It is. That's one thing I wouldn't deceive you about."

I'm about to reply when Xavier's voice comes from the shadows behind the cop who wheeled Charlene onto the stage. "Nobody move. I have a crossbow aimed at this man's back."

Plunge

8:42 p.m.
4 minutes left

"They drugged her, Xavier," I call to him.

"I heard."

"We need—"

The sound of a gunshot rips through the auditorium, another rifle shot from the lighting booth.

The cop Xavier is aiming the crossbow at jerks backward as the back of his head blows apart in a ferocious red spray from the bullet's exit wound.

His body drops limply to the stage.

Charlene cries out and Xavier stares dumbfounded at the corpse.

"Put down the crossbow," Akinsanya says calmly. "I didn't need him. I need you even less."

A second cop appears from behind the curtain and pulls a gun on Xavier. "He told you to set down the crossbow."

Xavier looks my direction and I nod for him to comply.

He lowers it to the stage, bolt still in it, and kicks it toward the curtain.

As I'm trying to sort out what just happened, Charlene gasps and starts convulsing.

"No!" I rush to her side.

"That's not a good sign," Akinsanya tells me. "You have maybe three minutes. But I wouldn't guarantee—"

"Alright. I'll tell 'em to you. Give me the antidote." I put my hand behind Charlene's neck to support her. Her breathing is strained, her fingers clenched.

"First the launch codes."

You can't give him the codes!

You have to!

The officer signals with his gun for Xavier to move toward center stage, and they walk past me.

Charlene's eyes roll back in her head and she begins to make harsh gasping sounds.

"I'll do it!" I whip around and face Akinsanya. "Write this down!"

He has his cell phone out. "Take it slowly. I don't want to make a mistake and have to reenter this. That would take time. And time is the one thing you don't have."

Concentrating, focusing, trying not to let my concern for Charlene distract me, I tell him the thirty-five-digit alphanumeric code that was written in Dr. Turnisen's notebook.

Fred Anders stood at the security checkpoint trying to explain what had happened to his walkie-talkie when he heard the harsh swish of the UAV rush past overhead.

A drone had taken off.

The test flight had begun.

"Now, the antidote," I shout. "Give it to me."

Akinsanya holds a syringe above the tank. "Happy swimming."

"No!"

He drops it in, and as I race toward the steps that lead up to the platform where he's standing, I track the movement of the syringe.

I have no idea if it'll float or not. Syringes are hollow, but if it's full enough it might sink. And that would be very bad, because I'd inevitably kick up sand going in after it and finding it then might take too long to save Charlene.

Akinsanya sets down the iPad and the phone, then stands at the top of the platform waiting for me.

It looks like before I can get to the needle I'll need to get through him.

Alright then.

Let's do this.

As I rush past Xavier and the second police officer, I hear the man say, "My partner's dead and I'm holding you responsible. Please, give me an excuse to shoot you."

"Does this count?"

Out of the corner of my eye I see Xavier whip out Betty.

As I reach the spiral stairs that lead up to the platform, I hear a gunshot and the sizzle of the Taser go off almost simultaneously.

A glance back tells me Xavier is still on his feet.

There's still someone in the back of the room. Someone with the rifle.

But at the moment I'm not as worried about that as I am about getting the antidote for Charlene.

I take the stairs two at a time, and when I reach the top, Akinsanya is waiting for me.

I go at him with a crescent kick, which he effortlessly blocks. He lands a crippling punch to my side and I almost stumble backward off the platform. It's nearly a fifteen-foot drop to the floor.

I take a swing at him, an uppercut, which he also deflects. The needle dips and tilts downward. "It's getting interesting now, isn't it, Mr. Banks?"

"What happened to your lip?"

"I had a feisty woman slap me at dinner."

I have an idea and punch him, going for the lip and connecting with his nose, but he brings an elbow down hard on the back of my neck, sending me sprawling to the platform.

"I don't think you can beat me, Jevin. It looks like this time you lose."

Beyond him the needle is beginning to sink into the water. Piranhas are circling it curiously.

No. You can't let it go down!

Blood is pouring from his nose. I might have broken it. "I don't have to beat you. Your face is bleeding."

"A little blood never hurt anyone."

"You haven't been in a piranha tank recently, have you?"

Climbing to my feet and rushing forward, I grab him and both of us hurtle off the platform and into the water.

He fights fiercely to get free, but I hold him under long enough for the fish to find his face. With my other hand I go for the syringe, but it's bobbing and floating awkwardly in the water and I can't get ahold of it while I'm fighting with Akinsanya.

He clings to me and pulls me down. I grab a breath before going under and manage to wrestle free of him in the churning, bloody water.

The weights are still at the bottom of the tank. The ones you used to keep you under.

I swim down, retrieve them, wrap their strap around his waist, and snap the clasp shut to keep him under the water. Then I kick to the surface to get the syringe.

His face is no longer visible in the school of attacking piranhas, still he snags my leg and yanks to pull me under with him.

I go for the needle but miss it.

I'm barely able to snatch in a mouthful of air before he pulls me under.

He has a fearsome grip and I have to stick my hands into the pool of frenzied piranhas to squeeze more blood from his nose before he finally releases me.

I kick free, get to the surface, and search frantically for the syringe.

Come on! Where is it?

It must have sunk to the—

No.

Wait.

It's near the edge of the tank. I swim over, grab it, and spin toward the platform.

Akinsanya reaches for me again, still intent on dragging me down, but I kick his hand away and climb out, then rush down the stairs.

There's no sign of Xavier or the other police officer, and I'm not sure if I should take that as a good sign or a bad one.

I sprint to Charlene.

She has stopped convulsing. Her body is limp and her mouth lolls open, spittle dripping from it. Eyes closed. Unconscious.

I find a vein in her arm and place the tip of the needle against it, then depress the plunger, injecting Charlene with whatever the syringe contains.

It better be the antidote. It better help.

Come on, you have to be alright. Please be—

From backstage I hear the sound of a fight and I hope Xavier is doing alright.

The corpse of the police officer who was shot in the head lies beside the wheelchair, and I notice he has a radio.

I grab it and call for help, relay our location, tell dispatch to get an ambulance over here immediately. "My friend was poisoned with Dalpotol. I gave her something for it; I don't know what it is. Hurry, she's unconscious."

Turning toward Charlene again, I clear the saliva away from the edge of her mouth and feel for a pulse.

Faint. Thready.

She's breathing. Her heart is still beating.

I pray for her, begging God to let her live.

But.

Then.

What happens next seems to happen all at once but also in slow motion.

I hear the rapid sound of semiautomatic gunfire spraying across the stage, and then the sharp, thunderous *crack!* of glass as the sniper in the back of the auditorium peppers the piranha tank with bullets and it bursts, sending water, glass, and fish exploding across the stage.

Whoever was back there with the rifle has a clear shot at me. I don't know why he doesn't kill me, but I don't have time to think about it because then Akinsanya is tossing the weights aside and coming at me.

Piranhas move fast, and nearly half of his face is missing. Bones are visible through the flayed, ragged flesh that still hangs in uneven patches. His nose is entirely gone, as is his left eyeball.

He sneers, ripping a new gap in the skin that's somehow managed to cling to the edge of his jaw.

I go for the dead cop's gun, but it's snapped in his holster, and while I fumble for it Akinsanya comes at me, kicks me in the stomach and then in the face, knocking me onto my back.

I'm scrambling to my feet when he reaches for the gun, swiftly unsnaps it, and raises it in one smooth motion.

His eyes flick toward Charlene.

He aims the gun at her, then at me, then back at her.

And he shoots her in the right thigh.

"No!"

She's still unconscious, doesn't cry out.

"I think I'll let her bleed out. Don't worry, I won't kill you until you've had the chance to watch her die."

421

Help is coming. You radioed for the cops. You called for an ambu-lance. They should be here soon.

"Why did you have Emilio killed?" I can still hear Xavier fighting the officer backstage. I wish I had his Taser, if I did—

No. Not his Taser.

His crossbow.

It's near the edge of the curtain and I'm maybe ten feet away from it.

Create a distraction. Get the crossbow.

"It wasn't my decision to make," Akinsanya answers me.

"Who, then?"

What kind of a distraction? You don't have anything with you—

"Tomás?" I ask.

Except for your Morgan Dollar.

"Yes. Your friend found out something he wasn't supposed to know."

"About the drone delivery."

"About the timeline."

"Your timeline."

"No. The person I report to."

"Who?" I repeat. "Who's behind all this?" I turn slightly to hide my right arm behind my body.

He doesn't reply.

Charlene's leg is bleeding heavily, blood pooling on the floor.

I brush my hand up along my leg, picking my own pocket, then deftly flick the coin to the side.

It clatters onto the stage, and Akinsanya turns instinctively toward the sound.

When he does, I dive forward, sliding across the stage on my stom-ach. I snatch up the crossbow and roll onto my back.

He spins around, faces me, levels the gun.

I aim.

And shoot.

Coordinates

The crossbow bolt embeds in Akinsanya's chest and he wavers, then stumbles backward, staring blankly at it. Dropping the gun, he grabs the bolt to pull it out, but that's not going to happen.

He drops to his knees and I hear him struggling to breathe, his hands still wrapped around the bolt, futilely trying to tug it from his chest.

When he falls forward, the bolt goes in the rest of the way, the tip protruding from his back.

I jump to my feet and fly to Charlene's side.

She's breathing weakly, yes, but she is alive.

I do my best to stop the bleeding from the gunshot wound in her leg. It's not spurting, so I'm hopeful he didn't hit any arteries.

I hear a heavy thunk backstage. "Xavier! Are you okay?"

"I am now."

Then there's a groan and the click of handcuffs closing.

Xavier appears from behind the curtain, dragging the cuffed officer he'd been fighting. The guy looks pretty worse for the wear, Xavier not so much. He puts one knee on the guy's back to pin him down, then sees me trying to stop the bleeding.

He yanks out his phone. "I'll get an ambulance."

"I radioed for one, it should be on the way, but call in and tell them she has a gunshot wound too. In the thigh. It might help them get ready at—"

The doors to one of the main entrances to the theater burst open and Agent Ratchford appears, gun in hand, four Arête security personnel by his side.

"Mr. Banks?" He stares at the bodies on the stage, the shattered glass, the piranhas flipping around in search of water. "What happened in here?"

The security guards flare out. I hear Xavier talking with emergency services, telling them about the gunshot wound.

"Agent Ratchford." I'm still doing my best to quell the bleeding in Charlene's leg. "Get someone from the Air Force on the phone, fast. Have them contact Area 51 immediately. There was a drone that took off from there a few minutes ago. It's flying toward Mexico to a drug cartel—are you listening to me?"

He's staring at me dumbfounded. "Yes. A drone test. Area 51. Mexico. A cartel."

"Make the call. Hurry."

"Area 51 doesn't exist."

"Trust me. Get someone as high up as possible. There's a launch code. I'll tell it to them. One of their drones is on its way to Mexico. They need to shoot it down."

I turn back to Charlene. "Hang in there. Help's on the way."

She opens her eyes.

Oh, yes.

Yes.

She nods slightly.

"I love you," I tell her.

"You too." Her voice is barely a whisper. But she's conscious. She's talking.

She winces in pain, and I ease back a little from the pressure I'm putting on her leg, but I still try to press hard enough to keep the bleeding under control.

I give Agent Ratchford the code, he writes it down and makes another call, then says, "You're not gonna believe this." He's staring at his cell. "But the Undersecretary of Defense wants to talk to you."

I reach out to take the phone from him, but he shakes his head. "No. I mean in person. She's at the Arête. She wants to know how you found out those codes."

That might take a little explaining.

The thought brings to mind what Akinsanya had said: that it wasn't his timeline, that it was the timeline of the person he reported to.

The drug lords? The cartel who was supposed to take delivery of the drone?

Who knows. I'll figure that out later. Right now we just need to get help to Charlene.

Agent Ratchford informs me that the military is tracking the drone, but it doesn't look like it's heading to Mexico.

Maybe the codes weren't correct.

Or maybe you didn't remember them exactly.

Possibly, but I'm pretty sure I got them right.

They were erased, then rewritten.

He changed them. Turnisen did.

I evaluate that as I call for one of the security personnel to get a key for the handcuffs shackling Charlene to the wheelchair. He scours the dead police officer's pockets, comes up with one. They're standardized locks, the key works, and I free her.

Clive Fridell arrives and speaks with his security team, then sends them out to find tubs. They fill them with water and rescue as many piranhas as they can. One of the men retrieves my Morgan Dollar for me.

At last the paramedics show up and help Charlene onto a gurney. I fill them in on what I know. Someone has turned the house lights on, and I can see a couple of the Arête security staff in the back of the auditorium. One of them has the semiautomatic rifle that was firing at the stage. It's attached to a pivoting turret. The other guy is holding what looks like a robotic arm.

A robotic arm?

Undersecretary of Defense Oriana Williamson strides up to me as I'm walking beside Charlene's gurney on our way to the ambulance.

"Mr. Banks, I want you to tell me how you found out the launch codes to an experimental aircraft test at a top-secret military installation."

"I'm on my way to the hospital. I'll tell you when we get there." That would at least give me a little time to try to figure out what to say.

I climb in beside Charlene, the paramedics close the door, and we take off for Fuller Medical Center.

The Only Honest Profession

Calista knew she was dying.

She could tell by the look on the EMTs' faces as they tried to figure out how to help her.

She could tell by the sharp pains in her chest, the way it was getting harder and harder to breathe.

Yes.

She could tell.

She was not going to remain young.

And she was not going to grow old.

Memories of all the crimes she'd been a part of passed through her head.

The murders she'd committed.

The pain she'd caused.

She'd told Derek that all he thought of was himself, but it had been the same for her.

You're no different.

Yes you are!

No.

No, you're not.

If love meant making sacrifices for another person, she'd never genuinely loved anyone.

Regret swept over her.

Calista had never been a big believer in God, but now she realized that he had every right to be mad at her, every right to punish her.

Though weak and getting weaker, she told the EMTs about what happened in sublevel 4 at Plyotech Cybernetics' R&D facility.

As Calista Hendrix died, she did what she could to help others live.

∙∙ ⟳

Charlene is quiet. The paramedics are bent over her.

I have no idea how I'll explain to the undersecretary how I knew the codes without lying through my teeth or getting Xavier and myself into a heap of trouble—Charlene, Fionna, and Fred as well, since we were all involved in getting the access to Groom Lake.

That's what I think through as I ride in the ambulance next to the woman I love.

Word comes through the radio up front that Dr. Turnisen has been admitted and is in stable condition. I don't know what happened to him, and when I ask the paramedics about it, they tell me quietly that they heard he'd been tortured.

Doctors are waiting for us at Fuller Medical Center and take over for the paramedics, wheeling Charlene immediately toward an operating room. The medics tell me her vitals are stable, but I can sense a hesitation to assure me that she'll be alright.

While we were en route, Xavier had called Fionna to tell her what was going on, and now he waits in the lobby for her and her kids while the undersecretary leads me to an exam room where we can talk in private.

She closes the door.

"The codes that you gave to Agent Ratchford were verified coordinates for a UAV the military is testing. You told us it was headed toward Mexico, but the coordinates just sent the vehicle to the desert south of here. I want to know how you found out about that code, why you thought it would send our drone to a Mexican drug cartel, and how you came to know it by heart."

"It's complicated."

"I'm a patient woman." So far I haven't exactly gotten that sense, but this isn't the time to argue.

Here goes nothing. "Akinsanya told me."

"What?"

"He showed it to me to verify it. He assumed I had the real one from a USB drive that my friend Emilio had with him when he was murdered in the Philippines."

"You're going to have to talk me through that."

I do.

"And you're saying that Akinsanya showed it to you. Where? Was it written down?"

"He had his people send me a text, but then one of his men destroyed my cell phone. As far as I know, whatever remains of it is still at the Arête."

"And you memorized the code just by looking at it?"

"I'm pretty good at memorizing things."

"Prove it."

Too bad I don't have a deck of cards with me. "Write down a list of random numbers. I'll show you."

"How many?"

"Thirty."

"Thirty?"

"Yes."

It goes well.

I remember my conversation with Charlene yesterday when I'd referred to Karl Germain's saying: "Magic is the only honest profession. A magician promises to deceive you and he does."

There are times to keep secrets and times to tell the truth.

"Is there anything else you want to tell me?" the undersecretary asks me.

Magic is the only honest profession.

"Would you believe it if I told you I snuck onto Area 51 and found those codes in a top-secret underground research facility?"

"I might. But I would likely be more interested in how you pulled it off so that other people, who might not have the best intentions in mind, would not be able to." She leans forward. "So, theoretically, how would you have done that, if you had?"

I'm a magician.

Involved in the only honest profession.

So I tell her what she needs to know.

As I wait for word from the doctors, Fionna and her children arrive. Xavier must have told her about me being in the tank because she hands me a set of dry clothes from my house.

After changing, I hear from the surgeons: Charlene is recovering well. It looks like she'll be spending a couple days in the hospital but will be alright.

I hear Turnisen is in one of the rooms on the first floor.

After checking in on Charlene and finding her asleep, I swing by Tim's room on my way to fill Xavier and Fionna in on Charlene's condition. The door is slightly open and the lights are off.

I decide not to disturb him and head to the lobby to update my friends, wondering how much trouble I might get into with the undersecretary.

And who the person Akinsanya reported to really is.

PART VIII

Fallen Princes

Monday, February 11
Fourteen hours later
11:32 a.m.

Here's what we know:

(1) Charlene is doing well.
(2) Dr. Schatzing got a pretty good gash on his head when he was attacked last night, but it looks like he's going to be fine.
(3) Dr. Jeremy Turnisen is getting the wounds that Akinsanya gave him treated.
(4) Tomás didn't commit suicide after all. Video surveillance at the police station showed a couple of cops walking down the hall to transfer him to another cell. But the transfer was never sent through from HQ. Turns out it was the two cops who'd been in the theater helping Akinsanya last night.
(5) There's nothing on the news about the drone incident, which comes as no surprise to Xavier.

Now, Fionna and the kids are out flower shopping for something special for Charlene, and Xavier and I are in the hospital room with her. I'm sitting beside her bed; Xavier has positioned himself on the wide windowsill where he's eating a pecan log roll.

Agent Ratchford swings by. "So, I just wanted to see how you were," he tells Charlene. "I was shot last year. I know how much it hurts."

He was shot?

This guy continues to surprise me.

"I'm feeling much better. Thank you for stopping by."

We talk for a few minutes. He isn't able to share much with us about the case. "But there is one thing you might be able to help me with," he says. "Did any of you hear the name 'Jesús Garcia' when Akinsanya and his men were around you?"

We all shake our heads.

"Who is he?" I ask.

"I'm not sure. His name came up yesterday. A woman who Akinsanya poisoned mentioned it before she passed away. That's all we have right now. That, and some unsanctioned research we need to look into at a robotics center. But who knows, maybe if I can get permission we might be able to subcontract a couple researchers to help look into Garcia."

"Fionna and Lonnie?" Charlene guesses.

"Let's just say that's a possibility."

After he leaves, Xavier crunches his way through a mouthful of pecans and nougat. "I still don't understand who Akinsanya was working for. You think it's this Garcia dude?"

They both look at me as if I might have some insight into it. "I don't know," I tell them honestly. "I really don't know."

As I think about it, that's not all I'm wondering.

Something else still bugs me.

After everything that happened, the drone didn't go where Akinsanya was trying to get it to go. The coordinates were wrong.

Or were they right?

Charlene asks if I wouldn't mind getting her a Coke, and mulling things over, I leave for the soda machines in the lobby.

As I pass the nurses' station I see a series of photos cycling across the woman's computer screen—her standing next to a broad-shouldered, smiling man, children playing beside a cabin, a collie running across the desert.

It gets me thinking.

"Say"—she looks at me knowingly—"aren't you the man who did that magic show for the children yesterday?"

"Yes."

"I was there. It was very nice what you and your friends did."

"Thank you."

There's a web of relationships here, and I can see threads leading from one person to another, but how they're all connected is still murky to me.

The photo of Emilio and Tim.

The RixoTray USB drive.

Emilio's notebooks.

The one person who might be able to shed light on everything is here at the hospital.

I'm not sure if I'll be allowed to see him, but this nurse seems to have an affinity for me from seeing the show, and she unreservedly gives me his room number when I ask for it.

I swing by the vending machines and buy the Coke. I'm on my way back to Charlene's room when I decide I can afford a couple-minute detour.

I knock on the door and Dr. Turnisen invites me in.

He's sitting up in bed.

When I see the extent of his grievous injuries, my heart goes out to him.

Akinsanya cut his face and then stitched him back up in ways that almost made you want to look away when you saw him. It's gut-wrenching to see.

His left hand is thickly bandaged. I heard he lost three fingers, sliced off by Akinsanya.

"Hello, Dr. Turnisen. My name is Jevin Banks."

"I've seen your billboards." He struggles somewhat to get the words out. "You must get that a lot."

"They're hard to miss. I'll have to get you into the actual show sometime."

A nod. "You're the one who found the codes at my desk."

"Yes."

Out of propriety I'm about to ask him how he's doing, but I figure I can already guess that by seeing his condition. "You went through a lot yesterday." I really can't think of any other way to get a conversation started. "You were incredibly brave."

"Thank you." He seems unsure how to respond to the compliment.

"We had a mutual acquaintance."

"Emilio Benigno."

"Yes."

"Agent Ratchford filled me in," he explains. "I was a little out of it last night."

"I can't imagine why."

After a moment he says, "You killed him. The man who did this to me."

"Yes, I did."

"From what Ratchford told me, he didn't die in a very agreeable way."

"That's true."

"It sounds like a strange thing to say, but I'm glad."

"Considering the circumstances, it doesn't sound strange at all."

As I think about what Dr. Turnisen went through yesterday and our visit to his research area at Groom Lake, a few things come together.

The photo on his desk.

The progeria research.

The launch codes.

They were the wrong codes.

Or the right ones.

Yes. It would explain a lot.

"You know, Doctor, a friend of mine once told me you can tell what's important to someone by looking at three things: his calendar, his checkbook, and his refrigerator door."

"That makes sense."

"Well, there's one other place."

"And that is?"

"His desk."

"His desk?"

"Yes." I walk toward the window. Look out across my city, with all of its filth. With all of its glory. "There was only one photo on your desk."

"Yes? And?"

I face him again. "Dr. Turnisen, how many people keep a photo of their friend and their friend's friend on their desk?" I shake my head. "No. People keep pictures of family members on their desks. And that's why you kept a picture of your son there, where you could see him every day."

He stares at me for a long time. "Close the door."

I do.

"How did you know? Just the photo?"

"No. The codes. You erased the original ones. Only yesterday's set was in pen."

"There has to be more."

"There were RixoTray USB drives in your drawer at work. And you allowed yourself to be tortured all day even though you knew the codes. You could have told them to Akinsanya at any time, but you held back. I was thinking about that, about how hard it would be."

He glances down at the hand that's missing three fingers.

"I did a show here yesterday, and the hospital administrator mentioned that a sizable anonymous donation was going to be made for the progeria research. How much were you going to get from the drug cartel for delivering the drone?"

He hesitates. "Twenty million."

"So you were the one. And you were going to donate it to RixoTray's transdifferentiation research with Dr. Schatzing . . ." I'm thinking aloud, tying the threads together. "But you didn't want Emilio dead . . . Is that when you changed the codes in your notebook? After Emilio was killed? Is that when you decided you didn't want the drone to get into the hands of these people after all?"

He looks at me curiously. "How do you know all this?"

"We were looking into Emilio's death. We stumbled across a few things. When I met Tim yesterday he told me his parents were divorced, that his dad wasn't allowed to see him."

"It's a long story. It wasn't my choice." He waits for me to say something, but I have no idea what to say, and at last he goes on, "I'm no saint, Mr. Banks. But I love my son."

"Yes." I'm not sure what else to say and finally ask, "How did you contact Akinsanya and the drug cartel?"

"Someone named Solomon. He has connections."

Solomon.

Why doesn't that surprise me.

Tim's dad looks at me concernedly. "Are you going to tell Agent Ratchford?"

I consider the wounds he suffered while holding out so that he could find a way to do the right thing. To both protect innocent people and help his son. He changed his mind about the drone when he realized what the consequences of turning it over would be.

Free will.

We are broken gods, fallen princes, with animal instincts and divine desires.

Incongruous. Able to go along with our convictions, or go against them.

Finally I answer, "How would it help Tim if I told anyone?"

He's silent.

It's hard to know where to take things from here. I hold up the Coke. "I should be going."

"Thank you."

When I'm halfway to the door I have an idea. "When you're feeling better, I'll get you some tickets to my show. Seat D4. Remember that." It's inadequate, but it's all I can think of at the moment and I go with it.

"D4. Sure. Thanks."

"There'll be a mutual acquaintance of ours in D5," I tell him. "If you ask him, I'm sure he'll do a French Drop for you. He's really very good."

PART IX

Lovelock

Thursday, February 14
Valentine's Day

"I think I got it." Lonnie is at my kitchen table, leaning over a pad of paper filled with algorithms and permutations.

Xavier peers over his shoulder. "So what are we looking at?"

"I've never seen anything like this."

"Like what?"

Donnie stands near the window texting a friend. Upstairs, Fionna is helping the girls get ready for today's drive across the state. Charlene, who can't tackle stairs yet because of the gunshot wound to her leg, has found a lounge chair in the library and is answering some get-well-soon emails on her laptop.

"Well," Lonnie says, "let's see . . . Think of space/time as a fabric. You've heard of the book *A Wrinkle in Time*?"

"Sure," Xavier replies. "It's a classic. That one's definitely stood the test of time."

"Yeah. Hmm. I think it has. Well—"

Donnie stops texting long enough to interrupt. "It's not that far-fetched. To travel through space, I mean, really through space, to the far reaches of space, you need a way to warp time to allow you to move

443

faster, to travel light-years in an instant. Otherwise the prospect of interstellar travel is just science fiction or wishful thinking."

He and Lonnie share a look.

I sense I can see where they're going with this. "And you're saying that these algorithms, what? Prove that time travel is real?"

Lonnie answers, "Not time travel, no, but a way to take a shortcut through space, like you might slice through a three-dimensional object." He backpedals a little. "Or at least they seem to point in that direction."

The algorithms he's been working on come from the chalkboards in the classrooms of Building A-13 at Groom Lake.

"So it's true," Xavier mutters.

"What's true?" Lonnie asks.

"The space/time continuum. They've got a ship there. At Area 51." He nods knowingly. "It might even be where they're getting some of their thought-controlled technology from."

Donnie lowers his phone. "You're saying that our unmanned aerial vehicles were created from reverse engineering a spaceship?"

"If you believe the stories."

"And do you?"

"You know me."

"Yeah." He smiles. "Wicked."

Fionna calls down that they're ready to go, the boys head into the other room, and Xavier comes over and holds up a knapsack.

"I got something for Fionna," he whispers.

"Something memorable?"

"I believe it is."

"What's that?"

He fumbles through the pack and pulls out a bottle.

"Mango perfume."

"Yup. Think she'll like it?"

"What gave you the idea to buy Fionna mango perfume?"

"It's fruity."

"Fruity."

"Yes."

"And?"

"And it was on special. Two for one. This way, I've got next year covered as well."

"I hope you're joking."

He looks slightly concerned. "You think I should take one back?"

"Xav, I'm . . . You know, I think Fionna would actually love a bottle of mango perfume coming from you two years in a row."

"Yeah." He puts it away. "I figured that too." He places one hand on my shoulder. "Listen, what you told me last night, about the truck, I mean, I've been thinking and—"

"No. It's okay. I was serious."

"I can't take your new pickup truck."

"Really, you need something to get around town in."

"Well . . . the RV is a little tough to parallel park," he admits. "But—"

"Besides, this way, if the opportunity ever presents itself, you can maybe visit Fred at work—by the way, any word on those photos being released?"

"Nothing so far. We're crossing our fingers. Hopefully that's all in the past."

When the girls come downstairs, Charlene joins us in the kitchen, and Mandie and Maddie hand around Valentine's Day cards to everyone.

I find a prominent place on my fridge to hang mine up.

We've taken a lot of pictures this week, and I have to remove one of the extra magnets from a photo of my dad and me fishing off the Oregon coast to put the cards up.

He never did explain why he wasn't able to come down to visit earlier this week, just that he had a doctor's appointment.

"Everything okay?" I'd asked him on the phone on Monday.

"Sure. Everything's fine."

But still, over the last few days I found myself worrying about him and decided that next week I'm going to fly up to check on him.

I replace his photo and straighten it.

Fionna grabs her purse. "So I've been curious about something, Mr. Wray."

"Yes?"

"What nuts are you eating today?"

"Almond Joy. In fact . . ." He digs through his knapsack and pulls out a heaping pile of candy bars. "I bought some for everyone. Happy Valentine's Day."

"Hmm. I was saving these for later today, but I suppose we can break them out now." She goes to her purse and offers us a bag of those heart-shaped candies with little sayings on them.

"Are those the ones that taste like chalk?" Donnie asks.

"I don't know, I . . ."

The kids all go for the Almond Joys instead. Charlene and I take some of Fionna's candies so her feelings won't be hurt.

It only takes me a few bites to discover Donnie is right.

They do taste like chalk.

Or at least what I imagine chalk would taste like.

We head outside.

Fionna, Xavier, and the kids pile into her minivan while Charlene and I head to the Aston Martin.

"How about I do some stories on the way," I hear Xavier offer the kids as he climbs in.

"I thought there were rules?" Mandie sounds concerned. "That you have to wait until bedtime?"

"Once in a while it's okay to break the rules. Right, Fionna?"

"Once in a while."

"I'll remind you of that, Mom," Donnie says, his mouth full of Almond Joy candy bars.

"Quiet now. Don't eat with food in your mouth."

Then the door closes, Charlene and I hop into the DB9, and we all take off for Lovelock, Nevada.

"So what's the big surprise?" Charlene asks me as I pull out of town. "Where are we going?"

"Can't tell you."

"Oh. Let me guess: or else it wouldn't be a surprise."

"See, we are operating on exactly the same wavelength."

We spend some time brainstorming a new finale for our show when it opens up again next month. "Everything Xavier has proposed to me so far," I tell her, "has to do with me being set on fire."

"Imagine that. Maybe I could get set on fire this time?"

"We'll have to see once your leg recovers."

As our conversation cycles around the events of the last week, I think of my talk with Dr. Turnisen, something I haven't told my friends about.

On Monday morning he'd mentioned the twenty million dollars that was going to go toward the progeria research, but since the drone never got delivered, he never received his payment from the drug cartel.

Now while I'm in the car with Charlene, I think about Tim and the possible breakthroughs in transdifferentiation research.

I make a decision to help move things forward.

Yeah, I have some money at my disposal, but a donation of that size would definitely put a crimp in things for a while.

Well, once in a while, crimps like that can be a good thing.

Charlene turns to me. "I've been thinking about the stuff we were talking about earlier this week—strong AI, machines making decisions like humans do, all of that. What makes humans different from machines: Consciousness? Self-awareness? Emotional intelligence? Can machines ever be taught to love? How to program them to be moral—it's a lot to, well . . . consider."

"They're not easy questions."

"Well," she says, "to create truly 'human machines,' they'd need to be able to worship or rebel against their creators."

"You mean, against us."

"Yes."

"But what kind of a creator would ever be bold enough to give his creation free will and the opportunity to kill him off if they chose to?"

"The real one," she says softly.

We arrive in Lovelock two hours before dusk.

The town capitalizes on its name and has become known as a place where you snap a lock on a never-ending chain in the center of town as a symbol of locking your love to someone.

Lovelock.

Lock your love.

Good for tourism.

But today I have something better in mind. When we arrive at Altitude Escapades, they have our hot air balloon waiting for us. A big enough basket for the whole crew, just like I ordered.

I arranged a special takeoff ceremony with our pilot. It took some convincing, but the management finally went for the idea when I offered to buy them two new balloons if there was any damage to this one.

But first, before we go anywhere, I need to give Charlene her present.

"I've got something for you." I move my hands in a circle around her neck, and when I pull them away a necklace appears.

"How did you do that?" Mandie gasps.

"Magic," I tell her.

It's a leather cross necklace that I picked up for less than ten dollars at one of the souvenir shops on the Strip. I have a feeling Charlene doesn't care one bit about the cost.

"It reminds me of the necklace I left in the Philippines."

"I was hoping it would."

"This necklace is going to be one of the most special things I own."

"Just *one of* the most special things?"

"You never know. Someday someone might give me a ring that ends up being even more special."

"A ring?"

"You never know."

"The right piece of jewelry can speak volumes."

"Yes, it can."

After we're all in the basket, I give Xav a nod, snap my fingers, and the ropes holding the balloon down burst into flames.

Donnie gives me an approving nod. "Sweet."

"Xavier's idea."

Everyone looks his way, and he gives us a sly half smile. "Fire," he says. "The only thing better would have been an explosion."

I'm not so sure about that.

The ropes burn away, but one line is still holding us down. The pilot nods to me and I'm about to untie it when Xavier stops me. "Do it with a flourish, bro. Why not? Come on, for the kids."

I object that I'm not a flourisher, that he already knows that, but he presses me and so do Fionna and the children.

Everyone is waiting.

"Oh, alright." I wave my hand above the rope, doing my best imitation of a magician doing a flourish. "I hope that satisfies you all."

"Got it." Lonnie winks at Xavier.

"Got what?"

He holds up his phone. "The video. YouTube, here we come."

Great.

As he taps at his phone, I undo the rope, Charlene takes my hand, the pilot blasts the burner, and we take off on our twilight flight.

What better place to watch the sunset than from the ceiling of the world?

I draw Charlene close and kiss her.

Sometimes you look before you leap.

Sometimes you just gotta take the plunge.

PART X

Aspera

Hayden Pennet stepped off the bus, carrying the one suitcase she'd brought with her from Ohio.

Eighteen years old. She'd finally done it, finally left home.

She was going to be a model.

A man approached her and introduced himself as Martin Yearling from the Aspera Modeling Agency. "I'm thrilled to see you, Hayden. You're even more lovely in person than you are in your audition video."

She found herself blushing. "Thank you."

"All of us at Aspera are glad you decided to come."

She'd been wondering something, and now just went ahead and asked it. "Online it said a billionaire owns this place. That true?"

"Yes. Clive Fridell. If things work out at the agency with you, I'll introduce you."

"That'd be awesome."

He gestured toward a limousine. "Let me get your bag." He moved her suitcase into the trunk and opened the door for her.

"We'll swing by the hotel first so you can freshen up," he offered.

"Then, whenever you're ready, I'll take you to a friend of mine from the agency who's been waiting to meet you ever since he saw your video."

"Cool. What's his name?"

"His name is Solomon. And he'll get you all set up in your new career."

Acknowledgments

Special thanks to Eric Wilson, Trinity Huhn, Ariel Huhn, Jennifer Leep, Jessica English, Heather Knudsten, Pam Johnson, Dr. Jimmy Lin, Dr. Todd Huhn, Shawn Scullin, Rigo Durazo, Mark Spicer, Kevin James, Seth Grabel, Kevin Curtin, Brian Gillis, Joe Castillo, Dr. Johnathan Kiel, Dr. Ray Hunter, and Jim Nyberg.

Steven James is the critically acclaimed author of many books, including the bestselling Patrick Bowers thrillers. He is a contributing editor to *Writer's Digest*, has a master's degree in storytelling, and has taught writing and creative communication on three continents. Currently he lives, writes, drinks coffee, and plays disc golf near the Blue Ridge Mountains of Tennessee.

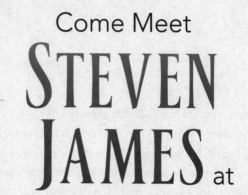
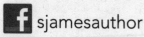
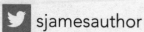

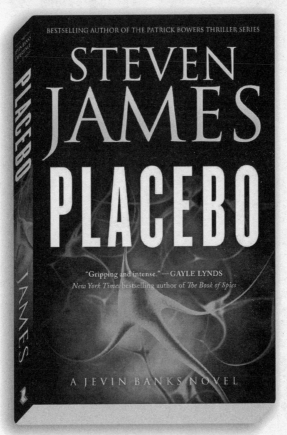

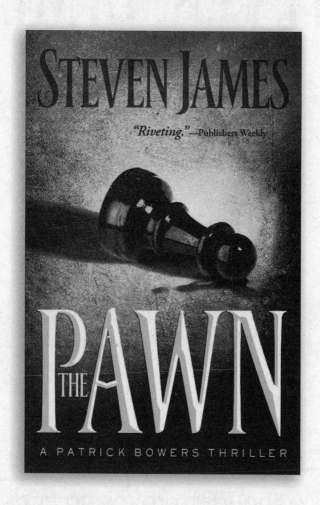

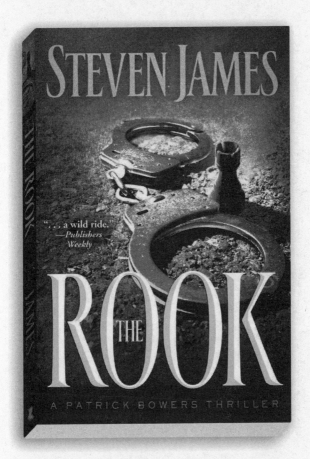

FROM CRITICALLY ACCLAIMED BESTSELLING AUTHOR

STEVEN JAMES

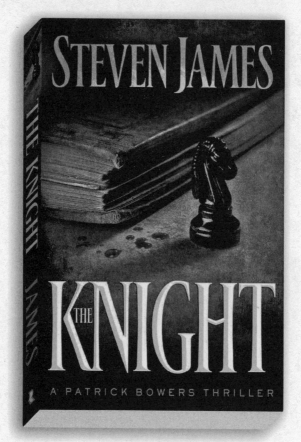

"Top-notch suspense!"
—*RT Book Reviews,*
★★★★½

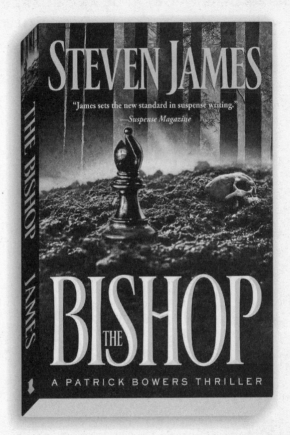

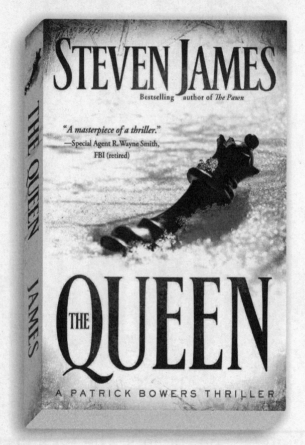